Jay Rayner was born in 1966. He is the author of one previous novel, *The Marble Kiss*. His journalism has appeared in the *Mail on Sunday*, the *Guardian*, the *Independent*, *Cosmopolitan* and *GQ*. He was named Young Journalist of the Year 1992. He now writes full time for the *Observer*.

DAY OF ATONEMENT

Jay Rayner

BLACK SWAN

DAY OF ATONEMENT
A BLACK SWAN BOOK : 0 552 99783 8

First publication in Great Britain

PRINTING HISTORY
Black Swan edition published 1998

Set in 11pt Melior by
County Typesetters, Margate, Kent

Black Swan Books are published by Transworld Publishers Ltd,
61–63 Uxbridge Road, London W5 5SA,
in Australia by Transworld Publishers (Australia) Pty Ltd,
15–25 Helles Avenue, Moorebank, NSW 2170,
and in New Zealand by Transworld Publishers (NZ) Ltd,
3 William Pickering Drive, Albany, Auckland.

This book proof printed by
Antony Rowe Ltd, Chippenham, Wiltshire

For Claire and Des, without whom . . .

Acknowledgements

I would like to thank: Max and Muriel Berk; Larwence Cohen of the Swiss Cottage Book Shop; Michael Freedland; Jack and Hannah Grant; Linda Greenlick and the staff of the Jewish Chronicle library; Nan Greifer; Anthony Julius; Oberlander, kosher caterers; Greg Williams; Dr Brian Wells; John Witton of the Institute for the Study of Drug Dependency.

Andreas Loizou gave me impeccable advice on matters financial. Jonathan Freedland played the Rebbe, as ever. Bill Scott-Kerr flowed with editorial wisdom. My agent ntony Harwood first encouraged me to consider writing a novel about Anglo-Jewry. Finally, Pat Gordon Smith combined the difficult task of reading every chapter as it was written and making concise and tactful suggestions, with the even tougher job of being my wife. She was endlessly patient with me in both roles; this book simply would not have happened without her.

All mistakes, of course, remain my own.

One

Jews do not like the sea.

Mal Jones was a Jew and he didn't like the sea.

He stared through his bedsit window at the endless stretch of rippling grey, smudged off to the horizon by a cover of heavy autumn cloud, and fell to brooding. We don't know what to do with it, he thought. You can't build on the sea. You can't buy the sea. And you certainly can't walk on it, whatever Jewish mothers may say about their sons. It limits possibilities and Jews hate having their possibilities limited. That's why they live in cities. In a city you always have somewhere to go. You can walk down roads and up streets and around corners. All life is there: cities are packed full of shysters and filchers, conmen and criminals. And that's only the accountants. There are hookers too, and people willing to pay them. In cities there are always people willing to screw and be screwed. In a city you can look for opportunities. And there's somewhere to hide, of course. Always somewhere to hide. On the seashore there's nowhere to hide. There's just the blank-eyed stare of the horizon, the foul breath of the salt-crusted wind and the endless crush-crack-crush of the surf on the beach. And someone in sensible boots walking their bloody Labrador.

Still this was where Mal found himself, hard by the water's edge. Outside, a gull called and clawed at the air, beak held high, oblivious to the silent, middle-aged man watching him from across his tatty sink in his tatty kitchenette. Perhaps he could learn to like it here. Perhaps he could become a new kind of Jew, a Coastal Jew. Maybe he'd even get a boat one day. It would be a nice shiny yacht with ropes and sails and a drinks cabinet filled with real drinks. The whole bit. Then again maybe he should get a car first. Or a bike. Better still, a new pair of shoes to replace these ones with their ragged man-made soles and putrid leather uppers. Keep it modest. Modest is good. Modest is great. Modest is all he has.

Mal Jones sighed and shook his head. Who was he kidding? He could never be a Coastal Jew. There's no such thing. A Jew with a boat? Really. The only Jews with boats are shipping magnates. He had no greater love for the sea than anyone else he knew or, to be more exact, had known. But it suited his purposes right now, being here in this dismal bedsit on Herne Bay looking out over these mind-numbing waters. And it suited him precisely because they were so dull. The problem with cities is that they don't just provide opportunities, they pose threats as well. Challenges hide in the shadows. The venal and malign hang about at crossroads waiting for you to trip just so they can say they were there when it happened. But the sea is just the sea. The seashore before him meant there was half the world he didn't have to worry about. Mal knew what was out there, knew better than most, and it couldn't throw up any surprises. Those who would want to gloat over the reduced circumstances in which he found himself were hardly likely to come sweeping up the beach in some gilt-edged armada. They would drive down in their BMWs and their Mercs and he would see them coming because the coast road in front of this block only went in two directions, east and west. He could keep an eye on two directions. He could manage that. If he kept to his usual routine, didn't do anything ambitious, he would be fine.

Not that his latest address was exactly a peach. Herne Bay, he decided, was the arsehole of the world. No, it was worse than that; it was an annexe off the arsehole of the world; it was a Portakabin in the car park off the annexe of the arsehole of the world. And he laughed a short, ironic laugh, heavy with fury at how right he was. Grey buildings clung apathetically to the north Kent coast like depressives who can't even summon the will to end it all and throw themselves in. The paintwork here was blistered by the wind and the rain and litter drifted and fluttered down greasy, oil-stained streets. In Herne Bay, watching the litter blow about was the nearest they had to a spectator sport. Although nobody could quite remember the rules. Here, at the edge of the town centre, he could look out over the skeletal finger of the pier stretching away across the sea to his right, deserted and sullen now that the season was done with. Below him, all but on the beach, was the grim jollity of an empty amusement arcade; when the breeze blew inland he would be taunted by the metal rattle of change flushing automatically through the machines, and the tuneless mutter of their electronic melodies. In the building next door to the one in which he lived, taking over half the terrace block, there was a nunnery. If ever he looked down at the pavement immediately below, it seemed constantly to teem with the angels of death, black-clad and severe. There was a pub he never entered and a take-away he had visited all too often. That was just about it.

And yet this was where it all ended. Or where the end began. This was where his business partner revealed what he had done and the last place Mal set eyes on him. This was where Mal Jones set out on the surprisingly swift transformation from millionaire co-chairman and chief executive of the Sinai Corporation to convicted felon, guilty of embezzlement, fraud and illegal share price maintenance. But now he had done his nine months in Classwell Grove Open Prison, along with all the other company secretaries and managing directors who had been caught up to their nipples in the till and for whom 'a few months in Class' was considered adequate punishment. He had, he was told, paid his debt to society. The formal part of his sentence was over. He was on probation now, undergoing a test period. Proving himself, that's what they said. Prison did not test enough, apparently. Prison was just about waiting; probation was about proving.

In a way they were right. In prison he did not need to dwell too much on what had occurred or what he had done. He had the torture of other people's stinking bodies to deal with, the endless smells and noises that only grown men can produce when shoved into tight corners with each other. Prison, or at least short spells of it, makes you feel self-pity, not remorse. Now he was out he felt something else was necessary. He felt the need to do something appropriate to his crime and this godforsaken place fitted the bill. They had history, Mal Jones and Herne Bay; something to share. It was as if they had been waiting for each other, both the crumbling and the broken, so when they released him he refused the offers of help: a few days a week at Uncle Morri's place, doing the books, adding up the numbers ('You had a head for numbers Mal, always did'); a berth in cousin Shirley's lilac spare room, sleeping on a mattress protected from sudden incontinence by a plastic sheet that crackled beneath you when you rolled over; stilted dinners where prison would be deliberately forgotten, or at least unmentioned. He turned it down and came here to stare at the sea and watch the litter blow around and work a few things out.

He saw the car draw up and heard the weak splutter of the doorbell echo up the stairwell. But he had no reason to start at the sound, even though it was the first time the bell had been rung for him in the two weeks he had been there. He knew who it was. Soon she was through the opened door and they had embraced, in the silent way only those with too much to say can embrace. They tramped to the top of the house, each footfall beating out a creaking rhythm on the wooden stairs, and found places to stand in the raw clutter of his bedsit. It was the first time anybody else had been in there since Mal had been shown it by the landlady, and suddenly it felt not just utilitarian but small and desperate. Natasha stood in the middle of the room, one hand holding the strap of her bulky shoulder bag. Mal took up a perch by the window, resting his buttocks against the radiator and its meagre dose of heat.

She wore jeans that defined her narrow waist and a white T-shirt that defined everything else. Her deep blond hair was cut back in what might have been a bob had it not been for the broad waves that broke its line, and at her throat she wore a cheap thin necklace of round, threaded coral. It had been only a few months since last they had seen each other, when she had visited him in Class, but again, Mal decided, her face had changed, although only in the way the features of the young seem so regularly to alter. It was as if her face had come into focus. There was more definition: a firmer jaw, starker brow, fuller lips. She looked more like her mother every day.

'You look good,' he said.

Natasha smiled. 'You look like shit.'

'Thank you.'

She gave a slight shrug. 'No problem. That's what family is for.' She studied the room. 'It's . . . how do you put it?'

'It's small, Natasha. It's small, and dingy, and it smells of damp. But it's only temporary.'

'I should fucking hope so.'

'Language, honey.'

She raised one eyebrow and heaved the bag off her shoulder and onto the floor, squatting down to open it. 'The jailbird lectures me on language. Really.'

He watched her dig around inside. 'How's your father?'

'Your brother is fine. Benny's just fine.'

'Does he talk about me?'

'He doesn't know I'm here, if that's what you mean.'

'Probably best that way.'

She found the paper bags she was looking for and

dragged them out onto the floor. 'No,' she said. 'It's not best that way. But if that's how you two children want to play things then so be it. I'm not going to get involved.'

'Were you able to get everything?'

'Everything but the wallies,' she said.

'No pickled cucumbers?' he said, a look of mock horror crossing his face. 'What is this? Has there been a cucumber blight? A cucumber famine?'

'Yeah,' she laughed. 'The whole of Eastern Europe has it. The crop failed and now the Poles are starving. Dad is planning Cucumber Aid.'

'Starving Poles? Oh, well. Maybe there is a God.'

'Mal!'

'Sorry. A joke.' She looked up at him, brow creased with distaste. 'You kids are so damn sensitive,' he said. 'It was a joke.' And then. 'I'll get a couple of plates.' He opened the cupboard above the gas rings. 'Hell, I'll just go mad and get all three of the plates.'

They laid the food out on the table, ripping open the bags of bagels and scooping the chopped liver and the herring and the cream cheese into bowls. It was good to see a table full of real food again, rather than just the industrial wrapping of aluminium take-away tins and sagging pizza boxes. Mal split one of the bagels and began spreading the chopped liver in thick slabs. Natasha watched.

'You not eating?'

'I'm not hungry at the moment.'

He waved his knife at the window. 'Better eat something. It will be night soon, and then . . .'

'This is the plan? The feast before the famine?'

'Sure. It's years since I observed the fast on Yom Kippur.'

'You've not discovered God on me? Please say you haven't.'

'No. Still no God in my universe.' He looked about the room. 'If there were a God I'm sure he'd hate magnolia. I know I do.'

14

'When was the last time you went to shul?'

He cocked his head on one side and thought, knife held high. 'It's been years. Maybe eight years ago. Maybe it was your cousin's Bar Mitzvah.' He returned to sculpting the liver onto the bread. 'But ritual can be good sometimes. I need a little ritual. It's not like I don't have things to atone for. So this year, I fast.' He took a bite and chewed. 'Christ, but is that good. I think that's the first real nosh I've eaten in a year. Seriously.'

She smiled and reached out to rest her hand on his. He looked up and swallowed. They stared at each other. 'Thank you for coming,' he said. 'There aren't many people these days I can . . .'

She squeezed his hand. 'Hey, don't worry about it. All part of the service. How could I let my favourite uncle down.'

'I'm your only uncle.'

'Whatever.'

They laughed and then fell silent. Mal returned to building his bagels.

'Tell me a story,' she said. 'You were always good at those.'

'What? Like "The Princess and the Pea"? You liked that.'

'I think I'm a bit old for "The Princess and the Pea".'

'What? Now you want sex and violence?'

'Nah. I get enough of that at home. Tell me about you and Solly. Tell me that story. I've never heard the full version, the way you met. You've always edited it when I've been around.' She saw him hesitate before taking a bite. Suddenly she thought how old he was. Mal had always kept his looks. His hair, even when it had lost its colour, had always carried a healthy sheen and wave. His skin had always seemed to have a warm glow to it. Now he looked grey and tired and she wanted to embrace him again.

'Of course, you don't have to tell me about it if you don't want to. You don't have to tell me anything.'

He put down the half-eaten bagel and dabbed a

crumb from his lip into his mouth in a delicate manner learned from other, more refined establishments. 'No, it's a good idea; the right kind of story. And appropriate. After all, it was a Rosh Hashanah.'

'When you still went to shul?'

'Honey, it was over thirty-five years ago. I didn't have much choice.' He looked out the window at the sea, now a solid mercury grey in the falling autumn light.

'So?'

He turned back to her. 'OK. So here's how it was.'

Two

When people later asked how they met, Solly and Mal would both refer to that particular New Year service, consciously playing up their Jewishness, challenging people with it. While they would never have bothered to explain it to others, they both knew it was where their mutual admiration had been born. In those days the synagogue to which their families belonged in the further reaches of north-west London was housed in a bunch of tatty prefab blocks originally thrown up to accommodate civil servants during the war, sited on the very edge of what would later become the green belt. They were meant only to have lasted ten years but shortly after the end of hostilities the thirteenth tribe of Israel, the wandering Jews of Edgware and Wealdstone, had scraped together enough to buy it up to use as their shul. They intended to replace it with a brick building by 1960 but, due to infighting and a classic bit of Semitic hubris – old Mrs Silverstein promised to fund half the work on the condition that she was buried in the foundations of the new building and then forgot to die – it was to remain the home of the Edgwarebury congregation of Reform Jews until almost the 1980s. Each autumn on the High Holy Days, Rosh Hashanah and Yom Kippur, the place would be packed to overflowing with the twice-a-year mob all turning up to remind each other they were still alive and that yes, they still had a moral centre if only they could remember where the hell they had left it.

The biggest draw at both services was always the blowing of the shofar, the sounding of the ram's horn, allegedly a rousing call to the guilty to repent, though when it rolled round in the interminable all-day Yom Kippur service it was taken simply as a rousing call; it was the only thing guaranteed to wake up the first five rows. In the old prefab blocks the throaty shout of the horn had a marvellous effect on the fabric of the place. It resonated with the building so that the windows rattled in their frames, the everlasting lamp swung on its electric cord and the walls shook and groaned on their foundations. It was a tradition that the more devout among the congregation would whisper to their small children that the stirring of the building was caused not by harmonics but by the breath of the Lord blowing against their fragile little shul. It scared the wits out of the under-fives and would swiftly be followed by the wailing and screaming of children whose parents had literally filled them with the fear of God.

The gnashing of juvenile teeth was the sign that the meat of the Rosh Hashanah service was over and that the older kids could now slip away into the car park to check out what wonderful tricks puberty had worked on the opposition's bodies, and for the boys to see if they could grapple with Judy Goldman or her pal Ruth Zatz. This was all but seen as a mitzvah by the parents: far better you be caught groping that awful Goldman girl than that you tumble about with some damned shiksa, like the Feldmans' boy did last Yom Kippur in the park behind the gasworks at Belmont. But that morning Mal, then 14 years old, felt fat and clumsy and desperately awkward in a scratchy brown suit two sizes too small for him, a sensation that he later came to suspect pursued him for much of the next decade. He passed up the dismal opportunity to stand around trading insults with the girls and instead made for a wide clump of horse chestnut trees down one side of the building, where he knew the lads always gathered to exchange fags and bravado. There were half a dozen of them there, younger boys like Mal starting now to burst out of their Bar Mitzvah suits, the older boys in the suits they had worn when it had been their younger brothers' turn. They stood in a huddle about the largest of the trees, backs to the path so that stray parents could not see what was going on, one hand in trouser pocket, the other gripping a stubby cigarette between thumb and forefinger as they had all seen the spivs and hoodlums do in those Saturday morning movies.

At the centre of the group was Solomon 'Solly' Princeton, a burly 17-year-old who had opted out of the ravages of adolescence by going straight from the curious uncertainties of childhood to manhood. He wasn't tall, certainly no taller than Mal back then, and while Mal continued upwards for a few years after that Solly stayed resolutely where he was. But even then he had all the other equipment the younger boys associated with maturity. He had broad shoulders and a thick neck and bulky thighs that stretched and strained against the thin material of his trousers as if trying to escape. And Christ, but he was hairy. On quiet days it was said you could hear his stubble growing. There was hair on the back of his hands and poking out the top of his shirt, and a little flicking from his ears. He had one long bushy eyebrow and more than just the hint of a moustache above his top lip so that if you squinted at him it looked like there was a train line running horizontally across his face. But it was a beguiling mush for all that, dimpled through the thicket and welcoming in a sarcastic sort of way. It was a face that said things. It said come here and let me humiliate you.

They had been members of the same shul for years and even attended the same school (though Solly, of course, was a few years ahead of Mal) and yet they had never before passed a single word. Not a syllable.

'Well, well. Moses Jones,' Solly said as Mal approached, stepping over the dog turds and rotting conker shells and the ground-down mulch of fallen leaves. 'Come to lead your people?'

Terrific. They had never properly met and yet Solly

already knew how to rile the new arrival. It was Mal's bizarre misfortune to be the paternal grandson of a cotton merchant from the Welsh valleys. His father's mother, his grandmother, was a Jewess so there were no question marks over his impeccable lineage, but he did carry about him a surname that was, he always said 'about as Hebraic as Prince Philip's dick'. To compensate, his dear parents had lumbered him with Moses. It made him sound, he complained, like a black American hoofer, all sparkly teeth and eager smiles. Since he could first speak he had asked people to call him Mal, which was by no stretch of the imagination a shortening of Moses, but seemed eminently preferable to Mo. 'Now you understand the depth of my tragedy,' he later said to friends. 'I hated my first name so much I wanted people to think I was really called Malcolm.'

'You can call me Mal,' he said, grabbing a light off one of the smaller boys and assuming the required position with thumb and forefinger.

'I know I can call you Mal,' Solly said. 'More fun to call you Moses though, innit.' He crinkled up his nose and jerked his stubble-spiked jaw up a little, challenging Mal to respond.

He spat on the ground, trying to think of a sharp response. 'Call me what you like. Don't promise to answer.' Damn.

'All right. I'll call you Mary. Or Doris. What do you reckon? Doris?'

Mal looked away into the bushes trying to drag on his fag and look inscrutable. Or about as inscrutable as a bloke who has just been called Doris can look. There was silence.

'Solly here's just had a blow job from Judy Goldman,' one of the other boys said, because he thought everybody ought to know.

Mal choked on some smoke. 'You what?'

'Haven't you Solly?' the lad said. 'Just now.' Solly shrugged.

'What? Really?' Mal said, unbelievably impressed. 'During the service?'

Princeton threw his cigarette down and ground it into the earth. 'Yeah. You know how it is,' he said. Though they didn't. A perfect Solly moment, this: all eyes turned upon him, admiring, waiting to be shocked and impressed. 'The rabbi was blowing his horn out front and there she was, blowing mine out back.'

'Where?'

Solly sank both hands into his pockets and leaned back against the tree, nodding towards the building. 'In his room.' Mal shook his head in disbelief. Solly Princeton had been blown in the rabbi's room. The cheek of it. The lucky bastard.

'Do you think you'll get a repeat performance?' said one of the others. 'You know. Yom Kippur?'

Mal reached over and gave him a light clip round the head. 'Don't be rude, Rosenthal. Judy Goldman may just have been crowned the Blow Job Queen but she's a good Jewish girl. She wouldn't want to break the fast.'

There was a moment's silence. Then Solly threw back his head and roared with laughter. 'Very good, Jones. This I like. Very good. Wouldn't want to break the fast. I'll let the Blow Job Queen know.' He looked down at the ground and casually dug a groove in the damp autumn earth with the toe of his shoe. 'I hear you've taken over my business,' he said eventually. There was a more respectful tone to his voice now. Mal nodded and allowed himself a long satisfied drag on his fag.

It was true. Until the end of the academic year before last when Solly Princeton had left the grammar school they both attended in Hendon, he had been the 'titty-card' merchant. Comparatively this stuff was innocence itself: postcards of women who looked no sexier than your racy aunt, tits out, hands on hips. If you were lucky, there would be the odd flash of pube, and most of them were very odd indeed. If you ever got to see anything below the navel it had been airbrushed or touched up so much that they looked less like pubes and more like someone had been going around colouring in their bits with a stumpy wax crayon. It was years before Mal found out that girls' pubic hair was the same as boys.'

Still this was, what? The early sixties? They took their thrills where they could get them, and compared with trying to get the rabbi's wife to rub her ample bosom against you when she leaned over your shoulder in Hebrew classes the titty cards were explicit. Rudeness itself . Solly bought them in job lots from a shop off the Tottenham Court Road every Saturday afternoon and then sold them at double the price the next week in school. It was a good business idea but it lacked that spark which could make it a great one. The problem was the boys soon grew bored of each card. Adolescent male fantasy is pitifully limited and there was only so much masturbatory pleasure you could get out of one titty card. So they would flog each one on to their mates for slightly less than they had paid for it and put the proceeds towards getting themselves a new original which, too, would later be sold on. And that was where Solly was missing a trick. He wasn't controlling the market in his own product.

When Solly left to go into his family's *pâtisserie* business Mal took it upon himself to carry on the fine social service already provided and became the new titty-card merchant, but with one fundamental difference. You couldn't buy the cards any more. You could only rent them. The hire charge for a week was very reasonably exactly the same as Mal had paid. The second time each card was rented he matched Solly's profit, but the third time round he began raking it in. It took a bit more admin, of course. He had a book with names, not just for clients but for the cards, too. There was 'saucer nipple girl' and 'Miss Russell', after Jane, and 'hand shandy Sandy' and one – a connoisseur's piece, this – was called 'Mrs Rubenstein' because the model bore a striking resemblance to the rabbi's wife, though obviously the only takers for that were the other boys at the school who went to Edgwarebury shul. He lost a few cards along the way, of course. Sometimes they came back torn or stained or creased, as if they had been rolled into a dick-sized tube, which didn't bear thinking about. And sometimes, when confiscated by an outraged parent, they didn't come back at all. But Mal drew up a business plan which allowed for a modest average of four rentals per card and, with losses and damaged goods accounted for, had little trouble achieving it.

By the time Solly and Mal spoke for the first time beneath those yellowing horse chestnut trees he was turning a clear profit of over a pound a week, which back then was serious cash for a 14-year-old kid. 'Got a head on you, there, haven't you?' Solly said, when he had explained the system. 'Should have done a partnership, me and you. Made you a partner. What would you have said to that? A partnership with Solly Princeton?'

'Depends whether you'd called me Doris or not when you put up the deal.'

And that was it: the first ever meeting of the two men who founded the Sinai Corporation, in a dog-turd clearing down the side of a prefab in Edgware. It was not exactly 'Dr Livingstone, I presume?' Not exactly glamorous. But we all start somewhere and this was where Solly and Mal began. Looking back, everything that eventually made it work was there. Solly had the genius for the original idea – the titty cards – but he didn't know how to make the best of his own cleverness. And yet he had all the charisma and charm to get you on side. Mal wasn't that good at hatching the initial plan, though he was great at spotting potential and making it work: hiring out the titty cards rather than selling them. And then again he also lacked whatever spark it was that Solly had to win people over. Apart, they were a waste of time, two no-hopers scrabbling about in the dirt for the key. Together they were dynamite. It was a double act that would make them both disgustingly rich.

Three

'The thing is, I never intended to be wealthy,' he said, chasing crumbs of chopped liver around the plate with the flat of his knife.

'No?' Natasha lifted one leg off the floor and rested her knee against the edge of the table, holding it there with clasped hands. 'You always seemed to be someone who knew how to have money. You knew what to do with it.'

'What? Some people, they don't know how to have money?'

'Sure. It doesn't suit them. Money makes them clumsy. Money never made you clumsy.'

He pointed at her with the greasy tip of his knife. 'You saying I've got taste?'

She giggled. 'Yeah. I always thought you had taste . . . until I saw this place, of course.' The magnolia walls were now turning a sickly grey as dusk fell outside.

'I told you. It's temporary. A stopgap, that's all.'

She lifted her hands in mock surrender. He piled another sweaty wedge of bagel into his mouth, as though it were the first food he had seen in a week. 'I'm not saying that I don't . . . that I didn't like money. It was just I never planned to be wealthy. Not that I planned to be poor either. What shmock plans to be poor?' He laid down his knife and sat back in his chair to look out at the view that he had been studying so closely these past days. 'And yet I've managed both, which if you ask me is a real achievement. It takes major talent to lose a £150 million fortune, especially if you don't have a big-time cocaine habit, and I

25

didn't.' Natasha dropped her head to one side and raised an eyebrow.

'Honestly. I never did drugs.'

'But I thought that was what this was all about. If it wasn't for the drugs all this would never—'

'Solly's thing. Not mine. Always Solly's.'

'Mal, I am not a child any more. I've been stoned, you know. I've done stuff. At college things happen.'

'Then you've done more than me. And don't try to shock. It doesn't suit you, being shocking.' There was silence.

'So?'

'So what?'

'You never did drugs?'

'OK, OK, once I did cocaine and it was a disaster.'

'Now we're getting somewhere . . .'

' . . . but I only did it then because Solly said it would be rude to the client not to.'

'Great. Another story.'

'Not another story, honey. Don't make me tell it. It's embarrassing.'

She fixed him with a stare.

'Look, OK. I was trying to do a line of coke and I overbalanced and almost broke my nose when I hit the table. That's all there is to it.'

'Sounds like a great story.'

'Maybe later, sweetheart. Maybe later.'

She could see he was uncomfortable with the memory. His head was turned away to the blank window. She decided on another approach. 'So you're saying the coke was Solly's thing.'

He looked back to her. 'Is this an interrogation? because I've already done one of those with frightening men in bad suits and I don't fancy another.'

'Yes it's an interrogation. So?'

'It was Solly's thing, not mine. I already said that. What kind of man do you think I am? I once tried to tell him as sensitively as I could that Jews don't really drink and that they don't do drugs either. I told him,

26

what was it? Ah yes. I told him he was turning into a kind of absurd cultural mongrel. I was proud of the phrase.'

'Solly understood words like that?'

'Solly was many things, but he wasn't stupid.'

'I believe you. What did he say?'

'Well, as his coke dealer was called Saul Israelson and his big-time using buddies were the Horowitz brothers from Mill Hill it didn't really wash.'

She laughed. 'I can understand that.'

It was dark now and the time for food was passed. Yom Kippur had begun. Mal began clearing away the plates, shovelling chopped liver and herring back into their plastic pots, wrapping up spare bagels, locking away food for the fast. 'I've been trying to think of the biggest contrast between before and now. And you know, I think it probably was that night I gave myself a nosebleed over the cocaine. Not nice. Not nice at all.'

'No, it wasn't but at least you now know that.'

'So?'

'So, it's beginning. Atonement. You're learning to regret. Of course, it shouldn't take a year in prison for you to realize that bleeding into your cocaine is bad manners, but if that's what it takes, so be it.'

'Please, Nat. This is a small bedsit. There isn't room in it for you, me and your sarcasm. But you're right. It's beginning. A little penance. I am starting to regret, learning how to say sorry and how to feel guilt and that has to be a good thing.' He began to wash the plates beneath a tepid stream of yellow water from the rusted pipes. Here in his Herne Bay fastness, he thought, he had the chance to learn how to be human again instead of superhuman. Even after the fall and he was in Class doing time he was still marked out as special. He was still Mal Jones, the man who was in for the Sinai conspiracy and that gave him a kind of infected celebrity. True, his business had been smaller than those belonging to some in there, but it had been bigger than most. Even in prison-issue gear he had his status, what the other cons called 'High-grade RC' or 'Respect Credibility'. But here in Herne Bay, he was just the weird middle-aged Jew up in the bedsit on the third floor who paid his rent with cheques on a bank account in Golders Green. The last few thousands he had in the world; what the authorities hadn't taken in fines, his dear wife had grabbed when she divorced him.

Mal looked about the room while Natatsha sat and flicked aimlessly through a magazine plucked from her bag. He had two small gas rings on a chipped enamel hob and a sink painted with tide marks. He had a lonely double bed that sagged on only one side, a transistor radio and – his one luxury, this – a small colour television. There was a kitchen table plus two chairs. There were a few books, mostly thrillers. There was a separate shower room with a toilet, which was so small you could stand in the shower and piss into the toilet bowl without missing, if you were ever so bored as to try (which he had been). And of course, he had the view. The endless, wretched, taunting plain of the sea. Perfect brooding material.

In the old days the house in Highgate would have been full of Jewish new year cards about this time. Hundreds of the damn things, each one as grim as the next, with their sentimental images of Torahs and Stars of David in silver and blue and white, their earnest inscriptions and their wishes and blessings and scribbled greetings from the Bessies and Friedas they had so long ago forgotten. Mal always used to resent their presence on his bookshelves because they reminded him that once again he would not be going to shul this year on the High Holy Days. It always struck him as something of a betrayal, despite his god-lessness. And yet, now things were different, he missed the cards. There was only one, from Natasha, but that was too tasteful, all autumnal golds and browns, not a flash of silver in sight.

'Thank you for the card,' he said. She shrugged, as if

it were nothing but she knew it was a lot. 'Heard anything from my brood? Have you seen them, the boys?'

She shifted awkwardly in her chair. 'I've seen Simon, talked to Jonathan.'

'They say much?' She shook her head. 'Not much you want to repeat?' She nodded, embarrassed. 'That's OK,' he said, drying a plate. 'Still too angry with me to get in touch. This I understand.' He stacked away the plates and wiped around the sink. She said 'You done?' and he nodded. 'Then come back over here and sit down. Tell me more stories.' He returned to his seat and leaned forward on his elbows. They stared into each other's eyes for a moment and he felt another wave of gratitude break over him. She had come when no-one else would.

Suddenly she gasped. 'Christ, I almost forgot.' She reached down into her bag and began digging around for a lost treasure.

'What?'

'This,' she said, victorious, waving a tape. 'Mood music. Atmosphere.' She looked around the room. There was no tape player. She dug around in her bag again and pulled out a personal stereo and two dwarf speakers. 'A bit tinny but they'll do.' Natasha clicked on the tape and a rich tenor voice soared to the echo, every word of Hebrew clear and proud.

'The Kol Nidre service,' she said. 'I didn't think there would be a shul nearby so if you're going to do the fasting bit, I thought . . .'

'I know what it is,' Mal said, his voice tight and uncomfortable. He stared at his hands as if desperately hoping there were something between them that he could fiddle with, a ribbon or a paperclip or a knife, but there was nothing. She heard him snort and reach to brush his eye, as if irritated by a speck of dust, though the air was clear. 'I'm sorry,' he said, swallowing heavily. 'It's just that I've always loved . . .' He swallowed again, trying to compose himself, and looked up into the shadowed corners of the room, blinking back a rogue tear that had determined to show him up. 'There haven't been beautiful things in this rancid flat since I got here. Apart from you, of course.'

She looked at the table top and said 'Do you want me to turn it off?'

He shook his head. 'Leave it. I'm fine. Just for a moment there, it all went a bit, you know.'

'I know,' she said, quietly. And then, louder: 'OK, the music stays. Now give me the stories. Tell me things. How did you get the money? What happened next? You and Solly, you've met outside the shul and you've made friends.'

He cleared his throat and sat back. 'Yes, we've made friends, but we don't see each other for years after that. He goes off to Manchester to work with his uncle for a while and I finish school and go off to study to become an accountant. So it's years. Next time we meet, I'm, what, 18 and he's 20 or 21. Anyway it's 1968 and it must have been November because your great-grand-father had just died.'

'And?'

'Patience, honey. Like all good success stories this one starts with a dead chicken.'

'Mal, stop playing with me. Success stories do not start with dead chickens.'

'Natasha, my poor child. If you don't start with a dead chicken how the hell are you going to make the chicken soup?'

Four

By the time they met once more the dead chicken, which was to have such a impact upon both their lives, was already in a large pot on Golda Princeton's cooker, drowning in salted water. It was, as far as her son could see, the most noble end a chicken could wish for. While the carcass rolled and bucked in the boiling stock, nudging the side of the pan as if making a feeble bid for freedom, Solly was half a mile away in the family's Edgware shop, wiping down the cake cabinet, rearranging the pastries and thinking about locking up. He watched his girlfriend flick through an edition of *Vogue*; watched her dismiss furiously the designs of expensive outfits he knew she so coveted with an impatient rap of her manicured fingernails upon the Formica of the shop's one café table. He watched her flick and rap and sigh and flick once more and wondered again at the bizarre behaviour of women, and why he found it so damn attractive. He was so captivated that he did not notice the younger man with the familiar square jaw and mop of indolent hair enter the shop until he was standing in front of him, head on one side, peering at his face.

'Solly?' the customer said, tentatively.

The other man started and looked up. 'Well bugger me sideways,' he said, his hairy cheeks folding up into a grin.

Mal heard a nasal shriek from the girl in the corner. 'Dirty words, Solly. I've told you. It's disgusting.'

'Sorry, darlin'. But as I live and breathe it's Moses, I mean Mal Jones.' He walked around from behind the counter, wiping his hands on his apron and reached out to shake. 'How are you, my old mate? Where you been hiding?'

'I've been here,' Mal said quietly, a little taken aback by the warmth of welcome. 'It's you that's been away.'

'That's true,' he said, with another broad grin. He turned to his girlfriend. 'Sweetheart you remember Mal here, don't you? Mal Jones, you know from Edgwarebury shul. And of course Mal you remember my girl, Judy Goldman.'

'My God, the Blow Job Queen,' Mal heard himself say, and felt a sharp elbow in the ribs. Judy looked up. 'What was that?' she whined.

'Nothing,' Mal said. 'I coughed. That's all.' And manufactured a cough worthy of a consumptive.

'Nasty,' she declared, with apparent admiration. 'Mr Silverstein died of a cough like that. Choked on his own phlegm,' she continued, the silent 'g' finding voice in her pronunciation. 'You should get that looked at.' As she spoke Mal found himself captivated by the sight of her thickly painted lips and the thought of what she was willing to allow past them. He watched her gather up her magazine, bag and nail file, the equipment that went with the job of womanhood, and make for the door. 'Now Solly,' she said, hovering by his shoulder. She puckered up and placed a kiss upon his cheek before turning to him for the same. 'You can call for me at eight tonight and don't be late.' And then she swept out.

'Lovely girl,' Solly said as she went, her heavy perfume still hanging about them in a cloud, like recently discharged fly spray.

'Lovely girl,' Mal agreed, because it seemed the polite thing to say.

'She's just so . . .'

'So what?'

Solly looked at Mal. 'Jewish,' he said.

Mal roared with laughter. 'Yeah and you're king goy.' He shrugged irritably. 'Fair do's. But you know what

I mean. With Jewish girls it always feels like you're snogging your sister.'

'Have you snogged your sister?'

'I don't have a sister,' he said, his eyes still fixed on the distant spot where Judy had been, as if he could see the perfume vapour trail she had left behind. 'But if I had one I know what it would be like to snog her.'

'You're an odd man, Solly.'

'No I'm not. Healthy Jewish lad with an enquiring mind. That's all. Now then, you just come here to eye up the Blow Job Queen or did you want to buy cake?'

'I came for cake, though Judy was a bonus. My grandad has died. Need to sort a few bits and pieces for the shivah.'

'Jesus Mal, I'm sorry, why didn't you say? I wish you long life an' all that. Here's me going on about a sister I don't even have and your grandad's . . .'

'It's all right, he was getting on. Some of us were beginning to think he'd never get round to it.'

Solly took off his apron and began closing up the shop. 'Come up to the house,' he said. 'We'll sort out what you need there and I'll bring it round tomorrow. My mum would love to see you again, give her condolences, all of that.'

'Your mum's never met me.'

'Ach,' he said. 'Then she'd love to meet you. Whatever. Anyway come up to the house. There's a chicken needs tending to.'

Golda Princeton was a short, bulky woman of middle years who wore blouses which strained above the cleavage, carpet slippers and, like her son, a dark moustache. She was, she would say, a martyr to her extremities. The centre was holding but the feet, hands and sinuses were all complaining in their own unique way. 'Come in,' she said to Mal. 'My sinuses are as blocked as Park Lane in rush hour, but come in all the same. And I must sit down. These feet of mine, they are telling me to sit. So I sit. You sit too. Solly will make us tea and we will sit. It is all a mother asks. That

33

she sits while her son makes the tea.' Solly told his mother about Mal's grandfather because he knew how much she enjoyed a good bereavement and she responded appropriately, tutting and rolling her eyes and shaking her head, and sometimes doing all three. In Golda's book there were few better deaths than the expected death of an old person. All the drama with none of the distress. And a funeral was so much more enjoyable than a wedding or Bar Mitzvah: you didn't have to bring a present. Mal made the right noises in return and watched as her son busied himself about the kitchen.

It was then that Solly performed the alchemy that would change their lives. He lifted onto a plate the chicken that had been boiling away on the stove and put it to one side. Next he reached into a cupboard to bring down the apparatus. It had a funnel and beneath that a glass tube with a tiny tap attached. At the bottom there was a sieve and in turn below that a bowl. The whole rested in a stand which kept it vertical. It was clearly home made, the soldered joins less than neat. But it was a fine piece of work, for all that. Whatever it was.

'It's for instant chicken stock,' Solly said, as he checked the tap was closed and began pouring the liquid from the pan into the funnel.

Mal walked over to watch. 'You cook?' he said with wonder.

'Of course I cook. I eat so I cook. You want to eat? You should cook too.' He finished filling the funnel and stood over it, watching the surface of the stock. 'Normally you want to make chicken soup, you boil the chicken and then you leave it to stand so that the fat, the shmaltz, it goes solid on the top. Takes an hour, at least. With this, there's no waiting. You see.' He pointed into the funnel. 'The surface has gone a little milky. So now all the fat is at the top.' Slowly, his gaze fixed on the clear tube, he opened the tap. The stock passed through the sieve which caught the parsley and onion skins and the occasional lump of chicken meat, and went into the bowl. After a minute or so, the layer of fat started to pursue the stock down the tube. Before it reached the bottom, Solly turned the tap.

'*Voilà*,' he said, 'all the shmakz in the funnel and all the stock in the bowl. Now we make chicken soup and it takes an hour less. Everybody needs chicken soup.'

'Everybody needs chicken soup,' Mal muttered under his breath, overwhelmed with admiration. 'Solly, that is close to a philosophy.'

'My son,' Golda said, as she rubbed one slipper-free foot between both hands, 'is the Einstein of the kitchen. There should be a Nobel prize for cooking. I tell you. Who cares about economics? Adding up never saved your life. But cooking, we all need to eat.'

'Have you made any more of these?' Mal said, flicking the tube with one finger.

Solly shrugged, as he decanted the fat into another bowl. 'My Aunt Gloria has one. Why?'

It was the titty cards all over again; Mal could see a way to improve on Solly's good idea. His proposition was simple: they produce another ten and try to sell them. Most of the parts, Solly explained enthusiastically, came from Mrs Hyman's kitchenware shop on the high street, apart from the tube with the tap – the most expensive part – which he had taken from an old chemistry set. 'They sell replacements in the toy shop next door to the kitchenware place,' he said. It took only three days (with a break for old Mr Jones's funeral and shivah, both of which Golda enjoyed hugely) to gather all the parts together and build ten of Solly's Stock Skimmers, as they had come to call them, on Golda's kitchen table.

'You build Airfix models as a kid?' Mal said, as he watched Solly construct the first. Bursts of grey smoke came dark and acrid from the end of the soldering iron as each piece was fused into place.

'Yeah, but only so I could crash them. Spent ages building jet liners and then I'd chuck them out the top window to see what a plane crash looked like. I reckoned I'd never get to see a real one.' Solly closed one eye against another dwarf-genie puff of smoke. 'Still haven't.'

'You were a difficult child?'

'Nah. Just liked breaking things. Built a doll's house once. Even gave it rooms and curtains and stuff. Little net curtains on runners made out of string. Then I burned it down.'

'What did your folks say?'

'They were really pleased. When I started building the doll's house they thought it was a sign I was a bit . . .'

'Obsessed by soft furnishings?'

'Yeah. Ready for a duet on the pink oboe. All of that. Didn't think they'd get to see the glass get broken.' Another lump of solder fizzed and liquefied on the end of the iron. 'So when I burned it down they were well chuffed. They were much happier with a psychopath for a child than a queen.'

Mal rested his head in his hands as he watched. 'If you know about building things, tell me this,' he said eventually.

'Try me.'

'Those big cranes. The ones they use on office blocks, the 200-foot-tall ones.'

'Yeah, I know the ones you mean. The big buggers.'

'How do they get the huge concrete counterweight onto the top if they haven't finished building the crane?'

Solly stopped soldering and sat back. He stared at the ceiling for a moment and then shook his head. 'Haven't got a clue. Leave those kinds of questions to the Gentiles. They work that sort of thing out.' Mal was pleased. Solly could build stock skimmers but he couldn't answer the crane question. He'd never met anybody who could answer the crane question. And he didn't want to meet anybody who could. He was sure their thoughts would work in a way he wouldn't like, all straight lines and angles rather than warm curves. He was sure he could never go into business with someone who thought in straight lines.

Solly had returned to the task before him, fixing the contraption into its stand.

'There,' he said. 'Finished.'

'Work of art,' said Mal.

'Work of an hour,' said Solly. ' Here's your soldering iron. There are the pieces. Get to it.'

With the skimmers completed all they had to do was convince Mrs Hyman, the local kitchenware maven, to stock their product.

Mrs Hyman was not a woman ideally suited to the task of selling kitchen equipment. She believed the modern world to be a conspiracy against her; that each new labour-saving device was the opposite, something designed to clutter up time and space. Specifically her time and her space. 'In the hours it takes to learn to use it,' she would say, of a new electric carving knife, 'you could skin a cat the old-fashioned way three times over'; which comment, many said, told you all you needed to know about Mrs Hyman.

Mrs Hyman, it was said, thought the gas cooker a pointless innovation when the open fire was perfectly adequate. Mrs Hyman, it was also said, was a terrible cook, but as no living person had ever eaten anything she had prepared there was no way to substantiate the claim, although the more malicious would point out that Mr Hyman had died early of a massive heart attack, suspiciously close to one dinner time.

'So show me, dear,' she said, arms crossed over her chest, thin lips clenched tight, as if Solly had laid a dead rat on her counter. He busied himself with the glories of the tap and the funnel, the wonders of the sieve below and the glass tube above. The old lady was unmoved.

'Mrs Hyman,' Mal said, when it became clear Solly was floundering. 'Everybody needs chicken soup.'

'That's true,' she said. She reached out and turned the little tap this way and that.

'That's all it takes,' Solly said; 'a twist on the tap. So simple.'

'Simple to you young man. But some of my old ladies have arthritis. Simple then, is it? And what if you have no hands?'

'If you have no hands,' he said, 'you will be well beyond the help of chicken soup.'

'Don't be clever with me, Solly Princeton. I've known you since you needed someone else to hold your little pipi.'

'He still likes it when people do that,' Mal said quietly and felt a sharp kick to his shins for his troubles. It was time for a new approach.

'Mrs Hyman,' Mal said. 'Let's do it sale or return. A little shelf space is all. If you don't sell any, we take them away. You sell, and we split the profit down the middle.' She looked up at a sparsely filled shelf on the wall behind them.

'What do I call it?' she said, turning it around on its base.

Mal was about to speak when Solly interrupted. 'The Pollo-Matic.'

'The what?' Mal said.

'The Pollo-Matic. Pollo. It's French for chicken soup.' Mal raised one eyebrow. 'Whatever,' Solly said through clenched teeth.

'Yes, Mrs Hyman, as my associate says it is called the Pollo-Matic.'

'And what are you two clowns called?'

'Er, Solly Princeton and he's Mal—'

'I know your names, child. What's your company called? God forbid, anybody should try to buy one of these but if they do they'll want to know who made it.'

They fell silent for half a minute and stared at the floor. Finally Solly opened his mouth. 'The Sinai Corporation,' he said. And after a few seconds more he added, 'incorporated. The Sinai Corporation Inc. That's who made it.'

Mrs Hyman fixed him with a dark stare. 'Why?' she said with a shrug that started at her navel. 'Why Sinai?'

'Because Moses here is trying to lead me to the promised land.'

Five

When things don't happen on Edgware High Street, they do so bloody noisily. In the days that followed the introduction of the Sinai Corporation's first product to the public, the sound of failure was deafening. Apparently nobody wanted instant chicken soup. Mal spent much of his time in Solly's *pâtisserie,* where the air smelt comfortingly of melted butter and warm bread, neglecting his accountancy studies and watching his new business partner sell cakes. If he'd had his way Mal would have stood all day at Mrs Hyman's shoulder in her shop two doors down, watching, nudging, talking up. But this was out of the question. So instead he camped out in Princeton's Pâtisserie, among the pastries and the poppyseed cakes and bridge rolls, in the hope of gathering intelligence on what was occurring across Mrs Hyman's counter. Sadly, what intelligence he gathered told him that nothing was going on at all.

Mal's life was not dependent on the success of the Pollo-Matic. He knew that. But his juvenile self-esteem was. He knew he had skills: a facility for numbers, a dull gift for organization, a comfortable, unassuming way with people which appeared to make them like him. These he took for granted. It was his eye for the great money-spinning idea upon which he really prided himself. Not that he had put it to much good use so far, or to any at all. Apart from the titty cards, which to his mind barely counted, all his great marketing successes had been of the imaginary kind. In his daydream – and there was only one – he found the perfect product whose virtue everybody else had failed to

recognize, and made it into something great. The daydream was so regular, and so finessed in detail and
colour and even flavour – it tasted only of copper coins
– that he had to remind himself that it was indeed
imaginary. It mattered little that in this daydream he
had never once been able to identify the wonder
product. He knew what qualities it had: it was carry-
able, it was relatively cheap, and it was something
women wanted. Sometimes it was shiny. Sometimes it
wasn't. But it was deeply utilitarian. This he knew for
sure, because he'd heard the word being used and
looked it up in a dictionary and become convinced that
whatever this thing was for, it was definitely 'designed
for use rather than beauty'. Later he decided that,
while being firmly designed for use, it could also be a
little bit beautiful.

Now he had found the product. It was called the
Pollo-Matic, it was on sale and the time for daydream-
ing was past. He was left with simple fear. If he was
wrong, then his belief in himself would be gone and he
would be bound for a life of accountancy, like his
father Samuel. His eyesight would be shot by the time
he was 40, he would develop a lump on his middle -
finger from where he squeezed the red pen; the mark of
servitude. He would always add up other people's
figures. He would, in short, become his father.

Sam Jones had long believed himself to be a great
businessman, but his faith had not been rewarded.
When he had started out as an accountant twenty years
before, the junior bookkeeper to a firm of dress manufacturers in Colindale, he had considered it his first
step on the route to what he called 'grandiose business
ventures'. Back then he had twenty-twenty vision.
Back then he had plans and schemes and visions, but
that was all they ever were. No ventures, grandiose or
otherwise, had ever materialized. He had progressed
only to become senior bookkeeper with thick glasses,
employed by the same firm of dress manufacturers in
Colindale. To his friends and relatives he was in the

shmatte business. But to Sam Jones, a large man with big ideas that had stayed small, he was merely in the number business and that was a source of endless disappointment to him.

Now at breakfast, living out his thwarted ambitions as fantasy, he would search for stories of success in the *Financial Times*, which he always referred to as his 'journal'. He would nod his large, round head in recognition, or run his fingers restlessly through his tight mop of greying, brilliantined curls. 'Marsha,' he would say to his wife, who was as slight as he was broad. 'This is what I'm always saying. That to have success in business you need the product. It says so here, on the page. Only a no-nothing shmock would disagree.'

Or he would say, 'Marsha, one day, this will be us. In the journal.'

Marsha Jones would no longer look up from her copy of the *Daily Sketch*. 'Samuel dear, I'm sure you're right,' she would say, pursing her narrow lips in irritation at being disturbed. It was all she ever said over breakfast to her husband. 'Samuel dear. I'm sure. You are right.'

Her indifference did not deter Sam from his view of the world as a place breathlessly awaiting his entry into high commerce. It seeped even into his social language. He did not greet friends with a 'hello' or 'great to see you' or 'where have you been hiding?' Always it was 'How's business?' At a wedding to the groom. At a Bar Mitzvah to the father. Outside Princeton's Pâtisserie on a Sunday morning, as he queued for onion platzels with friends from shul. Always 'How's business?'

If Mal arrived home late from school and Sam had arrived back from work before him he would welcome his son with a gruff 'How's business?'

'It's school, Dad.'

'So? What's to choose between school and business? If you don't make good in school you'll never make it in business.'

'It's not about making money. It's about learning stuff.'

'Things you can use, Mal. Trust me. I know about finance.'

Eventually Mal would give up, just as Marsha had done years before. 'Business is fine, Dad. Business is just fine.'

When Mal Jones went into partnership with Solly Princeton he was therefore going into the family business. Which for the Jones family was dreaming about having a great business success. As he told Natasha thirty years later, his strivings were not about wealth – he was honest about that – but they were about achievement, and achievement was measured in figures; figures which, if you had achieved, other people would be employed to add up for you. That was exactly what Sam Jones still did, and would always do for a living. He added up other people's figures.

Mal's only diversion from fear of failure was watching Solly perform. It had been a friendship made on the hoof. Until that afternoon around Golda's cooker and the dead chicken, they really had not known each other. They had understood each other, of course, in the way all north London Jewish lads understood each other. There was a language in common, which was not merely about exotic words of Yiddish – which were, in any case, more affectation than vocabulary – but about shared expectation and what kind of people they weren't.

They were not uptight Gentiles. They touched each other. They spoke. They did not comprehend silences. And they liked their families. Or if they didn't like their families they knew that family was part of them, in the way we know our legs are part of us, however much we might wish them to be another shape. We still need them to get around. Their understanding was in the detail: for example both Golda Princeton and Marsha Jones said to their sons that all they wanted was 'for you to be happy'. But both sons knew that what their mothers really meant was that they had fixed ideas about what exactly it was that would make their boys happy.

So they understood each other, Mal and Solly, and they understood Jewish mothers, because they each had one. This, however, was context, not friendship. It was one thing to know someone, quite another to admire them as well, and Mal found he admired Solly. Not in the way he had been in awe beneath the damp horse chestnut trees four years before. That had been mere deference to an elder. This was something else.

He admired Solly's enthusiasms and his ludicrous exuberance. Solly did not merely take money for cake. He sold cake, flogged cake, forced it out the door, like a sailor bailing out a sinking boat. He was a cake shop man who was only happy when there was no cake in his shop. He had a shtick. He knew all his customers by name and what they wanted and what ailed them and what ailed those around them. And most importantly he knew how to make them feel better.

'Mrs Gross,' he said to one hypochondriac, who complained that death was near on account of her aching legs. 'My dear Uncle Alf had varicose veins and he lived to be 95 if he was a day.' She would leave happy, and as she went Solly would wink and declare in a stage whisper that he had no Uncle Alf or that Alfie had died of thrombosis at 45. But what matter? Mrs Gross was happier going out than coming in and she had bought cake. When rain showers came he handed out cups of his terrible tepid coffee until the worst of the weather had passed. In the mean time the customers stood and gossiped with each other as Solly looked on indulgently, like a mother hen. When the bread had come out of the oven he implored them to hold it to their cheeks as they walked home for comfort against the cold autumn winds. For these reasons he was loved.

But for Mal all of this was a sideshow to the main event two doors up at Mrs Hyman's.

'Ah, the shmaltz moguls,' one customer said as she bustled in, her shopping trolley clanking behind her. 'The two boys who don't want to wait for chicken soup.'

'Everybody needs chicken soup,' Mal said a little despondently.

'If it's worth having it's worth waiting for. But why should I expect young lads like you to understand this? All you have in your minds is bosoms and tuchus,' she said, tapping her temple. 'Now give me a dozen bridge rolls.'

'Oh, the great Jewish metalworkers Mrs Hyman told me about,' said another. 'For 5,000 years no Jew has ever known how to weld. If we wanted welding we got a Gentile to do it. They did the welding. Now we have two Jewish welders. This, I suppose, is progress.'

'The Pollo-Matic makes great chicken soup, Mrs Roth,' said Solly.

'I make great chicken soup,' said Mrs Roth, 'and I don't need a blowtorch to do it. Are you criticizing my chicken soup?'

'No, Mrs Roth. Of course not. Here, have an extra bridge roll on me.'

After three days of this, Mal could take it no more and went next door to see what was going on. The shop was empty save for Mrs Hyman, who sat behind the counter reading the wedding announcements in the *Jewish Chronicle*. 'Brides always need kitchenware,' she said to Mal. 'They don't need quick chicken soup but they do need kitchenware.'

'I just thought I'd check how things were going,' Mal said.

Mrs Hyman looked up at the shelf, its contents undisturbed. 'Things are not going,' she said. 'They are staying. All of it is staying.'

'You could be, you know, a little more encouraging. You could sell it a little bit more.'

'Ha. Does this look like a street stall? Do I look like a hawker? I don't hawk. You want to hawk, get a stall and hawk, but there's no hawking goes on in my shop.'

Two days later Mrs Hyman had moved on to the death notices in the *JC*. 'In the winter there are always more funerals than weddings,' she said, sadly. 'This is not good for kitchenware. Dead people do not need kitchenware. And no, I have not sold any of your contraptions. We had one woman yesterday who was interested but . . .'

'But what? What happened?'

'Ach, she's mad as a hatter. Poor Elsie. She probably only wanted it because it was shiny.' She took off her glasses, rubbed the bridge of her nose and looked sympathetically at Mal for the first time. 'I'm sorry, child,' she said gently. 'I really think I need my shelf back.'

'Oh, Mrs Hyman, no, please, just a few more days . . .'

The bell above the door rattled in its hinge as a customer in headscarf and hound's-tooth wool coat came in asking to look at fish slices. It could have been a wedding gift, then again maybe she was catering a funeral. Who could tell at Mrs Hyman's? Mal slunk back into the depths of the shop, grateful for a few moments to come up with some way to convince Mrs Hyman to keep the Pollo-Matic on display. He ran his fingers over piles of glass bowls made by vast multinational companies with names he had heard of, admired the sets of kitchen knives held in wall cabinets, studied the cheese graters and copper cooking pans and cooling racks.

'And this one,' he heard the woman say, as she picked up a fish slice from the counter, its silver flat glinting under the shop lights.

'This one is twice the price of that one,' Mrs Hyman said.

'Twice the price?' the woman said. 'Is it better than that one?'

'What can I tell you? It's twice the price.'

'Twice the price,' the woman repeated. She turned it over in her hands, studied its fine bevelled edge and markings, nodding slowly as she did so, as if she were an expert in the art of fish slice manufacture. She ran the pad of her middle finger around the tip. 'Fine work,' she said. 'Twice the price, you say.'

Mal hovered by the Tupperware and watched, transfixed. He muttered the words to himself. 'Twice the price, twice the price.'

'I'll take it,' the customer said, eventually. 'Wrap it for me, will you?'

'Mrs Hyman,' Mal said, after she had gone. 'I have an idea.'

He was still grinning when he returned to the *pâtisserie*. Solly galloped around from behind the counter and grabbed Mal by the shoulders.

'How many?' he said. 'How many have we sold?' Mal shook his head, but the grin did not subside.

'None,' he said, 'but we will.' Solly frowned.

'We've sold none and you're happy? Explain.'

'It's all in the marketing,' Mal said. 'I'm standing there and I'm looking at the Pollo-Matics all lined up on the shelf. And do you know what I'm thinking? I'm thinking they look like really cheap pieces of crap.'

'Oi, I didn't ask you into my shop to slag off my invention.'

'Solly, calm down. I didn't say they *were* cheap pieces of crap. I said that's what they looked like. Cheap crap. And if that's what they look like to me then that's what they look like to everybody else. And who wants cheap crap?'

'So? They're home made. They're cheap and they're made from crap. What can we do?'

'What we can do is make punters realize just how good they are.'

'And that's what you've done?'

'Yeah.'

'How.'

'I've told Mrs Hyman to double the price. Instead of putting them on for ten bob, the Pollo-Matic now costs a pound. People appreciate expensive things. If it's cheap they think it's, well, cheap.'

Solly stared at him open-mouthed for half a minute and then threw the tea cloth in his hand across the shop so it smacked into the wall behind the counter and dropped into the sink. 'I am in business with a shmock,' he said, rubbing his stubbled chin with the back of one hand. He went back behind the counter. 'I am going to carry on stacking cake,' he said quietly. 'That is what I will do. I like cake. My customers like cake. Cake I understand. People always need cake.' He looked up at Mal, whose grin was only just beginning to subside. 'You arsehole,' Solly said, finally.

Mal was unmoved. 'Trust me,' he said. 'It will work.'

Except, of course, it didn't. For the rest of that week nothing happened. It didn't happen the following Monday or the Tuesday. Even Mrs Hyman turned on the pity. She didn't mock Mal any more when he came into the shop to see how things were going. She offered to make him cups of tea and it was these acts of unexpected kindness that most unnerved him. When you were offered charity by Mrs Hyman you knew you had to be in a bad way. He accepted the tea rarely and went to the *pâtisserie* less and less, afraid of Solly's barbs. 'You want a cheese sandwich?' he said, one lunchtime. 'Yours for a grand. Or maybe you'd prefer to pay two. That way you'll know it's a better sandwich. Shmock.'

By comparison a few hours with double-entry book-keeping seemed pure heaven. In any case, he reasoned, he was going to need it now. He studied his middle finger and the slight callus that was already beginning to appear just above the first joint, from where he held a pen. This is my destiny, he thought, and I deserve it.

One Friday afternoon, almost two weeks after they had first taken the Pollo-Matics to Mrs Hyman, Mal turned up at the *pâtisserie* clutching two crisp pound notes, half the cost of the materials which they had originally split between them.

'Here,' he said, placing them on the counter, side by side. 'Just wanted to give you this.' Solly looked at them and nodded without saying anything, as he dried his hands.

'If it's any compensation, I still think it's a great invention. You should patent it. Definitely patent it. You don't know. Maybe someone . . .'

'Maybe,' Solly said. The two of them fell silent.

'If it's all right by you, I'll keep the other ones and, you know, give them to people who . . .' Solly assented with a simple wave of a hand.

'Yeah, keep 'em. We've already got one,' he said, eventually.

'Yes, well then.' Behind him Mal heard the door open, and somebody come in, old shoe leather scuffing the tiled floor. 'I better leave you to it.'

Solly wasn't looking at him any more. He was frowning at somebody over his shoulder. 'Mrs Hyman,' he said tentatively. 'You are . . . I mean it looks to me like . . . that you're smiling.' Mal turned around.

'Moses Jones, come here,' Mrs Hyman said firmly, her lips fixed in a grin. He looked around the room, as if trying to see who she was talking to. 'Yes you, lad. There's hardly going to be anybody else here called Moses Jones, is there.' Other customers began filing into the shop to pick up their Friday night loaves of chola. Mal wandered over and she whispered into his ear while Solly looked on, serving the customers distractedly. After she had gone Mal remained by the door, jaw slack, shoulders slumped.

'Well?' Solly said.

'It's Shabbat tonight,' Mal said.

'Is it?' Solly said, sarcastically. 'I wondered why there were five dozen loaves of chola on the shelves.'

A grin spread across Mal's face. 'It's Shabbat,' he said again. 'The first Shabbat since we raised the price. And what does every housewife in Edgware do on Shabbat?'

They said it in unison. 'Make chicken soup.' Mal

skipped a little dance around the shop. 'She's sold them. Every single one of them. Mrs Hyman's shop is now officially a Pollo-Matic-free zone. She says she needs another ten by Monday. The Sabbath may be a day of rest but I'm afraid you're going to have to work.'

Six

Yankel Morowitz, ageing patriarch of a large, extended family of hirsute men and broad-shouldered women, had long held that banking could never be the salvation of the Jews of Latvia, nor of anywhere else for that matter. 'We must always be ready to leave,' he said to the equally sag-faced men he met in the synagogue or, more often, in the smoky coffee houses that cluttered Riga's waterfront, where the river chased the eels out to sea. 'If we must leave we shall move slowly if we carry with us only gold and the bad will of others' debts.' In a community where logic and rhetoric were more sport than a means of discourse, none could disagree with the first part of dear Yankel's argument, however much he larded it with pomposity. They each had knowledge of the pogroms that had hounded so many families from their homes on the Russian Steppes only a few years before. True, those who lived in the Latvian capital in the latter half of the nineteenth century considered themselves far more cosmopolitan and worldly wise than their counterparts who gouged an income from the frigid Russian earth. But they knew still that they were Jews and that Jews should never be complacent, wherever they might be.

With the second part of his argument, however, they could not agree. Banking, after all, was how many of them made their living. It gave the Jews mobility. If you were forced to leave, it followed that some time afterwards there would be a place in which you would be forced to arrive. How better to arrive than with sufficient wealth to re-establish business? Yankel shook his head, picked crumbs from the tangle of his beard and sipped his coffee, pushing the grains up against his crooked teeth with his tongue. Who could say you would be allowed to fill your pockets before leaving? But fill your head and that is always with you. Learning, he said, was the secret to survival. Do not keep a suitcase packed beneath the bed. Keep your mind well stored and you should never fear, because your mind is always with you.

He made certain that his eight children and his many grandchildren achieved an education, paid for by his furious efforts in the family firm of bookbinders. It was finger-blistering work that on cruel winter afternoons made his hands fold up like eagles' claws and his nose drip like a leaky tap, but he was certain that the next generation would labour only with their minds. In his lifetime, so it proved. As he moved into his seventh decade he was able to enjoy the knowledge that many of Europe's great universities – Paris and Vienna, Geneva and Milan – had been attended by a Morowitz at one time or another. But still he was not satisfied. In the 1890s news came all too regularly of outrages against the Jews in Russia to the east. He feared that Latvia would not be a place where his brood could prosper for long. Accordingly in 1892 he purchased passages for himself, his wife and three youngest sons – all he could afford – on a boat out of Riga, destined for New York. The rest of the family would follow when there was sufficient money.

Yankel never lived to see Ellis Island. What had started as a raw cough in the damp autumn of that year had become, by the winter of the crossing, the tuberculosis which would claim so many who made the trip. When the ship broke the journey at Surrey Quays in London's East End the Morowitz family disembarked and made for a reception centre hard by Brick Lane in Whitechapel where, three weeks later, Yankel died. He was just a few weeks shy of his sixty-fifth birthday. Before he died he left behind one last gift.

New beginnings, he had said, needed new names. As he had thought himself destined for the New World it was there that he looked for the title which he hoped would be his family's introduction to learned circles and a better life. There were a number of universities whose names were appropriate, but only one really appealed. Harvard and Yale could, he said, be given a Latvian pronunciation, the H and Y each coming from a unique place somewhere deep at the back of his throat when he tried them out. And so it was that when his family came to the head of the immigration queue at Surrey Quays he told the officials that he was Yankel Princeton and that this huddle gathered about him was the Princeton family.

'I should be grateful,' Solly said to Mal one afternoon. 'I could have ended up being called Solomon Massachusetts Institute of Technology.'

Yankel would have been sorely disappointed by what had become of the name he had so painstakingly chosen; he had meant it to be preceded by 'Professor', not followed by 'Pâtisserie'. But this said more about Yankel's prejudices than the achievements of his descendants, who had built for themselves a modestly successful business and moved, like so many before them, from the sooty intimacy of the East End to the London suburbs of privet and cherry blossom, shedding religious orthodoxies as they went. Equally, while it was true that Yankel's great-grandson had failed to fill his parents' walls with framed certificates of academic achievement, his facility for flunking exams had only obscured a more emotional intelligence. In the ten months that followed the introduction of the Pollo-Matic, Solly had designed a set of five other kitchen implements that might not have been as inventive as the original, but firmly complemented it. The Sinai range now boasted a can opener and an apple corer, a bell whisk, a potato masher with a lever for changing the size of the mashing holes and a pair of tongs. Each had a solid, clunky appeal which played well against the late Sixties vogue for the modern and the flash. These were rounded, dependable implements that, like heavy pebbles on a beach, begged you to wrap your fist about them. They were the sort of blunt food tools whose inflated price tag would always demand attention and that would sit in your kitchen drawer for a generation.

A small workshop in Mill Hill agreed to knock out a couple of dozen a time at low prices as and when required, if the boys would finish them off themselves. Ralph and Golda Princeton gave their son and his cautiously handsome friend the run of an unused storeroom up a flight of stairs at the back of the shop with the proviso that Solly would help out when business was brisk and, with some relief, Mal suspended his accountancy studies.

'I could spend my time in classrooms adding up false numbers,' he told his father, when he announced his decision. 'Or I could add up real ones.'

'If there are any real ones,' said Sam Jones, rubbing the ancient pen-made lump on the middle finger of his right hand with his thumb, as he always did when he was agitated.

'There will be real figures,' said the son, firmly. 'There are real figures already.'

'You think this is a business? A business isn't just two lads in a back room with a junior tool kit. Read the journal every day. Learn about what a business is. Then, when you have read the journal, maybe you'll be ready.'

'I'm ready now.'

Marsha Jones said, 'All I want is that you should be happy.' She licked the pad of one index finger and ran it fondly along her elder son's eyebrow to flatten the restless tufts. 'And kitchenware will not make you happy. Believe me. I am a mother and I work in a kitchen. Kitchenware has never made me happy.'

'I have to find my own way.'

'Your own way will make you unhappy. But if this is

what you want, to be unhappy, well then . . .'

'We have to make this work,' said the son to his friend, later that same day. 'I can never go back to college.'

'You trying to lead yourself to your own promised land then, Moses, my old mate?' Solly said.

'Sort of,' Mal said. 'And stop it with the Moses gags.'

Together they spent their days surrounded by boxes of implements, filing away rough edges and polishing to a shine, tying on printed name tags with the word 'Sinai' realized in a pastiche of Hebraic script, and preparing batches for the dozen or so shops in northwest London aleady willing to stock their products.

Rarely did they have to labour alone. To their friends, Mal and Solly were the first to have made a break. They had a place of their own, even if it was only a storeroom that smelt of dust and metal filings and clarified butter. Visiting them carried the rare pleasures of self-importance, as they marched about the back of the counter with a wave and shout to Mr and Mrs Princeton. Mal's younger brother Benny would often be there, feet up on the table, drawing on a surreptitious fag and talking loudly of the horses he was going to back with the money he didn't have. Judy came in as well to sit, rounded knees crossed one over the other, filing her nails more noisily than the boys filed their kitchen implements. Still, in Mal's mind, she remained the Blow Job Queen, the nice Jewish girl who did things nice Jewish girls weren't meant to do. Sometimes she would chastise Solly for bursts of ripe language. At other times when she felt he had said something 'sweet and gorgeous', she would shower him with plump kisses, that only made Mal obsess once more about her mouth and the wicked, supple tricks it could perform.

On the occasions they were alone, Mal and Solly filled their time discussing their version of 'The Jewish Question'.

'Here's the thing,' Solly said, late one afternoon. 'You

screw a Jewish girl and afterwards it's like you just showed her your best card trick. She's all "aren't you a clever boy". All that. And she pats you on the head. I don't kid you. Like you're a dog who fetched a bone.'

'And this is different from non-Jewish girls?'

'Sure. You screw a shiksa and she says thank you. No Jewish girl ever said thank you for sex.'

'If you're me, no Jewish girl ever said yes for sex.'

'Ah, Mal,' Solly said, with a dismissive wave, 'don't worry about it. Trust me. It will happen. But I tell you when it does you won't get thanks. She will expect you to thank her.'

'Believe me, when it does happen, I'll want to thank her.' Mal turned to look through the small internal window in the storeroom that looked out over the *pâtisserie* floor, where young Jewish women with carefully coiffured hair and expensive boots came to buy bread. 'But you're right. Girls are meant to be strange and there's nothing strange about a Jewish girl.'

'I told you before,' Solly said, wrapping up a pair of tongs in tissue paper, ready for despatch. 'It's like snogging your sister.' He reached for the next implement. 'Of course, Jewish girls do have tits,' Solly said. 'That's an advantage.'

'You what?'

'Tits. They have tits. Bosoms. Fun bags. You show me a flat-chested Jewish girl and I'll show you a shiksa.'

Mal looked back out the window, spying on the curve of breast and the plunge of cleavage standing before the counter below. 'I have just conducted a very scientific survey and from this random sample I can tell you it is true. Jewish girls do have tits.'

'Of course it's true. I've been conducting the same survey for years.'

'Ah, now that's what I call a shiksa.'

Solly looked up. 'What? Where?'

'Down there in the shop.' Solly came round to stare over Mal's shoulder. Her hair was a glowing deep blond and cut in what would have been a bob had it not been for the broad waves that broke the line. She had a lovely stretch of clear, honeyed forehead, a delicate nose that ended before it made a nuisance of itself and a heart-stopping smile of full lip and dimple. She was leaning over the counter to talk to Ralph Princeton so that her jumper stretched across her chest – next to no breasts, naturally – and her black stretch trousers pulled taut across her thighs. Ralph cocked one ear towards her as he wiped his thick *pâtissier*'s hands on his apron and then pointed at the window where Mal and Solly spied. She looked up at them, nodded and smiled a delicious smile of thanks at Solly's father. Up above the two young men tumbled back over each other onto the greasy linoleum as they tried to get away from the window and out of view.

'Christ,' Solly said. 'She's coming up here.'

'Why?'

'Fuck knows. But she's coming up here. Get back to your work. Look busy and important. File something. File like the wind.'

They heard footsteps on the stairs, a light rap on the door and then she popped her head in. 'Hello,' she said, 'I'm sorry to bother you but . . .'

'No bother darlin',' Solly said, leaning deep into his chair so that it rocked on its two back legs. He shoved his hands behind his head. 'Not botherin' us at all. What can we do for you?' She raised an eyebrow of fine down and sable and looked past him to Mal.

'I'm looking for Benny,' she said.

'Benny?' Mal said, incredulous. 'My brother Benny?' There was a crash as Solly's chair overbalanced and he landed on the floor, so that only his shoes flapped pointlessly in the air. Mal winced and sighed and felt his cheeks colouring. 'I'm sorry,' he said in a stagy whisper, nodding towards his partner's shoes. 'They've, er, they've only just let him out of the special school. Day release. You know how it is.' The girl giggled conspiratorially and nodded, as Solly scrambled to his feet, choking up a sarcastic laugh. 'Yes,' she said, 'I know how it is.' There was a moment's uncomfortable silence. Solly scowled.

'So, is he here?'

'Who?' Mal said.

'Benny. Benny Jones. Only he said this was where I could find him.' He loved the soft breath of her voice, free of nasal inflection or the hint of a whine.

'No, he's not here, but you can wait. He might be along later.'

She looked uncomfortably at the floor, as if suddenly she thought it had been a bad idea to come. 'No,' she said, 'It's all right. I'll leave it.'

'Can I tell him who . . .'

'Yeah, just say Heidi popped in.'

'Heidi,' Mal said, working the unfamiliar sound about his mouth. 'I'll tell him.'

'Now she,' Solly said, after she had gone, 'would say thank you after sex.'

'Don't be so fucking coarse.'

Solly laughed. 'This I like. Don't be so fucking coarse. Perfect. And don't you fucking swear so fucking much.' He leaned across the table to stare at his partner. 'The golden Heidi has you smitten, don't she.'

'Shut up, Solly.'

'Miss Honey Heidi has you smitten and it's your kid brother she just popped in to see. This must hurt.'

Mal shrugged. 'It's difference, that's all. They think in different ways, these non-Jewish girls. I'm just, you know, curious.'

'That's what sex is, Mal. Curiosity. You want to know all the secret stuff And once you know it, none of it's secret any more.'

'Unless they have lots of secrets.' Mal tapped the table with the business end of the potato masher upon which he was working. 'That's the thing. These non-Jewish girls, they have more secrets than Jewish girls. We know the Jewish girls' secrets before we even get their knickers off them. That's all it is. Fewer secrets.'

He stared at the implement in his hands and then threw it desperately onto the table.

'Awh Solly, this is ridiculous.'

'What is?'

'All of this. This poky room, no offence to your folks, Solly. It was kind of them to give us it. But really. And us sitting here filing our fingers to the bone, giving ourselves hard-ons to kill the boredom. It's just, you know, it's low rent.'

'Mal, it's not low rent. It's free.'

'Yeah well, it's a turn of phrase. You know what I mean.' He looked at the clutter about them. 'We should have other people doing this shitty kind of stuff. We should be the brains. We've got to move on. We need to have employees.'

'Employees cost money. You got any money?'

'No,' Mal said slowly, 'but I know where we can get some.'

Seven

George Cuthbert was short and thin. His nose was sharp and pointed and had at its tip a little groove that made him look not unlike a weasel. It required the very shortest of acquaintances with Cuth, as the bank staff called him with feeble respect, to know that he smoked far too much. His cough rumbled upwards from the soles of his brown slip-ons, a lank forelock bouncing upon his forehead each time his petrifying lungs twitched and lurched. Eventually his habit would kill him. But for now he was alive and in a position to wield the one bit of power that the fates, with blunt wit, had deigned to bestow upon him. Cuth stubbed out a full-strength Capstan in the overflowing ashtray by his right hand, lit another and instinctively flicked at the lazy flakes of ash that had settled upon the lapel of his brown polyester jacket. He peered at the application form and nodded his head.

'Eight hundred pounds is rather a large amount of money Mr . . .' he ran his finger down the page. 'Mr Jones.' The bank manager looked up and fixed Mal with a grin that revealed the full Technicolor glory of his yellowing teeth and bloodshot eyes.

'It's a modest amount for the returns we will realize,' Mal replied self-consciously, pulling on the sleeves of the old suit which was a size too small for him. Next to him Solly huffed, and turned to stare out the window at the high street in a miserable attempt to disguise his disdain for the whole affair. He had known it was a terrible idea. No bank was ever going to stand them the cash.

'My partner and I have a clear business plan and

guaranteed orders six months ahead,' Mal said, trying to put solid ground beneath his feet.

Cuth flicked once more at a little ash, dragged on his fag, flicked again and produced a sound from his chest that sounded like bubbles being blown through glue, but which Mal realized was his attempt at a laugh. Until the laugh became a vast cough that shook the windows and sent sprays of grey ash into the air to flicker in the weak sunlight.

'What's so funny?' he said, when he was finally certain the man was not about to project his own lungs across the room.

'It's just that I didn't think any of your people would ever come to me for such a loan,' he said, tilting his wizened head to one side and presenting another smile of pure ochre. Cuth felt powerful and in control. It was an uncommon sensation.

'What do you mean by that?'

The bank manager sniffed and looked at the sheet before him. 'Jones,' he said. 'Not a particularly Jewish name, is it?'

'My paternal grandfather was Welsh.'

'Hmm. And Princeton.' Solly turned from the window and jutted his jaw up.

'Yeah? What?' He did not try to hide the sneer.

'Not a very Jewish name, I said. Princeton. Is it?'

'It's a long story.'

'Yes, you people always have long stories, don't you.' Cuth ran one finger across the desk, sat back in his chair, yawned and considered the dust he had gathered. There was silence.

'So?' Mal said.

'Hmm?'

'The loan? Can we have it?'

'Oh that. I would have thought you could go to your own people for the money.'

'Our own people?' Mal said. 'What exactly do you mean by "our own people?"'

'You know what I mean,' he said, his face hardening.

'I'm not sure I do.' They stared at each other.

'You have to understand,' Cuth said, waving his cigarette at the world beyond his window, 'I have a responsibility to the businesses already trading. There's no point me providing you with funds if it's merely going to make our other customers go bankrupt.'

'We're a kitchenware wholesaler. There are no other kitchenware wholesalers on the street.'

'Leave it, Mal,' Solly said. 'This arsehole has already decided.'

'I suggest the meeting is over,' Cuth said, viciously stubbing out his half-finished cigarette for effect.

'You're making a big mistake,' Mal said.

'I don't think so Mr . . .' he looked at his sheet again, and gave a short staccato laugh ' . . .Jones.'

Mal stood up and leaned across the desk, resting his weight on his knuckles. 'Be careful or I'll come round and fuck your daughter. Then there'll be a little bit of our people inside a little bit of your people.'

The bank manager shrank back into his chair. 'She's only nine,' he stammered.

'That's all right,' Mal growled. 'I like 'em young.'

Outside a sharp September breeze was blowing up the high street. It tugged at their hair and made them hug their thin jackets about them.

'I'm impressed,' Solly said. 'Didn't think you had it in yer.'

'Well,' Mal said, staring blankly down the road, his anger only now subsiding. 'I hate anti-Semitic arseholes like that. Our fucking people indeed.' It was his turn to laugh. 'Jews are meant to be involved in a world banking conspiracy and we can't even get a buggering loan out of one.'

'I told you it was a bollocks idea.'

'You got a better one?'

_'Yeah. Dig out your kipah and meet me at the shul, 10.30, Saturday morning.'

'What? We going to pray for the money?'

'Nah. We're going to do what he said. We're going to touch our own people for it. Oh, and borrow one of your dad's suits. That thing does not fit you at all.'

The old, prefabricated synagogue was already full when they arrived late, pulling their prayer shawls about their shoulders and shoving their cupples into what, for Mal at least, was an unfamiliar position on his head. The windows were fogging now with condensation and the weak yellow overhead bulbs cast a buttery light that gave a comforting glow to the greying plasterboard walls.

'I haven't been in here for years,' Mal whispered.

'Shame on you.'

'Piss off.'

Solly gave him a dark look. 'Language, mate.'

'Jeez, you're beginning to sound like Judy.'

'Yeah, well, remember where we are.' Solly lifted his chin and looked down the room 'Grand. Just grand. We're in time.' Up on the bimah from where the service was conducted, the rabbi was arranging the Torah scroll in its gorgeous coat of red and gold velvet, for its journey around the shul upon the shoulder of the congregant who had been honoured with the task.

'When it comes by,' Solly whispered, 'tuck in behind the rabbi. We need to get down to Max Schaeffer.'

Schaeffer, a rotund man whose silver hair lay in a carefully combed slick across his massive head, was always to be found in the third row from the front, stumpy hands clasped in his lap, index fingers idly buffing the broad gold bands that he wore on both right and left. He was reputed to be the congregation's one millionaire on account of the road haulage business he had built from a single second-hand truck in Limehouse to a nationwide fleet of lorries, sleek of fender and shiny of hubcap. If he was admired, it was for his acts of quiet philanthropy; if he was pitied it was for Jeremy, the klutz of a son it had been his misfortune to father. And he was more often pitied than admired.

Jeremy Schaeffer, a contemporary of Mal's, managed to combine awesome ineptitude with a curious arrogance. Mal recalled him as a school bully who had taunted him over a public moment of wretched incontinence when they were children at the same primary school. Age had not improved him. Jeremy Schaeffer, it was said, had once burned down the family kitchen using a blowtorch to make toast, accusing the au pair of the crime, for which she was sacked; later he had argued to his few friends that it was her fault anyway because she had failed to change the fuse in the toaster. Women reported that he had a penchant for the sudden and rejected lunge, which failure he would always ascribe to *their* sexual inexperience. Max often fantasized that the boy was the result of an adulterous affair on the part of his dear wife Rebecca, but Jeremy had his bulbous eyes and his heart murmur and he knew it could not be so.

'Why don't we just give the old man a call?' Mal said, as the small procession carried the swaddled Torah towards them up the left aisle, the asthmatic electric organ playing in its usual minor key.

'He wouldn't take my calls.'

'So now in shul he talks to us?'

'It's worth a try.'

The men of the congregation clamoured about the ends of the rows, gathering the tassels of their shawls into their hands to touch the Torah with appropriate devotion as it passed. When the rabbi reached Solly, he stepped forward, touched the corner of his shawl against the warm velvet and kept walking, head bowed, in step with the other men. It was a few seconds before Mal realized his partner had left his side. Solly looked over his shoulder and hissed at him to follow. A couple of long steps and he was in. The rabbi looked around at them both and raised one doubting eyebrow. They replied the only way they could think of: with a little wave and a grin. The organ whined on.

'Walk like you're meant to be here,' Solly said.

'I'm trying,' Mal replied. He nodded sombrely at the men as he passed, some of whom he recalled, and some of whom he did not. Athough a few looked perplexed – what in God's name was the Jones boy doing on the rabbi's coat tails? – they were too polite to question him. Up ahead he could see Max Schaeffer, already out in the aisle waiting, tassels gripped.

'When we get there push your way into the row behind him before the other men get back,' Solly said.

'What? We just nick their seats?'

'It will work.'

'Arsehole.'

'Language.'

'Bollocks.'

'Now,' Solly gasped. They both fell out of line and thrust their way past the men trying to reach out to the Torah so that the crowd pushed and shoved against each other, shawls waving in the low-wattage light. Out of the corner of his eye Mal saw Jeremy Schaeffer leaning out over his father's head, his podgy, bulbous face fixed in an inane grin. All it took was one sharp, satisfying kick to the ankle and Jeremy tripped, falling sideways into the rabbi and knocking him in turn into Mrs Gold's remarkable cleavage on the other side of the aisle, where he landed with a thud like a walnut hitting soft butter. There was a howl of confusion as the younger Schaeffer hit the parquet floor. The other men had to hop and skip so as not to trip themselves up and the man carrying the Torah executed a little dance to keep himself upright, the heavy scroll teetering on his shoulder for a desperate second. Finally he steadied and moved on to the bimah, turning to watch the mêlée behind him as he went.

'Jeremy, get up and go wait outside,' his father barked. The congregation crowded around the sprawling figure on the floor.

'But I was kicked,' the son said, stumbling to his feet.

Max Schaeffer clenched his teeth. 'Get out.' The boy straightened his tie, checked his cupple was in place, and made miserably for the door at the back. A number of older men, shaken by the rumpus, shawls draped now around their waists, followed him out to get some air. In the confusion, Mal and Solly shifted in to the two now vacant seats right behind the old man's.

'That was lucky,' Solly said.

Mal craned his neck to watch Jeremy go. 'Yeah, wasn't it.'

Max Schaeffer humphed back to his seat, muttered to his wife darkly about their son and mumbled apologies to the others around him. Solly leaned forward so that his chin was all but resting on the old man's shoulder.

'Mr Schaeffer,' he whispered. Max Schaeffer turned his head until they were nose to nose and Solly could see the thick red blood vessels that traced their way across the man's aged pale skin towards the loose flesh beneath his eyes. He recoiled. The millionaire observed the young man with silent disgust.

'Mr Schaeffer. Solomon Princeton.' He extended his hand. Schaeffer glanced at it and then back at Solly.

'What?'

'I'm sorry to disturb you . . .'

'Then don't.'

'We have a proposition we need to discuss and we couldn't get to talk to you any other—'

'A business proposition?' Solly nodded nervously. Schaeffer turned back to face front. 'Get out,' he said. 'We don't talk business in shul.'

Mal grabbed his sleeve and pulled him away, before he could argue. Outside they slumped back against a wall, hands in pockets, considered sharing a cigarette and then thought better of it. They had been there a couple of minutes blustering away their embarrassment when Schaeffer appeared at the door. The two made to leave, desperate for no more humiliations, when he called to them.

'Stop,' he said as he stomped over, oblong legs

carrying his squat frame. 'We don't talk business in shul. Now we're not in shul, we talk business. You seen that boy of mine?' He looked distractedly around the empty car park.

'He's up by your car, Mr Schaeffer,' Mal said, indicating the shiny Jaguar parked across the road from where they stood; it was a mark of Schaeffer's confidence that, despite it being a sin to drive to shul on Saturdays – you were meant to walk – the only concession he made was to park just outside the gates rather than in the synagogue car park itself.

'Hmm. Shmock can stay there. Sweat it a bit. So talk.' He looked back to them. The air smelt of damp trees and wet concrete.

'We have this kitchenware business,' Solly said.

'I know. The shmaltz mavens, my wife calls you. They all call you.' He studied his fingers and picked casually at a thumbnail.

'Everybody needs chicken soup, Mr Schaeffer,' Mal said.

'So they tell me.'

'We need money,' Solly said.

'How much.'

'Eight hundred pounds.'

'That's a lot of money.'

Mal jumped in. 'We've got a lot of business.'

'Sure you have. You been to the bank?' They nodded. The older man snorted and looked about again, as if he had enemies lurking out behind the Ford Anglias and Morris Minors and Hilman Imps huddling alongside his Jag. 'And they turn you down.' Mal and Solly knew it wasn't a question. Max Schaeffer reached inside his jacket and found his wallet. He counted out ten £5 notes, the thin, white paper curling in the breeze, and handed them to Solly.

'I like initiative,' he said, tapping one finger against his temple. 'I wish that my boy had a little of that. A little gumption. But he hasn't, so what can you do?' Solly looked morosely at the cash in his hand.

'Mr Schaeffer, this is very generous,' he said. 'But it's not really what we—'

Schaeffer patted him on the shoulder. 'Don't worry yourself,' he said. He shouted out to the furthest corner of the car park in a roar that made the flesh on his bulging chest ripple beneath his shirt and the car windscreens stutter. 'Jeremy, come back in now.' And then to Mal and Solly: 'This is a start. That's all. Come round to the office on Monday. We'll sort you out with the rest.'

When the Schaeffers had returned inside, Jeremy dragging his feet behind his father, Mal extended his hand. They shook.

'I underestimated you,' Mal said. 'I'm sorry. You got the money.'

'Only just.'

'Nah, you got it. There's no only just. Either you got it or you didn't. You got it.'

Solly handed him the wad of notes. 'You look after this. That's your shtick.' Mal folded them away into his back pocket.

'So,' Solly said. 'What next? What do we do with it?'

'We find premises. Then we find desks. And then we each get desk blotters. I've always wanted a desk blotter.' And they laughed. They would not have laughed so hard had they known just how much an £800 loan was going to cost them.

Eight

For the moment what mattered was not what an £800 loan could cost but what it could buy.

'We need a lathe,' Mal said. He had drawn up a wish list of things the Sinai Corporation should own and a lathe was at the top of it. He wasn't sure what one was but he knew that the workshop in Mill Hill had three of them. And if they had three, Sinai surely needed at least one.

'What's a lathe?' Solly said.

'It's the means of production, and we need to own it.'

'Shouldn't we get some employees first?'

'OK. We get employees. Then we get a lathe.'

'And some ballpoint pens. Those we need.'

'Sure, we'll get stationery. Lots of it. And then a lathe.'

'And a telephone?'

'Three of them. And a bloody lathe.'

In the end the lathe was one of the last things they acquired. First came a few hundred square feet of disused space above Mrs Hyman's shop, empty save for a dozen tattered boxes of cheap, unsold fish slices. The room was filled by two school-leavers, lank of hair and attitude, employed to finish the kitchen implements at a long trestle table, who shortly became four and then six. They were joined by a secretary called Jenny who had constant sinusitis, brown woollen tights that sagged at the knees and perfect shorthand.

'In winter,' she told Mal when he interviewed her, 'I'm a delight. But in the spring? Forget it. My hay fever makes for disasters. So in the spring we get a temp. By then you'll be such a success you'll be able to afford it. Believe me.' Mal felt duty bound to give her the job. if he didn't he would be admitting that by the spring they would be failures. That, he could not bear. Next came three phones, later increased to five, two more trestle tables, two swivel chairs for Mal and Solly and desks for them to sit behind, a kettle and matching mugs, three dozen ballpoint pens, a ream of headed paper and matching invoices, an ancient adding machine, two desk lamps that crackled with static when you turned them on, three gross of paperclips, Sellotape, envelopes and five tons of stainless steel (always better to get raw materials in bulk).

Another desk was occupied by a young accountant called Gerry Bergner, whom Mal had met on his course and encouraged to join the company with wild and unlikely promises of advancement. He had wiry brown hair that appeared to have been styled with static electricity, and wore tortoiseshell glasses which he constantly reached up to adjust as if he was surprised they were there.

Bergner talked only in slogans. 'Cash flow must be maximized,' he would say, or 'stock must be minimized' or 'through flow is good'.

'Not much of a conversationalist is he?' Solly said, after his first day in the office.

'If I had wanted a conversationalist I would have made your Judy the financial director,' Mal said. 'But I wanted somebody who can add up. Talk to him in numbers. Those he understands.'

Finally, of course, they purchased two desk blotters. One morning Mal and Solly sat at their desks, facing each other across the high street end of the room, and practised their signatures on the stretch of thick, leather-framed paper. They filled up old mugs with pens and pencils, cheap, metal ashtrays with paperclips and rubber bands. At last they were gods in their own corporate universe. Mal picked up a single paperclip between thumb and forefinger.

70

'Now we are a real business,' he said, waving the clip at Solly. 'We have assets. Our company is worth something.'

'As much as a paperclip.'

'Three gross of paperclips, Solly. Three gross.'

'The other Moses takes his people to the land of milk and honey. Mine takes me to the land of paperclips and desk lamps.'

'Everybody needs paperclips, Solly.' Mal sat back and looked around the office, admired its peeling wallpaper, its dank, sticky carpet and the trestle table piled high with Pollo-Matics and potato mashers waiting to be finished by the six kids who even now filed and polished. 'And we owe it all to Max Schaeffer.'

'Literally, mate,' Solly said quietly. 'We owe Max the lot.' Mal knew that Solly was less impressed with the second-hand clutter their loan had bought them, and it bothered him. He knew Solly was not the kind of man to be impressed by 'assets' or 'balance sheets' or desk lamps that crackled with static when you turned them on. To Solly, Sinai had quickly become a business machine whose cogs needed only oiling. The machine was working for now and gathering speed. That was good. But it lacked the flash of spark and fire and the roar of noise and friction made by a machine meeting resistance. For now Sinai was not meeting resistance and only when there were obstacles did you need new ideas, which was Solly's speciality. He was there and he would help run things but, truth was, it did not enthral.

To keep Solly happy they took to holding their morning meetings over breakfast in the Monarch Salt Beef Bar across the road from Mrs Hyman's, where lonely pensioners came to nurse a coffee in the warm and the wall mirrors always held a veil of steam from the hyperactive cappuccino machines. Mal knew Solly was at his best when he had a plate of food in front of him. The Monarch also did breakfast bagels the way Solly liked them, all the ingredients laid out separately

71

so that he could build them for himself; each morning the cream cheese, smoked salmon, onion and lemon wedge were camped out at different corners of the plate, ready prepared behind the bar, awaiting Princeton's call. Big Reuben Lipsk, the owner, was a 40-year-old heap of a man with a garland of smooth pink chins that stood witness to his enthusiasm for his own food. He said he liked having the boys in there. 'Brings the average age of the clientele down,' he announced, with a thick laugh, one massive hand rested flat on his chipped Formica counter.

'Somebody should package bagels like this,' Solly announced one morning, as he constructed his breakfast. 'You would get the bagel, the smoked salmon, the cream cheese, all of it in one pack. Maybe we should do it.'

'Your best ideas come from just above your dick,' Mal said, poking Solly in the stomach.

'Yeah,' Solly said, finally biting into his masterwork. 'And my dick has a mind of its own too. So that's three brains in one body. Not bad, huh?'

'Pity they don't all think about the business.'

'They do all think about the business, just not at the same time.'

'What? Even the one between your legs? That thinks about the business too?'

'That one thinks about *my* business. It frees up the other two to think kitchenware business. It's a kind of delegation. Efficient management.'

'Judy doesn't mind what thoughts that dangling eye of yours has?'

Solly frowned. 'Judy's my girl. Simple as that.'

'But you look at others.'

'Sure I do.' He put down his bagel. Now Mal knew his partner was being serious. He rarely put down food. 'It's like going on holiday. You go on holiday to the same hotel every year, yeah? An' you go there because you like it, 'cause you feel comfortable, relaxed. You like the way it looks. That doesn't mean

72

you don't look at other hotels sometimes and wonder what it would be like to sleep in their beds. You do. But it also don't mean you're going to go and book into them. It's just curiosity.'

'So Judy's what? A stay at the Ritz?'

Solly had resumed eating. 'That's right,' he said, his mouth full.

'I never knew you were so deep,' Mal said.

'Neither did I.'

Mostly they talked about new opportunities, shops they could sell to and products they could develop and cheap ways of marketing themselves. But rarely could they just keep talking about Sinai. Solly's lowest brain was always too active for that. It kept butting in.

'There's a newsagent's in Enfield that's moving into doing other stuff,' he said, another day. 'I got a cousin there, goes in regular. She told me. Cheap crockery and cutlery. We should try them out with a narrow range . . .' His voice trailed off as he caught sight of a young, pretty dark-haired woman up by the counter, whose close-fitting jumper marked her out as his kind of woman. 'And look at those fabulous tits over there.'

The Sinai partners were in their usual place, at the table at the rear with their backs to the two walls so that they each had a clear view of the room. Mal stretched one arm out along the top of the red leatherette bench and turned his head casually, as if searching for a new piece of blank space to stare at it in deep thought.

'Good God,' he said, quietly, as he found the object of Solly's interest. 'How does that work? Surely no bra could stand up to the forces of gravity at work there. She doesn't need lingerie. She needs scaffolding.'

'Breasts, they have their own kind of gravity. They weigh less than the rest of the body.'

'Bollocks,' Mal said, but Solly was off on one of his raps and it was best not to try and stop him. Mal liked to hear him do the talk.

'No it's true. Thing is, Isaac Newton was only ever hit on the head by a falling apple. If it had been a falling breast it would have been different. Softer, know what I mean? And slower. Tits, they fall slower than the rest of the body.'

'Yeah?'

'Oh, yeah. It's a fact. Ask anybody.'

'Anybody? Should I ask Mrs Hyman if her breasts fall slower? Would that be good? She's anybody. "Mrs Hyman, do tell me about the velocity of your breasts".'

'Nah, not Mrs Hyman. Hers have fallen, already and too long ago. She won't remember. Anyway, it's true. Newton missed out the breast law, the one that says they are lighter than the rest of the body. At least at first.'

'Then what happens?'

Solly watched the young woman reach out to pay for her sandwich, now wrapped for take-away. 'After a few years they plummet like a stone. By the time she's 40 she'll be strapping those little darlings beneath her belt.'

She turned to leave, pulling her long coat about her self-consciously as if aware she was being watched by the two young men at the back of the shop. Mal felt guilty and said, 'They are too big.' As if that excused him from being a letch.

'What's too big?' Solly said. 'Explain to me too big.'

'Those. Those are too big. I like them, you know, smaller, neater. Hand size.'

Solly scoffed and stirred another sachet of sugar into his coffee. 'This is not a breast thing. This is a Heidi thing.'

Mal felt his face redden. 'What's Heidi got to do with this?'

Solly shrugged. 'You fancy Heidi. Heidi has small ones. So you say you don't like big ones. You don't want to be disloyal. It's unconscious. A bit like Pavlov's mouse.'

74

'Dog.'

'Mouse. The bell rings and the mouse runs up the clock.' The fingers of his right hand skittered up an invisible clock case in the air before him, as he lifted his coffee cup with his left. 'It's a reflex. Scientifically proven.'

'You're mixing up your psychology with your nursery rhymes. It's Pavlov's dog. The bell rings and the dog salivates.'

'Same difference, mate,' Solly said, indifferently. 'You see a woman with small tits and you salivate, 'cause you think of Heidi.'

'Rubbish.'

'Is Benny still seeing her?'

Mal grunted a yes. 'On and off.'

'Pain in the arse, no?'

'She can do what she likes,' Mal said, unconvincingly.

'You could ask him to step aside, pull big brother rank.'

'Life's simple for you, isn't it,' Mal barked, shifting uncomfortably. 'Just ask and people do.'

'I don't know. I was just saying—'

'Well, don't. Tell me more about the shop in Enfield. How much space they got? What's your cousin like? Could they do the sales job for us, for a small cut?'

Within a few weeks the breakfast meetings had begun to stretch into late morning, the back table now reserved as of right for the Sinai boys by Big Reuben. 'I like to see my boys in place,' he would say, one hand on the roundness of his belly. 'I like to see all the furniture in the right place.' Each morning breakfast would be ready for them when they arrived and it would be followed by a succession of coffees, watered down for Mal who found the caffeine made him restless if he drank too much too quickly, and double strength for Solly. They wouldn't have to ask. Reuben just made sure the drinks were there, and at the end of the week one or other of them would settle the bill. Sometimes they held meetings at the table with clients or sales reps, nipping back and forth across the road to the office for bits of paperwork and samples, each day delaying the inevitable return to their desks by a few more minutes. Mal even used the phone behind the counter for business calls, hoping the volume of clatter and talk from the cafe would convince clients the business was roaring ahead. Which it was, clatter or no.

He was on the phone one morning when he saw the young man with the familiar bulbous eyes and sickly pallor come in, snuffling the contents of his constant cold into a handkerchief. Mal turned around so that his back was to him and coughed at Solly to get his attention. Then he jerked his head in the direction of the newcomer. Solly peered down the shop, groaned and tried to sink down in his seat and out of view, but short of getting under the table there was little he could do. Jeremy Schaeffer saw him and arrived by the table at the same time as Mal.

'Mind if I join you,' he said with a sniff; sitting down before either of them could argue. 'I want to know how my investment is doing.'

'Your investment?' Mal said, lolling back on the bench.

Schaeffer ripped open four sachets of sugar and poured them into his coffee. 'Yeah. Dad said, you know, got to keep an eye on you two.' He sipped his drink, curled his nose in disgust and reached for another sachet.

'Did he?' Solly said, with undisguised contempt.

'Oh yes. As I said to him, you two shlemiels have got our money.' He shook his head. 'We've got to watch out. Soft touch, my dad.' Schaeffer pulled his damp handkerchief from his pocket, had a good blow and dumped the stretch of sticky, fetid cloth on the table by his cup, so the other two could examine what had just flowed from his nose. Mal and Solly recoiled. 'And he said, yeah always got to watch your investments. And here you are, drinking coffee when you should be down the office. Dad won't like it.' He drained his cup and called for another. 'You know what you should do, a real business opportunity this?'

'What,' Mal said, yawning.

'Pet food. You need a businessman's eye to see this, so I'm not surprised you haven't spotted it.'

'There's lots of people selling pet food.'

'Yeah, but nobody's delivering it, are they?'

'This is your big business idea?'

'Yup.' Schaeffer coughed up some phlegm, worked it round his mouth and swallowed. 'Meals on wheels for pets.' He sat back, satisfied. 'It's a winner.'

Mal and Solly looked at each other and then back to their unwanted guest.

'How's your ankle, Schaeffer?' Mal said.

'What do you mean?'

'I heard you got a nasty kicking in shul.'

'I tripped and fell over.'

'I thought you said you were kicked.'

'I tripped.'

'What, so nobody kicked you out of pure malice and spite?'

The two young men fell silent and stared at each other. Jeremy Schaeffer stood up and, after a last, dramatic blow bundled his handkerchief back into his pocket. 'Remember,' he said, with a snort. 'What I tell my dad to do, he does.'

'Yeah?' Mal said, with a slow nod. 'Then why don't you tell him to start a pet food delivery business?' But Schaeffer was already walking away up the café. They watched him go.

'What if he means it?' Solly said, eventually.

'What?'

'What if he can tell the old man to pull the plug.'

'Don't worry about that. It's business and Max Schaeffer's a businessman. All that matters is what's happening to his cash not what that arsehole of a son

77

of his says. We're on a roll. Orders are up. We're meeting demand. That's all we need to know.' For all his apparent confidence Mal Jones still felt a knot of tension pulling taut deep in the pit of his stomach. He waved at Big Reuben and ordered another coffee, in which to drown his worry.

Nine

Mal was right about the business, of course. Within a year, they were able to buy out the workshop in Mill Hill, and in the spring of 1971 he finally became the proud owner of the lathe he had so coveted, as well as a forge, half a dozen workbenches and enough Swarfega to de-grease an oil rig.

'What's Swarfega?' Mal said, when they came across buckets of the stuff stored in a back toilet, their lids crusted with a dark, industrial pus which firmly complemented the decor of the room. Black mould crept lazily up the walls and the room stank only of damp and a thousand missed reliefs.

'It's for washing up when you're dirty,' Solly said, whose hands had known dirt.

'So it's soap?' asked Mal, whose hands hadn't.

'Sort of soap. Special soap, for really dirty jobs.'

'Special soap,' Mal said, with wonder. 'I never imagined there was such a thing. I just thought there was soap. We need this much special soap?'

'Sure. We own a workshop. All workshops need Swarfega.'

'I'll take your word for it. These things, you know about.'

The six finishers, who shortly became ten, moved over to Mill Hill, while Mal and Solly, along with Gerry Bergner and Jenny, spread out to fill the entire room above Mrs Hyman's. Mal's brother Benny came in a few days a week to handle marketing and advertising, forever phoning up the local press or the *Jewish Chronicle* to talk up the company. 'We're at the cutting edge of the kitchenware revolution,' he would announce, with his usual bumptious enthusiasm, to whichever tired hack he had convinced to listen to him. 'Hey, Sinai is at the cutting edge of knife manufacture. You can use that line. Cutting edge. Knife manufacture. Good, isn't it?' Even though they didn't yet make any knives. 'Oh, and we do discounts for wholesale.' Eventually he too was employed full time. Business was good. Then business was better. Mal and Solly bought cars on the company – Ford Cortinas, executive models in red and blue respectively; new toys kept Solly happy – and rented separate flats, one atop the other, in a nearby mansion block with a wood-panelled lobby that smelt of furniture polish, which their parents could boast about to their friends.

'Our son,' Golda Princeton would say, 'he has a lobby, the like you can not imagine. Wood panelled. Not veneer. Real wood. We could not be more proud.'

One afternoon the relative peace of the Sinai office was disturbed by a crash from the shop beneath them that made their desk lamps shudder and the hairs stand up on the backs of their necks. Jenny stopped typing and blew her nose; Gerry was so agitated he laid down the accounts and reached up to push his glasses back into place three times. The sound was too loud not to have caused damage or injury. Something must have suffered from the rush of noise. Something had. They ran downstairs to find Mrs Hyman lying face down in a heap of Pyrex dishes into which she had fallen when her heart had decided that, without a few more weddings for which to sell fish slices, life was not worth living. It was a bad moment for Mrs Hyman and a good one for Pyrex. Not a single dish had cracked.

'Good workmanship,' Mal said, reaching down to check for the pulse they all knew would not be there. 'Pyrex. Survives Fatalities. PSF. Almost a slogan.' The secretary sniffed and blew her nose; Gerry adjusted his glasses once again and said, 'We could afford the lease on this place.'

Mal looked around at the shelves of kitchen implements, the racks of knives and piles of baking trays that he had once admired. 'What, take out the middle man? Sell our own product?'

'It's an idea.'

'Lads,' Solly said, nodding towards the corpse cooling at their feet.

'Sorry,' Mal said. 'You're absolutely right. I'm forgetting myself. Let's shift over to the Monarch where Mrs Hyman can't, you know, hear.'

'Mal, she's dead.'

'Whatever. Jenny, stop snivelling and call a doctor. If they want us we're across the road.'

The three of them slipped in around their usual table, Big Reuben brought them coffees and Gerry began to splutter out his usual staccato sentences about profit and overheads, like a mechanical adding machine clanking its way through each calculation. 'We would reduce distribution cost . . . offset it against the lease . . . save on storage . . . undercut the opposition.' Mal listened intently but Solly's thoughts were clearly elsewhere. He was watching Big Reuben who was now slicing a lump of salt beef, his bloated forearm tensed over the meat fork, just another piece of flesh on a counter packed full of it. Thick, red, slices of beef complete with their ribbon of yellow fat rolled onto the counter as Reuben sawed away, half his bottom lip held between his teeth.

'Selling our own products is a great idea,' Solly said quietly, cutting across the conversation. 'But it's time to expand our range.' Mal raised an eyebrow. It was clear Solly was having an idea and he liked it when Solly had ideas. He tried to sit back but his partner pulled him in, conspiratorially.

'Imagine this is the shop,' he said, arranging the cruet set, the ashtray and the tiny vase of plastic flowers that Reuben always put on the table, in a square.

'Where's the street?' Gerry said.

'In front of me,' Solly said, drawing a line on the table before him between the salt and the pepper. 'We put a food bar, here,' he whispered, indicating one wall. 'We sell soup and latkes, things like that.'

'Additional income,' Gerry said, leaning towards him and shifting the frames back up his nose.

Solly grinned. 'Exactly. We sell them the dish of the implement. They like the soup, they buy the Pollo-Matic. They like the latkes, they buy the grater. If there's something I know about, it's food.'

Mal looked over at the counter where the Monarch's proprietor was putting the finishing touches to the salt beef sandwich. 'Big Reuben won't like it.'

'We don't do many seats,' Solly said, with a dismissive wave. 'Or maybe none. No seats. Just take-away. Big Reuben keeps the sit-down business, we take the passing trade.'

Who was Mal to argue? Solly was a Jew by food. He worshipped at the stove. Recipes were his scriptures, preparation his ritual. He lived therefore he ate, therefore he cooked. So now he could cook for the company. He could cook for the balance sheet. This, Mal knew, would make Solly happy. It would give him the role in the operation which the production and sale of kitchen implements did not offer. Wholesalers could not evangelize. Not often, anyway. Once the first order was placed the second order would come. Only in retail could you convert the mass and that was Solly's gift. He was a retail rabbi.

When he heard about the idea Sam Jones shook his head and smacked his lips in disbelief. 'I said how's business? Not why don't you destroy the business?'

'Who's destroying the business?'

'You are, Mal, with this food idea. Who wants to eat in a shop? It's unhygienic in a shop.'

'The café and the shop will be separate, just under the same roof.'

'So now you're a roof expert already. In the journal you never read about cafés in shops. Never. I know. I read the journal.'

It was all the encouragement Mal needed. A few weeks later, then, the Sinai Corporation's first Manna From Heaven Kitchenware Café, opened on Edgware High Street, with Solly running the show. There was a blackboard listing dishes of the day and jars of pickled new green cucumbers on the counter labelled 'Kosher Style'. A fat-fryer bubbled with latkes and a large pot steamed with chicken soup. 'Simple stuff,' Solly said. 'Nothing fancy. Food to eat lying down.'

'Food you have to lie down after eating,' Mal said.

'Shut up and eat,' Solly said, handing him a hot latke wrapped in a greasy napkin. The punters came and saw and ate and bought kitchenware.

Only one person other than Sam Jones was unhappy with the arrangement. 'You can get out!' Big Reuben bawled, when they came over to cash up and drink a last coffee after the first day's trade. 'But Reuben—' Mal said.

'Get out. After all I do for you.' His cheeks were pink and swollen with rage and he held a long meat fork in his hand. 'Then you stab me in the back.' He made sharp downward thrusts with the fork that made Mal and Solly recoil.

'We haven't done anything to you . . .' Solly said. 'We do a different trade.'

'What? People eat latkes twice a day?' the proprietor sneered. 'Sure, I eat two latkes a day. I eat four a day. That's why they call me Big Reuben. Otherwise they call me Small Reuben and it don't sound right.' He prodded himself in the chest with the fork. 'I eat professionally,' he said. 'But I'm not everybody. One latke a day. That's all there is in a person. One chicken soup. One wally. No more. You're taking my trade. Get out. After all I've done.' He turned away and walked back behind the counter shaking his head.

Ontside Mal said, 'I'll see him right. I'll find a way. You'll see. Some day.' Business, he said to himself, is tough. You have to do things that are tough. Sometimes people don't like you for it. If everybody likes you then maybe it isn't working. The most important thing was that Solly was happy and Mal was happy that Solly was happy.

But Mal also felt sick with jealousy. Now that Solly had found a task he enjoyed – and he sold chicken soup as well as he had once sold cake – his life seemed complete in a way that Mal's was not. Solly had the business and Solly had Judy too; Mal had only the rigid corset of accounts. However they might bicker and tussle and row, Judy and Solly were firmly a unit, who even fell unconsciously into step when they walked alongside each other. Solly had learned that with Judy he could manage silence in the company of another. It was, Mal decided, a familial silence, the kind of peace that mothers can manage with their sons. But – and this was the great mystery of adulthood that had always escaped Mal – the relationship was still erotic. In Solly and Judy, Mal saw that it was possible to be familial and sexy. Mal was so far away from being sexy let alone familial that, for all practical purposes, there was no proof it would ever happen. At 21 years old, he was still infected by an unmovable stain of virginity.

In some ways he did have a new family about him and that was Sinai itself. Two or three evenings a week Mal, Solly and Judy would go to the pictures or out for something to eat with Benny – now the firm's marketing manager – and the delicious Heidi who had swiftly moved from the on-and-off deal to become his regular girlfriend. They would visit an ice-cream parlour in Chalk Farm or a coffee bar in Golders Green and Mal would always sit at the head of the table, the most logical place for a single person in a group of five to sit. It made him feel like he was shipwrecked on his own island, isolated from the mainland of the table where the new world was being built between the other four, who recognized so much of their new experiences in each other. Occasionally Judy invited a friend along for the evening supposedly to keep Mal company. Instead, all the two women would do was gossip and laugh, tearing at the secret lives of their friends, like vultures ripping carrion with their claws.

It would have helped if Mal's jealousies had been simple, if what he had wanted was to be in Judy and Solly's relationship with Judy. But he did not. He found Judy attractive but that, he knew, was because she was the only woman whom he knew to be interested in sex. And an interest in sex was, Mal had decided, one of the sexiest things of all. He still obsessed constantly about Judy's mouth and the whisper of its secret cabaret. Judy was an obvious sexual possibility, although in his wretched virginity, all women had to count as some form of possibility. But what he really wanted was to be in Benny's relationship with Heidi, and envy of your younger brother's life is a more virulent form of envy altogether. He adored the way Heidi smiled, a light crease defining the soft space between cheek and lip. He loved the way she laughed with a quiet splash of noise that seemed embarrassed even to announce itself. So unlike Judy, who was only happy if the foundations rumbled when she howled. And he was mesmerized by her calm sardonic wit, the way she could pick at Benny's boasts of betting prowess without him even noticing. The way she mocked the others' noise and clamour.

'Judy,' she would say quietly, 'don't let the boys squeeze you out of the conversation.'

'I know,' she would gasp, oblivious. 'Aren't men *pigs*!'

'Benny,' she would say, when he had finished recounting another night of heroic victories and more regular defeats, his pockets emptied by the bookies. 'Doesn't winning all the time ruin the fun?'

'I know, love. Can't help it if I have the eye.'

Here was true intelligence, bound in the utilitarian wrap of humour. What did she see in this buffoon of a brother? Of course, that was not the only question. Even if she had agreed to desert Benny and go with the obviously more appropriate Mal, was there not still a problem? She wasn't Jewish, for Christ's sake. It was only just acceptable for the younger son to date a shiksa. But the older Jones boy? What would his parents say to that?

He knew his mother would shout, 'That our own son should insult us like this. You would wish that we die ashamed? What is wrong with Jewish women? What is so bad with them? Your father, he married a Jewish girl. You think he did wrong?'

'No, Mother, it's just that . . .'

Jewish girls have fewer secrets.

And sex is all about secrets.

He would end these group outings in a morose fug, silently gouging away his ice-cream until it had all gone and the metal spoon clattered against the cold glass of the empty bowl, while the rest chattered on. This was his role: the spectator with the empty bed and the empty ice-cream bowl.

One evening they arranged to meet at the office above the shop before going on to see a film. Yet again Judy had said she would bring a friend. Mal was there first. He was at his desk studying the accounts, finger tracing the column of engorged figures, when he heard the door open down below and footsteps creak on the stairs. He listened. It sounded like only one pair of feet.

'All alone,' Judy said, gently pushing open the door. She pulled off her coat and shook out folds of dark curly hair from underneath her hat.

'Where's Solly?'

'Coming later,' she said, walking over and proffering her cheek for him to peck. He looked at his watch.

'You're a bit early.'

'Well excuse me,' she said, with a lift of her chin. 'I can go and wait outside.'

'No I didn't mean that, I was just saying . . .'

She stood behind him and reached over to turn pages of the accounts book. 'You work too hard,' she said. Mal could feel her breasts pressing against his shoulder. It reminded him of Hebrew classes. He muttered a fragment of a long-forgotten Hebrew blessing under his breath, as if to ward off the peculiar memory of rabbinical sexuality.

Baruch ata adonai . . .' He slowly closed the book.

'Just checking a few figures,' he said. She walked round and sat on the corner of the desk and studied him.

'You spend too much time checking the wrong figures.'

'The accounts are important.'

'Yeah, but so's a little, you know . . .'

Mal laughed, bitterly. 'Oh that. Didn't you know? I don't do that.' He tapped the book. 'This is what I do.'

Judy tutted. 'It's not right, Mal. A good-looking boy like you.'

He felt his cheeks colour and looked up at the clock to see how long it would be before the others arrived. He didn't need this. He didn't want anybody digging into him. The wound was already gaping and it did not need to be widened. But the clock ticked slowly. There would be no rescue for almost half an hour. He turned back to Judy. In one fluid movement she slipped her buttocks off the corner off the desk so that she was sitting in his lap, and hung one hand around his neck. He could smell her rich perfume and feel her bra-cased chest buffered against his.

'Judy . . .'

'Hush.' She rested a finger against his mouth and then leaned down to replace it with her own lips. Gently she let her tongue brush against him. Mal felt his crotch expand and shifted in his seat in the hope that she wouldn't notice. She giggled and leaned her forehead against his.

'Oh Mal, I bet accounts don't do that to you.'

'Judy, what is this? Solly will be—'

'Solly, won't be here for twenty minutes.' She glanced up at the clock for reassurance and then back to Mal. 'And that's all we need.' In another fluid movement she reached under her own thigh to his trousers and slipped his zip down, tumbling onto her knees before him as though gravity was now firmly in charge.

'Judy, for God's sake . . .' But, though he heard himself protest, he did not act to shift her hands or close his legs or even stand up and walk away. Instead he just stared down and thought to himself: Judy Goldman's got my dick in her hand. And now she's putting it in her . . .

She looked up and said with a grin, 'Think of this as a little therapy,' before ducking down once more and allowing his entire length beyond the lips he had fantasized about for so long. So women really could be interested. What he had heard was true.

For a while he watched the novelty of her head bob between his thighs. It reminded him of one of those dipping bird ornaments that constantly swing down to drop their beak into a little bowl of water, before swinging up again. Golda Princeton had one on her mantelpiece. Glass, it was. Red glass, with its own stand. Golda loved it. He shook his head. Why, in God's name, was he thinking about Solly's mum at a time like this? Did he want a blow job from Solly's mum? Was that what it was? Maybe he was in a worse state than he'd thought. Maybe he needed help. Then again, maybe he was getting it. To remove the thought he concentrated on the way Judy's cheek would bow out occasionally on the downward dip. He had come to imagine that nobody would ever be on eye level with his groin; what, he had wondered, would they ever find to do down there? Until sensation forced him to sit back and curl his toes against the gentle surges of pleasure. He rested his hand on hers as it gripped his knee for balance and squinted at the ceiling where, to his fury, he found himself focusing on a crack in the paintwork he hadn't noticed was there. First Golda. Now this.

Finally Judy's expertly lubricated touch shifted all thought from his mind and he felt the nerve reflex and the burst of pressure which, up until that moment, he had only ever given to himself. 'I'm coming,' he hissed, between gritted teeth, though Judy had already noticed. She ceased ducking her head and kept her mouth in place to take the flow. Finally she lifted her head from him for a second, lips and eyes closed as she swallowed. Then she looked up and smiled.

'There,' she said, running her tongue about her teeth. 'That's better, isn't it?' She tucked his fast deflating penis back into his trousers and zipped him up.

'Judy, I still don't understand.'

She stood up and straightened out her skirt. 'Three reasons,' she said, briskly. 'First, my friend Divinia Greenspan is coming tonight and I don't want your weird neuroses over sex getting in the way of you two hitting it off. You won't be worrying about getting some at the end of the night, because you've already had some at the beginning . . .'

'You planned this.'

'Don't interrupt. Secondly, you've been staring at my mouth for the past five years and I reckoned it was the only way to get you staring elsewhere.' She reached into her bag, pulled out a tube of mints and popped one in her mouth. 'Do you want one?'

'What's the third reason?' he said, taking the peppermint tablet and holding it in his sweaty palm until it began to crumble.

She leaned down and kissed him softly on the lips once more. 'You're cute,' she said. 'Think of it as a present from the Blow Job Queen.'

'Solly told you about that?'

'Solly tells me everything and I tell him everything.'

Mal gasped and stood up. 'Judy, you mustn't ever tell him . . .'

'Don't worry, darling. This is our secret and that's how it will stay.' Downstairs they heard the door open again and the chatter of voices. 'Oh,' she said in a whisper. 'And it's the only time it will ever happen.'

He was trembling. 'Of course.'

They both turned towards the approaching noise.

'Mal Jones,' Solly said, as he blustered through the door, pushing a short dark-eyed woman before him. 'Meet Divinia Greenspan.'

Ten

Oh, the subtle power of a discreet blow job. It was as if he had been jump-started. Judy was the battery, Mal thought to himself, and the jump lead was . . .

'Would you like some of my popcorn?' Divinia was leaning towards him in the darkness, one hand resting lightly on his forearm, the other holding the crackling bag. He looked over her to where Heidi was sitting further down the row, her head on his brother's shoulder. Now he could see only the back of her head as she turned to whisper something in Benny's ear. Then he saw her shoulders shake as she giggled silently. He imagined the tip of her nose caressing his cheek as she breathed out her hot little message. She'll always be whispering in Benny's ear like that, Mal thought. That's how it's going to be. He looked back at Divinia. The light from the cinema screen flickered against her cheek, she allowed herself a cautious smile and Mal decided there were definite possibilities sitting here at his side.

She laughed at his whispered jokes during the film and told him he was clever and afterwards, when they went for ice-cream, he no longer needed to sit alone at the head of the table. But he did so anyway because it meant he was just that little bit closer to her and could lean his head towards her across the table's corner and ignore everyone else, even Heidi. He knew his brother's girlfriend was watching him in her careful way from the other end of the table, head tipped to one side, thumb and forefinger fondling a gold earring. Mal imagined that she was even jealous that he was not giving her his full attention and laughing at her jokes before everybody else did. This was the gift that Judy had given him. He knew now that other people could be interested in him in the way he had been interested in them. Judy made only one reference to what had occurred that evening and even that would not have been recognized by anyone but Mal. When Solly asked her if she wanted more ice-cream she declined, saying she wasn't that hungry because she'd 'eaten a little something earlier on', and threw Mal the flicker of a wink.

'Come on darlin',' Solly said. 'That's not like you.' She shrugged.

'When your appetite's been sated there's no point having more, is there, Solly?' Mal said, because he was feeling brave.

Solly laughed. 'This from King Guts at the end of the table. The man who never said no to thirds.'

Mal lifted up his bowl which tonight was still full of ice-cream, and raised one eyebrow. Solly squinted at it. 'You feeling ill, mate?' he said with mock sympathy. 'Not like you, either.'

Mal leaned towards him. 'Maybe me and Judy already had dinner together earlier.'

Judy frowned and coughed. Solly returned to his ice-cream. 'If you did, you did it bloody quickly. She was only out of my sight for half an hour.'

'We don't like to hang about,' Mal said. 'Do we, Judy?'

She started furiously digging at her own bowl. 'I told you not to mention our little assignations,' she said, feigning mock horror. 'You know how jealous he gets if he thinks I'm eating without him.'

'Yeah,' Mal said. 'If you two ever split up Solly is bound to lay the blame on a dinner somewhere. He'll accuse you of having had an affair with a plate of saft beef because he wasn't there at the time to help you eat it.' What generosity, Mal thought, as the laughter died down. Judy had let him in on a secret and given him one of his very own at the same time.

But mostly his thoughts were of Divinia. She told Mal about her father who, she said, had seen 'horrible things but was still a love and had still made his fortune and isn't that admirable'. He told her that it was admirable and that he had never seen horrible things but that he still wanted to make his fortune. He asked if it was all right to be ambitious and she said that of course it was. She was warm and she smelt good and, best of all, she was smitten. When she talked to him she looked at his eyes and she touched him on the hand or on the arm and later on the cheek, as if he could not understand a word she had said unless they were in contact. The brush of skin on skin was a novelty whose pleasures took months to diminish. Three weeks later, to the clanking of the plumbing in Mal's flat and the rumble of an old fridge elsewhere, Divinia Greenspan relieved Mal Jones of his virginity, with a sharp, unobtrusive gasp of pleasure and a lift of her hips which he found endlessly erotic because he could not imagine its purpose.

As he had unshackled himself from his innocence so Mal felt it was time that Sinai be set free. By October 1972 the first Kitchenware Café had spawned a second and then a third along the tarmac ribbon of London's North Circular Road around which much of British Jewry had congregated, and the wholesale business was still expanding. Big Reuben had finally been mollified by being given the branch in Hendon to run, after selling up the Monarch to a family of Bengalis who wanted to turn it into Edgware's first Indian restaurant. Quickly the Hendon food operation had proved the most successful. 'I told you, Mal,' Reuben said one night, dabbing away jewels of sweat from his forehead with a handkerchief, as his boss studied the figures. 'I'm a professional eater. You got to like food to sell food.'

'You should meet my partner,' Mal said. 'You'd have a lot to talk about.' And Reuben laughed.

Big Reuben's figures were good. Everybody's figures

were good. It was time to repay Max Schaeffer's loan. They arranged to meet once again in the shul car park.

'What have you got for me?' Schaeffer stood with his back to the building, casually rubbing his rings. His breath hissed now from his ragged lungs and occasionally he slipped a hand under the lapel of his jacket and cupped his chest as if trying to stop something from escaping in there.

'It's a cheque, Mr Schaeffer,' Solly said, handing it over. The older man examined it. 'The £800 plus another £100 interest. I know you said it was interest free and all that but we felt, well, that we wouldn't have been able to . . .'

'How much of the company's value is this?'

'Sorry?'

'Sinai.' He waved one hand at the cheque. 'If I wanted to buy in, how much would I get for this £900?'

Solly looked at Mal for an answer but his partner was staring at the old man, studying his face, trying to work out if what he suspected was true.

'Ehm, 30 per cent, 35 per cent Mr Schaeffer,' Solly said. 'Maybe more.'

He smiled. 'Thirty five per cent of the company and you can afford to repay me. You must be clever businessmen.'

'Solly's mistaken,' Mal said through gritted teeth. 'It's 15 per cent. No more.'

'Mal,' Solly hissed. 'You always told me to talk the value of the company down, not up.'

Schaeffer stared at the cheque, laughed and tore it in half before handing both parts back to Solly. 'Stick with this one,' he said to him, nodding towards Mal. 'He's a clever lad.' He reached over and patted Mal on the cheek, so that he flinched. 'Got a head on his shoulders. If only my Jeremy . . . But then, you know about that. Maybe you can find him a place in one of your shops.'

'Maybe,' Mal said.

Schaeffer coughed and tensed his left arm, as though

checking that the muscle still worked. 'Yeah, maybe,' he said, putting out his hand for Mal to shake. 'Fifteen per cent you say and 15 per cent it is. We'll stick with that.'

Solly shook his head. 'I don't understand, Mr Schaeffer. Don't you want your money back?'

'Not yet,' he said. And then to Mal: 'You explain. I'll get the papers drawn up on Monday.' He turned and walked slowly back into the shul, shoes scuffing the concrete, slipping his cupple out of his pocket and onto his head as he went.

Solly watched him go. 'We got an extension?'

'No,' Mal said sullenly. 'We've got a sleeping partner. When you touched Max Schaeffer for the loan he bought 15 per cent of our arses.'

Solly let what Mal was saying sink in. Then he said, 'Can't we just refuse? Pay off the loan and leave it at that?'

Mal looked at him as if he had learning difficulties. 'And won't that just make us the most popular shmaltz mavens in town. Max Schaeffer takes a chance on us, stands us the loan when no-one else would. And then when he tries to claim his dues we tell him to sod off? I don't think so, mate. We need all the good will from the community we can get. And if we want good will it looks like we have to have Max too.'

The old man dropped dead only three weeks after he signed the papers, his crusted arteries and baggy pump finally refusing to provide the flow of blood his bloated extremities required. Mal and Solly were at their desks when they heard the news.

'It's like the end of an era,' Solly said. 'First Mrs Hyman, then Max. The people who got us going, gave us the chance. Must be what it's like when your parents die, this. They get you started and then . . .'

'He was a clever old bugger,' Mal said. He was staring out the window. 'Very clever. Huge fucking shame it wasn't genetic.'

'What? Jeremy?'

'Yes, Jeremy.'

'Yeah, poor sod. Losing his old dad and all. I should call my folks and get them to think about food for the shivah. We should do a lot of that, way of saying thanks. Jeremy always liked my mum's poppyseed cake.'

'Don't worry too much about Jeremy,' Mal said.

'Come on, mate, his old man's just gone. Have a bit of feeling.'

Mal turned to look at him. 'Max Schaeffer owned 15 per cent of us. That doesn't just come back to the company when he dies, does it. It's going to be in the will.'

'And you think Max . . .'

'He's going to look after that shmuck of a boy of his. Of course he is. See him right now he's on his own. Or more to the point, get us to see him right. Pound to a penny, Jeremy Schaeffer now owns 15 per cent of Sinai. And won't he just love that.'

Eleven

From the moment Schaeffer appeared in the Sinai office both Mal and Solly found themselves clenching their bottom lips between their teeth in an effort to control their rage.

'Can he do this?' Solly said, the first morning Schaeffer arrived demanding he be given a desk and the right to look at the books.

'His old man could do it so now he can do it.'

'You what?'

'Max Schaeffer put it in the papers. A desk in the office and sight of the books for his 15 per cent.'

'That's right,' the younger Schaeffer said, with a businesslike blow of his nose that shook the windows. 'Clever bloke, me old dad. Or God knows what would have become of this.' He waved one hand about the office, as if shooing away the smell of rotting flesh, a citric sneer etched across his face. Mal and Solly decamped to the sandwich bar up the road.

'Not the Monarch, is it,' Solly said, to make conversation, as they sipped their coffee.

'Can't have it both ways,' Mal snapped. 'Either we have Big Reuben working for us or we have the Monarch across the road.'

'I was only saying.'

'I think it's time you stopped only saying.'

'Oi! Don't take it out on me.'

Mal began rapping on the counter with a spoon. 'I'll kill him,' he muttered. 'Believe me. He stays in that office and I'll . . .'

But he did stay in that office.

'Solly,' Mal bawled one morning. 'I've just had a call

from the workshop. They've received five tons of the wrong steel. Lower grade. Did you change the order?'

'Why would I change the order?'

'I didn't ask why. I asked *if.*'

At his desk in a far corner, next to where Gerry was doing the accounts, Schaeffer was sniggering and blowing his nose at the same time, which was a neat trick if you could pull it off. 'I changed the order,' he said. He shook his head. 'You boys. No idea, have you?'

Mal's jaw dropped slack. 'Why did you change the . . . ?'

'The materials you are using are way too expensive. Low profit margins.' Schaeffer opened a page of the red bound ledger in front of him. 'Look at this. We can't pay this much. Do that and you make nothing. Trust me. You boys.'

Mal picked up a lump of metal from his desk that served as a paperweight and weighed it in his hand for a moment. It was a garlic press – part of their self-consciously new, continental range for 1972 – that was yet to be cut from the extra steel from which it had been moulded. Its edges were round and raw. He lifted it into the air and chucked it across the room so that it crashed into the back wall above Schaeffer's head, gouging out the plaster where it impacted. The secretaries stopped typing. Gerry stopped adding up. Benny stopped studying the latest advertising flyers. 'Cheap materials are a false economy,' Mal said slowly, as if he was talking to a child with learning difficulties. 'You can't make reliable kitchen implements with cheap steel. You can't make holes in the wall with cheap materials. Gerry, call 'em up and change the order.'

Three days later it happened again. 'Gerry, I've just had Mrs Hirsch from Southgate on the phone. She was in tears, said someone here refused her order.'

Gerry pushed his glasses back up his nose, shrugged and nodded towards Schaeffer, who was humming quietly to himself as he uncurled paperclips.

'Schaeffer, did you refuse Mrs Hirsch?'

'Of course,' he said, without looking up.

'Why?'

'She hasn't paid her last invoice. We can't do business with people who don't pay their bills.'

'Mr Hirsch died three weeks ago,' Solly said, surprisingly calmly. The rest of the office thought he was about to throw something but, to be safe, Jenny had removed anything of weight and heft the day before. 'She still hasn't sorted out the will.'

Schaeffer paused momentarily over his paperclip and then said, 'We're not a charity.'

'Gerry, phone Mrs Hirsch and make nice with her. Tell her she can have however much time she needs.' Mal stormed from the office, Solly in pursuit. Outside Solly found his partner stamping his feet.

'Give me a cigarette,' Mal said.

'I thought you'd given up.'

'Give me a cigarette. I'm starting again. If I die you can blame Schaeffer. If anything happens you can blame Schaeffer.' Solly cupped his hand around a burning match as he lit their cigarettes. 'It will probably be his fault anyway. I think you better go on Schaeffer watch for the time being, while I think of some way to get rid of him.' There was no threat or recrimination in Mal's voice any more, just a clear and distinct intent to be done with the man.

'We can't buy him out?'

Mal shook his head. 'If he doesn't want to sell he doesn't have to. We need to do something serious.'

A week later, when Mal discovered that somebody in the office had phoned the firm's estate agent and withdrawn from a deal to take up the lease on a shop unit in Ealing, he didn't even bother to question the staff. He walked across the office and, resting all his weight on his knuckles, shoved his face into Schaeffer's.

'Why?'

'No passing trade,' Schaeffer said, damp nostrils twitching. 'I know that area.'

'Did you check the planning permissions?'

'I know that area.'

'A 15,000 square foot supermarket will open next door in the autumn.' They stayed nose to nose, chins up, dogs spoiling for a fight. 'And now somebody else has that shop.' The room was silent again. Solly walked over and laid his hand on Mal's shoulder.

'Let's go and get a coffee,' he said gently. Mal did not move. 'Or a cigarette.' He squeezed the cloth of Mal's suit into his palm and slowly pulled him upright. Solly stood in front of his partner and stared into his eyes, but Mal was looking away into a forgotten corner of the office. Were those tears of frustration he saw. Behind him Schaeffer rocked back in his chair, a satisfied grin seeping evenly across the fleshy pudding of his face.

'You OK?' Slowly Mal nodded. He turned and walked out of the room.

Solly found him back in the coffee bar, on a stool by the window. 'We should have got the loan elsewhere,' he muttered.

Solly sat down next to him. 'So now you're blaming me for this?'

'You set up the deal.'

'You were happy enough when it happened.'

'Yes, well . . . I wasn't thinking straight.'

'And so you blame me?'

Mal stared out the window. Across the road a pigeon flapped and fluttered by a kerbside puddle, pecking at a rancid scrap in the water. Why did he always focus on pointless detail at the wrong moments? The cracked ceiling, a pigeon, Golda Princeton and her red glass dipping bird?

'Well?' Solly said. He was angry now. He could feel the blood pumping in his throat and his mouth going dry. 'Well?' he said again. He was leaning towards his partner, mouth against his ear. 'You want to blame me? Come out and say it.' Mal said nothing. The bird turned away from the kerb and strutted towards the middle of the road, oblivious to the traffic, head cocked left and then right, as if listening for the call of others. Mal saw a truck approach, dented chrome bumper a dull grey in the pale afternoon light. He wondered if the bird would die, it's neck broken by the wheels or crushed by the vehicle's metal snout. He became excited by the prospect of a small but sudden drama. At the last moment it skipped into the air and lifted itself to the other side of the road. Mal felt cheated.

'We have a problem,' he said slowly. 'And we need to solve it.'

Solly sensed the challenge was passing, if only for now. There were words to be said, sharp and acid, but they could wait. 'What do you suggest?' he asked.

Mal turned to look at him. His face was still. 'We need to get rid of Jeremy Schaeffer.'

'Keep him out of the company? Not let him get involved?'

Mal picked up a discarded spoon from the counter and began tossing it in his hand so that it somersaulted before he caught it. He concentrated on its spin and roll, eyes turned to the air before him. 'I think we have to come up with something a little more permanent than that,' he said. 'Don't you? Something to solve the problem altogether.' He reached out to catch the spoon once more but this time he missed. The narrow strip of cheap steel clattered onto the tiled floor.

Solly flinched.

Twelve

The private detective lark is a waiting game, Harry Phat always said. 'It's about doing nothing until there's something to do,' he would announce to those who took an interest, and who would soon wish they had not. 'That's what the punters do not understand, you see. They think they can read a book or look at a newspaper at the same time as doing the waiting. This is fully and firmly out of the question, out of the picture, out of bounds. If you get my meaning.'

Phat was eminently qualified for waiting. As a toddler he had waited for childhood to end. As a child he had waited for adolescence to arrive. As a teenager he had awaited adulthood, measuring out his life in gluey units of passing time. Phat had waited too for the moment when he would no longer be thin, so pigeon-chested and slight of waist that only child's sizes could get any purchase upon him. But that was to be a wait too far, even though he now consumed vast quantities of carbohydrate and fat, wrapped up in donut and Danish pastry, in an attempt to hasten the day. Of course he never ate when he was working because that would not count as pure, unsullied waiting. That would count as eating and the two could never be reconciled. Nevertheless there remained constant about the edges of his mouth and upon the lapels of his Dunn & Co. tweed jacket a fine dusting of sugar, that had fallen from the food he had eaten before work. This was all that anybody who met Harry Phat ever recalled about him: the slimness of his hips and the fine coating of sugar.

Even by his own standards, which were low, the

Schaeffer job had been dull. The intense pleasures of a wait well executed were only justified if there was something interesting to observe or record once the wait was over. In Schaeffer's case that justification had never arrived. Phat flicked through the pages of his notebook, where he had recorded the target's comings and goings for the previous seven days, dusting away stray grains of sugar from the leaves as he went. Not that he could easily distinguish one day from the next. Jeremy Schaeffer awoke every morning at 7.45 a.m., the light in the front bedroom of the large double-fronted house beside Stanmore golf course going on at exactly the same moment, a weak spread of hepatitis yellow against the veiled glass. The curtains would stay drawn. At 8.30 a.m. he would leave the house and drive in his late father's black Jaguar to a café (terrible donuts; not enough sugar) on Stanmore High Street where he would drink a coffee and read a copy of the *Daily Express* before arriving at the offices of the Sinai Corporation in Edgware. The client would be fully conversant with what Schaeffer did in there. An hour for lunchtime in the sandwich bar up the road (much better donuts; lots of jam) this time reading the *Evening News*. Come 5 p.m. Schaeffer would leave the office and drive home. It was the same every day. Morning coffee. *Daily Express*. Lunchtime sandwich. *Evening News*. Home.

After work on the Tuesday he had entered a newsagent's and purchased a number of magazines dedicated to vintage cars. On the Thursday, his one night out, he had visited a house in Golders Green, hedge of privet cropped short, path crazy-paved in Play-Doh colours. Phat had noted both of these. Very carefully. What else was there to note? There the target had played a game of chess with a young man who wore glasses, which contest Phat had observed from a safe distance with the aid of a pair of binoculars. After two hours Schaeffer had conceded defeat. Then he had returned home. The high point of the target's week had been losing at chess. The private detective studied the last page. Not a lot to report for a week's work. Even less to report for a week's life. Still he had only to observe it, not live it. He had completed the seven-day project for which the client had paid in advance, claiming a 10 per cent discount for what he called 'going wholesale'. He couldn't help it if Schaeffer was an intensely dull man.

Phat put away his notebook and peered through the windscreen. The client had finally left the office and was now striding towards him across Edgwarebury Lane. He reached over and opened the door, allowing in a gust of cool air that churned the warm fug of sweaty vinyl seat and damp tweed jacket, and let him slip into the passenger seat.

'Mr Phat.'

'Sir.' They shook hands. The client ran his finger along the dashboard, collecting grains of what he swore looked like sugar.

'What have you got for me?' he said, studying the crystals.

'Hmm, indeed. What have I got for you?' Phat retrieved his notebook from his inside pocket, with a theatrical flick of the wrist. 'Well, then. Let's see.'

'Yes.'

The private detective sighed, deep and long, or as deep and long as his shallow chest would allow. 'I have to tell you it's not promising.'

'Tell me.'

'Bugger all, I'm afraid.'

'Nothing?'

'I looked for smut, sir,' he said, as if he had been employed to survey for damp or subsidence. 'But there was no sign. Not even a minor indiscretion.' Briefly he described the details of Jeremy Schaeffer's week.

'When he was in the newsagent's . . .'

'Yes sir?'

'He didn't linger by the, you know, the top shelf?'

'Didn't appear to notice it, sir. The nearest thing we

have to a perversion is an interest in vintage cars.'

'It's hardly illegal, is it.'

'No sir, I'm afraid it isn't. I suspect he has strong feelings for that Jaguar of his, but so far there's no sign of him trying to express it physically.'

'Amazing how this man can be both venal and dull.'

'Indeed, sir. Having pursued him for a week I must admit to feeling rather sorry for the poor fella.' The client raised one eyebrow.

'Though, of course, as a professional in your employ I consider Mr Schaeffer to be a disgusting little reptile who is beneath contempt.'

'That's more like it.'

'Thank you, sir.' They were silent for a moment. 'Perhaps,' Harry Phat said eventually, 'it is time to approach the matter a little more actively.'

'Perhaps.'

The private detective reached into a briefcase at his feet and pulled out a large black and white photograph. He studied it for a moment, checking the image was the correct tool for the job, before passing it on to the client.

'She might do the trick,' he said. He turned to stare out the window at a passing bus, as if the picture were now none of his concern. It was a photograph of a young woman with dark hair that fell in thick glossy black curls, about a bold face of high cheekbones and full lips and eyes the colour of ink. She wore a smile that said she knew how to please and that she liked doing so.

'Who is she?'

'She,' Phat said, with a little more emphasis on the word than seemed strictly necessary, 'is a professional, like me.'

'Private detective?'

'No. Not exactly. Eddie is a . . .'

'Her name's Eddie?'

'That's what I call her.'

'Short for?'

'Never asked.'

'What does she do?'

'Most things.'

'What can she do for us?'

'It's more what she can do for Mr Schaeffer, I should think.'

'Is she discreet?'

'She is a master of discretion.' The client dropped the photograph into his lap and stared away across the road to the Sinai office. Even now Schaeffer sat there behind a desk, ledgers open before him. The only case of human damp rot known to science, Benny had called him. Human slime, Solly had called him. Bastard, Mal had called him. Many times, and to his face. He handed the photograph back to the private detective. 'Do it,' he said. 'Do whatever it takes. Just do it quick.' He opened the car door and clambered out. 'And I'll call you,' he said, before he closed the door. 'I don't want my partner knowing about this. Not till it's done.'

'Right you are, Mr Princeton,' Harry Phat said. 'Call me day after tomorrow.' He watched the stocky man with the stubble-black jaw lollop back across the road, before turning the key in the ignition and pointing his old Ford Anglia in the direction of a unique little massage parlour he knew in West Hampstead.

Thirteen

On a greasy Edgware street stood a vision of cultured femininity, her black patent leather knee-length boots reflecting the cherry glow of brake lights from cars winding their tired way home at day's end. She checked her appearance in the window of the shoe shop, pointlessly tugging her red leather hot-pants down a fraction to mid-thigh and reaching deep into the folds of her hair with both blue-taloned hands, to plump and flounce. A dish and a delight, she thought to herself. Pure perfection. Eddie Flowers lifted her chin and gently stroked a long milky stretch of neck with the back of her hand, as if smoothing it out. 'Irresistible,' she whispered to herself huskily, pursing her ruby lips, and turning slightly to catch the eye of the man in the driver's seat of the Ford Anglia parked by the kerb. Harry Phat dusted a little sugar from his lapels and nodded towards the doorway of the newsagent's three shops up, from which a customer was shortly to exit, a pile of magazines clutched beneath his arm. Eddie took the cue, stretching her lissom figure to its full six-foot-two-inch height, wrapping a hand about the strap of her shoulder bag and striding headlong into Jeremy Schaeffer's life.

Before they collided she registered in his mind only as a faint blur of red and black advancing up the pavement towards him, an irrelevance compared to the crisp, unsullied pages of the vintage car magazines beneath his arm. Oh, the curve of metal body contained within, the length of running board, the stretch of bonnet! And the bliss of contemplation to come. He never even had a chance to arouse himself further with oiled thoughts of gaskets and carburettors. She ran into him side on, buffeting his hip with one leather-clad knee and thigh, and flinging the magazines into the air to flutter down like a flock of broken-winged pigeons, joining him where he lay sprawled on the ground.

'Oh my God. Oh my God. Oh my God!' she screamed, resting a hand on his shoulder and kneeling down so that her impressive bloused chest was at his eye level. 'I'm so sorry. Are you OK? Tell me you're OK?'

'I think I'm . . .' Schaeffer looked around at the magazines scattered to each side, his legs stretched out before him. 'I think I'm all right,' he said eventually, still clearly dazed.

'Oh look,' cooed Eddie, 'you've got some mud on your face. Let me clean you up.' She reached into her bag and drew out a tissue, licking one corner before dabbing at Schaeffer's cheek. He stared at the way the leather of her hot-pants drew taut across her thighs and curved deep into the dark-shadowed apex of her gorgeous, silken legs. She hesitated. 'Your skin,' she said. 'It's so . . .' She stroked it with her fingertips, making sure to avoid the area beneath his nose which even now ran damp and sticky, as she had been told it might. 'It's so soft.' Schaeffer looked at her face, at the full pout of her crimson lips and at the rise of her cheekbones. She shook her head, so that stray curls flicked soft against him. 'I'm forgetting myself. I really mustn't . . .' She stopped again. 'You have such lovely eyes.'

Like a stray cat, fur matted by years of neglect, Schaeffer was unused to such displays of affection. These days even his mother tried to avoid physical contact with her son. 'My doctors say I have a tendency to myopia,' he stammered.

'How lovely,' Eddie said. 'Myopia. It sounds so exotic. You must be very proud.'

Schaeffer gazed longingly. 'I suppose so,' he said. 'It's a family trait.'

'Are all your family as beautiful as you?' she said softly. And then gasped, her fingers to her mouth, fluttering against her lips. 'What am I saying?'

'It's all right,' Schaeffer said, slowly getting to his feet. 'Really.' They stood before each other in the half-light, he looking up and up her towering frame. If he fell forward his nose would land in her cleavage and for a moment, as the blood rushed giddily to his head, he thought it just might.

'My name's Eddie,' she said extending one hand which Schaeffer decided was the most gorgeous, delicate thing he had ever seen. Even though it dwarfed his own.

'Eddie?' he said, as they shook.

'No that's my name.' She let out a bell ring of a laugh. 'It can't be yours too.'

'No, mine's Jeremy.'

'Hello Jeremy,' she said, in a voice hot with welcome. 'Well,' she said, lifting her bag onto her shoulder and tugging half-heartedly at her hot-pants. 'I suppose I ought to be on my . . .' She turned to go and then stopped. 'I don't suppose . . .' Eddie giggled and looked at the ground. 'No. It's too ridiculous.'

'No, please. Say it.'

'I don't suppose. I mean I was wondering if you would . . .'

'Yes?'

'Have dinner with me?'

Schaeffer gasped. 'Well of course,' he said, his voice almost a whisper now. 'I mean to say . . .'

'Tonight,' she said so forcefully that her voice plummeted headlong into unnaturally low, yet intoxicating registers.

In the warm sea cabin of his car Harry Phat allowed himself a thin smile and shot off a few more pictures, the motor drive dragging the film through his camera at triple speed. 'What a pro,' he muttered. 'If you get my meaning. What a performer. What a star.' He saw Schaeffer point to where his own car was parked and

109

the two of them begin to cross the road in front of him, arm in arm. 'Attagirl. That's what I like to see. Physical contact. What a night Little Miss Eddie has in store for you, my boy. What a night.' He threw the camera onto the passenger seat, started up the car and pulled out into the traffic to follow Schaeffer's Jaguar through north-west London to a pizzeria on the Finchley Road, where they could drink cheap red wine and, as she was putting it at that very moment, 'turn a nasty collision into a happy accident'.

Jeremy Schaeffer, who had always assumed women to be some sort of bizarre invention designed specifically without him in mind, took easily to Eddie's company amid the candlelight and gingham flicker. Such attention, he reasoned, was entirely reasonable. His due. Yes, she was striking and dramatic. Rather more than ordinary. Extraordinary, in fact. Even her name was extraordinary. Eddie. He turned the shape of it about his mouth, pressing it against his teeth with his tongue. Truly extraordinary. But then so was he. An original, in his own careful, unoriginal, unassuming way. He dabbed at his nose with his handkerchief and watched her eyelids and her fingertips flutter once more as she talked of the problems of meeting 'real men like you' in Seventies London. Schaeffer nodded and sipped, dabbed and blew and imagined introducing the delightful Eddie to the shmocks at Sinai.

And *this* is Eddie, he said to himself.

And this *is* Eddie.

And this is *Eddie.*

Outside in the car Harry Phat finished off another of the donuts he had allowed himself in what he had concluded would be his one break of the evening before he returned to the important job of waiting. He fired off a couple more shots just to be on the safe side, a few pictures to confirm Jeremy and Eddie had spent the evening together, checked his watch and then drove to West Hampstead and the flat above the massage parlour where the evening was to finish. He let himself in and made for a bare room hidden behind the pink chintz and lace bedroom, where the tripod had already been erected, in front of a two-way mirror. It had a full view of the softly cushioned low-lit arena where the end game would be played out. The observation room was a cheap bit of conversion which, with Eddie's help, had already more than paid for itself. There was always someone somewhere who needed their services. They might not always know that they needed them, but Phat could soon bring them round.

He did not have to wait long. Half an hour after his arrival he heard the key turn in the lock downstairs and the thump of footfall on stair. Then they were in, Eddie taking Schaeffer's coat and depositing him on the edge of the bed while she went to fetch him a drink. Like an eager child he could not stay seated, soon moving to the large picture mirror on one wall to check that his hair was neat, and his tie, carefully knotted.

'God you're an ugly swine,' Phat said to himself, as they stood eyeball to eyeball on either side of the glass. 'And blow your nose, boy. For God's sake. Blow it now.' As if having heard, Schaeffer reached into his pocket for the crumpled cloth and, putting it to his face, made a noise like a hippo on heat. Phat knew the text of the drama from here on in; they had played it out so often neither of them needed to go over the script. And so it began. Eddie returned, a glass of red wine in each hand, heaving open the door with her knee, while apologizing for the quality of the booze. She advanced across the room towards the grinning Schaeffer and at the exact moment found an imagined ruck in the carpet upon which to trip, leaning forward and chucking the contents of both tumblers all over him with such force that a significant amount splashed against the mirror, a crimson wave breaking on the glass.

'Take it easy, woman,' Phat said as he recoiled from

111

the liquid heading towards where he stood, eye firmly fixed to the camera lens.

'Oh my God. Oh my God. Oh my God!' she screeched, for the second time that night. 'I'm so clumsy. So, so clumsy.' She grabbed a towel with which to mop him down. Schaeffer stood, dazed once more, as the wine began to seep through the thin cotton of his shirt.

'It's no good,' Eddie said, stretching forward with her sharpened fingernails. 'It will have to come off. All of it.' Within seconds Schaeffer was standing bare chested, loose folds of grey flesh hanging apathetically about his hips, with nowhere else to go. Eddie gasped.

'What a beautiful body,' she said, running her hand across his clammy flesh. And then, in one fluid movement, it was done, the other hand pulling his head towards her so that they were locked in what Schaeffer believed to be a passion of darting tongues, and Eddie considered just another night's work. Once more the camera went into overdrive, frame after frame ripping past the lens to record this momentous night in Jeremy Schaeffer's life. All that remained was what they both termed 'the reveal': a touching scene from which Schaeffer would surely recoil and run. For it to be a success he had to be positioned in such a way that Phat could record both the event and the target's reaction. Suddenly Eddie disentangled herself from Schaeffer's embrace, walking away from the bed to put a clear space between herself and her charge. He sat up on the edge of the divan.

'What?' he said. 'What is it?'

'I have something,' she said, silkily. 'Something unusual. Something you may not have been expecting. But I hope you like it.'

She reached around with one hand to release the careful construction of straining clips and zips which would strip away the hot-pants to leave her standing only in blue satin briefs, that bulged with unimagined goods. In a second those too were gone, and Jeremy

Schaeffer knew for sure that Eddie was short not for Edwina or Edith or even Edina, as he had imagined, but for plain old Edward.

Eddie had expected a few seconds of stasis, Schaeffer fixed to the spot as he took in the full scene, leaving just enough time for Phat to get the photographs. Then he was meant to get up and run from the room and the flat and the street, shirt or no. But he did not. For dear Jeremy Schaeffer it was simply too much to hope for; that the stuff of fantasy, both feminine and yet so tumescent, should be realized in such graphic terms. The vain hopes of his mind's blue movies, rich in their secret Technicolor glow, had been more than superseded by the revelation before him. Obedient to the last, he reached for the flies of his trousers to undo himself and then turned over to lean loosely across the bed, a willing sack of flesh. Beyond the glass Harry Phat, glowing with voyeuristic thrill, continued to fire off photographs. Now he knew it was going to be a long night. And not a donut in sight. Eddie stared at the mirror as if hoping it would deliver up some suggestion about what to do next but none came, save his own startled reflection. He shrugged and stared at the prone form on the counterpane before him. Oh well, he thought, as long as he stays facing that way it can't hurt. In for a penny, in for a pound.

Behind the mirror the camera clicked and whirred.

Fourteen

Mal leaned down over the black and white photograph so that his nose was touching the page. He could still detect the sour tang of the darkroom. 'I don't believe it,' he said.

'What, mate?' Solly was standing behind him, peering over his shoulder.

'Schaeffer's about to be screwed by a shiksa.' His finger rested on a delicate part of the image. 'Look.'

'See what you mean. Our Edward was definitely never the star attraction at a bris.' They stared at the novelty of the transvestite's foreskin, caught by Harry Phat's lens in the sad gloom of bedroom lamplight.

'Weird things,' Mal said.

'What? Foreskins?'

'Yeah.'

'Yeah, weird,' Solly said. 'Always look like uninvited guests at a party. Never know what to do with themselves.'

'Just hanging there.'

'Hanging about.'

'Doing nothing.'

'Apart from hanging.'

'What do you think people do with them, exactly?' Mal said.

'What do you mean do with them? You don't do anything with them. A foreskin isn't something you take on an outing. Today, dear foreskin, we're going to the zoo. I don't think so.'

'Another one to leave to the Gentiles, then.'

'Oh definitely. One for the Gentiles.'

They stared at the photograph again, took in the

114

tensed muscles of Schaeffer's bared thigh, the blissful clench of his jaw. 'Mrs Schaeffer's not going to be very impressed, is she,' Mal said. 'Her lovely boy doing it with a goy.'

'If Mrs Schaeffer ever gets to see these pictures I don't think the religion of the other participant will be the first thing she notices.'

'No, I suppose not.' Mal flicked through the rest of the photographs. 'This private detective of yours, he sorted these out for you?'

'He didn't tell me what he was going to do, but it's his work.'

The image in his hand showed Schaeffer being stripped of his shirt by the delicious Eddie. 'So this is what Schaeffer does of an evening. These two been going long?'

'What, those two?'

'Yeah, Schaeffer and this—' he tapped the photograph with one finger – 'this, what do you call her? Him? Eddie?'

'Not exactly.'

'Short-term affair, then?'

'You could say that.'

Mal looked up from the picture to his partner. They were silent for a moment. He could hear the second hand of the clock on the wall as it slipped around, the sound of a penny dropping. 'What are you saying?'

'Nothing. I'm saying nothing. It's a short-term affair. Yeah. Very short.' Solly clicked his fingers twice. 'Short, short.'

'How short?'

'One night short.'

Mal watched his partner pace out a small circle on the carpet.

'Did you set this up?'

Solly gasped. 'Christ, no. Me? Set up Schaeffer with the bloke in the skirt? No. Never. Not at all.' He turned to look out the window at the high street. 'Harry Phat did that,' he said, in a whisper.

'Solly, this is entrapment. It's worse than entrapment. It's . . .'

'He seems to have had a nice time,' Solly said, indignantly. 'Look at that one.' He pointed at another photograph. 'He's grinning.'

'I don't doubt he is, but you set him up. It's obscene.'

Solly walked over to his desk and sat down, checking his watch. Schaeffer wouldn't arrive in the office for another ten minutes. By now he would have received his own set of photographs passed to him in an anonymous sealed brown envelope by the owner of the coffee bar on Stanmore High Street. Harry Phat had delivered them there at six that morning. Solly had checked that.

'We need to be rid of him" he said. 'It's my fault he's here. So I'm sorting it.'

'There's sorting and there's sorting.'

'Well this is sorting it for good.'

'I've already sorted it,' Mal said.

'Mal, we can't just threaten him or beat him up in the hope that he'll run away.'

'Beat him up? I wasn't going to . . .'

'Could have fooled me. Two weeks ago you chucked half a ton of steel at his head,' Solly said, waving at the paperweight which had now returned to its place on Mal's desk. 'You said you were going to kill him.'

'It was a figure of speech. I don't do violent,' Mal said, genuinely aghast. 'You want know how bad at violent I am? When I make a fist, I fold my thumb up inside, like this.' He lifted his right hand to prove his point, the thumb tucked away, so that only the knuckle protruded. 'If I hit anybody with this, I break my bones. Seriously. I break my hand. Christ, Solly, I'd never do that stuff. Never. It's true I think Schaeffer's the lowest scumbag in north-west London, but still . . .'

'What's your plan, then?'

'My plan?'

'Yeah. Yours. This great plan of yours.'

Mal leaned back in his chair and grinned. 'Sell the company.'

'You what?'

'Sell the company. I've already made the deal. You know my Uncle Morri? Got the stationery shop? He's going to take the whole lot off us for a couple of hundred quid and . . .'

Solly shook his head. 'This is a plan? Why don't we just all drink a gallon of Swarfega? There's enough of it out the back of the workshop. We can get them to send it over in a taxi. Be here within the hour. Swarfega cocktails all round.'

'Let me finish. We sell off the company for a tiny sum. Give Schaeffer a 15% per cent share of bugger all, and then Morri sells back to us for the price we sold it to him.'

'This sounds too good to be true.'

Mal cleared his throat. 'It is. A bit. It's a bit too good to be true.'

'What? In the way Eddie Flowers was a bit too good to be true? Is this idea another gorgeous girl with seven inches of uncircumcised dick which is going to screw both of us good and proper?'

Mal leaned forward conspiratorially and pressed his fingertips together. 'Thing is, it's illegal. Breaks the Companies Act in fifteen places. It's called operating at arm's length. So Schaeffer could sue. But it's simple. We just settle out of court, make a deal. He'll go. He won't hang around. Once we pull a stunt like this he'll know we mean business.'

Solly stared at the empty desktop before him. Across the four years they had been in business together a clear divide had opened up between them on who did what. Solly thought ideas. He thought projects, ranges and innovations. Mal thought about how to make them work. That was the system. It wasn't Solly's place to call Mal on business decisions. But this time the plan didn't seem right. It felt like violating Sinai, making it dirty, unclean. It was like giving up your sister's virginity to the neighbourhood slob. Of course, giving up Jeremy Schaeffer's virginity was also rather less than clean, but that was personal. If Solly was done over for setting up Jeremy Schaeffer he'd be the one with the black mark against him, not the company. Sinai would still have its virtue. Surely that was the most important thing?

Solly sat up straight, though he still remained shorter than Mal. 'We can't do it,' he said. 'We can't do your plan. The company is what counts. Break company law and we're screwed too. With all due respect, Mal, you know your stuff. But don't give up Sinai like that. It's crude.'

Mal waved one hand across the photographs. 'And this isn't?'

'That's different. That's me being crude. Not Sinai. They are different things. I take the rap, not the company.' He stared up at the ceiling, noticing the crack that had caught Mal's attention one evening a few years before. 'Too many people depend on Sinai for us to go risking everything. Your brother Benny for one. All the people we've got down the workshop, Gerry and Jenny here. Us, for Chrit's sake. If business is bad, so business is bad. We did our best. There's nothing we can do about it. But we don't play games with the company. It's got to be the rule. We've got to stick to the rules. They are all we've got.' Mal heard him out and then shuffled through the photographs one more time.

'OK,' he said eventually. 'Tell me your plan.'

Schaeffer arrived five minutes later, his stride slow and uneasy as if he were a pallbearer burdened by an unreasonably large coffin. His skin was the colour of tracing paper and his forehead was set with toxic beads of sweat. The boys did not let him sit down; grabbing him gently by each elbow, they led him back downstairs and out to the sandwich bar down the road. The three of them sat on tall bar stools at the counter in the front window staring out at the street, Mal and Solly on either side of the compliant Schaeffer. He said

118

nothing. Solly collected the coffees, filling Schaeffer's with four sachets of sugar and then, having studied his sagging, greasy profile one more time, added another just to be on the safe side. After all, the lad had clearly received a shock. They sat in silence. In front of Mal lay a manila file, unopened. Schaeffer did not look at it. Outside, cars purred by. An elderly woman walked past, a Yorkshire terrier on a lead at full tension drawing her towards the kerb. The postman stopped to study a haphazard guess of an ill-addressed letter.

'We've received some photographs,' Mal said, tapping the file with one index finger. He did not look down at it.

'Surprising photographs,' said Solly, sipping his coffee.

'Terrible business,' said Mal.

'Awful,' said Solly.

Mal pushed the file down the counter towards Schaeffer. 'Do you want to have a look at them?' Schaeffer glanced down and then back to the dead spot on the other side of the street upon which he was trying to focus.

'No,' he said, in a voice throttled by emotion. 'I've seen them.' And then: 'Did you do this?'

Mal shook his head. 'No. I didn't do this.' As Solly had reasoned with him before, it wasn't exactly a lie. As long as Mal did most of the talking they really wouldn't have to fib. Too much. 'But Solly thinks he might know who did it. Don't you, Solly?'

'I do,' he said. 'I think I might know.'

Mal rested one hand flat on the file. 'It would be awful if these got out, wouldn't it? Your mother would . . .' Schaeffer released a tight gasp, as if he had just been stung. Still he did not look at the file. 'Yes, well,' Mal said. 'It would be awful. That much is clear.'

'Maybe we can help,' Solly said.

'Yes, maybe we can. Thing is, if Solly can find out who did this . . .'

'And I think I can . . .'

119

'. . . then we should be able to make sure they never fall into the wrong people's hands. We should be able to do that shouldn't we, Solly?'

'Yes, Mal.'

The three of them fell silent again. Schaeffer reached into his pocket for his handkerchief, blowing his nose and then dabbing at the sweat on his forehead. 'What,' he said, in a tight voice, 'do you want from me?'

'Your signature,' Mal said. 'Only that.' He slipped a second manila folder out from under the first and opened it up. Inside were two identical documents. 'Sell us back your share. We offered your father £900 for it. We're offering you £1,200.' He pulled a ballpoint pen from his inside jacket pocket and marked two crosses by where the signatures were required on each sheet. Mal had already signed. Schaeffer reached across with one shaky hand and scribbled his name. A cheque was clipped to the file, which Mal now eased off and passed to Schaeffer. He folded it into his pocket without even checking what was written on it.

'We'll pay for the coffees,' Solly said.

Slowly Schaeffer eased himself from his stool. 'Right,' he said, quietly. Mal handed him the folder of photographs.

'You should have these.' Schaeffer stared at it in horror, as if it were his own severed head. 'And we'll try and track down the negatives. Won't we, Solly?'

'We will, Mal.' There was nothing more to be said. Jeremy Schaeffer turned and walked out the door, letting in a gust of wind that caused a stray paper napkin to flutter prettily across the linoleum floor. They watched him go, a broken man and an enemy for life.

'That's what you call sorted, isn't it,' Solly said.

'That's what you call a relief.'

'Yeah, well. Sorry I got us into this.'

Mal shook his head. 'Nothing to apologize for. I shouldn't have blamed you. I should have blamed old man Schaeffer for breeding. That was the mistake he made. He had sex with his wife.'

120

'We weren't in a position to stop him.'

'No. That's the problem with sex. It's hard to stop people doing it.'

'As we're talking about having sex with your wife . . .' Solly said, staring into his coffee.

'You want to have sex with my wife? I don't have a wife.'

'Nah mate, but *I* will, soon.'

Mal leaned back and took a good look at his partner. 'You and Judy . . .'

'Yup, asked her last week.'

'Why didn't you tell me this before?'

'Well, things have hardly been settled here, have they?' Solly said.

'No. No of course not.' A grin spread across Mal's face. 'So when are you two doing this?'

'Next May. Already sorted the date.'

'That's terrific. Mazeltov,' Mal said. And they hugged. 'My partner the married man.'

'It'll be the biggest wedding of '73. I'm telling you. The works. Three kinds of fish.'

'That's serious. I didn't even know there were three kinds of fish. I thought there was just fish.'

'You'll be best man?'

'Of course, mate. I wouldn't let anybody else do it. Seriously.'

'Then it's settled,' Solly said. They grinned at each other again. And into Mal's mind slipped the image of a wedding: of tables laid and planned, of platters filled and speeches made. Only the startled bridegroom wasn't Solly, but himself. It was Mal in the suit. It was Mal leading the dancing. It was Mal making the speeches. He searched his mind for his bride, delved deep into the recesses of his imagination to find the adoring Divinia, dark-eyed and certain, there by his side. But she was nowhere to be seen. Instead, where his new wife should have been was nothing more than a stark, hollow absence.

Fifteen

If one included the mound of chopped herring that greeted the guests as they arrived to celebrate the wedding of Solomon Princeton to Judith Goldman, there were actually four kinds of fish. As they sipped their pre-dinner drinks and nibbled their canapés in the Regency Suite of the Bayswater Garden Hotel hard by Hyde Park not many people noticed the herring. This was because it had been formed in a chicken mould.

'This is chopped liver?' Solly said, pointing at the carefully shaped chicken on the silver platter, the colour of old window putty.

'Ah, no, Mr Princeton,' said the elderly caterer, with an earnest bow of the head that revealed his black cupple. 'It's chopped herring.'

'In the shape of a chicken?'

'At the last moment we found we had mislaid the fish mould.'

'So you put it in the chicken mould?'

'What can you do when you have no fish mould?'

'There is a logic, I suppose.' Solly scooped a little onto a cracker and tasted it. 'Almost as good as my own,' he said. 'So tell me. What mould did you use for the chopped liver?'

'Ah, something very special,' said the caterer, pointing down the table past heaving platters of vol-aux-vents and gherkins and waxy cubes of cheese on sticks. 'We have just received from my cousin in Tel Aviv a mould that is the likeness of Mrs Golda Meir. The newest thing.' Solly stared at the bust, a deep luscious grey, as though it had only recently been manufactured from wet clay. There were the soft round cheeks and the narrow eye slits, and the two deep jowls like a coat hanger upon which was suspended her wide mouth. It was definitely Mrs Meir. The mother of the nation stared out reproachfully across the ranks of men in their velvet suits with wide lapels and even wider flares and the women in halter-neck dresses. Somebody had already attacked the nose, so that the Israeli Prime Minister appeared to have suffered a great misfortune.

'We have chopped herring that looks like a chicken and chopped liver that looks like Golda Meir in advanced stages of the clap,' Solly muffered. 'Now I know this simcha will go with a swing.' And then to the caterer: 'I think perhaps we should put a label before both of them just so guests know what they are.'

The caterer nodded his head and wrung his hands. 'Very good, Mr Princeton. Of course, Mr Princeton.'

The chopped liver became a talking point. In the following months other moulds would be pressed into service at Jewish weddings across London, including one of Moshe Dayan, complete with eye patch. 'Golda Meir at your wedding,' said one aunt – said all – with a rapid nudge to Solly's ribs. 'Imagine that.'

Then again, everything was a talking point, as was the custom. The guests paraded in for dinner and huddled by tables to point and count. 'What do we have?' said one man, who in middle age had spread to fill the space of two. 'Is it eight to a table. No, ten.'

'But how many tables, Bernard, how many tables?' said his wife, golden hair frozen by lacquer. Her eyebrows could be guaranteed not to register surprise whatever the answer, having been encouraged into that shape already with a pencil.

'I count twelve tables. Twelve of ten. At, what? Ten pounds a head?'

'Ten pounds a head, Bernard? With three kinds of fish?'

'Three kinds of fish?'

'So it says here,' she waved the menu card at him. 'Salmon, pike and carp. And stuffed carp, yet.'

'They stuffed the carp?'

'That's what it says.'

Bernard gave a little whistle. 'Well then £12.50 a head. For stuffed carp.'

'And the rest. And you forgot the top table. Always, you miss things.'

There were indeed salmon, pike and stuffed carp, with sauce hollandaise, or mayonnaise. There was Galia melon to precede them and a choice of a Roast Surrey capon exotique or Norfolk turkey with mushroom sauce to follow. There were cucumber salad and potato salad and a garniture of vegetables. There were cheese blintzes and sour cream and fresh strawberries, fresh fruit platters and home-made pastries, pineapple crush sorbet and *petits fours*. There was food. This was what was expected of a wedding.

Solly and Judy sat side by side at the top table and grinned indulgently at their guests' pleasure. 'Everybody needs to eat,' Solly said.

Judy laughed. 'Darling, you wouldn't let them escape without eating.'

'It's a mitzvah. At a wedding you eat.'

'You telling me it's in the Torah?'

'It's in the appendix to the Torah,' Solly said. 'The appendix to the appendix. Small book. Not many people have read it.'

'Only you?'

'Only me.'

'Come here you gorgeous man and give me a kiss,' Judy said, wrapping her soft, bare arms about his neck. 'It's legal now. You're my husband.' The rest of the table applauded. Solly's only concern was, he said, to make sure that everybody remembered Judy's wedding day. He was in the food business and if he could not make his own wedding work, well then, he would be 'like a chauffeur who did not know how to change gear on his own car'. But that did not rule out having a

124

little fun. And so the two official toasts of the night –
to the President of Israel and to the Queen – had been
handed to the most inappropriate people possible,
only because Solly knew they could not refuse the
honour and this made him laugh. The toast to
the Queen was therefore given to Solly's cousin Roger
who had emigrated to Israel in 1948 – changing his
name to Avi, though none of his family in Britain ever
used it – and who since referred to himself as a pioneer.

'Pioneer?' his detractors would say. 'He landed an
hour before the Declaration of Independence. And this
makes him a pioneer? If there had been fog at Luton
airport he would never have made it.' Nevertheless, he
retained the commitment of the convert and regarded
the British State as the enemy for the enforced blocks
they had put on immigration to Palestine both before
and immediately after the war. 'May she choke on a
fish bone,' whispered Roger, after he had implored the
room to raise their glasses to the monarch.

To Solly's Uncle Ronnie fell the task of toasting the
President of Israel. Ronnie was a Bolshevik who still
lived off Brick Lane and who had helped fight Mosley's
Blackshirts at the Battle of Cable Street in 1936. The
State of Israel, he said, with the emphasis on every
third word, whatever it might be, was 'a hole in the
ground. We should all go and live in the desert? That
way we say to the Fascists they have won. I will never
live in a desert hutch, like that putz Roger. If we are to
proclaim victory over the Fascists we must live here, in
the world.' As he toasted President Shazar, he too
added a little prayer of his own, in the hope that the
head of state's gonads might soon drop off.

Mal muttered no expletives under his breath when it
came to his best man's speech. 'Solomon Princeton,' he
began, 'is a bit of mouthful, as I'm sure Judy has
already realized.' He looked down the table, to where
the Blow Job Queen and her new husband were seated,
both with one eyebrow raised. 'So, I'll call him Solly,

because that's how we know him.' They relaxed. In the shul as they had been married and now in this room, before a sea of warm velvet and silk and pale blue eyeshadow, Mal had found himself dwelling on the idea of marriage. He had clasped Divinia's hand as she sniffed through the service and thanked the stars that they were Reform Jews, and not therefore separated, men from women. He enjoyed the warm touch of her skin on his, which made him feel that he too understood the point of the union. But compared to Solly he knew he was only a spectator. It seemed as if his grasp on intimacy were as slight as his physical hold on Divinia. It was no more than two sets of fingertips touching.

'Solly Princeton,' he told the party, 'treats life as if it were like this bash, as if every day were a seven-course wedding banquet. He fills his plate with nosh and then he fills it again. And he tries to make sure that you fill your plate too.' A ripple of giggles passed about the room, from those who had already been implored to eat and eat some more. 'This,' Mal continued, leaving a delicate pause, 'makes him an ideal partner for a catering and kitchenware business.' The room erupted in laughter.

But Solly's success, his completeness, was more than that. It was not simply the enthusiasm of the eager puppy, desperate to please. He was at ease with himself. He was at ease with his wife. 'Judy,' Mal said, 'is not just Solly's wife. She is his best friend.' Judy laid her hand, sparkling now with fine-cut ice, upon Solly's and he in turn leaned down to lay one spare kiss upon her bare shoulder. That was it, Mal thought, as he talked his way through the anecdotes so carefully ordered upon the page before him. Sanitized fragments of a life, party-safe. Solly does not mind throwing himself in. Me, I sit on the beach dabbling my toes in the surf, scared of jellyfish and sharks and mystery creatures with spines. He is out there, up to his nipples in the breaking waves. Mal could feel Divinia by his side, looking up at him as he held the room. He imagined he could feel her warm breath against the material of his suit.

'You will do fine,' she had said to him, as she straightened his bow tie that morning. 'You like a crowd.' But he hadn't been reassured because it was only Divinia. He was not immersed in her. Maybe his mistake was not diving in. Maybe that was it. Cowardice.

Mal Jones, coward.

'I have known Solly ten years now,' he said, 'and he hasn't changed. He still needs to shave three times a day. Unfortunately he only gets round to it once a day, but what can you do. He still lives to eat rather than the other way round. He still talks for Britain. And that's the way he should always be. To be frank I'd come to think he was mine. We're partners. We do everything together. We have bank accounts together. We even have breakfast together every day.' There was a wolf whistle from the further reaches of the room. Mal raised one hand, to silence it. 'Thing is, I now have to face up to the fact that he's leaving me. That he's found someone else. He won't be there for breakfast any more. Worst part is he's leaving me for a woman. And you know' – he picked up his glass from the table – 'I really couldn't be more delighted. Rabbi, Ladies and Gentlemen, Relatives and Friends. I ask you to be upstanding for the bride and groom.' Beside him he heard Divinia's blue satin dress rustle as she stood and raised her glass, one hand clutching Mal's forearm. 'The bride and groom,' came the response from the crowd, and the band struck up. Mal leaned across and kissed Divinia gently on the cheek. Maybe it was time to dive in. To swim in the waves.

As the music played and the guests danced Mal began to wander about the room. He found his parents sitting, hand in hand, to one side of the dance floor.

'How's business?' Sam Jones said, as he pulled out a chair for his son.

'Look at the room, Dad. I think everybody's having fun.'

'They have a good thing going here, this hotel,' he said, nodding slowly in admiration. 'Simchas like this. A fine product.'

'Oh Samuel,' Marsha Jones said, with a fond nudge. 'Can't you just enjoy a party.'

'I'm only saying.'

'Mal, darling, ignore your father. One day soon, please God, this will be you.'

'Mother!' Divinia's face swept into Mal's mind and he felt goose bumps expanding on his chest although he was more than warm enough.

'To Divinia Greenspan,' Sam Jones said with a wink, as if reading his son's thoughts and knowing what would make him feel most uncomfortable.

'I think we're getting a bit ahead of ourselves.'

'All we want, your father and I, is that you should be happy.'

'That's all we want,' Sam said.

'And with Divinia we know you would be happy.'

'Happy.'

'And so Divinia is all we want for you.'

'And that Syd Greenspan. Oi! what a businessman.'

'Samuel! Really.'

'All I'm saying is he's a good businessman. What's so bad that I should say that?'

Mal kissed his parents patiently and moved off to explore the party further. Benny and Heidi were at a corner table, she hugging his arm, head rested on his shoulder.

'Nice speech, big brother.'

'Thanks, kid,' he said, squeezing his younger sibling's cheek between thumb and forefinger, as their grandmother used to do.

'Hey.'

'Memory from the past,' Mal said.

'Are you having a nice time?' Heidi said sleepily. Mal guessed she had drunk one glass too many. Her delicate lips glowed with a light spread of fashionable orange lipstick and her black silk dress was tied back behind her neck in a way that begged you to undo it with one hand.

'I'm having a lovely time,' Mal said, pulling up a chair. 'You used to weddings like this?' He nodded towards the surge of well-upholstered humanity on the dance floor.

'You Jews,' Heidi said, with a soft smile. 'Nothing ever happens until it's happened noisily.'

'Got to make sure people know about it.'

'I think the guests on the top floor of the hotel know about this one.'

'We like smaller things,' Benny said, reaching out to squeeze Heidi's knee, making contact and building a wall with her at the same time. 'Quieter, you know.'

'The king of the racetrack does intimate?'

'Yeah. Seriously, brother.' He shrugged, and looked shiftily at his shoes. 'Track's one thing, but otherwise, keep it small.'

'You've never done anything small. You're the family bigmouth.'

'Not in everything,' he said. He looked at Heidi and she nodded at him to get on with it.

'What?' Mal said. 'What you two want to ask me.'

'Is it that obvious?' Benny said.

'Yeah, it's that obvious. Go on. Ask.'

'We don't want to ask you anything. We've got something to tell you.' Mal felt a lump rise in his throat; this, he was not expecting. Not so soon.

'So? Tell me.'

Benny coughed. 'Heidi and me. We've got married.'

'When?' Mal said, trying to make sense of what he thought he'd just heard. 'When are you doing this?'

'No bro, Mal, we've done it. Two days ago.'

Now Mal noticed that Heidi was playing with a simple gold band on the third finger of her left hand. It reminded him of his father stroking the callus on his finger from where he held the accountant's pen. The

129

mark of servitude. 'You're the first to know,' she said. 'We wanted it that way.'

He looked from Heidi to Benny and then away to where his parents were sitting. 'Mum and Dad? Do they . . .'

His brother shook his head. 'What with Heidi not being . . . well, we just wanted to sort it out first and then talk to them about . . . don't tell them, Mal. Promise me that.'

'You'll tell them soon?'

'Of course, mate. Tomorrow. Or the day after.' The three of them were silent. Around them the room spun and turned. 'So . . .?'

'So what?' Mal said. He was thinking about Divinia. Or he was trying to think about Divinia because he imagined it was what the moment demanded.

'Aren't you going to congratulate us?'

'Forgive me, Benny. Mazeltov. Seriously. L'chayim.' He wrapped his arms about his brother and breathed in the smell of dry-cleanig fluid on his hired tuxedo. 'Do I get to hug my . . .' He hesitated. 'My sister-in-law.'

'Better than that,' she said, stumbling woozily to her feet. She stretched out one hand towards him. 'Come and dance with me.'

He looked to his brother. 'May I?'

Benny waved him away. 'Go. Go dance with my wife.' And then, with a grin he added: 'My wife. I like the sound of that.'

They threaded their way to the dance floor, past tables now being laid with pastries and cake and sandwiches, where older women sat massaging their shoeless toes through their tights. The band played a soft ballad of even chord changes and Heidi hung her arms around Mal's neck in much the same way as her dress hung about her own. His hands found the soft bare skin of her back. He kept his palms away, touching only with fingertips, so as not to lay too much flesh upon flesh. She looked into his eyes. 'Relax,' she said.

'You can hold me. We're family now.' He let his hands fall soft against her back.

'I could have held you before.'

'You didn't though.'

'I didn't know there was so little time.'

'What do you mean?'

'I didn't know you were going to be a married woman.'

She looked up at him. Her breath smelt of stale apples and white wine.

'Did I get the right Jones?' she said.

'I don't know. I can't choose. I don't fancy Benny.'

'No, but you love him.'

'So do you.'

She grinned. 'I do,' she said, and rested her head on the wide lapel of his velvet suit that, ten years hence, would serve as an embarrassment whenever they examined the photographs of the day.

'You're lucky to have found someone you love so much,' he said softly as they moved around the floor, each trying not to tangle their feet in the other's.

'You have Divinia,' she said.

'I know. You're right,' he said, a little anxiously. 'I do have Divinia.' Even she can see it, Mal thought. I have Divinia.

'And you have me.'

He reached under her chin to turn her face up to his. 'What are you saying?' She leaned her head on one side.

'Well I'm always here now, aren't I,' she said. She stroked the back of his neck. 'Part of the family. And you boys love your families. I'll always be here. If you want anything I'll always be here.'

'Is that a promise?'

She stood on tiptoe to kiss him on the cheek. 'Of course,' she said. 'And I never break a promise.' The new Mrs Heidi Jones rested her head back on his chest and he looked out over her at the turning, dancing crowd. The problem was the one thing he really wanted was now the one thing he could not have.

131

Sixteen

The older man opened the box. Inside it smelt of earth and burnt leaves. He picked out a long, fat cigar and sniffed it, running the roll of tobacco beneath his nostrils.

'You want one of these?' Sydney Greenspan said, his speech sharp with the staccato consonants of an earlier life, lived elsewhere. Mal reached in and took one. He studied the two candles burning in the centre of the table. The flames reflected off the clusters of ornate silver picture frames scattered across sideboards and shelves and windowsills, that held aged photographs of people he took to be relatives.

'I thought you weren't meant to smoke on Shabbat.'

Greenspan grinned so that his eyes folded away into tight knots of shadow, and his narrow bald pate creased up. 'You didn't know the Kiddush but this you know?'

'Was it that obvious?'

'That you don't know the blessings? Sure.' Greenspan closed the cigar box and slipped it back into a drawer of the heavy coffin-black sideboard. 'My wife meant well,' he said. 'She wanted our Divinia's boy . . .' He smiled again and Mal found himself blushing. 'Her intended, to feel honoured. So she asks of you to do the blessing. But I could see this is not for you, so I do it.' He stood at the end of the table, legs slightly apart, unlit cigar held between third and fourth finger, as he cut the end. 'You blushed then, like you do now when I mention my daughter.' Now he leaned down, and placed the flat end of the cigar to the first Shabbat candle, puffing on it, mouth open to help him breathe in a little air as he drew it aflame. He passed the cutter to Mal, who copied as best he could. He felt edgy and unsure of himself. Even as he pumped his own cigar he wondered whether he was being tricked into an unholy act by a father who, from the devotions just shown over the Shabbat meal, took his Jewish rituals seriously.

Syd Greenspan sat down at the head of the table, his chair at an angle, the hand that held the cigar rested on its elbow. 'You know, there are two reasons for Shabbat. The first is the day of rest, that God rested on the seventh day and so must we. Fine,' he said, puffing again, a soft cloud of blue-grey smoke rising up about him. 'So I rest.' He pointed at Mal with his cigar. 'But there is the other reason. As memorial to the exodus from Egypt. Only those who are not slaves may rest. It makes sense, no? Only those who are not slaves, can rest.'

Mal nodded. 'It makes sense,' he said, chugging on his own cigar. It was hard to pull any smoke down such length.

Greenspan held a little smoke in his mouth, puffing out his cheeks, before releasing it. 'In 1946, I make it out of the transit camp to Geneva,' he said. 'I was lucky, my father, before he . . .' Divinia's old man licked his lips. 'He was organized. He has put the account in Geneva in my name as the eldest son. So many people, they could not reach their money because it was in the name of someone else. So many others they were not there, even to ask for it. There's not a lot in my account. But there's enough. I take it out, take out some, and I go to Davidoff on rue de Rive.' Mal noted the perfect pronunciation. The Dutch have always been good at languages, he thought.

'Have you been to Davidoff?' he said. Mal shook his head. 'Then you should go. The best shop for cigars in the world. There is one in London. So . . .' He yawned and puffed again. 'I go to Davidoff and with my money I buy a big cigar, like this one.' He held it up, studying it. 'And I leave the shop and I light it, out there on the street. That, for me, is freedom at last. A big cigar that I buy with my own money.' He looked around the room at the silver-framed photographs and then pointed at them all with his cigar. It was his prop, his shtick. 'All these people, they never made it to smoke their own cigar in Geneva. May their souls rest in peace.'

Mal looked at the photographs. Young women with rich dark eyes and young men in fine starched collars stared back at him, fixing the lens with certainty. This was an audience not just with Sydney Greenspan but with the entire Greenspan – or, as they once were, Grunweld – family. As his eyes scanned the cluttered dining room, Mal found more and more photographs, tucked in corners, hidden in shadows. Wealthy family groups picnicking on a warm summer hillside, looking both pleased with themselves and a little self-conscious, because of the vulgar debris of lunch about them; old men with white eyebrows dripping over their eyes like Virginia creeper, gripping their sticks and staring away into the distance, sure it no longer mattered what anybody else thought; old women with sagging chin and bosom, indulging the young photographer, with a smile. Must all these people consent to my marrying Divinia, he thought? Will my easy life be judged by the standards of their suffering?

'And now,' Mal said, 'you smoke a cigar on Shabbat to mark your freedom?'

Greenspan laughed. 'You are even more sentimental than me, young man. No, I smoke cigars all the time. I just don't deprive myself on Shabbat. Anyway . . .' he said, nodding towards the candles. 'It is my wife who believes in all of this. Not me. For me, God died in the camps, with all of them. I am still a Jew, without him. I choose how I shall be a Jew my own way. We light the candles, it reminds me I am still a Jew. That's good enough. My Divinia, your Divinia, she will want to light the candles.'

'I will like that,' Mal said, wondering if what the

older man had said about his daughter were true, and feeling a knot tighten in his stomach at the thought of it.

'Maybe you will,' he said with a slow nod of the head. And then: 'Your business is successful?'

'We're doing fine.'

'You're not doing fine. You're doing good. I've been in business long enough to know when someone's doing good. And you'll do better.'

'You think so?'

'Sure.' Greenspan blew on the end of his cigar so that it glowed orange and red. Flakes of ash spun and fluttered in the air. He dusted a little off his knee. 'Millionaire before you're thirty. It takes one to know one. Business for me has worked here so I know what to look for.' Mal knew the older man was rich. He had read about his success as a property developer. And even if he had not done so, he could see it here in this house with its wide hallways and thick carpets.

'Thank you for your confidence but—'

'The thing is, always protect the business. That's the most important thing. Protect.'

'I will.'

'Do you give?'

'Give?'

'To charity?'

'Oh, well I give to the Yom Kippur collection. I do that.'

'You should give regularly, young wealthy man like you. Every month, something. What you can afford. And it's tax deductible. Makes sense for everyone.'

'I see.'

'You're rich now. You can afford it.'

'Sure, I'll see to it.'

'It makes good business sense.'

'Of course, tax deductible . . .'

'Feh . . .' he said, waving Mal away. 'Tax deductible is only half of it. All the time when you are a Jew in business there are disasters for which people think you

135

should put your hand in your pocket. Always palaver.'

'What sort of disasters?'

'Disasters. You'll see. Calamities. As I say, palaver. Everybody is running around panicking, giving and giving. More than they can afford. Me, I didn't do it. I already gave. I gave all the time. I gave when there weren't calamities. Don't lose your business to guilt and panic.'

'I won't.'

'All of us, we must look after ourselves. You must look after yourself.' He was staring away into a corner now, as if trying to understand a memory.

'Who do I give to?'

'Whoever. You just make sure you give now, so you don't do silly later.'

The two men sat in silence, puffing on their cigars. Mal decided he liked the taste, its bitter astringency on the tongue. If only he needed to commemorate his own freedom rather than Syd Greenspan's. On the sideboard a carriage clock rang the hour. They both turned to look at it.

'Time is talking to us,' Greenspan said, with a sniff.

'Mr Greenspan?'

'Mal.'

'Divinia and me. It's OK? We can get married?'

He stood up. 'Hah,' he shouted. 'If it wasn't for my wife I would marry you myself. But I'm taken and so are you. Divinia doesn't marry you, I disown her. Come on, let's go find the ladies.' And he was gone from the room, leaving behind him only a trail of smoke and the dull echo of his laughter.

Seventeen

It was only a few weeks later that Mal came to grasp exactly what his father-in-law-to-be had meant by the word 'calamity'. On 6 October 1973 Mal, like so many other 'twice a year' Jews, was locked in an uncommon act of observance, seeing out the all-day Yom Kippur service in the overcrowded, overheated shell of the Edgwarebury shul's prefabs. By early afternoon condensation was fast climbing the windows and the plasterboard walls were beginning to smell of chalk dust and damp. If British Jewry had been true to their devotions that day then none of them would have known about the simultaneous invasion of the Golan Heights by Syria and the crossing of the Suez Canal by Egypt until nightfall, when finally they could have switched on television and radio to hear the news. But the Day of Atonement is the one High Holy Day guaranteed to be observed by those who do not observe; it was inevitable that somebody would hear the bulletins, however accidentally they claimed the news fell into their ears, like a bad smell passing beneath their nose. And so it was that Yom Kippur 1973 became the one sacred day of the year upon which the unrighteous were kings.

Word first reached the Edgwarebury Synagogue at a little after 1.30 p.m. when most of the congregation was beginning to think of the lunch they were not eating and the breakfast they had not eaten before that. The whisper began three rows back from where Mal and Divinia were sitting, with the arrival of an Edgware housewife, make-up applied just so, nostrils aquiver both at the thought of being the bearer of the news and at the possibility of having been beaten to it by someone else. 'Geoffrey,' she hissed, as she made her way towards her husband, a quiet solicitor with a long top lip and thin veined neck that made him look not unlike a turtle. 'Geoffrey.' At the sound he jutted his head forward as if to escape the hard shell of his loose shirt collar. Soon she was upon him, powdered cheek pressed against his to deliver a kiss but clearly also imparting something far more valuable.

'War.'

'No.'

'Yes. War. An invasion. This morning. Can you imagine it? On Yom Kippur.'

The turtle craned his neck to tell his neighbour who brought into the huddle a third person and then a fourth, so that those who turned to see what all the fuss was about found only a scrum of bowed heads and broad-suited backs draped in a slack spread of prayer shawl. Those nearer the front assumed at first that, as every year, some poor soul had proved unequal to the deprivations of the fast and had fainted, but wondered who could be so fragile as to have succumbed so early in the day. Soon, however, word was passing from row to row, from ear to ear, a stream of boiling information pouring like water through the channels and passages marked out by chair and aisle. The initial news soon gave way to barks of disbelief and outrage so that the rabbi, head bowed over the text, looked up to find the entire congregation concentrating not on him, but on each other. For a moment his mouth fell open as if he were about to call them to order, until the shul secretary, a self-important little man who revelled in his status as community gontser macher, mounted the bimah to whisper the news in his ear. The rabbi hesitated, his head still tilted to one side to hear what the deplorable fool had to say. Then he stood up straight, quietly thanked the secretary, and stared out at the hall. Slowly a kind of peace returned to the room as one by one the congregation realized the rabbi was watching them. They expected an announcement or an unscheduled prayer. Surely the moment deserved something? A word? When at last peace had descended he simply bowed his head and returned to reading.

It was a fragile and uneasy peace. Throughout the afternoon gossip and news continued to arrive in the hall, where the windows seemed to steam up even more than usual until they glowed a dull orange from the dirty overhead lights. Men, digging about in the velvet bags that carried their prayer shawls, feigned surprise when they found the car keys they should not have been carrying, to a car that should not have been parked nearby, and absented themselves to listen to their car radios. Women returning from feeding the children who could not go all day without food, muttered about troop numbers and conflict. Soon, very soon, the information became mangled by a desperation to be in possession of some piece of news that trumped the offering recently provided by a neighbour. All about the room the search was on for new news, for breaking events with new novelty and new drama.

'It's just a small incursion,' said one. 'Not a war.'

'The Soviets have given the bomb to the Syrians. In Tel Aviv they are already in their air raid shelters.'

'Gas. I hear the Egyptians are using gas.'

'There is hand-to-hand fighting in Jerusalem.'

'Already, Syria has surrendered.'

But they hadn't. One woman, whose son was serving in the Israeli army, was led from the hall, white faced and shaking. Another remained standing, eyes staring dead ahead, when all around her everybody else was sitting. Slowly, gently, her husband eased her back into her seat whispering, 'It will be all right. He will be all right. They will be all right.'

In the late afternoon the Edgwarebury Schul, like so many other parts of north-west London that October day, was affected by a power cut that extinguished the lights and plunged the hall into a deathly gloom, as if the Yom Kippur service had slipped from a stinging Technicolor into black and white. Nobody bothered to comment; the symbolism was too bald and too obvious to bother with.

'Solly, meet me outside,' Mal said, as he shuffled his way out of the row and past his partner seated in front of him.

In the empty car park men huddled in twos and threes, hands shoved deep into pockets against the chill autumn wind. Mal watched as three teenage lads wearing what had once been their Bar Mitzvah suits – or what they had worn when it had been their younger brothers' turn – sloped off around the back of the shul, eyes over their shoulders in case any parent should catch them. Off for a smoke, Mal thought, and allowed himself a half-smile. He felt tired and hollow, but he could not tell whether that was because of the news or simply because he was hungry.

'Mal,' Solly said, arriving by his side. Spontaneously, he embraced his partner as he might have done at the funeral of a relative. Mal held him a little stiffly, surprised at the intimacy.

'Can you believe it?' Mal said.

'No.'

'On Yom Kippur?'

'I know.'

'Amazing. Arab scum. On Yom Kippur, holiest day of the year.'

'I know.'

'Awful.'

'Terrible.'

Mal took a deep breath and stared out over the car park to the newsagent's across the road. The early billboards for that day's edition of the *Evening Standard* were carrying the news. 'We have to decide what we're going to do now,' Mal said.

'I know.'

'What Sinai's going to do.'

'Yeah, of course. Back inside people are talking

about what they're going to put into the Yom Kippur appeal. Obviously it's all going to Israel now.'

'Of course. Where else.'

'Mr Frank, you know him, the greengrocer?'

'Marcus Frank?'

'Him. He says he's selling one of his shops and putting the money into the appeal.'

'He's what?'

'Said he was thinking of selling it anyway. Just a question of what he does with the cash. So he says he's putting it in. We've got to do something too.' A gust of wind blew old crisp packets and fallen leaves about their feet.

'Do you have Gerry's number in your head?' Mal said.

'Gerry? He's not going to be home. He's a bit of a frummer, belongs to Stanmore United. Even if you rang and there was someone there they wouldn't pick up, not for a couple of hours.'

'Of course, yeah. Look, we're due at yours tonight to break the fast?'

'You're still coming?'

'Wouldn't miss it. Do you mind if I stop by and pick up Gerry first? I think we should talk this over, first opportunity.'

'No problem. Tell him to bring the whole family. Judy would love to see them. And since we've moved into the new place we've more than got the room.'

That evening the three men sat around Solly's new kitchen table in his new kitchen with its new varnished pine units, pulling at gefilte fish. Solly had catered for forty, even though there was less than half that number in the house. 'It's a mark,' said Solly, as he attacked his plate, 'of just how important food is to us Jews that our holiest day of the year is signified by a lack of it.'

'After all, what greater hardship could there be for a Jew than going without lunch?' Judy and Divinia came and went, filling plates and pouring drinks.

'You three putting the world to rights?' Judy said as she stood over Solly, running her fingers through his thick black hair. He laid his hand upon her belly. She was a couple of months pregnant, and he loved to imagine he could feel a roundness growing there, although so far there was no sign.

'Getting something sorted, darling,' he said.

Divinia stuck her head round the door 'Mal, come and talk to us.' He sniffed with irritation. 'In a bit, my love. Gerry and Solly and me, we need to talk.'

He looked at Gerry, who was feeding a piece of fish into his mouth with one hand while pushing his glasses back up his nose with the other. 'How are the cash reserves?' Mal said.

Gerry wiped his hand on a napkin and ran his tongue around his teeth. 'Good,' he said. 'Healthy.'

'Five figure healthy?'

'Without a doubt. There's a cash sum of at least £20,000 in the bank and with the payments we're due . . .'

'We going to put the whole lot in?' Solly said. 'I think we should. I think that's what we should do.'

Mal glanced at his partner and then back to Gerry. 'Have we got any big expenses coming up? Anything urgent?'

'Workshop says one of the lathes could do with an overhaul but it could wait.'

'How much will it cost?'

'Three hundred pounds. Maybe £400.'

'OK get it done first thing. I want all the plant working properly.'

'Sure, Mal.'

'What are you thinking, mate?' Solly said.

Mal sat back in his chair and rolled his head from side to side. His neck was stiff and his head ached from the calculations he had been doing all afternoon. 'I want to put the workshop on double time, triple time if we can.'

Solly gasped. 'What?'

'I want the workshop going full time, for the next two months or for as long as we've got.'

'I thought we were going to put the money into the Joint Israel Appeal.'

'Yeah, that's what you thought. But it's not what I thought. I never said that.' Mal stood up and made for the fridge to get himself another glass of orange juice. The fridge bulged with cheese and eggs, bread and smoked salmon, butter and milk. Mal found the sight of a full fridge comforting. Obviously so did Solly. 'Listen, Solly,' he said, leaning back against the door. 'You are free to give whatever you want to the appeal. Give them this lovely new house of yours, for all I care. But we can't give away Sinai because of a calamity like this. We've got to survive. It's no use us going down as well as Israel.' In his head he heard the precise Dutch syllables of Syd Greenspan.

'You put the factory on triple time,' Gerry said, 'and we'll be left with too much stock. Quickest way to go bust.'

'Yeah,' Solly said. 'Too much stock.'

'Have you boys been reading the papers recently?' Mal said. They stared back at him, blankly. He sat down, and gripped his drink. 'The Arabs have been upping the price of oil for months now.'

'That, I know,' Solly said. 'We all know that.'

'Let me finish. It's not going to get better. If you ask me it's going to get much worse. If America backs Israel in this war, and they will, pound to a penny the price shoots up three or fourfold. In a few months' time, we won't be able to afford fuel to run the workshop, at least until it's sorted.'

'Oh come on, Mal . . .'

'I'm telling you Solly, trust me on this. Businesses like ours will go to the wall by the dozen if they don't sort themselves out now.'

'Seven years of fat for seven years of thin?' Gerry said.

'Exactly. A man who knows his Bible. Stock up now

because in a couple of months we may not be able to.'

'What's more important?' Solly said. 'Us surviving or Israel surviving?'

'The war's already started. If they're not sorted out there yet then they're fucked. I'm telling you. These wars are always short. By the time the money they collected this afternoon gets out to Jerusalem it will all be over one way or the other. And there's no point us going down too. We've got to survive. Sinai can't do anything to help anybody if it doesn't exist.' Solly dropped his head into his hands. 'I'm doing just what you told me that time,' Mal continued.

'What time?'

'When we had the Schaeffer business. You told me not to sacrifice Sinai.'

'This is different.'

'Yeah, it's more serious.'

'Gerry?' Solly looked at the financial director. He raised his hands. 'I've got shares but it's your business. The decision's up to you. If what Mal says about the price of oil going through the roof is true then he's maybe right. We should stock up now.'

'Thank you, Gerry,' Mal said. He turned to smile at Solly but his partner was looking away and refusing to meet his gaze.

'I'm hungry,' Solly said and he stood up to fill his plate for a fourth time.

Eighteen

When business students came to study the history of the Sinai empire they all agreed it was that dark October night in 1973, when the forces of three desert armies were still assaulting each other by bullet and shell, which was the defining moment. Mal was right about the difficult times ahead, even if for the wrong reasons. It was not the seemingly endless surge upwards in oil prices that did for British industry, although that was trouble enough. It was the miners' strike, an industrial dispute that would eventually plunge the country into a three-day working week and unseat a government.

'I'm not surprised they're striking,' Solly said, when he heard the news. 'I mean, really. Spending your life down a nasty black hole, digging stuff out of the ground. Sounds like torture to me.'

'They're not striking about having to be miners,' Mal said. 'They want to be miners. They're striking because they want to be paid more for it.'

'They want to be miners? Sorry. Explain this to me. Who would want to be a miner?'

'Face it, Solly, coal mining is not a great part of Jewish culture. Nobody is ever going to write a folk song about Coal Face Cohen the great Jewish coal miner who dug 16 tons in an hour.'

'No, I suppose not.'

In the ten weeks between the outbreak of war and the introduction of the three-day week in the middle of December the Sinai workshop went into overdrive, producing stock for twenty out of every twenty-four hours. Not that everybody knew about it. Gerry announced that it was too expensive to put the regular shift on overtime. What he actually said was 'it will minimize cash-reserve return', but they all knew what he meant. The only solution was to employ cheap, unskilled labour and ship them in quietly after the first lot had gone home, so as not to enrage a dispute of their own. Thus, each evening, with the help of the foreman, the manufacturing floor was closed down at 5 p.m. on the dot and, with over-dramatic display, all the doors locked. An hour later Mal, Solly and the foreman would return quietly to reopen the back entrance and allow in the curious collection of Bengalis and Ugandan Asians that Benny had recruited from the shabbier tenements of the East End, where their own family's life as immigrants had begun.

'They've worked lathes before?' Mal said to his brother, as they trooped in on the first night.

'Not precisely,' Benny said.

'Not precisely? What does not precisely mean? These are precision implements.'

'They're technically minded.'

'Oh yeah?'

'Well, most of them have got driving licences.'

'Great.'

There were errors, of course: colanders produced with holes large enough to allow through new potatoes; garlic presses without holes, so that bulbs were pulverized rather than merely pressed; Pollo-Matics with all the pieces joined in the wrong order, so that the wide end of the funnel was at the bottom, inverted, rather than at the top. But, by the time the short-hour working began, Sinai had a secret warehouse packed to the rafters with chrome and steel implements, which glittering, polished store Mal compared to a pharaoh's tomb.

'You die, Solly, and we'll inter the body in here,' he said, as they stacked the last of the boxes in place. He was still trying to convince his partner that they were doing the right thing. 'You'll be surrounded by your great treasures: 15,000 pieces of kitchenware.'

'It's not *my* death I'm worried about,' he said, sullenly. 'Let's just hope this place doesn't end up as Sinai's tomb. The place where they come to bury the corpse of our great company.'

'It won't. Trust me.'

It didn't. Other companies suffered. But not Sinai. It took months for the poison to work its way through the sluggish, tattered arteries of the economy; for those firms that had failed to stock up in times of plenty to feel the referred pain of not now having goods to supply demand. But still it happened. For them 'cash flow' became a wicked, mocking phrase rich only in contradiction as revenue went from a rolling pumping river to a parched stream. Sinai did have problems, but in comparison they were minor. They too had to absorb the cost of short-time production while paying full-time wages. But they still had a warehouse full of implements ready for people to buy. When other companies supplying the same market started going to the wall, Sinai were still around to pick up the slack. Later, much later, even Solly had to admit that if it hadn't been for Mal's plan the company would never have survived and he would never have been able to embark on his own peculiar brand of charitable work.

In the autumn of 1974 Mal finally married Divinia, with all the grandeur and excess and fine napery that Syd Greenspan's deep pockets could afford, although no members of the Israeli cabinet were represented among the canapés, either in the form of chopped liver or chopped herring. 'A good marriage should be like a good business,' Greenspan told Mal just before the ceremony. 'You should be only a part of both but also be vital to both. Without you both should be nothing. But when you are there you are just part of the team.'

'It's a contradiction, then.'

'Forget contradiction. It's hard work, I tell you. That's what it is. Hard work.'

But more and more Divinia did not feel to Mal like

147

hard work. She felt right when she was by his side. She was the sort of woman that a man who was going to be a millionaire before he was thirty, should have by his side. Immaculately turned out, hair fixed, nails shining, electric with smiles and wired with small talk. She was correct and proper, the perfect north London Jewish girl, who could name a dozen designer labels and say the blessings over the candles. She made him feel good about himself. He was the lion-maned prince and so she was the . . . But no, she was too modest for that. Too careful and too understated to be a caricature. He would never marry a stereotype.

True, she wasn't Heidi but who gets to marry their Heidi? Did even Benny manage that trick? Already it seemed his brother spent more time at the track than at home, frittering away note after note on the capriciousness of the fates. Already he was neglecting his wife. And she *was* Heidi. Maybe he had his own version of Heidi elsewhere? So no. People didn't get to marry their ideals. That much was clear. But marriage isn't about ideals. It's about getting it right. That was what Syd Greenspan had meant. Divinia was right.

'A few years ago my friend Moses here told me he would take me to the promised land,' Solly said, inverting the real story, when he came to make the best man's speech. 'And you know, he has. Now he has found someone else to take to the promised land. I know she will enjoy the trip as much as I have. Because Mal knows the route. He always knows where he is going. He may not tell you where you're going but he'll have it there, in his head.' Solly tapped his temples with one finger. 'And when you get there I can tell you the view is always lovely.' They stood to toast the bride and groom in wine whose magnificent cost was all but wasted on a room full of non-drinking Jews. Mal sucked noisily on the cigar his father-in-law had given him, as the guests murmured their congratulations.

'This is all Samuel and I have ever wanted,' Marsha

Jones said to anybody who would listen. 'That he should be happy. That is our only ambition for our son. And with Divinia he will be happy.'

Like Solly and Judy before them, Mal and Divinia moved into a large house in the manicured avenues of Hampstead Garden Suburb, alongside all the other young families on the up. Two cars in the drive. Fondue set in the kitchen. Mezuzahs on the doorposts. For a few months Mal and Divinia's empty extra bedrooms, papered and carpeted in the latest style, stood sentry as breathless question marks beside their own, with its wide expanse of double bed. Until the question marks were shooed away with pregnancy and the birth of Simon, all fearsome lungs and searching limbs; a son to match Joseph, whom Judy and Solly had presented to the world a year before, his furious, pink brow capped by a mop of leather-black hair. On Sundays the two families would meet for lunch at one or other home, both to eat – always to eat – and to take mutual pleasure in their success.

'The next generation,' Mal said, as he held Simon before him at arm's length, and watched him dribble enthusiastically down his chin.

'Hey, he can dribble,' Solly said. 'Deserves a place on the board for that alone. Simon and Joe, the next chief executives of Sinai.'

'Of course. We should get them desk blotters of their own.'

'Is it all right by you if my son learns to crawl before we sort out his career?' Divinia said, taking Simon back. 'Anyway, this one will be a doctor,' she said, as she smoothed her child's cobweb of hair. 'Just look at his hands.'

'I wasn't thinking anything stressful,' Mal said, with a grin. 'Just a couple of board meetings a month. The two of them could dribble onto the blotters for us, just to check they work. Put them on a salary for that.'

'Maybe our boys don't want to be in kitchenware,' Judy said, heaving the weighty Joseph up onto her lap.

'Not want to be in kitchenware?' Solly said. 'Who could not want to be in kitchenware?'

'Yeah,' said Mal. 'The glamour of the sieve, the excitement of the potato masher. Who could not want that?'

'Someone with a weak heart,' Solly said, with a wink. 'They couldn't take it.'

It was the first time either of them had acknowledged, however obliquely, that the business they were in might not be the most thrilling. There was still a warm place in both their hearts for the Pollo-Matic; every Saturday Solly used the silver-plated version that Mal had given him one birthday, to make chicken soup. They were both proud of what they had achieved. But neither wanted to go to their grave saying, 'What I gave to the world was quick chicken soup. For this, I should be remembered.' Once Mal had imagined his success in heaps of steel and chrome, kitchen implements stretched out across a field as far as the eye could see. Now, when he tried to give it form, it appeared as a pile of dripping chicken carcasses.

He imagined himself being interviewed by the *Jewish Chronicle* at his retirement, old man's trousers belted beneath his nipples, and saying proudly, 'I have measured out my life in chicken wings. For me this is enough.' The thought made him shudder. How would that achievement compare to the fate of the Grunweld family, who now stood framed in Syd's memorial dining room? Could it ever be enough to be the chicken soup mogul?

But still Sinai continued to grow apace. By early 1975 there were twenty Kitchenware Cafés dotted around the country – a dozen in London alone, spread out like a crude necklace of paste and pewter across the wealthy suburbs. Likewise, the wholesale business was now supplying major chain stores throughout the big cities. When a large northern firm that Mal had always seen as their opposition finally succumbed to the financial sclerosis that had done for so many others, Gerry informed him they were in a position to acquire it from the Official Receivers.

'What do you think, Solly?' Mal said. 'Should we buy up Plantagenet Kitchenware?'

'We can buy up Plantagenet? Are you kidding? A company called Sinai gets to buy a company called Plantagenet? This I love. We have to do it. And while we're at it I don't suppose there's a company called Aryan Industries that the Jew boys can buy too?'

So they bought Plantagenet, with its aura of faded aristocratic grandeur, and temporarily closed down the dozen dedicated stores the firm owned. Within a few weeks they reopened those that would not be in competition with their own, as Kitchenware Cafés, with Big Reuben running the entire catering operation. Then they opened a second administration office amid the industrial smudge and clutter of Sheffield, alongside the old Plantagenet factory. An extra warehouse in Manchester followed to handle supply to the North-West. Within a few short years their two delivery vans had expanded to become a fleet of trucks, complete with an Hebraic swirl of Sinai livery in gold and black, to move all the stock that came out of the factory in Sheffield. Sales rose, as did profit. And yet still they stayed in the office above Mrs Hyman's.

'It keeps us in touch with our market,' Mal said, when questioned. 'Mrs Roth and Mrs Gross, they buy their kitchenware on Edgware High Street, not in the West End. Here at least, I'll be able to keep an eye on my customers', although they didn't have ime to keep an eye on Mrs Roth or Mrs Gross or even the grey spread of the high Street. Now most of their time was spent travelling the country, driving from shop to shop to warehouse to factory, buttocks stuck to acres of sweaty leatherette, to check all was as it should be and to make changes where it was not. But they stayed at Mrs Hyman's nonetheless, because it was what they knew in a business that seemed now to become unrecognizable every other week.

'Some days,' Mal said, over a Sunday lunch, 'it feels like we are trying to drive a horse-drawn chariot with all the bloody horses pulling in different directions.'

'And every day we add another horse,' said Solly.

One afternoon in the late spring of 1976 Solly took Mal to see a derelict shop unit on Baker Street, in the West End of London. It had clearly been empty for years, a victim of the recession of the early Seventies, that had never found anybody willing or able to nurse it back to health. The wide frontage was clad in boards of graffittoed plywood, ragged with ripped posters for rock concerts that had taken place so far back that the featured artists' outfits had long ago fallen out of fashion. On the pavement, ignored, lay bags of putrid rubbish from which seeped a stream of foul brown liquid.

'I love exclusive addresses,' Mal said, staring at the devastation before him.

'You just have to use your imagination, mate,' Solly said pulling keys from his pocket. 'Let's go and take a look.' The first key fitted a padlock on a plywood door cut into the cladding, behind which was what had once been the shop entrance, glass smashed out, so that it now lay in glittering shards on the concrete floor within. Solly unlocked that too.

'Mind your feet,' he said, nodding to the wreckage by the entrance. 'Don't want to get any of that embedded in your nice leather soles.'

Mal squinted into the darkness, while Solly felt around on the slimy walls for a light switch. The long, wide room stank of damp and urine and in the distance Mal could hear water trickling from a pipe. There was a wide puddle, black as an oil slick, that started at the back wall and stretched towards them, ending only a few yards before where they were standing, lapping at the bare concrete floor as if it were a lake shore.

'Solly, for Christ's sake what is this?'

His partner flicked on the one bulb. It cast a deathly

orange glow about the room. Old shop counters and display cases emerged from the shadows.

'It's an idea of mine,' Solly said, staring at the mess.

'There's nowhere near enough residential near here to make it worth opening this as a shop. And anyway we've got a branch on Finchley Road . . .'

'I'm not thinking about opening another shop.'

'I'm glad to hear it.'

'There's an alcohol licence out on this place, you know. Always easier to get an alcohol licence granted on a joint if it's had one before.'

'Alcohol? You don't even drink.'

'Sometimes I drink. Anyway it wasn't me I was thinking of.'

'So who are you planning to invite down here for a drink? That will be a night they won't forget.'

'Oh it will be. Believe me.' He breathed in deeply, as if he were standing on a mountain top and wanted to draw upon the fresh air. 'When I'm finished here everybody will have a bloody marvellous time.' He turned to his partner. 'This, my friend, is our future.'

Nineteen

The Sinai Diner, Solly said from the very start, was going to be one big confidence trick. But it would be a nice confidence trick, a sweet sleight of hand, so nobody would mind.

'Home-made nosh, but restaurant style. No Formica tables. Always tablecloths. Lots of nice polished glasses to drink from. Fancy cutlery. Wedding cutlery. You know the kind of thing.'

'But the food is like Momma makes?'

'Exactly,' said Solly. 'But it's not like my momma makes because she can't cook to save her life. So it's food like me and Reuben make. Actually it's not *like* the food me and Reuben make. It *is* the food me and Reuben make. Salt beef plates. Chicken soup with kneidlach, latkes and gefilte fish. And of course the Reuben sandwich. Pastrami, sauerkraut, cheese, all on rye bread.'

'Named after our Reuben?'

'No. Another Reuben. A dumb New York Reuben. But we've got our own Reuben so we can borrow it. Trust me.'

It wasn't just the Reuben sandwich that came out of New York. The whole idea was imported from there. Except it wasn't an idea. In the hands of Larry, the lissom interior designer who wore purple velvet shirts and far too much silver jewellery, it was a concept. The diner on Baker Street was to be modelled on a New York deli on Broadway, only grander.

'Think crisp,' said Larry. 'Think sassy. Think New York style.' And they did. They thought crisp and sassy and New York until the creases in their trousers

154

ached. Even Big Reuben tried to think crisp, when all he'd managed up to then was soft and round. It happened that none of them had ever been to New York and that their only experience of crisp, sassy style came distilled through the eye of the movie camera's lens. But then, as they reasoned, they had this in common with their clientele.

'Like they've all just flown in from Manhattan,' said Larry, right hand raised, palm forward. 'No, sir. I do not think so.' In any case, he said, lots of his friends were New Yorkers so it was as if he had been there.

'I see you've got royalty working on this project,' Mal said one afternoon, when he arrived to survey the building works. Already the walls had been panelled and the long blond-wood bar, complete with brass foot rail, was taking shape. Larry was standing in front of it shrieking 'I love it I love it I love it!'

'Yeah. Every palace needs its queen and he's ours.'

'And it will be a palace,' Mal said, as the carpenters sawed and the electricians wired. 'Are there any forests left? Or is all the wood in here now?'

'Forget forests. Have you ever tried to eat dinner in a forest? It's uncomfortable. Vermin eat their dinner in forests, and they do not make for good eating partners. Far better the wood ends up here.'

Lots of things were ending up there, including large, steaming reservoirs of Sinai cash. Money appeared to flush through the place without even touching the sides, a damburst of numbers and notes: money for brass and glass, for wood and varnish. Money for carpets and mirror and lights. Money for art.

For art!

When had Sinai ever needed art before? Never. The nearest they had come to art was the garlic press with the rounded handle. But now Larry said they needed art.

'Norman Rockwell art. Americana art. We need lots of Americana.'

'If Larry says we need art,' said Solly, 'who am I to disagree?'

'Do they come to stare at the walls or at their plates?'

'They come to stare at everything, Mal. We're in the service industry now. They come to stare at the walls, they come to stare at the food, they even come to stare at Big Reuben.'

'Now even Big Reuben is art?'

'Well,' the chef said, rubbing his girth with one downturned palm. 'I'm all my own work.'

'They don't have to be real Norman Rockwells,' Larry said, with a delicate sniff and a twitch of the nostrils. '*Faux* will do if *faux* it must be.'

'*Faux*?' Mal shouted. 'It's all fucking *faux*. It's all very fucking expensive fucking *faux*. The whole place is *faux*.'

'*Faux* schmo,' said Solly. 'Just give us the money for the art.'

So he gave them the money for the art.

'Do you like looking at pretty things when you're eating?' he said to Divinia one evening.

'I always like pretty things,' she said. 'Why should it be any different when I eat?'

He put the question to Judy.

'Do I like looking at pretty things? I'll tell you what I like looking at. I like looking at my husband, but now I don't even get to see him. He's at Baker Street, all day every day. Dawn till dusk. I'm beginning to show the wedding photographs to Joseph just so he won't forget what his father looks like. He thinks Daddy is a man who always wears bow ties. Now I take him past the local Italian place and he screams because he assumes all the waiters are his father.'

'Solly's committed, that's all.'

'Committed? He ought to be certified.'

Solly knew he was neglecting his family but he knew why, too. Kitchen implements were fine. They had been great things to work with for a while. They were useful and people liked useful things. But nobody remembered a kitchen implement fondly; well, no-one apart from Mal and Solly when they discussed those first Pollo-Matics. No, what people remembered were occasions. He saw that now. People still talked about their wedding and the four kinds of fish. ('My dears, a stuffed carp!') People liked to have other people do things for them. Nobody had ever come and bought cake from the Princeton family *pâtisserie* because they sold the best cake in the world. That wasn't why they walked through the door. Fact was, the Princeton *pâtisserie* did not sell the best cake in the world. No, people came and bought cake there because Ralph and Golda and Solly knew how to sell cake to them. These customers liked it when someone made them feel good about themselves.

And it made Solly feel good about himself; he adored the approval, the sense that he was of value. He might not have Mal's business instincts, his steel-trap mind or his financial self-assurance. He might never spot that the time had come to put the factory on double or triple time. But he had a talent for pleasure. Other people's pleasure. His own pleasure.

'Here, we will be selling them experiences,' Solly told Mal one afternoon as the diner was nearing completion, 'and they will pay more for experiences than they will for things. Trust me on this.'

'And *faux* Norman Rockwell is part of the experience?'

'Exactly.'

'I think I almost understand,' Mal said.

'Darlings,' screeched Larry, who had overheard their conversation. 'Mal's one of us now.'

Mal looked from Larry to Solly. 'Is there something you want to tell me?'

'He means "one of us" in the business sense. Just the business sense,' Solly said.

'Right.'

'Right.'

But still, the cost! Mal's calculations saw the place coming in at three times the budget of a new Kitchenware Café. And then, once it was open there would still be the expense of running the restaurant: all those people you would need to make all those other people feel nice.

'You will have to sell a lot of Reuben sandwiches,' he said.

'We will,' Solly said. 'Don't worry about that. And salt beef, and sodas and milk shakes. We've got lots of ideas, me and Big Reuben, about how to sell stuff. We're going to do a coffee special called the Stuyvesant Cup.'

'The Stuyvesant Cup?'

'Yeah, after Bedford-Stuyvesant in Brooklyn. Comes with a single cigarette on the side. You know. Peter Stuyvesant. For people who don't smoke much. Just want a coffee and a cigarette.'

'Make sure they don't try to stir their coffee with the cigarette by mistake.'

One afternoon, a week before opening night, Mal arrived at the diner to find his way blocked by cardboard boxes of *faux* antique telephones. He picked one up, and watched the earpiece fall off the tall stand, so that it dangled at the end of its cable.

'Nice, aren't they,' said Solly, as he appeared at his side.

'Very nice,' Mal said cautiously. So far he had counted five boxes and there appeared to be eight to a box. The phone was a piece of heavy, shaped Bakelite, that weighed comfortably in his hand. Serious quality. 'You have, what, forty phones here?'

'Yeah. They were ten short. The rest are coming tomorrow.'

'I don't know why but I have a feeling I am going to regret asking this question. Why does a restaurant this size need fifty telephones?'

'One for every table,' Solly said brightly.

'One for every table.' Mal repeated the explanation

quietly under his breath. 'One for every table. OK. I'm all ears. Explain.'

Solly marched off happily down his new, polish-fresh, varnish-rich restaurant. There was a broad central bar area and then, rising away in three tiers, terraces of tables each separated from the one below by a low darkwood wall. Brass light fittings, shaded by green glass, hung low from the ceilings so that the room was swathed in a golden glow and the engraved mirrors all around the walls glittered and shimmered. Mal had to admit that even the Norman Rockwell prints were attractive. Two workman were fixing 'specials' blackboards high up the walls so they could be seen from every table and a sign painter was working on the Sinai logo for the window.

'Here's how it will be,' Solly said, standing on the first terrace so that he was addressing Mal from above, the ruler of his own kingdom. 'Every table will have a telephone.'

Mal was still holding the handset. 'One of these?'

'One of those. And they'll all be wired into an exchange. Now then. All these tables will have numbers . . .'

'And when you want to,' Mal said slowly, 'you'll be able to call up another table. Just like in *Cabaret*.'

'You've got it. Just like Liza Minnelli in *Cabaret*.'

'You know in *Cabaret* the Kit Kat Club was a bar where people went to pick up transvestite hookers.'

'That bit we won't do,' Solly said, with a sardonic raise of his black bristle eyebrows. 'Apart from maybe in happy hour. But everybody likes to use the phone. Judy likes to use the phone. All the time she's on the phone. So she can come here and still use the phone.'

'To call the next table?'

'Sure, if she likes. It's fun.'

'Is it necessary?'

'I told you, mate. It's just fun.'

'How much will this bit of fun cost?'

'It's worth it. People like fun stuff.'

'I said, how much will it cost?'

Solly shrugged and stared into a distant corner. He'd been working on the diner for twelve hours a day. Every day for weeks. Months, even. Who was Mal to come in and call him on details? A good restaurant wasn't about detail. It was about experience. The whole. From getting through the door to paying the bill. What was a few telephones between friends? Nothing. A bit of fun.

'I've not got the exact figure in my head.'

'I don't need pence. Pounds will do. Round it up for me.'

'You can't think short term with this stuff,' Solly barked.

'I said how much.'

'Enough.'

'How much.'

'Fifteen hundred pounds.'

'Fifteen hundred fucking pounds?'

'I told you. Fun costs.'

'Have you paid yet?'

'No,' Solly said, with a self-satisfied grin. 'Negotiated terms. Full payment isn't due until a week after we open.' He imagined his partner would be stopped in his tracks by that. Solly didn't usually do negotiating.

Mal went over to the boxes and replaced the phone he was holding. 'Then send them back.'

'You what?'

'I said send them back. We can't afford them.'

'Who says we can't afford them?' He was shouting now. He'd had enough. Twelve hours a day. Seven days a week.

'*I* say we can't afford them.' Mal was trying to keep his temper in check.

'And who the fuck are you?' The workmen had stopped hammering at the blackboards. The sign painter placed his brush in the jar of turps. He couldn't keep his hand steady with that kind of noise going on behind him.

'I'm your sodding partner,' Mal said. 'I'm the one who watches the money. And you are spending too much on this.'

'The diner is my idea and my project,' Solly bawled. 'Mine. So sod off. Go back to your fucking books and your fucking numbers while I get on with my work.'

'Nothing is just yours in this business. Nothing. Everything is ours.'

'This place will never be yours. It will always be mine.'

'You don't get it, do you.' Mal shook his head.

'There's nothing to get. You're jealous of what I've done here so you want to see it fail.'

Mal gasped. 'Bollocks to that. Why would I want to see it fail? All I want to do is see it succeed or I'm down as much money as you are.'

'There you are. That's all you care about. The cash. The bottom line. Nothing else going on up here, is there?' He slapped the side of his head with his hand. 'Just budgets and the great green-eyed, limp-dicked brain-dead number monster.'

Mal shook his head. 'Fuck it. I don't need this. Just send them back because I won't be authorizing the payment.' He looked Solly in the eye. 'And go and get some rest, mate. You're losing it.' He turned on his heel and walked out.

For a few seconds the room was silent until Solly turned around and shouted at the crew to get back to work. He could feel his heart pumping and his lips were plump from the rush of blood. He knew he was trembling now. An argument. He and Mal had argued. Properly. Shouted. Bawled. Argued. They'd never done it before. Not like that. Not with both of them meaning it. He felt a little sick, as if he'd been punched in the stomach. But the bastard had asked for it. That was certain. He'd cried out for it. Had done for months.

Slowly Solly wandered up to the top terrace where

the dark wood shadows were deeper, and the corners smelt only of new paint and varnish. He pulled out a chair and sat down, resting his head in his hands. He felt so tired now. So terribly, terribly tired. He didn't even hear the approaching footsteps of the person who was now at his side.

'Well my, what a dirty-mouthed lad we are. What was it, now? Ah yes. The great green-eyed, limp-dicked brain-dead number monster. Wonderful.'

Solly smiled at the thought of it but didn't look up. 'Fuck off, Larry,' he said quietly.

'He's right though.'

'Don't you start.'

'No, not about the phones. About the rest. You look tired. Why don't you go home?'

He looked up blearily at the interior designer. He was wearing a particularly silky purple shirt, that shimmered even in this darkness.

'Can't. Reuben's coming by in half an hour and we have to go through a few trial dishes. I'll be fine,' he said. 'Just rest up here for a bit.'

Larry nibbled his bottom lip for a moment. 'Look,' he said, dropping his voice to a whisper. 'I've got some-thing that will help. Just to get you through the evening. Let's go down to the loos and—'

Solly laughed and shook his head. 'Larry you're a great guy but I'm really not into that, and even if I were I don't think I've got the energy.'

'Oh please. Don't flatter yourself. You're not my type. I hate men with hairy shoulder blades.'

Solly sat bolt upright. 'I do not have hairy shoulder blades.'

'Bet you do.'

'Seriously. I do not have hairy shoulder blades.'

'Well, everything else is hairy. You could lose small children in your chest hair.'

'But not my shoulder blades.'

Larry raised both hands in surrender. 'You win. You win. No hairy shoulder blades. Still. Are you going to come with me and try what I've got? It will work. I promise you.'

Solly sighed. 'All right,' he said. 'If it will perk me up and shut you up at the same time I'm definitely on for it.' Slowly, ever so laboriously, he dragged his heavy aching limbs down to the newly painted toilets at the back of the restaurant.

Twenty

They opened for business on a hot, steamy Sunday night at the beginning of July 1976. As it happened, every night that summer was hot and steamy, the pressure-cooked air sitting thick and heavy in London's streets; an unseen but rotting ballast that spawned many an ill mood. It was freak weather with which the Sinai Diner's air-conditioning system had not been designed to cope. Then again the air-conditioning system was no more than an open front door and a few bowls of ice cubes on the tables to be rubbed across sticky flesh. Every evening the few customers who could manage it sat over stomach-bulking plates of latkes and dumplings and salt beef – food designed to defend against chill winds off the Russian Steppes, rather than *émigré* Saharan weather systems – dabbing away the sweat with paper napkins and fanning themselves with menus.

That first night, however, nobody seemed to mind. Earlier in the day news had broken of an attack by Israeli Commandos on the airport at Entebbe in Uganda. The soldiers had flown 2,500 miles, landed at the airfield and freed over a hundred hostages held by Palestinian and German terrorists in the terminal building, before flying back home again. As a result, while there were no telephones on the tables that evening there was a small television set on the corner of the bar, around which guests at the opening party gathered to watch the news bulletins.

'Can you believe what we did?' said Benny. Almost every Jew in the room was an Israeli that night. He was standing at the bar resting his weight on his elbows, cold drink in hand, watching the pictures on the set. Relatives of the hostages were shown hugging their loved ones as they were released from the care of the Israeli army; tanned commanders in battle fatigues, chins up, lips pursed, marched through adoring crowds.

'Two thousand miles we flew,' Benny said again, in wonder.

'Two and a half thousand,' corrected another, as the crowd stared at the pictures. 'Don't forget the half.'

'And we did it.'

'And we did it. What chutzpah, eh. What chutzpah.'

Even those who found nothing in Israel with which to identify had to admit a grudging admiration. 'They got away with it. God knows how, but they got away with it.'

'Because God was on our side,' said one woman.

'Because we knew what we were doing.'

'Because the Israeli army is the best in the world.'

Big Reuben took breaks from the stir and clamour of the kitchen to curve his thick neck around and look at the television. Sweat rolled in oily streams down the pink folds of his face. 'Look at these soldiers,' he said, jabbing at the screen with one stumpy finger. 'So strong. So disciplined. When they say Never Again this is what they mean. This here. This.'

Everybody around the set knew what he meant. How could the Holocaust happen again when Israel was blessed with an army of soldiers, built of sinew, bone and muscle, so willing to fight? These were not the pale intellectual soft-handed Jews of Germany and Poland and Russia, who worked more with their minds than their bodies. Who had not imagined they might need to defend themselves. These were a different kind altogether. Dark browed. Strong. Determined. In charge of their own destiny.

Never Again, the crowd muttered. Never Again. If it means flying 2,500 miles and storming an airport, then so be it. But Never Again.

Solly dipped in and out of the crowd around the television as he dipped into every crowd, hopping from table to table, from shoulder to shoulder, meeting and thanking and nudging and chivvying.

'How's the soup?' he would bark. 'Is it hot enough for you? Is all of it hot enough for you? The weather? I know. Too hot. Too hot.' A quick wave in the air with both arms. 'Made with my own fair hands, it was, the soup. These hands. Solly's soup. You want more soup? I'll get you more. You don't want more? Are you sure you don't want more? Well if you change your mind then ask one of the girls. They'll get you more.' And then onwards and around the room and back again.

'Solly's on form,' Divinia said quietly to Mal as they stood by the bar, a little way from the crowd by the television.

'Isn't he,' Mal said, watching his partner chart his course through the tables. 'He was born for this. If there were only two tables of customers he'd still manage to work the room.'

'He's a good man, isn't he?'

'Yes,' Mal said quietly. 'He is a good man.'

Peace had been negotiated by the wives, who had been determined to hold their Sunday lunch regardless of whether their men would take part. Both refused, even Solly, and the meal was to be at their place that week.

'I'll stay upstairs. Work on my menus. If he wants to come he can come but I'll stay upstairs.'

'Don't be ridiculous,' Judy said. 'You can't sit in the same house and not talk to each other.'

'Just watch me. The man's an arsehole.'

'Solly, please. And don't talk like that in front of Joseph.'

At first Solly didn't have to sit in the same house as Mal because his partner didn't come. Divinia arrived alone with Simon and her fast-growing second pregnancy, heaved herself down and admitted that Solly's assessment was correct. 'My husband *is* an arsehole,' she said. The word sounded much ruder coming from Divinia.

It didn't take much plotting to solve the situation. Divinia telephoned Mal and told him that Solly was there and desperate to talk to him; when, finally he arrived, Judy shot upstairs and told Solly that Mal had come and had something he wanted to say. Fooled into meeting each other they sat silently about the table, staring at their plates, until Mal poked at the potato salad and said, 'Is this going to be on the menu?'

'No.'

'It should be. It's good.'

And so they made their peace over food. Just as they did everything else over food. Mal admitted he had interfered and Solly admitted he had been over-extravagant. Mal agreed the diner could have the tele-phones when they broke even and Solly promised that would be soon. On the doorstep they hugged and parted company feeling better than they had when they arrived.

Now Mal stared out over the crowded restaurant, at legions of happy customers roaring with pleasure, as his partner wandered among them oozing pleasure at their pleasure.

'He's Sinai's real asset,' Mal said.

'What do you mean?' Divinia

'All of this could happen if I wasn't here. You could always find someone else to do the job I do, but you couldn't find another Solly.'

'Don't be silly. He needs you as much as you need him.'

'Maybe you're right.' He rested his hand on her tummy. 'Go sit with Judy. Take the weight off our child.' She kissed him gently on the cheek and made her way through the crowd.

Solly bolted over to where Mal was standing.

'What do you think?' He was still watching the room, eyes flicking from side to side, only occasionally catching Mal's gaze.

'I think there's going to be a lot of washing up.'

Solly laughed. 'Hah. You're right. Lots of washing up.' And then he was gone again, muttering 'washing up washing up. Hah. Washing up', under his breath.

While Solly had been talking Mal had noticed his father standing a few feet away, uneasily, as if waiting for their conversation to finish before he felt entitled to address him. Sam Jones had just turned 65 and, as he conceded inches with age, the son had become taller than the father. There was a roundness to his shoulders and his belly now, and his fine curling hair had turned a yellow-white with age. With Solly back on the prowl, he made his approach.

Sam Jones wrapped one arm about Mal's shoulder and turned to look at the full tables. 'Business is good,' he said.

Mal turned to look at him quizzically, but Sam wouldn't meet his eye. 'What did you say?'

'I said business is good.' He turned to his son. 'Well, isn't it? Look at them all. In heaven they are, these customers of yours.'

'I know, Dad, it's just . . .'

'They're having a marvellous time. Business is good. That's all I'm saying.'

'Usually you ask me . . .'

'Usually I ask you how's business?' Mal nodded. 'Feh! What kind of putz do you take me for? That your father should need to ask when everything is so good.' He looked away. 'Me, I hoped one day . . . that, you know, that I would . . .'

'I know, Dad.'

Sam Jones suddenly embraced him wrapping one heavy palm around the back of his head. 'I'm proud of you, Mal,' he said into his ear, squeezing him hard. 'That's all I wanted to say. Me and your mother, we're proud of you. I would have liked this for myself. But that you know. You're a grown-up. Why should I lie. I would have liked it for myself. But it wasn't to be. So the next generation gets what the first could not.'

He let go and they looked at each other. He patted his boy on the cheek. 'You've done well, son. That's all.'

'Thank you. It means, well, you know . . . a lot.'

'What can I tell you? We just want that you are happy.' And then a soft kiss on the cheek. 'Go attend to your guests. Me, I'm going to go find your mother. Help her boast about you. It's a big job, boasting about you. She needs help.'

Later in the night Mal found Heidi sitting by herself on the top terrace, chin rested on one of the dividing walls, watching the scene below.

'Hello, sister-in-law.'

She looked up slowly, like a cat uncurling itself 'Hello, brother-in-law.'

'Where's Benny?'

She waved one hand off in the direction of the door. 'Gone.'

'Left?'

She nodded and rested her head miserably back on her arm. Mal stared towards the door as if he just might be able to see his brother leaving and could stop him.

'Did he say where he was going?'

Heidi didn't look up. 'Cards,' she said. 'Poker. Sunday nights. Always poker.'

'He's still gambling, then?'

She scoffed at his naivety.

'Yes, well,' Mal said. 'He always did like the risk.' He looked at his watch. 'It's getting late. Do you want me to take you home? Divinia can get a lift back with Judy.'

'Would you, Mal?' she said, softly. 'I'm tired and I want my bed.'

'Get your coat and I'll meet you outside.'

They drove in silence through quiet Sunday night streets, across Tarmac that shone from the heat of the day just gone. The sky was clear and starlit and the air smelt of stale petrol and dust. Outside Heidi and Benny's mansion block in Maida Vale, Mal parked the car and they sat silent and still, staring at the empty pavements glowing orange beneath the sodium lamp-light. A bus drove past them and the car shook in the rush of air. Heidi let out a deep sigh, a hiss of breath like a tyre being slowly deflated.

'Things between you two are not good?' Mal said, because he couldn't bear the silence any more. Maybe it was true. Maybe non-Jews really did like silence.

'Things have been better,' Heidi said. 'He gambles. I tell him not to. He tells me not to tell him not to. I shout at him.'

'Shouting's not nice.'

'It's horrible.' She sounded like a little girl when she said that and Mal wanted to wrap his arms around her.

'You can tell me to shut up but have you thought about having kids? It might snap him out of it, kids. Children are wonderful. Really focus the mind. And you two have been married, what, three years now?'

Heidi sniffed. 'Yes, we've thought about having kids. There are days when I don't think about anything else.'

'Then why don't you do it?'

She turned to look at him, resting her head against the seat.

'We've tried,' she said. 'But we can't.'

'Can't?'

'Your brother, he . . .' She stopped herself. Mal reached out to hold her hand.

'Sweetheart, it's all right,' Mal said. 'Nothing you say will go any further. You look like you could do with a friend to talk to.' He felt her caress his hand with the soft pad of her thumb.

'Your brother, Benny, he's . . . He can't have chil-dren.'

'What's wrong?'

'Don't ask me for details. Doctors say he's infertile. Your little brother's firing blanks. That's all I know.'

'Christ, Heidi I'm sorry.'

'Not as sorry as he is.'

'Do you think that's why he's out playing poker and . . .'

170

'What do you think?'

'Fair do's. I'll shut up.' Heidi shuffled across, wrapped one arm about his neck and rested her head on his shoulder.

'You don't have to shut up.' Mal found his arm wrapping itself about her soft waist. They sat staring at the street again. Moths fluttered beneath the spread of light from the lampposts. A cat padded past, eyes reflecting emerald green in the darkness. Mal looked at his watch, uneasily. He felt too comfortable here, entwined with Heidi. His sister-in-law. Too warm. Too at ease.

'I should be going,' he said.

'Don't.'

'You said you wanted your bed.'

'It can wait.' And then, 'Come up. I make a great hot chocolate. No water, just milk.' She smiled at him broadly.

'But you need to sleep.'

'Best hot chocolate in London.'

'That's the kind of offer a lad can't refuse.'

'I knew you couldn't,' she said. She kissed him so that he could feel her breath on his cheek and then pulled herself away to open the car door.

Twenty-one

There were never any telephones on the tables at the Sinai Diner. The hot summer of 1976 saw to that. Made fractious by the sweat and effort of the heatwave, the punters chose to avoid the dead weight of Solly and Reuben's cooking. Their absence turned the terraces of empty tables and chairs into an expanse of dark woodwork and delayed for months the point where the business broke even.

'They're all at home eating mangy salads,' Reuben would say each night, as he mopped his brow, surveyed the silent gloom and mopped his brow once more.

Only when the weather broke in late August, dampening the dust and turning the roads into a slick of greasy puddles, did the trade return, and then in droves. Still Reuben had to mop his brow, but now it was from the heat of the kitchen rather than the sun. By the early winter, when a golden wave of chicken soup swept the restaurant firmly into the black, Solly had all but forgotten about the telephones. It was yesterday's idea. A fragment of a shard of a memory. In any case by then he was preparing a second branch on the King's Road in Chelsea, where the punks roamed, and a third in Camden Town.

'Each diner,' he told Mal, briskly, 'must be the same as the others. Different location. Same food. Same experience.'

'Same heartburn?'

'Exactly. Same heartburn.' He rested one hand on his solar plexus and frowned at the thought. 'That's the definition of Jewish keep-fit lessons, you know. You

172

eat three bowls of my chicken soup with kneidlach, and say "feel the burn". What kind of meal would it be without heartburn to follow?'

A year after Solly had first shown Mal the derelict Baker Street site, they met there for lunch, taking their usual table at the end of the second terrace where nobody could avoid seeing them. The proprietors, in their rightful place.

'Business is good,' Mal said. 'In all three joints.'

Solly shrugged and sniffed. 'We do our best,' he said. He stopped eating and pulled a handkerchief from his pocket to blow his nose.

'Got a cold?'

'Nothing major. Don't seem to be able to shake it.' He put the handkerchief back in his pocket. 'I'm sure I won't die of it.'

'Better not, mate,' Mal said. 'Or I'll kill you.' Solly managed something trapped halfway between a snort and a giggle. Mal studied his partner. He looked tired, as if he had slept badly every night for the last week. There were dark grey shadows under his eyes, the colour of troubled winter clouds, and he had lost weight. His stubbled cheeks weren't round any more. They were flat and followed the line of his cheekbones. He looked angular and drawn. Too much work, Mal thought. Pushing himself too far. Then again maybe he was just getting older. Solly had just turned thirty. Early white hairs peeked out now from the thicket around his temples, a gentle dusting of grey that Mal, three years his junior, found himself envying. He could do with a bit of white-haired gravitas, he thought. Just a little. Not too much. Something to take away the gloss of youth.

'I've got a proposition to make,' Mal said.

'I thought you might.'

'What do you mean?'

'You're always quieter when there's something on your mind.'

Mal laughed. 'Christ, it's like being married.'

'I'm sleeping on the left of the bed.'

'Deal. I'll take the right.'

'So?' Solly said, after a few seconds' silence. 'Talk to me.'

'We've had an offer for the kitchenware company.'

Solly laid down his fork. 'You want to sell the firm?'

Mal shook his head. 'No. Not all of it. Just part of it.'

'How you going to do that?'

'I'll show you.' He picked up a paper napkin from the table and patted his jacket pockets until he found a pen. 'Here's what Sinai looks like at the moment.' At the top of the napkin he drew one big box inside of which he wrote 'Sinai Corporation'.

'That's the parent company,' he said, jabbing at it with the pen. He drew three arrows down from the main box. The first ended in a box marked 'Sinai Manufacturing', the second in 'Sinai Kitchenware Cafés', and the third in 'Sinai Diners'.

Solly studied the diagram. 'How long's the company been like this?'

'Gerry and me, we sorted it out about six months ago. Separated out all the various businesses in case we ever wanted to flog part of it.'

'You didn't say anything to me.'

'You were busy. Would you have told me not to do it?' Mal waited with his pen held above the napkin, certain of the answer.

'No,' Solly said, with a sniff. 'Suppose not.' He felt excluded even though he knew he would simply have told Mal to get on with it.

'OK,' Mal said. 'Here's how it will work. Clearview Holdings. You know them?'

'The fitted kitchen company?'

'The same. They buy Sinai Manufacturing. It makes sense to them. It gives them the unit in Mill Hill, the factory in Sheffield, the warehouse in Manchester and the entire fleet of trucks.' Mal put a cross through the first box as if scrubbing it from the record. 'They also

174

buy the Kitchenware Cafés.' He put a cross through that as well.

'Those too?'

'Bear with me. The majority of the Kitchenware Cafés. Twenty-four of them. I've identified four which could work as Sinai Diners. I'd like you to look at the list and see if you agree.'

Solly sat back. He was beginning to understand. 'How much will we get for this?'

Mal grinned. 'A lot of money.'

'How much is a lot?'

'Eight figures a lot.' Solly grabbed the pen from Mal and started writing down a one and zeros on another napkin until they stretched in a line eight long. He slipped in the commas where he thought they ought to go.

'More than ten million?' he said in whisper. 'Ten million?' A shiver ran down his spine. He saw the money stretching away from him in a column of curled pound notes until it disappeared over the horizon.

'Only just,' Mal said. 'A little over ten. Yearly profit times fifteen. Simple. But you'll definitely be a millionaire.'

'I should fucking say so. It's a shitload of money.'

'We're going to need it.'

'Keep talking.'

'You and me, we take half our money each. Benny and Gerry and Reuben will get a few quid too, for their shares. I want us all to be secure. Not to have to worry about cash. The rest we reinvest in the Sinai Corporation and in your Sinai Diners. You were right. You always are. The future isn't in selling people things. It's in selling people experiences.' He was leaning forward over the table now, firing out the words in rapid succession, like slimy apple pips squeezed out between thumb and index finger. 'That's what you know how to do, what I'm learning to do. And I want us to do it big. Roll out the diners across the country. One in every major city. Half a dozen here in London. There's a site coming up on Piccadilly . . .'

Solly whistled. 'A diner on Piccadilly. There's smart.'

'No,' Mal said. 'This is a big site. Huge. You could fit ten diners into it.'

Solly squinted at Mal. 'But you're not planning to fit ten diners into it, are you?'

'No,' Mal said. 'No I'm not. I want it to be the Sinai Grand. A hotel. Serious, plush, pukka. Trouser press in every room.'

Solly sat back and dabbed at his nose with the napkin upon which Mal had scribbled. He'd never been as impressed by good creases as his partner.

'You could do it, mate,' Mal said.

Solly pointed at the paper napkin on which he had scribbled the digits. 'It doesn't add up. OK we put, what? Four, five million pounds in between us. Lot of money. Stupid money. Enough for the diners. But not enough for a hotel too.'

'That's the thing. Sinai has to change.' Mal was on a high. 'We'll have investors on board to spread the risk. Venture capital, a lot of it.'

'So we don't own the company any more?'

'We'll have the controlling stake. And we'll still be co-chairman and co-chief executives. Sinai will be nothing without us. The money men know that.'

'You've already sorted that out?'

'Pretty much,' he said, waving the thought away. 'And we have to move up West. There's an office block in Golden Square and . . .'

'Soho?'

'Yeah. Going cheap.'

'We're leaving Edgware?'

'Solly, we left Edgware years ago. All we're doing is getting our bags sent on. It's time.'

As far as Mal was concerned it had been time for a long while. Sinai was a big company but it was deeply parochial too. The suburbs in which they did most of their trade were the same kind of suburbs, whether

176

they were in London or Leeds or Manchester. They were neat and carefully tended and full of nice middle-class people whose only goal had been to live in the suburbs alongside lots of other nice middle-class people and watch their children succeed. It was very unlikely that the whole of Sinai's revenue came from the pockets of the Jewish community. The company had grown too quickly for that. But Mal had long ago realized that if an idea played well with Jews, it was certain to play well with the rest of their core clientele. The Jews did not have a monopoly on liking things that were expensive and shiny. They could merely be guaranteed to do so.

The problem was it all seemed too intimate and claustrophobic now. What was it Solly had once said about going out with Jewish girls? He recalled the phrase. 'It's like snogging your sister.' They have no secrets, these Jewish girls. Well, none of their customers had any secrets any more either. Mal knew what made them tick. He knew how to get inside their heads. Now he wanted to escape into something alien and unfathomable just so he could try and fathom it. He wanted to play the grown-up game out on the bigger pitch. He wanted to escape the confines of the Jewish community and give his company an identity outside of it.

He wanted more.

'Why are we doing this?' Solly said, staring now at his empty plate.

'Why are we doing what?'

'I mean what are we doing selling up just so we can expand when we have a perfectly good business already?'

Mal nibbled his bottom lip. He hadn't even thought about it. Not clearly. 'We're making sure we're rich enough so nobody can ever tell us to do something we don't want to do,' he said, eventually.

'Instead we end up telling ourselves to do things we don't want to do.'

'Exactly.' Mal said. 'We're in charge of our own destiny.' And then: 'We're making sure that our sons get to do what they want to do.' Solly had no answer to that.

Ten weeks later the new board of directors of the Sinai Corporation met in Mal Jones's office on the third floor of the building in Golden Square. Mal was seated at one end of the rectangular apple wood table with his back to his new antique, leather-topped desk, which stood in stark contrast to the sharp-edged modernism of the décor. Solly was at the other end, with his back to the double doors. In between, Gerry and Benny sat opposite each other, each of them flanked by a pair of representatives from the four institutional investors. They were men with thin, flimsy faces and blond hair and thin flimsy names like James and Piers and Gavin and Francis. They wore Oxford brogues and shook hands with such firmness that Solly assumed it was a grip they had each been sent away by their employers to learn.

Mal and Solly knew they should have had the home advantage here but they did not. After the tat and squalor of Mrs Hyman's, which retained her name in Sinai's lexicon for years after her death, the new headquarters was a culture shock. There were thick carpets and white walls and subtle lighting. There were rubber plants with broad shiny leaves and a lift. Above the front door were the words SINAI CORP in blocky brushed aluminium letters a foot high. At Mrs Hyman's they had never managed to get beyond a scrawl on a piece of paper taped to the bell.

Mal and Solly had a wide office each at opposite ends of the corridor, each with a board table, each with a settee and a private bathroom. Here Jenny, who was seated between the doors to both offices with her two assistants, had a bigger desk than either of them had ever managed at Mrs Hyman's. They had no-one else to blame for this ostentation. The grand offices had been their idea. They had thought it was what millionaire businessmen would need, and in time it would be.

But for now they felt gauche and awkward, like little children who had been allowed to stay up late for dinner with the adults. The adults, James and Piers and their acutely chiselled friends, were entirely at ease, lounging back in their soft leather executive chairs, pens poised, brows furrowed over the business plans in their hands. This, their body language said, was their natural habitat. They understood how the world worked here. Mal sat tall and straight-backed in his chair, trying to imagine himself into the role of chairman. Solly went the other way, slumping into a fidgeting, muttering heap, huffing under his breath whenever one of the investors spoke.

'Hmm, we *like* it,' said James assertively.

'Yes we *do*,' said Piers who looked like Gavin.

'Oh they like it" hissed Solly to himself. 'Delightful. Delighted. They like the business plan.'

The City men appeared not to hear.

'We *love* the scope,' said Gavin.

'We *applaud* the vision,' said Piers.

'We *admire* the prudence,' said Francis.

'Marvellous,' whispered Solly. 'Francis admires prudence. There's no-one in this company called fucking prudence.' He threw his pen down onto the table so that it clattered hard against the polished surface.

Mal frowned at his partner but Solly merely groaned and looked up at the newly painted ceiling.

'Gavin does however have a couple of thoughts on the way forward for the diners,' said James. 'Don't you, Gavin?'

'Yes, James,' said Gavin. 'I do. Thank you.' He pulled a few sheets from a leather folder in front of him. Mal sat back in his chair, trying to look relaxed. 'Please,' he said. 'Go on.'

'Yeah,' said Solly. He leaned forward and fixed Gavin with a deep, malarial stare. 'I'm all ears.'

'I note the American style to the diners,' he began. 'The décor. The design and so forth. And I'm just thinking that, given the current popularity of the

American dining experience in the UK we might take this further. After all, McDonald's and Dayvilles' Ice Cream are doing very well in their own franchise markets. Great jumps in market share. Impressive jumps.'

Mal said 'Please, continue.' Solly scowled. Mal had promised him the bankers on the board would be there only to protect their investment. 'They won't interfere with your work.' This was beginning to sound very much like interference.

'I was looking at the menu,' Gavin continued, 'and I was thinking we could reflect the American décor further in the food. Hamburgers, milk shakes, baby back pork spare ribs. Spare ribs are very popular.'

'Fucking great,' Solly shouted, slapping the table with one hand.

'Solly,' Mal barked.

'Fuck this, Mal, I mean really.' He stood up and resting his weight on both hands leaned down the table towards his partner. 'Spare ribs? Pork fucking spare ribs? Did you tell these people that Sinai was a Jewish business?'

'Mr Princeton,' Mal said. 'Will you sit down and control yourself.'

'Don't Mr Princeton me, Mal Jones. Or shall I call you Moses? I mean, what in God's name did you tell them? That we're a couple of Greek Cypriot wide boys from Finsbury Park who just thought it would be snappy to call our company Sinai?'

'Solly, sit down and control yourself. We can't hold meetings like—'

'Solly is it now? Not Mr Princeton. Shall I get my dick out and whack it on the table for Franky and Jimmy here to have a good look at just so they know where we all stand on the pork spare ribs idea?'

'Get out, Solly!' Mal shouted. Benny and Gerry stared at their hands. The other four looked at each other and raised one golden eyebrow each.

'Get out now.'

Solly stood up straight and said, 'It will be my

pleasure', before pushing his chair back from the table and leaving.

In the low-lit bathroom off his own office at the other end of the corridor, he stood in front of the mirror and took deep breaths. 'Fool, Princeton,' he said to himself. 'No control. You should have been controlled. You only win by being controlled.' He closed his eyes. He could hear his heart pumping and deep in the pit of his stomach a familiar pebble of anxiety was growing into a familiar rock. He took a long breath, opened his eyes and reached into his inside pocket, feeling for the soft plastic of the bank bag that he knew would be huddling down in there against the silk lining.

Solly pulled it out, opened it up and tipped a little of the white powder it held onto the cool dry marble surround that he had demanded be fitted about his sink. He felt in another pocket for his gold American Express card, gripping it between thumb and forefinger, to chop and cut the powder into a fine white line across the stone. Finally he dug into his trouser pocket for the pound note that still held its curl from the night before. That was the great thing about cocaine. No cumbersome apparatus. No pipes or syringes or cigarette-rolling machines. Just an everyday, un-incriminating wallet full of plastic and paper. He rolled the pound note back into the tube to which it was trying to return, held it to his nose with one hand, closed down the free nostril with the other and leaned down to hoover away the line. For a couple of seconds, as the drug sparkled and flashed its way through the damp membranes of the nasal cavity, he remained bent double. Then he stood up, took a deep breath and opened his eyes. A broad smile spread across his lips.

'Control,' he said to himself. 'This is control.'

Twenty-two

Years later Mal would admit that he was never really sure when Solly's coke problem had begun. Then again, nor was Solly. According to the drug dependency literature, the dry medical papers that both of them would eventually end up reading, it began the day Larry took him into the half-finished toilets at the back of the first half-finished Sinai Diner and chopped him up that first line. But the literature was only a map and like all maps it did not show you what the world really looked like on the ground; his time in the toilet with Larry did not change the way Solly dealt with the world. It just made the inside of his head buzz and fizz a little. No more. Within a few months, however, a shift had occurred. By the time Mal and Solly banked their money from the sale and the company moved to Golden Square, cocaine was not just a part of his life. It defined the geometry of his every day. He could measure out the hours in the distance between two sharp snorts.

But it loomed large in his life even before that point. Less than a year after the opening night party at Baker Street, Heidi gave birth to a long-awaited, long-limbed daughter, as beautiful as she was unexpected. She and Benny decided to name her Natasha and everybody gathered at the flat in Maida Vale to toast her arrival in champagne. Solly's memory of that night was not of suffuse joy at a life begun and a marriage apparently saved, but of a sudden nosebleed in the bathroom, the blinding white of the porcelain scattered with crimson spots of evidence, which he quickly washed away.

At the beginning the drug was merely part of a ritual

he associated with Larry and the preparation of each new Sinai Diner. As afternoon turned into evening the two of them would disappear from the shell of the nascent restaurant to 'reinvigorate ourselves,' as the interior designer put it.

'I find it helps me reach decisions,' Larry would say, as mentally he recalculated the bill for his services to take account of the free coke he had lavished on the client.

'I know what you mean,' Solly would say. 'You can pinpoint what you want.'

'Makes you sharp as a razor blade, my dear.'

'Ready for anything.'

'Tip-top.'

Then Larry, fed up with forever sharing his stash, introduced Solly to his dealer, an expatriate American called Saul Israelson, who wore little round glasses and let his hair fall in shoulder-length curls. He had spent a year on kibbutzim, farming plums and cabbages and killing chickens for the kibbutzniks because it seemed the right thing to do. Now, having arrived in Britain, he could think of no better way by which to make a living than importing coke from the US and flogging it. 'I sell the catalyst for clear thought,' he would say, dangling a plump bank bag between thumb and forefinger, his pupils almost as wide as his eyes behind his glasses. Israelson, long ago wooed and wed by his own product, liked to imagine himself as the alchemist who used cocaine to turn good men into great men. His clients liked to think of Israelson as the coke dealer who used to kill chickens for a living.

Through Israelson Solly soon met the Horowitz brothers from Mill Hill, two ex-public-school boys who talked in bold phrases about cash flow and profit margins and triumphs and deals.

'Charlie is our friend,' Daniel Horowitz would say, before each line, talking fondly to his narcotic of choice. 'That's the great thing about cocaine. It's a drug you can be on first-name terms with.'

'Yeah,' Simon Horowitz would say. 'Charlie understands us.'

They made their money from property, wore sharp suits, drove matching Mercedes and took lots and lots of cocaine. Enormous amounts. They had bought the whole coke package; the entire glass coffee table, leather upholstered, matt-black nightclub and sports car shebang. With extra added bravado and go-faster stripes. And yet, despite the endless nights he spent in their company Solly still viewed himself as merely a coke tourist, who made excursions to Horowitz Land to see all the sights that this sovereign state, ruled by sparkling King Charlie, had to offer. He was not a resident like them. How could he be? After all, he had a wife and a child and a multimillion-pound business.

So he was the man with two lives. His ambitions and appetites were so big, he would think to himself, as the drug shot its ice-fresh, jade-cold way through his centre, that he needed more than one life to contain them. Not that cocaine mattered, he would mutter. Not really. Back then, before the white tide of the Eighties, cocaine was still rare and exotic; the safe drug, guilt free and non-addictive. An adult's plaything, imported from the US for the precious few who knew about these things. The problem wasn't the nose candy. It was what those who knew nothing of it imagined it to be. A perception problem. In the late Seventies cocaine users would still tut and shake their heads at stories of acquaintances using heroin, even as they dragged their greasy noses across the mirror.

A part of his brain was reserved entirely for Solly Princeton the cocaine user. Here, in his back memory, he turned over the facts of his drug life; a habit which he argued gave him the dangerous edge he feared the money they were making would take from him, like a leech sucking away at his lifeblood. Without the dangerous edge, he said, he could not be the great innovator that Sinai needed him to be. He could not create. It mattered little that Solly Princeton had never been more dangerous than a kitten with fleas. It was a perception problem. His perception problem. He would never have mentioned the 'F' word in his defence. To admit that 'Fear' was eating away at him was to admit defeat. His heroic act of denial did not change the facts, however. He was terrified of his own success, terrified of his own wealth, terrified of the shiny black chauffeur-driven Jaguar that was available to him at all times and of the fine silk suits that hung in his wardrobe. Cocaine turned terror into a creaking bravado. It was a salve to an overloaded soul. As a result the milestones towards true psychological dependency rested in his mind, not as danger signals but as badges of honour. He failed to recall exactly when they had arisen or even necessarily where, only the intense feeling of drama that went with them.

At the top of the list, of course, there was the first time he did it. With Larry. In the unfinished toilet.

Then the second time he did it.

Then the first time he did it two weeks running.

The first time he did it twice in a week.

The first week he did it every day.

The last time he went a day without doing it.

Judy knew, or at least she thought she knew. Solly told her that occasionally he took a little cocaine. 'Just to keep me going,' he said. 'Once in a blue moon.' That way it felt like he wasn't lying to her. He had told her part of the truth. The important part of the truth.

She had said 'Don't do anything silly.' He had said 'Would I?' And she had said 'No.' Because he was always in control, wasn't he? How could a man who had just received millions of pounds from the sale of his business not be in control? How could her Solly be losing it? To Judy the only outward sign that anything had changed in her husband's life was his sudden fascination with gold jewellery. He took to wearing a thick name bracelet, made from hard, square links of butter-yellow metal. He wore a gold sovereign ring and a thick gold necklace that buried itself deep in his

185

abundant chest hair. These things said money, and a man with a coke habit had to speak that language.

She had quickly come to accept his long days and long nights as the price to pay for the wealth and the comfort and the status. Why ask what he was doing late at night when it was clear he was building a multimillion-pound business? This was what her husband did. He moved fast. He designed restaurants. He planned hotels. He signed single orders for building materials worth tens of thousands of pounds. In any case there were times when he seemed even more attentive than he had been before Sinai moved into the restaurant business. When she gave birth to Rachel, a sister to Joe, he was by his wife's side, there to feed and change and manage whatever needed to be managed.

Moving fast.

For Solly it was a matter of pride that he could maintain work, home and coke in careful balance like this; surely the great man pulled more from each day than the simply mediocre? Nothing could be allowed to fall by the wayside. All had to be maintained.

Perhaps if the Sinai partners had not carved up their duties between them so clearly, Solly would have been unable to indulge his appetites with such abandon. But his role as the creative half of the pair had finally been confirmed by the success of the diners, and he had been rewarded with an ever greater freedom to misbehave.

'I told them you suffer from an artistic temperament,' Mal told Solly, when the first board meeting had come to an end and James, Piers, Gavin and Francis had departed the building for their pigeon-bombed money towers in the City.

'Did you?' Solly said coolly. He was behind his own desk now, calm. In control. In his mind's eye he could see the cool marble surround of the bathroom sink next door. The source of his strength. In his hand he held one of his new business cards. He tapped its longest

186

edge flat against the desk, in a repetitive cutting motion. It had become a habit, almost a reflex. Mal was spread out on the sofa.

'Well, I had to tell them something.' Mal yawned. 'Anyway. It's true. You've always been temperamental.'

'Perhaps,' Solly said. 'But it doesn't make what I said wrong.'

'About what?'

'The spare ribs.'

Mal shrugged.

'No, mate,' said Solly, assertive now. 'It's not something we can shrug off. We're a Jewish business. We don't put pork on the menu.'

'What's your problem? You don't even keep kosher.'

'I know I don't. Not properly, though I don't eat pork. Never had lobster either, actually.' He swivelled round in his chair to look out at the square below. 'Or crab. Or oysters. Amazing. There are lots of things I've never eaten. Seems odd to me now. Food I've not tasted.' He turned back to Mal. 'Anyway this isn't about ritual. It isn't about the Beth Din. It's about business. The Sinai Diners are Jewish restaurants. Kosher-style Jewish restaurants. That's what they're about. It's our image. We start putting pork on the menu and we're nothing. We start doing that and we'll end up running a Christmas special and nailing crucifixes up behind the bar. We'll be like every other tuppence-ha'penny joint on the street.'

'Why didn't you say that in the meeting?'

Solly laughed. 'Didn't get a chance. You threw me out.'

'Yeah, well. You started shouting.'

'And anyway I don't think the foreskin brothers would have got it.'

'Don't worry about them. They don't have any real power. They just have to make it look like they're paying attention.'

'Well next time tell them that if I want to paint a

six-foot Star of David on the window and put mezuzahs on every doorpost then I will.'

'And a ritual circumcision thrown in with every salt beef plate?'

'Not a bad idea,' Solly said. 'Not a bad idea at all. And those four could be first. We could sell tickets.'

'Less of this,' Mal said. He sat up on the settee and straightened his tie. 'Let's go look at Piccadilly.'

'Now?'

'Why not.' Mal looked at his watch: '4.55,' he said. 'Exactly the right time to move into the hotel business.'

'No better time,' Solly said, standing up. Another challenge for the man with two lives, he thought. Another adventure. And he dragged the edge of his business card across the desk once more.

Twenty-three

There were benefits to having a creative director fuelled by cocaine. Years later Solly would even admit that, if it hadn't been for his habit, he would never have managed to get so much done in so short a period of time. 'They always say you achieve things in spite of drugs not because of them,' Solly said to Mal one day. 'But I don't think that's always true. In fact I think, back then, I could have come up with a convincing argument for making my coke supply a tax-deductible business expense.'

'Yeah, but you'd have explained it so bloody quickly that only someone else who'd stuffed a gram up his nose would have been able to understand a word you were saying. Anyway I don't think the Inland Revenue would have gone for it.'

'Oh, I don't know. I once knew a tax inspector with a massive habit. He'd have understood.'

Still, it was true, up to a point. Only a man on chemical stimulants could have launched half a dozen restaurants and then, without blinking, moved on to starting up a 250-bed hotel. With Larry and Reuben's help he approached the job exactly as he had the Sinai Diners and the Kitchenware Cafés before them. Every stateroom and public area was designed around a central focus – a bar or a sunken area for seating or, in the basement nightclub, a tiered dance floor.

'People look into the middle of rooms,' Solly would say, buffing his gold sovereign ring on his tie. 'They never bother to look at the edges. Who cares what happens at the side? All they want to know is what's going on in the middle. That's what I want to know.'

Even the men's toilets off the lobby received the same treatment, the urinals arranged around a vast, round central column, so that it looked like a fair-ground carousel, made of smooth white porcelain and well-grouted tile.

'Why?' Mal said, staring at the plans.

'When we need a slash we need a slash,' Solly said. 'Shorter distance between the door and the middle, than the door and the wall.' He traced out the space on the plans with his finger.

'Solly Princeton, you are a genius. The Michelangelo of urinals.'

'Piece of piss,' he said, and howled with laughter.

Mal had been right, of course. A hotel was indeed something Solly had been born to do. He had an in-stinctive understanding of how to make people feel good. At one time, ten years before, he had done it by telling customers in his parents' *pâtisserie* to press warm bread to their cheeks against the chill winds on the walk home. Now he did it by finding soft coloured curtains and perfect beds and by buying more gold-plated bath taps than existed in the whole of north-west London. He simply created the place in which he wished to spend the night, in the same way as he had created the restaurant where he wanted to eat, and the machine he had needed to make his great chicken soup. He poached managers from hotels all over London, plundered their concierge desks and their bars, mounted dawn raids on the laundry rooms and the housekeeping departments. He booked himself into rooms across the city, made entirely unreasonable demands, and then offered jobs to those who didn't flinch.

'My bitch is having puppies,' he announced to the concierge desk of one particularly grand hotel, without any explanation. 'Send me a vet.' And although they did not allow dogs in the rooms, and had not even seen him enter with a dog in tow – because he did not have one – they still dispatched a vet to his room. He tipped the vet and sent him home; he tipped the concierge and told him he would double his pay.

'I need a wet suit,' he demanded in another hotel. 'And a snorkel. And a tub of Vaseline.' They sent him the flippers too. No questions asked.

He asked Judy's friends for the names of the best cleaning ladies in north-west London and then offered every single one a position, making him deeply unpopular in households all the way from Northwood to Southgate.

'Mine may be good,' said Mrs Glinsman, when she heard the news. 'But she'll never bother to get the dark rings off the bath. This, I can tell you. If you want that doing you have to do it yourself. Remind me never to take a bath at the Sinai Grand.'

Solly designed a brace of grand restaurants and employed the best chefs to cook in them. 'Not my deal,' Reuben had said. 'Leave me the coffee shop and the room service menu to think about. The kind of nosh I do is the kind that's good to eat lying on your bed.'

He even employed one sous-chef specifically because of his experience with seafood. 'I want you to cook for me, lobster and oysters,' he told the young Frenchman, when he offered him the job. Solly was determined, now he was a restaurateur, to fill in the gaps in his eating experience left by what he had come to realize was a merely passive observance of the laws of kashrut. He had never eaten pork or seafood because no-one he knew ate those things, not because he believed. He'd simply never been offered the opportunity. 'Yeah, cook me lobster and oysters. Those I have never eaten.'

'But Monsieur, the best way to eat oysters is not cooked. The best way to eat them is alive.'

'No kidding? I don't want a lecture, I just want you to make me dinner.' The chef did not smile. 'Ah fuck it, just a joke. Welcome to the Sinai Grand. Go find me a lobster.' Solly decided he liked lobster very much

191

and thereafter ordered it every time he dined in the Sinai Grand's Grill Room.

There was no blueprint for what was right, he said. 'You just know it's right when you see it in the same way you know food is good when you taste it. The way you discover lobster is good, when you haven't tasted it before just because the rabbis said you shouldn't.' In the matter of defining rightness he believed cocaine to be a genuine benefit. It gave him not so much an eye for detail as an obsession with it. He became consumed by the smallest weave in the cloth used for the bed-spreads, the direction of the grain in the wood veneer, the gloss on the marble tiles, the iridescent glow of the coloured glass lampshades on every bedside table. He filled the nightclub with a hundred flat mirrored sur-faces, because he assumed that everybody who danced there would want to take cocaine (eventually he was right); he made sure there were fine white lines carved onto the black dance floor that would flare only beneath the ultraviolet lights.

Sometimes he recalled events and places solely because of the details. When later he thought of the night in May 1979 when the Conservatives under Margaret Thatcher came to power, all he remembered was the depth of varnish on the walnut dashboard of the hired vintage Bentley in which he and the Horowitz brothers had cruised about town. No other moment remained with him. He couldn't remember being pleased at the poll result or who he had voted for. He couldn't remember who they saw that night. He couldn't even remember snorting cocaine, but he had to assume he had done a lot of that, because of all the other things he couldn't remember.

'Spoken like a true Edgware Jew,' Mal said, when Solly told him the story many years later. 'All you remember of great moments in history is the quality of the furnishings.'

'No. Spoken like a true hotelier,' Solly said.

But his drug habit brought him problems too, which

he recognized less readily. Decorators and curtain makers, builders and designers found themselves confronted by a man who babbled and blustered out his commands at such speed, his tongue tripping fiercely over every third word, that they could barely understand what he was saying. Either they would ask for clarification and Solly would huff and bang the table or, having seen what happened when they asked for clarification they would go away and execute the job poorly, which would lead to more banging of tables.

'What they all need,' Solly told Larry one afternoon as the Grand was nearing completion, 'is a bit of Charlie. It should be a requirement of the job. All contractors should take a quick toot so they are on my wavelength. Can get a grip. Understand. Have the knowledge. Know what's what. I'll even pay for it.'

'That would make a nice change,' Larry whispered to himself under his breath, as he tapped out yet another line from his own stash. He had returned once more to hiding the cost of Solly's on-the-job cocaine in his bills to Sinai.

More pronounced was the divide that opened up between Solly at the Sinai Grand and Mal at Golden Square. In Solly's mind the Square, as he called it, was a place only of meetings and budget constraints and rubber plants. Nothing else. It helped him to refer to it as the Square. That way, when he railed at the decisions of the management – among whose number he should have included himself – it meant he did not have to criticize Mal directly to other people; it was something he could not yet bring himself to do, but in time even that would happen. Time spent at the Square, Solly announced, was time not spent on the hotel or the restaurants. After his first display of histrionics Mal had agreed that his partner need not attend board meetings; they could discuss anything of importance between themselves. Now Solly visited only to talk to Benny about marketing or to badger Gerry into releasing more money. Occasionally he went there to see Mal for lunch, but for the most part he preferred to work from his own office at the hotel on Piccadilly.

He felt safe there, in his own universe of room service and plump cushions. Reuben was nearby and so was Larry. People who knew how he ticked and what he wanted. Who could understand him. They had no other agenda apart from the well-being of the hotel and the diners, which was exactly what Solly cared about. To those looking in from the outside the arrangement appeared to be perfect. Mal had been left in charge of the business, which was what he understood. Solly created the vehicles which made the business work, which was what he understood.

But it was not perfect. Swept along on a sparkling white tide of cocaine and overwork, Solly came first to rely on those who were around him and then, later, to assume that anybody who was not around him could not be relied upon.

'The Square is trying to tie my hands,' he would announce, whenever one of Gerry's staff telephoned to query a bill. 'The Square has no bloody idea how to run a hotel business.' He sensed plot and deceit in every business shadow, every call and memo. Soon his absence from the board meetings, from which he had begged to be excluded, became proof in his mind that he was being marginalized. They did not want him in the decision-making process. They did not think he mattered. It never occurred to him that he still owned just over a quarter of the firm; that, to all intents and purposes, he was the Sinai Corp. In his chemical paranoia the Square was now the enemy. He had built around himself a high wall, each brick glued into place by a toxic paste of narcotics and suspicion. But it was a fragile wall and all it would take for the entire edifice to collapse was one brick to fall out of place.

And then a brick fell out of place.

Twenty-four

One afternoon in June 1979, a year after the successful opening of the Sinai Grand, Reuben arrived at the hotel to find the kitchens deserted. The head chef of the Grill Room had released his brigade to rest their feet for half an hour before the evening service began, and now they were slouched outside the delivery doors in the back car park reading the sports pages and smoking. The peace of the kitchens was broken only by the clatter and bubble of a clutch of stockpots and the gentle hiss of the burning gas beneath them. Reuben lifted the lid of each in turn, hoping the rush of steam would clear his head of the severe, jellied cold that had smothered him for the past week, but all it did was make him choke and splutter. He bent over and, bracing his arms against his legs, tried to clear his lungs. His back ached and his head spun and he felt a little faint. For the past four weeks he, Larry and Solly had been working on a new hotel in Knightsbridge – The Sinai House – smaller and more intimate than the Grand, but still as indulgent. Solly had been moving even faster than usual and Reuben had simply not been able to take the pace; the first virus through the door had made straight for his throat and met no resistance at all.

He stood up and, wiping away the sweat from his forehead with the back of his hand, moved to the next stove where a pot of clear chicken soup was standing over a low heat. It appeared on the menu as *Consommé de Poulet aux Boulets de Matzo*, but Reuben was happy to do without the extras. He went to the crockery store and found a soup bowl. Then, catching site of the virgin white porcelain curve of a salad bowl, he put it back and took that instead. He was a big man, it was a big cold and he needed a big serving of chicken soup with which to nurse it. He filled the bowl with six large ladlefuls of broth and then, making sure not to spill any, shuffled down to the prep table at the far end of the kitchen. Reuben pulled up a chair and sat down, spoon in hand. Steam rose in delicate ribbons from the surface. He watched it curl about the overhead lights and sniffed the air, his eyes closed. Already he felt better. Much better. Now he leaned down, just to inhale once more before taking a first, palliative sip.

It was then that he felt the pain, a sharp blow just beneath his left shoulder blade, as if a meat fork had been thrust straight through his soft, fat-blanketed flesh. For a second he thought he had pulled a muscle. Had he not been stretching into high corners all week? But then the sensation radiated out from his back and eased its way along his left arm, like ink spreading across blotting paper. He gasped and dropped his spoon, to reach out and grip his left forearm, but he couldn't move. He couldn't even sit up straight. He was struggling for air now, desperately trying to pull oxygen into his throat, but it felt as if a tourniquet had been tied around his bulging neck. The last sight Big Reuben Lipsk saw in his truncated life was a heavy bead of sweat fall from his forehead and land dead centre of the soup, so that the liquid rippled away in perfect concentric rings, to wash and rise against the sides of the bowl.

How beautiful, Reuben thought. And then he passed out.

The chefs found him ten minutes later, face down in his soup. If his weak, overworked heart had been given a chance it would most certainly have been able to take the blame for the death. But it wasn't.

'I'm afraid Mr Lipsk drowned in his chicken soup,' the attending doctor said, as he packed away his instruments.

'His own recipe,' one sous-chef said, sadly, staring at Reuben's body. He had been pulled upright in his seat and covered with a sheet, so that he looked like a sculpture awaiting unveiling.

'Smells good,' said the doctor sniffing the air.

'Would you like some?' the chef said, nodding towards the large pot still resting on the stove at the other end of the kitchen.

The doctor looked at his watch. 'Well,' he said. 'Just a little, then. Thank you.'

Solly did not eat for twenty-four hours after hearing the news. He either ran about the building works at the Knightsbridge site trying to tidy away rubbish that was not there or sat in his makeshift office staring at the wall. He felt paralysed. Reuben had become the one fixed point in a working life that seemed constantly to change; he was a physical buttress against that part of the world with which he did not wish to deal. What, in God's name, would he do without him?

He would snort a little coke just to settle himself.

At the end of the day Mal came over from the Square to see him.

'He was my rock,' Solly said.

'He was a good man.'

'He was the best.'

'You two made a good team.'

'He understood me.'

The implication stood heavy in the space between them. There was silence.

Eventually, desperate to fill the void, Mal said, 'Was it your chicken soup?' because he could think of nothing else to say.

'Are you saying I killed him?'

'No, I was just . . .'

'What do you take me for?' Suddenly Solly started weeping, dropping his head into his hands, so that his neck folded away into the black collar of his suit jacket. In the corner of this half-decorated room he turned into a dark, rumpled shadow. Mal reached out to squeeze his shoulder but Solly shook him off.

'Would you like me to leave?' Mal said.

Solly nodded.

The funeral took place at Golders Green Crematorium the next morning.

'He told me he never liked the idea of being buried,' Solly whispered to Mal as they stood, side by side, staring at the simple wooden casket, unvarnished and free of expensive decoration or line metal handles, as was the custom.

'Scared of being buried alive, was he?' Mal said.

Solly shook his head. 'No. A kind of claustrophobia. Said big men hate the idea of being in small places, even when they're dead. Couldn't bear the idea of being locked up like that. Said he wanted to be cremated so that everything he was associated with was well cooked, even himself.' He heard Mal try to stifle a laugh. Solly smiled. 'That's what the bugger said. I'm not kidding you. Seriously. That's the kind of thing he said.' Solly felt in control here, in the warm gloom of the crematorium. Judy was on his other side, her hand reassuringly in his. He liked it here, he decided. He felt safe, as if darkness dissipated his anxiety. A cool breeze blew about the room as the door at the back opened to allow in latecomers. The wind felt sharp and cold against his cheeks. He reached up with one hand and found liquid running down his face. He looked at his fingertips as if expecting to find them smudged with blood, but instead they were damp with tears. I'm crying and I didn't even know it, he thought.

'It's a big box,' Mal said.

'He was a big man,' Solly said, and tightened his grip on Judy's hand; she rested her head on his shoulder.

Afterwards, in the gardens behind the main building, where Reuben's ashes were to be scattered, Mal said, 'I'm worried about you.'

'You should have worried about Reuben.'

'I did, but I never got to see him. I don't get to see much of you these days, either. Or Judy, Joe and

Rachel.' Their family Sunday lunches had become intermittent months before and now, like a train service suspended due to lack of custom, had ceased altogether.

'It's too late for worrying now,' Solly said, answering both points at once. He was feeling edgy out here, in the sunshine. The confidence he had felt in the darkness was gone. Why was the sun shining when Reuben was dead? Where was the logic in that? A great man was dead. What was the point of the sun? His mind was beginning to race. He felt anxiety piling rocks up against his stomach wall and lodging hard pebbles of flint and quartz in his gullet.

'For Reuben it's time only for the final reckoning now, I suppose,' Mal said uneasily. He was certain there was nothing after the flames of the cremation, but he suspected his partner wanted to believe in that sort of thing.

Solly recalled the chef's heavy folds of flesh, the girdle of fat that fought constantly to escape the unequal grasp of shirts and trousers that were invariably too small for him. Then he thought of the fire which had just engulfed his body. 'The final rendering,' he said staring away over his partner's shoulder. 'That's what it was.'

Mal sniggered again. 'What are you laughing at?' Solly said sharply. His jaw was held tense so that Mal could see the thick ridges in the muscles.

'Your joke about—'

'What joke?' He didn't wait to hear Mal's answer. Turning, he walked away to where Judy was standing talking to Reuben's parents.

'I really am worried about you,' Mal muttered, but there was nobody there to hear him.

At the Lipsk family house in Edgware, after the funeral, Solly excused himself and made for the bathroom. It was an old person's bathroom, that smell of cheap talcum powder and liniment. On each side of the bath there were heavy chrome handles to help the weak-hipped, and over it, from a fragile curving rail, hung a curtain of thick yellowing plastic. He closed the door and looked about the room. Quickly it dawned on him that there was not a single flat surface. The surround to the sink was narrow and curved, the edges of the bath equally rounded. Even the top of the toilet cistern was bell shaped. He opened the medicine cabinet, in the hope that the glass shelves were removable, but they were packed top to bottom with the collection of obsolete medication, in bottles of brown and blue, that only the aged collect. Finally he noticed the toilet lid, which was resting in the up position above the seat. He knelt down in front of the bowl, eased it down and tugged back the pink woollen crocheted cover with which Mrs Lipsk had tried to disguise it. Still looks like a toilet, Mrs L, Solly thought, as he cut a particularly long line on the aged plastic. Even with the woolly thing. He remembered with curiosity his tears during the funeral and tipped another little heap of the drug onto the toilet seat lid and cut that into a line too. Tram lines he thought, even as he snorted it away at double speed. To help you travel faster.

Solly stood up and took in a deep draught of air through his nose, feeling the cold wind against the thin flesh of what remained of his nasal lining. He closed his eyes and took another deep breath, waiting for his mind to sparkle or at least for the knot of anxiety in the pit of his stomach to fade away. Instead he felt a familiar and disturbing sharpness deep in the centre of his head. However long he tried to breathe in he knew he could not beat the inevitable. Gravity would always win out. The fluid soon began to run from both nostrils, quickly breaking onto his bristled top lip. Solly looked down and saw the first thick, heavy drops of blood splash in Technicolor against his white shirt. Lurching now towards the sink, he placed a hand under his chin to catch the flow but it sprayed over his fingers and sent droplets flying onto the dark carpet.

Deep in his chest his heartbeat doubled and tripled. He had suffered nosebleeds before, too many times, but nothing like this; not from both nostrils at once, not each pouring forth in an apparently endless steady, untrammelled stream. It looked as if an artery had been slashed with a knife. He tried to pinch his nostrils together but it was no good. The blood merely piled up behind the feeble dam of flesh.

There was a knock at the door. 'Solly, are you in there?'

It was Judy. He glanced at the sink: the stoneware, yellowed now by age, was all but obscured by thick smears of his blood. His heartbeat shot up once more. It felt like it was pumping in his throat. Now in his jaw. Now in his temples. His heart was in his head. And in his fingertips and deep, so very very deep, in the pit of his stomach and in the soles of his feet. Solly tried to respond to his wife but his hand was across his face and anyway, waves of panic were choking his throat. He tried to stand up straight. As he did so, an iron band fixed itself hard against his chest so that waves of pain broke across him.

This is it, he thought, even as the flow of blood began to slow. This is the end. He fell to his knees as Judy entered the room, saw her husband's blood-soaked shirt, and screamed.

'I'm finished,' Solly croaked, as if he wanted her to know that she really wasn't over-reacting. 'I'm dying.' And then he collapsed.

Twenty-five

He wasn't dying, of course. He was suffering a massive anxiety attack brought on by overwork and particularly enthusiastic drug abuse. They heaved him from the Lipsk house and took him, by ambulance, to a private clinic in St John's Wood. There a Dr Levy, who possessed a constantly startled air on account of eyebrows that rested half an inch too far up his forehead, informed Judy that 'Mr Princeton appears, most curiously, to have developed a pronounced, rather surprising dependency problem'. Solly waved the diagnosis away.

'I don't have a dependency problem. I have a dead friend problem,' he said, as he lay in bed, his nostrils stuffed with cotton-wool swabs, his chest wired to a heart monitor, gold necklace glinting under the sharp hospital lights. 'I get upset at my friend's funeral and the doctor says I'm a drug addict. How many years at medical school for him to learn that?'

'What about the nosebleed?' Judy said. 'The doctor says the lining of your nose is almost not there. I do not want a husband with no nasal lining. Joseph and Rachel, they do not want a father without nasal linings. All my friends' husbands, they have nasal linings but not mine.'

'Stress,' Solly said. 'Death is stressful.'

'You go on like this and you'll find out just how stressful death is. It will kill you, this stress. That's all I'm saying.'

'Judy, I'm fine.'

'And the bag of drugs you dropped in poor Mrs Lipsk's bathroom?'

'I told you, my love, something to get me through.'

'Mrs Lipsk, she almost took it for indigestion.'

'That, I would have liked to see.'

Mal said, 'You've been overdoing it.'

Solly said, 'I've been doing just what you wanted.'

'I never wanted you to end up like this.'

'I've been doing what the business needed.'

'The business needs you alive.'

Mal and Judy accepted Solly's explanation over Dr Levy's. 'Maybe I let the coke thing get a little out of hand,' he said. 'Maybe that. But no more than that. How could I have achieved so much if I was a drug addict?' For his partner and his wife this made sense. It was certainly far easier to handle than the brutal alternative, because it fitted in with what they knew of Solly; serious drug abuse did not fit in with anything they knew. That could not be part of the scenario. They paid Dr Levy's bill and ignored his diagnosis.

'Solly a drug addict?' Mal said. 'As likely as Golda Princeton running the marathon.'

'My Solly with a cocaine problem?' Judy said. 'Feh! And Divinia earns pin money as a stripper.'

Despite his stubbornness and his denials, Solly knew something had to change. Two weeks after his release from hospital he returned to work, but at Golden Square rather than at the Sinai House, whose launch was now being overseen by the deputy manager of the Grand.

'If this firm is going to survive,' Mal said, on Solly's first morning back, 'then we need you to survive too. Which means we can not have you doing every hotel yourself and running yourself ragged. It makes no sense. We have to start finding people who can do it the way you would do it. It's called delegation. We need you in one piece.'

Solly was standing by the window staring out at the tidy geometry of the square below, feeling a little uneasy. Under Judy's watchful eye he had been forced to stay clear of coke for the past two weeks. But then, it hadn't been difficult. Under Judy's watchful eye he hadn't even left the neat avenues of Hampstead Garden Suburb. Few coke dealers hung out on those carefully cultivated street corners.

'Have I behaved like the biggest arsehole in the world?' Solly said. He wanted reassurance, to know that nothing had changed even though everything had. He also wanted a quick toot. Nothing much. Just a short line to get him through the first day back.

'No mate, of course not. You could never be the biggest arsehole in the world.' He hesitated. 'Not while Jeremy Schaeffer's still alive. He'll always have first claim on the title.'

'Why does he get to live when people like Reuben have to die?'

It was a question so plump with melancholy that Mal could manufacture no answer. He stared at the ceiling and said, 'It will be nice for us two to work together again. Properly to work together. And will you bring Judy and the kids to lunch on Sunday?' Solly said he would like that.

He spent the following days reacquainting himself with the Square. In the previous nine months he had visited the building less than three or four times a month and then, usually at day's end when most of the offices were quiet. Now he saw just how large the company had become. On the second floor there were teams of accounts staff he had never met, young slick youths straight out of college, with letters after their name and ambition carved on their foreheads, who made him feel desperately old and unburdened by certificates.

'My nursery,' Gerry said.

'Do you have to stop for milk at break time?'

'Up to now. But we're moving them on to solids tomorrow. Everybody is very excited.'

He was taken to a room on the fourth floor which he was told was 'the estates office' and introduced to a vaguely familiar man with carefully chiselled features and what he later told Judy was 'blond hair an SS storm-trooper would have died for'.

'You remember Piers Grafton from the Heston Bank?' Mal said. Solly recalled that first board meeting very clearly.

'Oh yeah. I remember. Piers now works for us?' Solly said. 'For Sinai?'

'On attachment,' the banker said, perching on the corner of his desk, a delicate smile barely altering the smooth line of his face. He buried his hands in his trouser pockets and casually jangled his change.

'Piers is setting up our estates office,' Mal said. 'It's an area he understands and we all thought it would work well . . .'

'Forgive me,' Solly said. 'But what exactly is an estates office?'

Grafton stood up and waved at sets of blueprints pinned about the walls. 'The hotel trade is part service business, part real estate . . .' He stopped himself. 'Obviously, Mr Princeton, I don't have to tell you what the hotel business is.'

Solly accepted the man's deference and sat down on a sofa.

'Piers is here to oversee property acquisition,' Mal said. 'We need to have a rolling schedule of what we're going to buy and where, how much we can afford to pay per room, how much the financing will cost and so on.'

'And so on.' Solly repeated.

There were plans for two more hotels in Britain – one in Manchester and one in Edinburgh – followed by one in Paris and another in Madrid. Drawings of imposing buildings decorated the walls of the estates office, showing grand lobbies and state rooms, complete with what Grafton called 'original features' and 'defining motifs'. Alongside each building plan was a map of the city in which they would appear, the new hotel outlined in red.

'We're *very* excited about the development plans,'

Piers said, with an inflection Solly found depressingly familiar. 'And I'm *so* looking forward to working with you on it.'

'I'm sure you are,' Solly said.

'And then, of course,' Mal said, 'there's New York.'

'New York?' Solly said.

'Yeah, a small chain of three dilapidated hotels in mid-town.'

'Dilapidated?' Solly said.

'Totally fucked,' Mal added helpfully.

Solly grinned at the sudden expletive, even as Piers bristled. It was a Mal he remembered and loved and seemed to have heard so little of in recent years, as his partner had settled into an expletive-free life of chauffeured cars and smart suits and shiny-leafed rubber plants. Foul-mouthed, in his enthusiasm.

'We're talking bent over backwards fucked,' Mal went on.

'That fucked?'

Piers was now staring awkwardly at his shoes, excluded from the conversation by an ancient intimacy the partners had formed over profanity.

'So,' Solly said, warming to the theme. 'We can get these buggered-up shite-bombed hotels for less than market price?'

'Exactly.'

'Good locations?'

'Perfect.'

'Let's do it. Let me do it.'

Mal grinned. His partner was here. Back on the settee. Back on board. 'Of course, mate.' He turned to Piers. 'You don't mind if Mr Princeton leads on this?' The banker gave his assent, though it was clear to Solly that he had been jealously guarding the deal as his own. Solly hummed quietly to himself. One morning back in the firm and he had re-established his position.

New York in the late 1970s was not a good place for a man like Solly Princeton. On his first night in the city, strung out on jet lag, buzzing with anxiety, he visited friends of Larry's and, in an apartment high above Columbus Circle, was introduced to the less than subtle joys of freebased cocaine, the drug washed of its alkaloids in ether. He liked New York. It was coke city. In London, having a cocaine habit was still a minority interest, like white water rafting or sky diving. Eccentric and wild with a unique lingua franca that could not be shared. In New York everybody seemed to start their evening by powdering their noses. All of them: the club people and the hotel people and the money people. Here, he was among his own. He could be a coke head. And he could be a Jew. Be a loud-mouthed, in your face Jew, because everybody in New York was a Jew, even the non-Jews.

'No more nosebleeds?' Solly said as he gulped down the smoke for the first time.

'Say goodbye to nasal haemorrhage,' said his host, a languid costume designer called Brett, who seemed only to get more languid the more he smoked. 'The days of crimson handkerchiefs are gone, my friend. Away with them. Away.'

To Solly it seemed such a pure and unsullied way to take the drug. Fresher, more invigorating. Like swallowing bright, white clouds on a breezy summer's day. Here, high above the fastest city on earth, the roads below streaked by the red glow of a thousand taillights, he felt truly calm and free of stress for the first time since the 'incident' in the Lipsk bathroom. The high was so acute, so fierce and livid without being threatening, that he was even willing to dump his opposition to drug accessories. It seemed only fair that an action movie buzz like this should demand preparation, as if the high-class, top-drawer drug experience needed to be sanctified by ritual. He watched with fascination, only intensified by the high, as Brett diluted the coke in water, mixed it with ether and added a touch of ammonium hydroxide.

'Add salt and pepper to taste, my dear,' Brett said, as

he shook the sealed tube and the solution separated.

Onto the coffee filter paper. Watch the crystals grow, children. Watch them grow. Out with the dinky pipe. Crytals into bowl. Just add flame. Learn to suck. Solly the novice learned to suck with the best of them, to hold and not exhale until there was barely anything left to exhale. This was the way of freebase, and what gadget-fun it was.

And so he returned the next night and the night after that to stand by Brett's portrait windows to smoke drugs and stare out at the shimmering lights of Manhattan, a jewel-studded carpet spread out below him as a welcome to the United States. It completely passed him by that one of those glittering, shimmering jewels marked out the window behind which Piers Grafton was closing the deal he should have been closing.

'You went ahead without me?' Solly said the next morning.

'You weren't here,' Grafton said. 'They were ready to close so I closed.'

'You didn't consult me.'

'You were . . .' He paused. 'Elsewhere.'

'I own this company,' Solly said.

'So does Heston Bank.'

Back in London Solly swiftly returned to an uneasy pattern of cocaine abuse, hiding the best part of a chemistry set in the bathroom off his office, with which to produce enough freebase. He smoked to smother his paranoid suspicion that once more he was being undermined from within the company, and the drug abuse only exacerbated his paranoia. During site visits to the latest hotel in development he would sit with Larry, preparing more of Larry's coke ready for the fire that would vaporize it. 'The fuck wits are trying to carve me out,' he would say, muttering darkly of conspiracy and deceit.

'Piers Grafton is something we do not need,' he announced to Mal, one afternoon. He was sitting at the head of the boardroom table, trying to focus on his own reflection in the varnish.

'Piers is a good businessman.'

'He's an arsehole.'

'He knows his stuff.'

'He's a dickhead.'

'Oh right. He's a dickhead. Why, exactly? Can you be a little bit more specific on this dickhead diagnosis?'

'He knows fuck all about hotels.'

'No, Solly. He knows everything about hotels. He knows which ones we should buy. The thing you don't like is that he's not Jewish.'

'Sure. You're right. I don't like that he's not Jewish. I take shit from non-Jews every day in this business. Why should I have to take shit from non-Jews in my own house?'

'You don't take shit from anybody, Solly. Jew or non-Jew. And anyway we're not an Edgware business any more.'

'No. That much I'd noticed. More's the pity.'

When Piers Grafton announced just two weeks later that he thought it would be better for all involved if he returned to the Heston Bank, Solly took it as a moral victory. 'We should never have allowed a goy shithead like that into the building in the first place.'

Mal and Judy recognized the return of his mood swings, but tried desperately to pretend they were the after-effect of his having kicked his occasional drug habit, rather than the result of further use. Just as they couldn't accept the scale of his first drug problem so they couldn't handle the thought that it – whatever it was – had returned.

'Solly wouldn't go back, would he?' Judy said, one Sunday lunchtime, when he had left the room.

'Solly doesn't look backwards,' Mal said, eager to keep with the riff. 'He doesn't have a reverse gear.'

'Doesn't know where the past is,' Judy said.

'Exactly,' Mal agreed.

'He's still good with the kids,' Judy went on.

'And with you?'

'Ach, nothing I can't handle,' she said with a dismissive wave of one carefully jewelled hand.

'That man loves you,' Divinia said simply. 'He wears your heart on his sleeve.'

In the sweet domesticity of this suburban kitchen with its Teasmade and its ceramic tea caddy and spice rack, it seemed nothing short of obscene to harbour dark brooding thoughts about Solly's state of mind. Only when they came to close what had become known as the Topkaki Deal did Mal finally begin to discover the truth about his partner.

Twenty-six

On a scouting trip to Istanbul his partner had found a run-down hotel, close to the Topkapi Palace, which he felt had potential.

'These amazing Arab decorations,' he said. 'Like a brothel, only classy.'

'How many brothels have you been in?' Mal said.

'Not enough. That's why we should buy this one. So I have my own brothel. No millionaire should be without one.'

'That's your third brain talking again.'

'What? You want that it should stay quiet? Dream on.'

Now the owner, a wealthy Turk, was in London and renting a flat in Hampstead.

'We just have to make nice with him,' Solly said. 'Come with me. You're good at that.'

'Of course I'll come with you,' Mal said. There was no way he was going to let Solly go by himself.

Kemal Usak was a large sweaty man of middle years, whose body had fought a long war with gravity and lost. Rolls of fat were held down beneath his belt so that the wide stretch of his cotton trousers between the top of his legs and his waistband, ballooned. When he sat down on the deep leather sofa, the material rose up in front of him as if he had a space hopper stuffed down there. Mal felt a desperate urge to prod the mound of flesh just to feel his hand sink in, a desire tempered only by the thought that he would be perilously close to the man's undoubtedly sweaty genitals.

For a while they talked banalities: the weather in London and Istanbul; the hotel business and the nuisance posed by defecating pigeons on their roofs. Then Kemal said: 'We play with some fun dust?' He pulled a bank bag of coke from a trouser pocket. 'Then we talk business?' A broad smile swept across his soft, fleshy face.

'Of course,' Solly said. 'Lots of fun dust.'

Mal hissed, 'Solly, what in fuck's name . . .'

'Don't worry about it,' Solly whispered. 'It's just a little coke.'

'Just a little . . .' Mal turned around and addressed the Turk. 'Mr Usak, my partner and I, we just need to have a quick chat, something I forgot to mention.' Their host shrugged and weighed the bag of drugs in his hand. Mal dragged Solly off to stand beside the window.

'What in God's name are you doing?' he said.

'Mal, control yourself. Mr Usak, he likes to relax a little before doing a deal. That's how he works. We want the deal to go through, we just do a couple of social lines and we're fine. We're out of here. Coke is part of the deal.'

'Fine. What am I supposed to do while you two are emptying that bag of yours? Play with myself?'

'Why don't you do some too?' Solly said, simply. Mal stared at him.

Solly laughed. 'Look at you. Anybody would think I had just asked you to shag your mother.'

'You know I've never done coke before.'

'Then it's about time. It will loosen you up.' As far as Solly was concerned the conversation was over. He walked back to the glass-topped coffee table and started cutting up lines of Mr Usak's coke, watched by their eager host, his heavy hands resting on the bulge in his trousers. 'This should be fun, no?' Usak said.

'Lots of fun,' Solly said, as he scraped the third line into place.

'So, my friend,' Usak said, turning to Mal who was still standing behind the settee, watching. 'You are my

212

guest in my house, so you will be going first.' He grinned so that Mal could see a mouth full of gold and silver, glinting through the fetid saliva dampness. Solly held up a pound note, already rolled into a tube. Mal wanted to refuse, to casually raise a hand and say no, as if he had been offered a whisky and soda. He had refused so many whiskies so many times before. Said no. But this was different. To say no here would be to stand in judgement. He didn't care what Mr Usak thought. He didn't know the man. But he really didn't want to stand in judgement on Solly. Here they were, about to close a deal together for the first time in years, and he was going to ruin it by simply raising his hand and saying no.

After all, it was only one line.

It couldn't do any harm.

It might even be fun.

It would close the deal.

Slowly Mal walked around the settee and knelt down in front of the table. Glass filled his entire field of vision. Enough glass to clad an office block, he thought. To his right he could just see Usak's hands. He was playing with his own pound note, carefully rolling it into a tube and unrolling it again. Solly handed him his money tube and whispered, 'Hold it to one nostril, close down the other one with your hand and just inhale.'

As he shifted into position Mal registered that it meant he would have no way by which to support himself as he leaned down, but already it was too late. Gravity was playing as evil a trick on Mal Jones as it had played on Kemal Usak's hips. He saw the glass rising up towards him and had time only to release a little whimper before the impact. There was a sharp cracking sound of fragile matter meeting resistance and then a violent bitter taste on his tongue, as a plume of white dust blew up around him.

'Shit!' he shouted.

For a few seconds he lay dazed face down on the

table, until he noticed the puddle of blood that was spreading in front of him.

There's some blood, he thought to himself. And then: It's my blood. Now it was rolling across the glass and seeping into what remained of the drugs. Wasting neither time nor narcotics, Usak dropped to his knees and, using his own pound note, raced Mal's lifeblood to the cocaine. When he was done, he sat up.

'Ah,' he said. 'Now I feel much better.'

Afterwards, outside in the car, Solly began shouting: 'You blew the deal. And it was a good deal. A great fucking deal on a great property. You bled into Mr Usak's cocaine. And you blew it.'

Mal was still dabbing at his nose. 'Strictly speaking I head-butted the deal.'

'Ha fucking ha.'

'Thank you for your sympathy.'

'You blew my deal. The one I worked to set up.'

'Mr Usak is a contact you're proud of?'

'It was great deal. He was going to give that hotel away.'

'Frankly, I wonder whether we should be doing deals with people like that.'

'For Christ's sake,' Solly said. 'We're grown-ups. A little coke is a little coke.'

'What's a little coke? Define for me a little coke. A bag full? Two bags full?'

'You don't know what you are talking about.'

'Yeah, because I don't do drugs.'

'It's nothing.'

'Nothing? I thought you said you'd stopped the coke.'

'I never said anything of the kind.'

'You gave the impression . . .'

'There's no such things as impressions. There's just assumptions. I do a little coke now and then. So what? I'm allowed a little quality partying time.'

'Quality partying time? With Mr Usak the human beach ball?'

214

'I work hard. I play hard. It's nothing special.'

'I don't get it,' Mal said, his voice burning with sarcasm. 'You're a nice Jewish boy from Edgware. Jews don't drink and Jews don't do drugs. You're turning into, I don't know. You're turning into some absurd cultural mongrel.'

'Oh yeah? Absurd cultural mongrel? Jews don't do drugs? Listen to you. Have you ever met my dealer Mr Saul Israelson? Ever met the Horowitz brothers from Mill Hill? They're hardly kings of the goyim.'

They fell silent, their anger all but burnt out. 'Fuck this,' Solly said eventually, his rage catching aflame once more as he opened the car door.

'Where you going?'

'To get a cab. I'll see you in the morning.' He climbed out, walked up Hampstead High Street and away into the night.

Twenty-seven

Late on a March day in 1981, when the skies were still darkening before their time, Mal left his office to hand his signed letters to Jenny and found Judy in the waiting area. His secretary hunched uncomfortably over her typewriter, as if trying to pretend that pressure of work had stopped her from noticing Solly's wife was there at all.

'Judy?' Mal said, taking off his steel-framed reading glasses. He had only recently acquired them and he still enjoyed sweeping them dramatically off his nose. 'How long have you been here?' She smiled weakly and chewed her bottom lip. 'Jenny, why didn't you tell me Judy was here?'

'I told her not to,' Judy said. 'I didn't want to disturb you.' For the first time she appeared slight and vulnerable. Even the curls in her hair were flat and ill-defined. She was wrapped up tightly in an overcoat that would have guarded against the chill outside but was more than unnecessary for the centrally heated offices.

'You know Solly's not here,' Mal said.

'Yes I know that,' she said flatly.

'Come into the office.' He held open one of the double doors with an outstretched arm. A pornographic memory of what once had passed between them many years before expanded into his mind and then subsided. That was a postcard from another life. Nothing else. Slowly, miserably, she stood up and went inside. She pulled out a chair from the boardroom table, sat down and started crying.

'I'm so, so sorry,' she said. Tears, rich in diluted mascara, flowed down her cheeks, and dribbled onto the table top. 'This, I didn't mean to do. It was the last thing. You do not need me to come here and do this. With your work and your meetings. I just . . .'

'Judy, sweetheart. Really. It's all right.' He sat down in the next chair and held her. 'It's all right.'

'That's the thing,' she said. 'I don't think it is all right.'

He hesitated. 'It's Solly, isn't it,' he said to the top of her head, now pressed against his chest. She nodded. 'How is he?'

She looked up and sniffed. 'I don't know. How should I know if I haven't spoken to him? I can't speak to him. I've tried to . . .' She sat up and felt around in her coat pocket for a tissue with which to dab away the froth of tears and make-up. 'But he won't take my calls.'

'He is still in Paris, isn't he?' Solly was meant to be overseeing the last few days of trials at the Sinai de Rivoli. Checking systems, overseeing kitchens, inspecting rooms.

She nodded again as she dabbed at her nose. 'The telephonists say that he's there. But he won't pick up the phone. They say he has made a few calls out but none of them are to me. I spoke to the concierge yesterday. What's his name . . .?'

'Gérard.'

'Gérard. That's him. Gérard. Lovely voice. Gérard, he says Solly hasn't been out of his suite for three days, maybe four. That he orders room service food . . .'

'We know he's alive, then.'

'Mal!'

'Judy, sorry. Weak joke. It's just that . . .' Mal stood up and began pacing the room. Outside in the square, early leavers were beginning to make their way home along damp, puddle-splashed streets. Mal wished he were one of them. The winter evenings, when night

217

came early, always made him think of home. 'If you haven't spoken to him in three days then you won't know what's happened.'

'Tell me.'

'Three, four days ago I cancelled our rolling contract with Larry.'

'Interior designer Larry?'

'Yeah, interior designer Larry. The Queen of Sheba. I sacked him.'

'Why?'

'Oh God.' Mal sat down and rubbed his face with his hands, pushing his glasses far up onto his forehead. 'It was Gerry who noticed it. All of Larry's invoices up to now have been OK'd by Solly. That's just the way it's been. Solly deals with it, because he oversees the jobs. Makes sense. This one comes in, Solly's away so it goes to Gerry and it's huge. I mean vast. Mid-five figures. Partly, it's because it covers a longer period than normal, but that can't be the only explanation . . .'

'Go on.'

'So I get Larry up here and ask him why and after a lot of prodding he admits that it also includes the cost of Solly's coke.'

'What?'

'Yeah, exactly. He's been giving Solly drugs and then charging it to the company. For years. God knows how much has come out of the firm's accounts.' Figures flitted into his mind on wings made of tenners, but he swiftly waved the thought away. 'Look, I knew Solly was using a bit of coke again. I've known for months, since the night the Topkapi Deal went west, but I didn't realize it was this bad. Maybe I didn't want to know.'

'How much was it?'

'The coke money? Over ten grand.'

Judy bit her bottom lip again. 'Oh Christ,' she said. She looked like she was ready to cry once more.

'I tried to call him myself, to talk it through. I wanted him to hear it from me. But he didn't take the call when I rang the suite. I left messages and he didn't come back to me so I assumed he was busy with the trials and . . .'

'He hasn't been around to do any trials,' Judy said. 'He hasn't been around to do anything.'

'No,' Mal said. 'No he hasn't.'

Mal walked over to his desk. He stopped for a moment with his back to Judy while he decided what to do and then picked up the phone. 'Jenny,' he said. 'Get me on a flight to Paris. Tonight.'

Gérard was waiting for him at the deserted reception, the desk still covered in a veil of dustsheet, when Mal arrived at the Sinai de Rivoli a little after ten that night.

'A good journey, Monsieur?' he said taking Mal's overnight bag. The concierge's beautifully manicured nails shimmered and his shirt looked fresh on even though his shift had begun at eight that morning. It was a trick Mal knew he could never manage.

'Fine, thank you, Gérard,' he said, slipping uneasily into bizarre hotel pleasantries. 'Thank you for sending the car. Can you get someone to take that bag to my room – whichever room that is, and find me the duplicate key for the suite.'

In the lift Mal said, 'Have you seen Mr Princeton?'

'No, Monsieur.'

'At all?'

'On arrival, Monsieur.'

'That's it?'

'I gave to him a telephone message he had received. He took it and went to the suite.'

'Did you see who the message was from?'

Gérard bristled. He had recently left the concierge desk at the Crillon to help launch the Sinai, the brand new act in town, and already he was beginning to regret his move. One chairman appeared to be a madman. Now the other was questioning his probity. 'Monsieur, I would never . . .'

'That's OK, Gérard,' Mal said. 'I know.' And then: 'I

219

am sorry about all of this.' Mal had never felt comfortable around senior staff like Gérard; it was an uneasy character trait for a hotelier.

At the top floor the lift shuddered to a stuttering halt and they clambered out, stepping up a little because the machine had stopped two inches shy. 'Ask the engineers to check the lifts,' Mal said, looking behind him. 'Where is the suite?'

'In this direction, Monsieur,' Gérard said, leading the way. Mal and Solly had recently decided to install a private suite in every one of their hotels, designed and decorated in exactly the same style, so that they would not have to put up with hotel living during long stays in their own hotels.

'Sometimes I like my own things around me,' Solly had said.

'So you choose your own things and we'll buy ten of them.'

'Makes a kind of sense. Hotels are about duplication.'

Mal had not yet had a chance to visit this one but he knew what it would look like inside, where the living room and the bedrooms and the two bathrooms would be. The only problem was whether he could get inside. As they walked he admired the wood-panelled corridors, still rich with the scent of fresh varnish, and the art deco costume prints that had been hung irregularly along the walls. The dark wood and low lighting gave a comfortable night-time feel to the corridor. A thick, moneyed, thousand-franc-a-night feel. The concierge stopped and pointed down a dead end corridor that finished in a simple oak door.

'There, Monsieur,' he said bluntly, handing Mal the key and holding his position.

Mal walked to the door and was about to knock when he looked back down the corridor. Gérard was still standing there, silhouetted against the pale light, head held just so, legs together. 'It's OK,' Mal said. 'You can leave me to it.'

The concierge gave a sharp nod of the head and said, 'Very well, Monsieur.' He walked away. In the carpet-muffled half-light Mal could have sworn he had heard him click his heels together.

Mal banged on the door. 'Solly? It's me, Mal. Will you let me in?' There was silence. He pressed his ear against the door but the wood was far too thick for him to be able to hear anything. All the doors had been designed that way. He banged again. The only sound was the rolling echo from his own fist. He slipped the key into the lock, turned it and gently pushed the door open but it stopped after only a few inches. At first he assumed it was the security chain. But then he noticed that, while it was in place between frame and door, it was hanging slack. Something else, pushed up against the door, something heavy, was holding it closed.

'Solly? Mate? Come and let me in.' There was clearly a light on in the living room which was spreading a dull yellow glow against the stretch of wall just visible through the partially open door. The air smelt of chemicals and old sweat and day-old food. 'Solly? For Christ's sake. Come to the door so we can talk.' Far off in the depths of the suite there was a rustle of material. Movement. The noise became a little louder. It was the sound of stockinged feet scuffing against carpet.

'Solly?' Mal said. Before he could finish the word there was a roar of noise as somebody ran at the door from the other side, throwing themselves against it and slamming it shut.

Mal recoiled in shock. 'Solly?'

'Fuck off,' a voice said.

'Solly?'

'I said fuck off.' It was his voice, all right. Rough and overwrought but it was his voice.

'And nice to hear you too, mate. I was beginning to think you'd snuffed it.'

'You'd like that, wouldn't you.'

'What?'

'Me, dead.'

221

'I just want to talk to you.'

He heard another shout, but Solly was walking away and the sound was muffled by distance. Gently Mal unlocked the door and opened it again as far as it would go. He looked about the dim corridor for something to keep it from being slammed shut once more, but there was nothing. He removed one shoe and shoved it into the gap.

'Solly?' He sighed. 'I am getting seriously bored with this. I just want to talk to you. I want to talk to you about Larry.'

Mal turned around and, pressing his back against the wall, slid down so that he was sitting on the floor, arms rested on his knees. He stared at his feet, one shoe on, one shoe off. Mal Jones, millionaire hotelier, he thought. Again Solly rushed the door but this time it would not close.

'I want to talk to you about Larry,' Mal said.

'Fuck—'

Mal interrupted him. 'Yeah, I know. Fuck off. Haven't you got anything else to say to me?'

'Why did you do it?'

'You know why I did it.'

'You want me out of the company.'

'What?'

'You want me out. First Reuben. Now Larry.'

'Solly, Reuben died. I didn't sack him. He died.'

There was a moment's silence. 'Why did you get rid of Larry?'

'He was charging us for drugs, Solly. For your drugs.'

'My business. That's my business.'

'Nothing's just your business. It's our business. Sinai is our business. And you taking drugs is doing damage to our business.'

'Is that the only thing you care about?'

'No.'

'Just the business?'

'No. I care about . . .'

'Yeah?'

'I care about you. You're my friend.'

'Ha!'

Mal shook his head. 'Solly, all of this was you and me before it was Sinai. That's what it was. I did it because it was fun. Being with you was fun.' There was silence. 'That's all I ever want it to be. If it's not fun it's nothing.'

'Then why are you trying to carve me out of the business?'

'I'm not.'

Solly shrieked 'Fuck off, Mal Jones, you lying shyster!' Mal could hear his partner walking away. He stood up and pushed against the door. Oh sod this, he thought. He retrieved his shoe from the gap, put it on and, lifting his foot, started to kick in the door. The first impact only dented the veneer. With the second and third he heard the wooden frame begin to splinter and crack and with the next, the security chain broke from its moorings. Now he leaned against the door, desperately trying to gain purchase on the corridor carpet with his smooth leather soles. Slowly the door slipped open as, behind it, the chest of drawers that had been placed there began to move. Finally there was just enough space for Mal to slip through.

'Solly?'

There was silence. Mal looked around. Just ahead, to the left, was the first bathroom. Only a low wattage strip light above the mirror was on but he could see, laid out beside the sink, what seemed to be a wooden rack of test tubes, as if from a child's chemistry set, bottles of chemicals and soup bowls lined with coffee filter papers. He moved on to the living room. It was a scene of devastation. The light he had been able to see from the corridor came from the one standard lamp that was not broken. The rest lay in shards of china on the carpet. Paintings and mirrors had been smashed, occasional tables overturned, settees ripped and stripped of cushions. By his feet Mal found the broken stem from an ornamental glass dipping bird. Solly had insisted every suite have one, to remind him of the one his mother kept on her mantelpiece. And so they had bought ten. Now, clearly there were nine.

Mal held the shattered bird in the palm of his hand. He's lost his mind, Mal thought as he turned the pathetic piece of glass over and over.

A short corridor led off the living room. The first bedroom off that lay dark and untouched. Mal moved on to the next. It too appeared to be dark. As his eyes became accustomed to the light, Mal began to see that the same interior designer who had remodelled the living room had been at work here. Broken glass and splintered wood littered the floor. Furniture had been turned over. In the corner, upended against the wall was the base from the double bed, positioned as if to make a lean-to. A feeble light spread out from what looked like the entrance.

'Solly?' Mal walked delicately across the carpet, glass crunching underfoot, and hunkered down in front of it. The mattress was on the floor of the lean-to. There was a blanket, a plate of half-eaten food and a torch, the source of the light. At the back, huddling into the darkened corner, was his partner.

'Solly?'

'Please go away,' he said. It was a plaintive voice now, high-pitched and uneasy. As if he were merely frightened.

'Solly please, we need to talk.'

'I don't want to.'

'Can I come in?'

Solly said nothing so, getting down on his hands and knees, Mal climbed inside. Now he could see that the mattress was littered with drug debris. There was a small brass pipe, surrounded by a clutch of singed metal filters, a couple of bank bags, now empty, dozens of burnt-out matches and a heavy brass lighter. Up the walls Mal could just make out burn marks. He shuddered at the thought.

'How much are we charging you for this fine

accommodation?' he asked. But Solly said nothing. His head was down on his neck and obscured by shadow. Mal tried again. 'Judy's worried about you.'

'I love Judy.' He sounded like a child. He was shivering and his breathing was coming in short uneven breaths.

'I know you love Judy. She just wants to hear your voice.'

'What would I say to her?'

'That you're fine.'

Solly didn't respond; they both knew it wasn't true.

'I sacked Larry because I was worried about you,' Mal said.

'I've been doing my job.'

'God, Solly. Of course you've been doing your job. You've always been doing your job. Without you this business would be nothing. I've said so, to Divinia, lots of times. I add up numbers. That's what I do. I think business. But you—' Mal knew he was babbling but he seemed unable to stop – 'you create. You're a genius. Brilliant. I mean, really. Brilliant—'

Solly interrupted. 'I don't want to be a genius,' he said. His voice sounded thin and uncomfortable.

'I hate seeing you like this.'

'I just want to sell bread and cake.' There was a quiver in his voice. Mal couldn't be certain, but it sounded like Solly was crying.

'What do you mean? Cake?'

'I just want to be selling cake.' He was definitely sobbing. 'I just want to go to the *pâtisserie* every day and be behind the counter and sell bread and cake and . . .'

For a few seconds, as Solly roared on, Mal sat rooted to the spot. Then he reached out into the darkness, wrapped his arms around his partner's shoulder and pulled him to his chest. Solly didn't resist. He fell against Mal, crying like a child. 'I just want to go home,' he said, between sobs. 'I just want to go home.'

Mal rocked him gently, as he rocked his children, one hand stroking his partner's wiry, greying hair and murmured, 'It's all right. Really. It's all, all right.' As he rocked and soothed he stared at the drug wreckage on the mattress and a line from an old song came into his head. 'I wonder what the poor people are doing tonight,' he thought. And he stroked Solly's head once more.

Twenty-eight

There were two kinds of men in the room. There were the younger Jewish men who had smoked and snorted away their parents' money. And there were the older Jewish men who had smoked and snorted away their own money. The latter said they could not help but feel a certain superiority over the former.

'The thing about me,' Solly said, during his first meeting of Drugs Anonymous, 'is that I'm a self-unmade man. Everything I spent I also at some time earned.'

'Me, I'm self-unmade too,' said a company director from Maida Vale, who wore expensive knitwear and a hangdog expression, even when he smiled.

One of the younger members slapped his palm against his thigh and said, 'You two do not know the pain of being born to money.' Others in the circle nodded their heads and pursed their lips in agreement, at the very thought of the torture they had each suffered by trust fund. 'Our parents say to us that we should succeed. But how can anything we do ever compare with what they have done?' He was heir to the Pekel family fortune, built on their venerable surgical appliance company, whose advertising slogan had long been 'You always have our support'.

'So do *I* have their support? No, I do not. If I suffer from a bad back then maybe my parents will give me a corset to wear. That's the only support they know. Is it any wonder I used drugs? The high gave me the kind of support I needed.'

Solly shook his head. 'My heart bleeds for you,'

he said. 'Almost as much as you bled your parents' bank accounts.'

Dr Gideon Needlebaum looked up from the clipboard where he had been taking notes, blinked behind his thick glasses, and said, 'The point in this group, gentlemen, is to share our experiences. It is not for us to compete with each other.' The twelve men turned to stare at the psychiatrist. The only sound was the echoing tick of the clock on the lounge wall and the gentle hum of the wall heaters. What in God's name did the shrink mean? Not compete? They were doing their best to give up drugs. Did he now also want them to give up the very essence of their culture?

'We're all still finding our way here,' Dr Needlebaum said, to answer the silence. 'Me as well as you. Remember it's one day at a time.' He held up the small blue-bound book that each of them was holding, a copy of *Twelve Steps and Twelve Traditions*.

'That's all it is. One step at a time.' He laid the book back in his lap and tried on what he imagined to be his most sincere and open and non-competitive smile. Needlebaum's was the first Drugs Anonymous group in the UK; he could be no more certain of its success than the men who had agreed to try it but boy, did he want to see results. He was desperate to have a paper accepted for publication in the *Journal of Psychiatry*, if only to establish his organization over and above Narcotics Anonymous, which was also just starting up on this side of the Atlantic. This, surely, was his chance? The twelve-step programme used by Alcoholics Anonymous had been proven to work in the US with other kinds of addicts; maybe it could also work here with the growing number of those with cocaine and prescription drug problems who were checking into the clinic? Perhaps, but only if the patients were genuinely willing to talk about themselves. Lay it on the table. Spill their guts. Talk the talk. It had therefore seemed a good idea to fill his pioneering group entirely with mouthy north London Jews.

Or, as he said to Solly the day Judy and Mal checked him in for his stay at the clinic in Belsize Park, 'We want you to feel free to express yourself here.'

'Really?' Solly said. 'I thought my problem was I'd been expressing myself a little too much.'

Two, long drug-free weeks later he was in the clinic's lounge, where the grey carpet tiles flashed with static electricity and all the plastic moulded chairs were a bright confectionery orange. They were seated in the kind of a circle he had not been part of since infant school.

'Go on, Solly,' Dr Needlebaum said. 'Please. Talk to us. Share with us.'

'OK,' Solly said, rubbing his chin with his hand. 'Here's how it is. My name's Solly Princeton and I'm a recovering cocaine addict. I used drugs for five years. Over five years. Always cocaine, nothing else. Why did I use cocaine? First I used it because it stopped me feeling tired and worn out at the end of the day. Then I decided I liked the way it made me feel, that it made me better at what I did. I liked not to feel tired and worn out. Eventually I found that if I didn't use cocaine I felt tired and worn out.'

There were laughs of recognition from around the circle.

'You know I've been doing some maths since I've been here. Maths is not my good point. My business partner, he does the maths for us. But anyway I've been working things out, adding up the numbers, and I think I must have spent £100 a day on drugs every day for the last five and half years. When you average it out.'

'Yeah,' said another man. 'I've been doing those sort of sums too.' He blew his nose on a paper tissue and, as of reflex, checked the colour. When he was satisfied he went on: '£110 it came out at. Can you imagine that? £110.'

Solly gave a 'well-there-you-go-isn't-life-ludicrous' jerk of the head and was about to carry on when somebody else spoke.

'For me it was £125. What can I tell you? £125 every day of the week. Every week of the year.'

'You call *that* a cocaine habit?' said one of the younger trust-fund casualties. 'For me it was £175 a day.'

'£175 a day?' said a man with long black curly hair, tinted glasses and a gold-plated Rolex. 'Why are you even here in this clinic? I spent £250 a day. God's honest truth. Why would I lie?'

Needlebaum tried to jump in. 'Gentleman, I really think—'

'Of course,' said Solly, furious now that he had ceded ground. 'When I give you a figure of £100 that's only the average. There was one weekend I smoked £3,000 of freebase.'

'With a friend?' said the man to his right

'Who needs a friend when you have three grands' worth of freebase?' said the man with the gold Rolex.

'We all need a friend,' Solly said. 'Luckily I had one. But he didn't smoke freebase.'

Afterwards, when the group had wound up for the day, the company director from Maida Vale invited Solly to go with him to eat cheesecake at a local coffee house.

'You and me, we're of an age,' Arnie Sussman said, extending a hand and a sly wink, building an alliance. 'Let's leave the younger boys to their own devices.'

They sat over coffee and baked cinnamon cheese-cake, made just the way Solly liked it, New York style, with a hard crust, and they talked about their families. Arnie showed him photographs of his children, wreathed in lurid grins, and said he felt guilty every time he looked at them. 'The youngest, she has only ever known me high.'

'Same with my Rachel,' Solly said, running the pad of his finger pointlessly across the picture of his frown-ing daughter. 'Conceived on coke.'

'And all that money we wasted,' Arnie said.

'Yeah, all that money.' They sat in silence, grieving

about what was past. The children they had not talked to. The wives they had troubled. The pound notes they had rolled up, snorted through. Spent.

'You know the thing about drugs that I can't get over?' Solly said.

'What's that?'

'How good a business they are.'

'What?'

'How good a business they are. Look, what is it that makes a good product?'

Arnie Sussman raised his eyebrows. So tell me?

'It's something the consumer wants. Right? Better still, if it's something the consumer needs. Then you want the product to be something not too bulky so you don't get transport costs. Drugs fit the bill. OK so there's unique transport problems with drugs but let's forget those for a moment . . .'

Arnie Sussman was sitting back in his chair, jaw slack, hangdog jowls dragged lower than usual. He was only just getting used to saying drugs were a really bad thing; he didn't feel ready to start finding the good in them as well.

'So with drugs there's demand and they're not bulky. And the best thing about drugs,' Solly continued, 'is the mark-up. Because the consumer really wants it you can charge what you want for it, more or less. True?'

'I suppose so,' Sussman stammered.

'But do you know why most people fuck up in the drug business?'

The other man shook his head.

'They fuck up because they use their own product. It's a unique feature of the drug business. Every other product, you sell it, so you should use it. Me, I'm in the hotel and restaurant business and I like to stay in hotels. Before I was in hotels I was only doing restaurants and I liked to go to restaurants. Before that, kitchen utensils.'

'And you liked to cook?'

'You cook?'

'Yeah, I make the coleslaw in the family.'

'Right, so you get my point. You're well placed to go into the coleslaw business because you eat it. You know about thin cut over thick cut. Mayonnaise coleslaw over vinegar dressed coleslaw. Am I right?' He looked at the other man. Arnie Sussman did indeed look like a coleslaw person, Solly thought. The kind of guy who would niggle about the best way to shred cabbage and add dressing. A details man. Not good at the big picture.

'So?' Solly said. 'Am I right?' Sussman said he was. 'Sure I am. But with drugs, you should never use the product because first, you're too screwed by the drugs to control the business and second, you're always snorting away your own profits. Did you ever meet a drug dealer who wasn't also a drug user? Who wasn't dealing drugs so they could afford to do drugs?' Sussman said he hadn't. 'And weren't these drug dealers all fuck-ups?' Sussman said they were.

'So you see—' Solly forked away another lump of cheesecake – 'If you didn't do the drugs yourself you could drop the price, undercut the opposition and still make a profit.' Another forkful of cinnamon cheesecake. Just like Momma never knew how to make. 'There's another problem with drugs, of course.'

'What's that?'

'Well,' Solly said. 'It's which bit of the business you control. Usually the business is horizontal rather than vertical.'

'Horizontal?'

'Yeah, horizontal. You've got different people controlling different parts of the business. The guys who import the drugs, they don't do the wholesale. There's someone else over here does the wholesale. And the wholesale person doesn't do retail. They pass it on to somebody else over there and maybe they pass it on to somebody else again. They each control their own bit of the business, taking margin as they go.'

'So?'

'So the big boys, the wholesalers and the importers, are missing out on the real profits. In the drugs business the real profits, the big mark-ups are in retail. Providing the product to the end user. That's where the cash is. But that's where all the little people, who sell drugs to pay for their own drug use, are working. See. That's the problem with the drugs business. It's dysfunctional.'

Solly laid down his fork. 'Listen to us,' he said, oblivious to the fact that he was the only one who had been talking. 'We sound like we could be discussing kosher chickens or Pekel surgical appliances. Wholesale this, retail that. Profit margins. The whole bit.' He chased away the last piece of crumbling cheesecake and ran it around his mouth, pressing the fragments against his teeth with his tongue. 'And you know the thing I didn't mention?'

'No,' the shell-shocked Sussman said.

'The thing I didn't mention is that drugs fuck up your head, burn your money and stop you from being a good father to your kids.' He studied his empty plate, waiting for a smart-arse wisecrack from the other side of the table. Only when nothing came did he look up and remember that Arnie Sussman was not Mal Jones, and that few men were.

Twenty-nine

Dr Needlebaum said, 'We do not have to be literal about this.' He held the little book aloft, index finger wedged between the relevant pages, the covers held closed around it so that *Twelve Steps and Twelve Traditions* looked like a pair of blue-bound jaws gripping his hand. Consuming him.

'This is just a way in.'

The group stared at the book in their laps.

Step One: We admitted we were powerless over our addiction.

Solly could handle that. He *was* powerless. Like a boat out at sea with no engine. Afraid of sinking. Afraid of drowning in an infinite stretch of salty water robbed of horizon.

Just afraid.

Step Two: Came to believe that a Power greater than ourselves could restore us to sanity.

'You told us it wasn't religious,' Arnie Sussman said.

'It isn't religious,' said Needlebaum. 'Not in the classic sense of the word.'

'What's a power greater than ourselves then? A power with a capital P, yet?'

'That's for you to decide.'

'My mother is a power greater than myself but she's not going to help me, is she?'

'All you need is an open mind.'

'But look at step three.'

Step Three: Made a decision to turn our will and our lives over to the care of God as we understood him.

With a sharp intake of breath Sussman said, 'Here.

234

Look here. It says God. You're saying that's not religious?'

Needlebaum said, '"God as we understood him".'

'My mother already thinks *I'm* the Messiah,' muttered another member of the group. 'So now do I pray to myself?'

'What you need to concentrate on is the idea of a power greater than yourself. Just that. This group, us, Drugs Anonymous could be that power. Don't you see? With our support you could get through this. One day at a time. All it's saying is you don't do this alone.'

Solly raised one finger. 'What,' he said 'if you do believe in God?'

There was an uncomfortable silence, of the kind that follows the smashing of a plate.

'Well then,' Dr Needlebaum said, 'you understand what is meant by a power greater than yourself.'

In the ten weeks he had spent with the group, attending meetings every other day, drinking tepid coffee, sitting on uncomfortable plastic chairs and forever talking, the Twelve Steps had infused Solly not so much with belief, but with memories. When he heard the word 'God' he recalled a childhood punctuated by warm mornings in shul on his father's lap, when Ralph Princeton still thought it was his duty to make sure his only son attended. There was the soft satin rustle of his father's tallis against his face and its earth and dust smell carried from the bottom of the wardrobe, where it lived in between Shabbat services. He recalled tying together the tassels at its fringes, to produce unsolvable knots of silvery thread, and his father irritably trying to untie them. He remembered the unconvincing smile of the rabbi, tall and thin and austere in his shadow-black robe, an admonishment for sins not yet committed, and the little biscuits arranged on plates for the Kiddush after the service which never tasted as nice as they looked.

He remembered his mother cleaning out the kitchen cupboards for Passover, each year being appalled by the dust and dirt and grease that had gathered in the back, each year swearing she would not wait for the next Passover to do the cleaning. And each year leaving it until the next Passover. He remembered his grandfather, hunched and grim with the task at hand, grinding his way through the seder service in a gruff Hebrew that sounded more like the noise a television makes when heard muffled through the wall, than a real language. And his mother imploring the old man to hurry up lest the dinner be ruined.

Solly remembered all of this and he thought: I am a Jew.

One afternoon, he found himself near the West London Synagogue and, with time to spare before his group meeting at the clinic, went inside. He took a black crêpe paper cupple from the pile stacked at the back and sat quietly in the shadows staring at the bimah. He felt ashamed of the piece of paper perched upon his head. It was temporary. It made *him* feel temporary. They were meant for Gentiles attending weddings or Bar Mitzvahs. I am a temporary Jew, he thought. No more. Later he wanted to claim that he had simply lost track of time, to make his hours in there sound like a mistake, but he knew exactly when he should have made a move and chose not to. He found the sight of the scrolls, sheathed in their bejewelled velvet coats of gold and red, altogether too intoxicating; these were his memories made solid. Here he could begin to gather back fragments of a life he knew he had mislaid. To make the temporary permanent again.

I do not need to invent a higher power, he thought to himself as he looked upwards and away into the grand vaulted ceiling. There *is* a higher power.

When Solly had been staying at the clinic Mal had visited each morning to keep his partner up to speed with business. It was as much ritual as practical, the discussion of hotels and restaurants relevant only because it gave them a point of contact within the alien world of group meetings and therapy sessions. Now that he was out and back working at the Square they continued their meetings, poring over maps, studying hotel specifications, discussing financing deals.

One morning, while Mal was crunching his way through a calculation Solly said, 'Me and Judy, we've decided to move shuls.'

Mal continued to tap away at his calculator. 'Makes sense. It's a drag from your place back to Edgware. Where you going? West London?'

'No. Temple Fortune.'

Mal continued to work the calculator for a few more seconds then stopped and looked up, over the top of his glasses.

'Temple Fortune's a United synagogue.'

'Yeah, I know.'

Now Mal put down the machine and sat back. 'You're joining an orthodox shul?'

Solly nodded. 'Yes,' he said. 'I'm joining an orthodox shul. Rabbi Grearson there, me and him, we've been talking a lot of late. He's a good man.'

'I didn't know you gave a damn.'

'I didn't. But, you know, things have changed recently. I'm doing a bit of a personal audit.'

'Anything I should know about?'

'Maybe. Nothing heavy. Just been thinking things through. Came to the conclusion that I'd seriously undervalued one of my assets.' Anybody catching fragments of the conversation would have assumed they were still talking business.

'So now you're bumping up its book value?'

'That's a way of putting it.'

Mal stared at his partner, and tried to work out what was going on in his head.

'Really, mate,' Solly said. 'It's nothing for you to worry about. You should be pleased for me. I've been doing this Twelve Step thing. It's all about, you know, going to the meetings to keep yourself on the straight and narrow, having something to believe in, trusting that will keep you clean. And I've realized that I don't need that because I'm lucky enough to be Jewish.'

Mal was surprised at how uncomfortable Solly's announcement was making him feel. Mal knew his Jewishness was a part of him in the way tall men know they will always be tall. They can't pretend to be short or even just of average height. They can't pretend to be anything other than that which accident of birth has made them, nor would they wish to. But their tallness is not what they want to be recognized for. It is only a part of them. When they were out in the suburbs, Mal and Solly had not needed to think about these things. Who there would draw attention to what was obvious? But they no longer were in the suburbs. That was another history.

'If you want to go to shul a bit more why don't you just stick at Edgwarebury?'

'That's stuff from the past. I've got to move on, look at things in a new way. I've decided to stop going to Drugs Anonymous. The solution for me lies elsewhere.'

'And you think Temple Fortune will give you what you're after?'

'The shul I go to is only a part of it. I like them and they like me. But for me it's about, you know, the rituals. Keeping the laws. I'm nothing if I don't observe.'

'You're not going to turn Hasid on me are you? Grow yourself a beard and get a heart murmur.'

Solly laughed. 'No, trust me. Though they're good people too. I had conversations with them. The Lubavitch, they run this outreach programme for people recovering from drug dependency . . .'

Mal could not believe what he was hearing. 'Those snaggle-toothed medieval throwbacks?'

'Don't judge them on their dress sense. Seriously. It just makes it easier for them to decide what to wear in the morning. Shall I wear the black, the black or the

238

black?' He mimed riffling through a wardrobe. 'Oh to hell with it, I'll just go with the black.'

'You talked to these people?'

'Sure, but it wasn't right for me. I want to live in the world.'

'I'm glad to hear it.'

'There's a contribution I've got to make.'

'Too fucking right.' Mal slapped his palm across his mouth even as the expletive escaped his mouth. 'Sorry.'

Solly waved him away. 'All I'm doing is going to shul, keeping kosher, the basic stuff. Laying tefillin. It's still me, though. I'm still Solly Princeton. Nowhere in the Torah does it specifically say you can't say fuck.'

'Yeah, but I'm sure it says you mustn't talk dirty.'

'Well, I've made my choice. I'm living here in the world. I'm being a Jew my way which is being more of a Jew than I was. But I'm a Jew who still says fuck.'

'Sounds like that song. I'm just a girl who can't say no. I'm just a Jew who still says fuck.'

'Wouldn't sell. Stick with the original lyrics.'

Outside a police car roared past, blaring horn dampened by the thickened glass. Instinctively they both turned to look but already it was gone. Just another day in Central London. Street dramas, quickly played out.

'What does all this mean for Sinai?' Mal said. It had sounded like such a simple question in his head, but the moment it had escaped into the room it seemed to be weighed down by its own self-importance.

'What do you mean?'

'You and me, we're Sinai. The moment something happens to us it changes the business.'

'You think so?'

'Of course. Something Divinia's old man said to me once. Syd said to me that a business was like a marriage. You are part of both and vital to both. Something happens to you it means something happens to the business too.'

Solly scratched the back of his neck a little uneasily. 'Well . . .'

'Yes?'

'I was thinking about the way we do food.'

'At the diners or the hotels?'

'Both, I suppose.'

'What's the problem?'

'Kosher style is the problem.'

'What do you mean?'

'Nothing we serve is truly kosher. It's just kosher style. Meaningless. It's that thing about being Jew-ish. We make like we're just a bit into the Jewish thing, not the whole deal. Now, only if I stick to vegetarian can I eat in my own restaurants. It's a bit odd, no?'

'You want that all our kitchens should go kosher?'

Solly shrugged. 'We're Jews. We're a Jewish business. I think we forget that too easily. Let's make an issue out of what we are. Anyway at the diners it won't change what we do. Same menus. Just kosher. The regulars who don't care won't notice the difference but we'll get lots of new customers who will. It makes business sense.'

'It will cost.'

'I'll pay, then.'

Mal thought for a moment. In principle this was completely at odds with what he wanted for Sinai: he wanted the firm to be free from the burden of its own history. Deep in his gut he felt certain that only if they stopped looking backwards could they ever hope to move forwards. But Solly had thought it through. He was talking this up in terms of business, not the Talmud. Mal could hardly argue against his partner on a point of principle that he could not prove. He certainly did not want to challenge him. 'No need to pay. This is a company expense. What about the hotels?'

'No big deal. Just get the kitchens certified for kosher caterers. That way we can start doing Bar Mitzvahs, weddings. Become the simcha kings. It's ludicrous. All the goys in town are getting the trade and we're not. It's about time. It makes good business sense too.'

'You have a point.'

'Just been thinking these things through.'

'Anything else? Want to put a yeshiva in the basement of the Grand?'

'No, the nightclub is fine as it is. There is one more thing, though.'

'Should I brace myself?'

'It's no big deal. The Department of Trade and Industry is mounting a trade mission to Latvia.'

'Where?'

'Latvia, on the Baltic. Part of the Soviet Union.'

'Oh, right.'

'Riga is the capital.'

'Of course.' Now his partner was giving him geography lessons.

'I want to go.'

'What will you be doing on this trade mission?'

'I think we tour tractor factories and steel plants.'

'Sounds . . .' he paused. 'Thrilling. After all, Jews have always been big in the tractor business.'

Solly managed a fixed smile. 'Riga is where my family came from. I want to go back and, you know, find my roots.'

Mal said 'Be my guest' because he could think of no particular reason why Solly should not go. What troubled him more was that he could also not come up with an explanation for why the man should want to go at all. To a place he had never heard of? To search for signs of people he had never met? Was not life complicated enough without this? 'And don't forget to bring me back a tractor,' he said. 'Maybe we'll break with 2,000 years of tradition and move into farming.' Beneath the usual currency of their jokes and gags the two partners had always exchanged, Mal couldn't help but wonder what kind of man would return from such a trip.

Thirty

For days after Solly's announcement Mal carried himself about uneasily, on account of an emptiness in the pit of his stomach that he could not quickly identify. At night he would lie awake, focusing on this space, trying to define its shape. He took to prodding at his stomach, three fingers held together as he had seen doctors do on television when diagnosing appendicitis, searching through his vital organs in the hope of finding one that was not there. A physical emptiness. Would that not be a relief? To find that something from his centre really was missing? Mal Jones, born without a kidney. Minus a spleen. Have pity. The man has no pancreas.

He can not pancreate. Would that not explain everything? This lack of function?

'Divinia,' he said one night, nudging her from the narcotic depths of sleep. 'Feel here. Right here. Is there not a gap? Should I make an appointment to see a doctor? Am I missing my pancreas?'

His wife dragged her hand sleepily onto his stomach and played with the lazy layer of fat that had recently gathered there. 'You've got everything you need,' she mumbled, 'and a little bit more.' And returned to unconsciousness.

The next Friday Mal sat in his office, palms laid flat on his desk, trying to understand the meaning of Solly's new-found interest in Judaism. Was it a discovery? Or a rediscovery? A return, maybe? A conversion? Surely not a conversion? Conversions are what you do to lofts, not people. He settled on the phrase 'He's become a bit of a frumer', precisely because it described nothing apart from his own lack of comprehension. As he considered the practicalities of Solly's new life that Friday afternoon, he pictured in his mind the lighting of candles which would take place in only a few hours' time; the saying of prayers and the conspiracy of intimacy that accompanied them. This, he thought, is what Judy and Solly do together. It is what binds them. She has followed him into this life. The Blow Job Queen has become the good Jewish wife.

It was only then that he came to understand his emptiness. It was envy. The same wretched envy he had felt ten years before when he had last recognized the completeness of his partner's life. Then Solly had been blessed with work he enjoyed and a woman he loved. Now he had the woman he loved, the work he enjoyed and a faith by which to understand it all.

Full house. Five years on coke seemed almost a price worth paying for the prize of such certainty.

'Where is God when I need him?' Mal muttered under his breath.

In the first few months after they married, Divinia had continued to light the candles on Friday nights, just as Syd Greenspan had said she would. She had cooked the dinner and said all the blessings because she had come to understand that Mal could not. These were her rituals and not his. As time passed he even began to search out events to keep him away from the house on Friday nights. He would take business meetings or organize trips that would keep him out of town or simply stay late at the office. 'It's the firm, my love,' he would say. 'The firm has to come first.' It bothered him that the woman he had married should observe something he couldn't even start to take seriously.

Occasionally, when he was not there, Divinia too would decide to miss a week, and then another. Absence was habit forming, made easier by upheaval. Six years after moving to Hampstead Garden Suburb Mal, Divinia and the boys packed up once more and shifted to the green inclines of Highgate and a brand new house of crimson red brick with a carriage drive and a dramatic portico above a balcony supported on brand new Doric columns and real gold-plated taps in every bathroom.

'It's taken me ten years to get from Edgware to Highgate,' he said to Solly, when he announced the move. 'Not bad, eh?'

'It's better than the forty years it took the Children of Israel to cross the Sinai, I suppose. Then again you did have a map.'

'Yeah, but what use is a map to a Jew? We've got a terrible sense of direction. Why do you think it took them those forty years to cross the desert? They kept arguing over which way was north.'

Just as Mal and Solly's ancestors had shed devotions in the journey from the East End to the suburbs, so Divinia all but gave up observing Shabbat when they shifted south. Now the lighting of the candles was little more than a stunt, reserved for when Divinia's parents came to dinner.

'Look what good parents we are,' Mrs Greenspan would say to her husband, as the flames guttered in the breeze from their breath. 'That they light the candles. So we have done our job. From generation to generation.'

Divinia would smile uncomfortably just as Mal would ask Syd to perform the honour of blessing the bread and Syd would do so, with a nod and a wink.

Later, in the office, Solly said, 'For me the lighting of the candles and the saying of the blessings is a way to remind myself that I'm Jewish. If we do not follow the halakha we are nothing.'

'Who needs blessings?' Mal said. 'If I want to be reminded that I'm Jewish all I need to do is go to that pub over there.' He pointed out of his office window to the crumbling local frequented by Irish navvies, pink-faced and whale-bellied, who gathered there from across the building sites of Soho. 'I go in and I feel like

244

a Hasid, I'm telling you. Frock coat, the lot.'

For another reminder of his Jewishness he could try listening to the nagging of his loins. Divinia was his wife and between them lay a careful mixture of admiration, respect and the odd spark of attraction which, when combined, Mal took to be marital love. But whenever he was with Heidi he still found himself desperate for a taste of the forbidden. It was her laugh. Her stillness. The curve of her waist. The exotica of her clean-scrubbed, Protestant soul. When they were alone he would ask desperate questions in search of desperate answers.

'Things between you and Benny these days . . . ?'

'Perfect,' she said, holding her daughter by both hands and swinging her this way and that to a chorus of giggles. 'Since this one arrived . . . and up goes Natatsha and down goes Natasha . . . everything's been great. Changed man. Doesn't go near the bookies.'

Mal could not help but feel disappointed. If things had been going badly for Heidi then she would have needed to be consoled. And if she had needed to be consoled, well then . . .

He buried the thought.

Instead his pornographic mind spied on women, his eye picking out the single features that matched Heidi's most, from those he saw in an airport crowd or passing by on the pavement. There, he would see a mouth; here, a clear stretch of forehead; and look at her with that perfect button nose. So Heidi. So very, very Heidi. From these he could assemble the part-work woman of his fantasies, who was not his sister-in-law and therefore not forbidden. Who was not Divinia, and therefore not grossly familiar. Better still, who was not Jewish.

He thought to act on these fantasies and once did, bedding a young woman with a voice as soft and un-demanding as Heidi's, that he had met in the bar of the Sinai Manchester one quiet Friday night. But it had been a desultory and unsettling kind of sex, full of single-word sentences and sharp gasps which sounded as if they were made in fear. He did not learn her secrets. Afterwards, as she lay uncertainly in his arms, she had said 'thank you'. It had made Mal smile for the first time that evening and think of Solly and what he had been doing that Friday night. Which in turn made him feel homesick. He decided that fantasy was better left unfulfilled.

In any case was not the reality of his life more than a match for certain kinds of fantasy? Of course it was. He was a wealthy man, worth millions. A few million, anyway. And he would be worth much more as soon as the company was floated on the Stock Exchange, as soon it would have to be, to repay the investors. Still, he already had the baggage of wealth. He owned a Mercedes and so did his wife. There was a driver for when he did not wish to drive, and the house with its brand new cherry tree and freshly laid turf, for when he sought privacy. There were marble floors and thick carpets and leather armchairs, just like at Syd Greenspan's place, and a rose garden out back. Divinia bought couture and met her ladies for charity luncheons. She entertained at home when entertainment was called for, with canapés and salmon, and took her tennis lessons. The boys went to expensive nursery and preparatory schools where they learned to pray to a God in three parts and speak like little boys who had never been anywhere near Edgware. Mal smoked thick cigars, sipped tiny measures of ancient Cognac from enormous glasses and even collected art.

Collected art!

'Landscapes only,' he would say, cigar in hand. 'Only buy something you like. That's the rule. Never buy as an investment.' Although every painting that was chosen for him by dealers soon doubled in value – and some never even hung in his home. Such was the way of the rich.

Now Mal and Divinia Jones sat at wealthy dinner tables, with captains of industry and minor politicians who talked of the new dawn that was breaking over Britain, colouring about the cheeks when they but uttered the name of the Prime Minister, as if they, like Solly, had recently been infected with a religion. Mal was a young businessman on the up and they liked him, these blue-eyed men in their pin-striped suits. He represented the spirit of the age, they said. He was an entrepreneur. A man who understood the imperatives of the service industry and how it could be made to replace the cumbersome demands of manufacturing. Mal made money from money from money and sold Britain abroad. What could be better?

'Have you met Margaret Thatcher?' said the chairman of one bank, when Mal went, as he did so often these days, for lunch in the City. Mal said he had not yet had the pleasure.

'Ah, well then you must,' said his host. 'You really must.'

And he did.

It was at a reception, at 10 Downing Street, hosted by the Secretary of State for Trade and Industry, for leading figures in what had recently become known as 'the leisure industry'. Solly was in the Baltic, guest of another part of the DTI, and Divinia had simply absented herself, bored now with what she called 'those dull men in their heavy suits'.

'You go,' she said. 'You'll have more fun without me. Anyway I cannot stand those grand houses and the way they always go on about their original features. For me, there is nothing wrong with reproduction. Lasts longer. And who can tell the difference?'

And so he stood alone in the corner of a large crowded room, trying to ignore the reproachful gaze of the painted and varnished grandees hung on the wall, in their gilt frames. But he could not avoid staring at the portraits. They each of them looked like the kind of men to refuse a Jew a loan; bold and cocksure. The Cuthberts of their day, with the authority to refuse. Now they were dead, no longer in power, no longer the gatekeepers. And he, Mal Jones, was here, at the heart of Government. A leading figure in the leisure industry. Mal Jones, the Edgware boy, he thought to himself sipping his white wine spritzer and rolling it about his mouth as if it were whisky. 'At Downing Street.'

'Good evening. Gerald Fulker and you are . . . ?'

Mal turned away from the paintings. He recalled the man's face slightly, from television news: the greasy crimson baldness; the capillaries that scampered away across his cheeks as if trying to escape his inflamed nose. Fulker wore a classic heavy suit, pinstriped and ash smudged, the uniform of the Tory MP, and he gripped a tumbler of liquor. Wasn't he a junior minister? An under-secretary? Bag-carrier-in-chief?

'Mal Jones, Sinai Corporation.'

The other man threw his head back slowly, mouth open. 'Aaaah,' he said. 'Sinai. Yes of course. The great Sinai.'

'Thank you.'

'The wonder company.'

'We do our best.'

'Of course you do. Your lot always do.'

'Well thank you again. We're a young company but we're trying to think ahead.'

Fulker dropped his voice and leaned towards Mal so that he could smell the raw alcohol on his breath. 'Of course, Maggie loves your lot.' He nodded towards the Prime Minister who was already being glad-handed about the room, stopping at huddles of suits to greet and shake.

'She loves Sinai? I didn't realize . . .'

'No, no, no,' Fulker said, eyes flicking hither and thither, as if checking that no-one was listening. '*Your* lot.' He grinned. 'Of course, I'm sure she thinks Sinai is marvellous too. We all do. But she really has a soft spot for your crowd generally. You know. Generally.'

Mal studied the man's face. What crowd? He hadn't been part of a crowd since the days they all went out to eat ice-cream in Chalk Farm. 'I mean, for example,' Fulker went on 'she adores Leon. Thinks he's just the thing.'

Now he understood. Leon Brittan. In the cabinet as Chief Secretary to the Treasury and tipped for bigger things. Also Jewish.

'Do you know Leon?' Fulker said.

'No.'

'Oh, I thought you people all knew each other.'

'There are more than a quarter of a million Jews in Britain,' Mal said taking a sip and looking round the room, trying to appear uninterested. Thatcher was advancing towards him.

'A quarter of a million? Well who would have thought it. I never knew we allowed that many in. Do you know why Maggie loves Jews?' He hadn't paused for breath between thoughts. Mal shook his head. 'Because you're the Americans of Britain.'

'Sorry?'

'Maggie loves Americans, you see. Can't stand them myself. So bloody full of themselves. But her nibs adores them. Likes their noisiness and the way they are always out there trying to make money. That's why she likes your lot. You're all immigrants too. And you're noisy and you're not afraid to make money either. Jolly well done, say I. Just don't start sounding like sodding Americans, that's all I ask. And look, here she comes now.'

'Good evening, Gerald,' she said in her hinged see-saw of a voice, and turned her gaze on Mal. She was wearing a turquoise two-piece suit buttoned to the neck, and was standing with her legs just slightly too far apart on low heels, one foot positioned a little behind the other so she could lean her head backwards towards the civil servant taking up the rear. Her hair was solid, in thick lacquered curves, and her eyes sparkled and bulged. A man with a clipboard leaned into the Prime Minister's ear and whispered to her. 'And this is Mr . . .' He hesitated over the name on the sheet in front of him. 'Mr Malcolm Jones of the Sinai Corporation.'

'Ah, Mr Jones . . .' They shook hands. Mal was about to correct his name but She was already speaking.

'I do so like companies like yours . . .'

'Thank you very much.'

'Family companies . . .'

'Well yes, up to a—'

'Built up from hard work in one generation.'

'Of course . . .' It was not a conversation. His words merely punctuated what she had to say. She emphasized her thoughts with one arm held up at chest height, hand clasped in a tiny fist, making little jabbing movements as She spoke. Her eyes were focused, he thought, on the spot between his own.

'But then you do believe in the work ethic . . .'

'We try to . . .'

'Rabbi Jakobovits talks so much about the family. Do you know the Chief Rabbi?'

'No, I'm afraid—'

'A pity. A very great man. You must meet him.' She nodded her head at every word. 'He believes strongly in the family and so do I.'

'It's important—'

'Without the family we are nothing. Nothing at all. And companies like yours make all the difference. Keep up the good work.' One last jab of the fist and she was gone.

'See what I mean,' Fulker said, as she moved on to the next group. 'Quotes the Chief Rabbi before the Archbishop of Canterbury. Hates the Archbishop. Think he's a bloody Trotskyite. But she loves your Jakobovits.'

'He's not *my* Jakobovits,' Mal said briskly. 'I'm a Reform Jew.'

'What's that, old boy? I know you're a Jew. What do you think I've been talking about all this time?'

'I'm not entirely sure,' Mal said. 'You must excuse me.'

250

Outside, on Whitehall, he hailed a taxi. The driver leaned across to the open window. 'Where to, mate?'

Mal looked back up Downing Street behind him. Until that evening he had been certain of his achievements. He was the Edgware boy who had travelled. Granted, there wasn't exactly an ocean between his childhood home and his present one. And nor was it a rags to riches story. It was more off-the-peg to bespoke. But even so. He had made it. He owned a house with pillars. He believed himself to have become a solid, copper-bottomed part of the establishment. Not someone who was just playing at it, but a serious, important figure who had been given the keys to the door. Now he wasn't so sure.

He turned back to the taxi. 'Do you know the way to the Warsaw Ghetto?' he said, grinning.

The driver looked suspiciously at him. 'Is that in south London? 'Cause I don't go south of the river . . .'

'Forget it,' Mal said. 'It was a joke. I live in Highgate. Take me there.' He climbed into the back.

Thirty-one

Solly had expected to be haunted by ghosts in Latvia, but instead it was the emptiness that struck him most. The road from Riga airport was clear of traffic, as if the locals had turned their backs on the automobile in disgust, and the verges were free of advertising bill-boards, save for posters proclaiming the wonders of the Soviet Union. The view of the fields and woods was broken only by the occasional road sign for the city ahead and by tall spindle lampposts, stretching vainly upwards like saplings seeking out the nourishment of the sun. As dust fell the lamps, those that worked, cast a sickly white light over the cracked and broken con-crete of the roads below, which meagre glow only emphasized just how dark the city would be at night. In London the night skies always glowed rust and umber from the sodium burn of the suburbs. To Solly it was the colour of home. Here, the city seemed to retreat into itself, as the daylight drained from the sky.

'It makes you wonder if the morning will ever come again,' Solly said to the man next to him on the trans-fer bus, an official from the British Embassy in Moscow, who had introduced himself simply as Cosgrave.

'In winter it barely does,' he said. Solly shuddered at the thought and gave thanks that they were there in May. To be in such blackness. Hidden by shadow. What horror.

Everything about Latvia and its capital city seemed empty or half finished or neglected, as if the super-structure had been completed but somebody had forgotten the details. In his room of beige and plywood, high up in the Hotel Latvija, a brutalist tower block thrown up with devotion to utilitarianism, there were stains on the carpet and sagging holes in the bed. The walls were bare and above the unstable, rattling sink was a strip light that flickered and buzzed when he turned it on the first time but then failed completely afterwards. In the morning, from his window, he would be able to see over the fractured roofs of the old town and down to the river beyond, but now it was just so much shadow and black. He picked up the phone to call Judy, just to hear her voice, but was told there would be no international lines until the morning. He asked for a local phone directory. After waiting an hour for it to arrive, he was ordered to come and collect it himself from a man with a cigarette glued to his lip by stale saliva. These were the joys of the Soviet Union in the spring of 1982.

Solly knew Yankel Morowitz's name as part of family lore, but that was all. Running his finger down the 'Ms' in the phone book he found only half a dozen people called Morowitz. When he tried the numbers, on an old plastic phone whose dial stuck constantly on the five, he discovered they were either for lines that were unobtainable or for lines which belonged to people who spoke only Russian. That had been Solly's plan. To phone up the Morowitz families of modern Riga and introduce himself, a fragment of the old, sent abroad. Already, the idea was exhausted. The next morning, over a breakfast of pale, sweaty cheese and dark rye bread, he asked Cosgrave if he would mind acting as an intermediary, translating on the phone for him.

'Morowitz?' the diplomat said with a frown. 'It sounds . . .'

'I'm Jewish,' Solly said, with what he hoped sounded like pride.

Cosgrave nodded slowly. 'Things are not . . .' He looked uncomfortably away to a thin man with a hint of moustache on the other side of the dining room who had been billed as one of their state tourist guides, but who was clearly there to keep an eye on them. 'Things are not great for Jews in the Soviet Union right now.'

'I know that.'

'It might be better if you tried to contact them from London on your return.' He looked down at his plate, embarrassed. 'For their sake as well as yours. Then again even phoning from London may put them at risk. I'm sorry.'

That morning they took a short walking tour of the old town, along narrow cobbled lanes from which countless stones had been gouged and not replaced, leaving raw gaps, like the holes that children develop in their mouths as they discard their first set of teeth. There were Romanesque and Gothic arches and spires, heavily sculpted façades and once-grand Hanseatic warehouses for the merchants who, in another time, had made the city their home. But all of the buildings were now in deep need of repair and many seemed dead and deserted. Shop fronts were indicated only by a wider stretch of window, most shelves empty beyond, or a patient queue from a doorway hidden in gloom. Their guide told them of great plans to remove these 'obsolete old buildings. And then we can have something the people can use, worthwhile buildings all the way to the river. That is our plan.'

On a corner Solly stopped and closed his eyes and breathed in, hoping that in that draught of foreign air he might catch the scent of an ancestor, or at least a visceral idea of what it had been to live in Riga when it was not as it now was. But instead all he felt was gratitude that a relation he knew nothing of had decided this was not the place in which his family should live. It was his good fortune to have grown up in Edgware. Those roots were exotic enough.

The tour was only made worthwhile by a glimpse of a building down a side street that made Solly stop and stare. For a few seconds, as the group moved on, he stood studying that part of the façade he could see. He thought to peel off there and then to check if it really was what he thought it was but, as the tour guide's brittle voice began to echo away from him, he decided it was not the right time. Instead he noted the street name and marked it on the map he had been given at the hotel.

On the Saturday morning two days later, after endless tours of tractor factories by fat men in bad suits, he returned to the old building at number 6 Peitavas Street. It was three storeys high, and built of a grey stone that glowed with a pinkish tinge in the watery morning sunlight. He looked upwards, across the ornate if dilapidated façade to what he thought he had seen during the walking tour. And there it was. A Star of David. The building was in need of repair, like every other building in the area. That much was clear. But it did not appear to be empty. There were grey net curtains at the windows of the upper floors and he thought he could just see the smudged glow of an electric light somewhere deep inside one of the rooms. Solly walked up the two low steps at the front and, feeling in his pocket for the reassuring soft velvet of his cupple, pushed open the wooden door. It took him into a narrow lobby. Before him was another set of doors behind which he could hear the murmur of voices. Softly he pushed those open too and went inside.

The synagogue was simple, to the point of being spartan. He could see none of the rich colours that signified a shul to him. Just a few rows of wooden benches around a central bimah, encased in the same kind of plywood with which the hotel had been decorated. There were a dozen men in there, and most were elderly. Barely a minyan, Solly thought to himself. And soon even they will die. Only a few of them were wearing prayer shawls. The galleries, where the women would sit, were empty, so that the naked walls vaulted upwards to a cracked and shabby ceiling.

An old man with a ragged covering of white beard noticed him first. He stopped reading aloud, as if disturbed by a noise, and looked up from his book. One by one the other men looked up until the murmur of noise had ceased altogether and Solly felt backed up against the door by the intensity of their stares. The first man stepped out from his seat and spoke in a language Solly took to be Latvian. It certainly was not Russian.

'I'm sorry but I'm English.' The man shrugged and looked across to one of his friends, a round man with dark, sad eyes, who put down his book and walked over. He extended his hand and in a thickly accented English said 'Shabbat, shalom. Would you like to join us?'

'Yes,' Solly said. 'I would like that. I would like that very much.'

He could follow the service, despite its local eccentricities, and gave full voice to the Amidah and the Aleynu and the Shema when they were reached. For a moment, as he recited the prayer – 'Shema yisrael, adonai elohainu adonai echad . . .' – he felt the warm glow of recognition, as if finally in these simple words he had found a point of connection with Yankel Morowitz. But as he looked about the room, at faces which would not have seemed out of place at his own shul in Temple Fortune, he realized the connection was simply with other Jews. There were no ghosts here. None, at least, with family connections.

Afterwards, when the service was done, he was invited back for Shabbat lunch and after making the necessary protestations that he did not wish to be any trouble, swiftly accepted. The round man with the sad eyes introduced himself as Yosif Feldman and said, 'We do not get many visitors here. There are so many people who would like to talk to you.'

They drove, six of them crammed into the car with more following on behind, to an apartment block amid many like it on the edge of the city, and walked up grey concrete steps to the third floor. The door was opened by Feldman's wife, who held Solly's hand in both of hers and said, 'We will try to make you comfortable in the space that we have. It is not much, but . . .'

Eight of them squeezed around the table for a heavy lunch of chicken and dumplings and fried cabbage with caraway seeds; others perched on chairs about the room, a plate on their lap, to listen.

'There are so few of you,' Solly said.

'There are more of us in Riga than this morning,' Feldman said. 'But not everybody feels happy to be seen in synagogue. The authorities, they . . .'

'Is that true? I had heard in London that you couldn't even go to shul but I didn't really believe it.'

'Oh, they won't stop us from going, not often. But they keep an eye on us and some people, they do not like to make waves. That is why it is only us old men who go to the synagogue. What do we have to care now at our age?' He translated his last comment for those around the table who did not speak English and they all laughed.

Feldman pulled at a piece of chicken with his fork. 'But more come to Hebrew lessons and to history lessons.'

'Where do you hold them?'

He shrugged. 'Here. And in Gregory's apartment.' He pointed down the table to another man who had been at the synagogue that morning. 'It is a squeeze. Sometimes with thirty or forty people in here, maybe more.' Solly looked around the cramped living room and tried to imagine it filled to bursting. There was a pair of black, vinyl-covered armchairs and to one side a cheap wall unit, once more made of the familiar veneer plywood, stacked with books and papers and in pride of place, at the centre, a silver menorah.

Another man spoke. 'But often they don't let us hold even those meetings. The militiamen come, they arrest us, take our names. Lock us up for a while. They don't like it when they see so many Jews in one place.' Solly looked nervously at the numbers already gathered there. Occasionally there was a knock at the front door and others arrived, stepping in quietly to the room with a gentle nod of the head to the crowd at the table. 'Don't worry,' said the man. 'The militia only come when we organize in advance. When we do not organize, like today, then they do not come for us. Chaos is better than order.'

Somebody said, Why are you here?'

'My family is from Riga.'

'Their name?'

'Morowitz.'

A gentle mutter went around the room. People had been making calls from the telephone out in the hall throughout the meal, bringing in the steady flow of new arrivals. Now someone lifted the receiver again and dialled.

'Do they talk of us much in London?' Gregory said. 'The refusniks?'

Solly had seen the word used in the *Jewish Chronicle* and occasionally Rabbi Grearson had asked the congregation to pray for the Jews of the Soviet Union, but he had never thought he would hear anybody use the term to describe themselves. It seemed so melodramatic.

'They do talk of you,' Solly said. 'There are appeals. Charity.' Feldman looked satisfied. 'How many of you have applied to leave the Soviet Union?'

A dozen hands went up around the room. 'So many? Have none of you been told you can go?'

'My daughter,' Gregory said proudly, 'is in Brooklyn, New York, since last year. I have asked to join her.'

'What have they said?'

'Why should the Americans have the profit of my labour?'

'You should protest,' Solly said, genuinely outraged, and the room rang with laughter.

'So we should all be like Shcharansky?' Feldman said. 'To be a prisoner of conscience is honourable but still you are a prisoner, whatever kind of prisoner. We have families to care for. It is enough of a protest that we go to shul and hold Hebrew lessons.'

There was a knock at the front door and a muttering of voices from the hall. Feldman looked up over Solly's head and his face broke into a wide grin. 'Ah, at least, Stefan is here.'

Solly turned round in his seat. 'Mr Solomon Princeton,' Feldman said, making Solly's name sound improbably exotic, 'meet Stefan Morowitz.'

If Solly had hoped that genetics would hold out down the generations he was to be disappointed. Stefan Morowitz was a man in his early thirties and was as thin and tall as Solly was short and stocky. He had a prominent Adam's apple set in a scrawny neck, and a mop of brown hair flecked with grey. The only feature they shared was their one long eyebrow. First they shook hands, the tall man grinning broadly to show a mouthful of yellowed and twisted teeth. Then, to the applause of the room, they embraced. Stefan spoke a few words in Latvian.

Solly turned to Feldman for a translation. 'He says he is glad to see the family is doing all right. They were beginning to wonder what had happened to you all because you do not write letters.' Another gale of laughter swept the room.

'Tell him we're doing fine. Just fine. That we've been busy.' They were still holding hands from when they shook.

'He says when they let him go he will come to London too.'

'He has also applied to leave?' Solly looked back to the man he was now certain was his relation, though he had no proof

'Of course,' Feldman said.

'And the authorities?'

'Nothing yet. He has a cousin who soon may go but for Stefan, well, it is time to wait.'

The two men stared at each other again, and grinned. But Solly's smile hid a dead weight of fury. How could so many people be robbed of their religious rights?

And for what? For being Jewish. Nothing else. Surely there had to be a way round this? To make the necessary happen. Not just for Stefan or Gregory or Yosif Feldman, but for all of them, all the refusniks. Solly had money. Cash made things happen. He knew that. Maybe he could find lots of money and make things happen for all of them. Why should these people not have what he had? Solly turned back to Feldman and said simply 'I would like to help.'

Thirty-two

A crumpled copy of that day's *Evening Standard* lay on the table between them.

'This is a terrible thing,' Syd Greenspan said, jabbing at the front page. It read ISRAEL INVADES. Below was a grainy black and white photograph of a tank, soldier perched on top, rolling along a dusty track. It was June 1982 and Israel had just begun its offensive against the PLO in Lebanon. 'Israel should not be the one to invade. This is not what we do.'

'I agree,' Mal said. 'It makes me uncomfortable.'

'Uncomfortable? War makes you uncomfortable? Feh! Prickly heat, now that makes you uncomfortable. Nylon bed sheets are uncomfortable. War and invasion, this palaver, I suggest, should make you more than uncomfortable.'

'It was a figure of speech, that's all.'

Syd leaned across the table and grinned. 'Shmock is a figure of speech but I didn't use it. Even though it applies.'

'Shmock is an expletive. Not a figure of speech.'

'Mal! Syd!' Heidi said. 'It's Divinia's birthday. We don't want arguments.' The entire family, and then some, had gathered at the Sinai Diner in Baker Street for the occasion. There was Solly and Judy, plus Joseph and Rachel, Mal, Divinia, Jonathan and Simon, Sam and Marsha Jones, Divinia's parents, and then Benny, Heidi and Natasha. One long table taking up an entire terrace of the restaurant, rattling with chatter and noise.

Syd shrugged long and hard. 'Who's arguing? Me and Mal, we're discussing.'

'You sound like you're arguing.'

'What? Because I call Mal here a shmock?'

'Syd! Please. Not in front of the kids.'

'Like they know from shmock.'

Joseph shoved half a Vienna into his mouth and said, 'I know what shmock means.'

'Joseph!' shouted Judy.

'But Mum, I do. Paul Golding at school, he told me—'

'I don't care what he told you.'

'But Mum . . .'

'What does it mean?' Natasha said. 'What does shlumk mean?'

'When you're older, darling,' Heidi said.

'It's shmock not shlumk.'

'Joseph!'

'I said shlumk.'

'Natasha!'

'It's not fair,' Natasha said, thumping the table with her tiny fist and pouting. 'Nobody ever tells me anything. I want to know now.'

'The quest for knowledge is a good thing, little one,' Syd said, reaching across and pinching Natasha's cheek between thumb and forefinger. 'That way you won't turn out a shmock like this shmock of an uncle of yours.' He winked at Mal.

'Syd, please.'

'It's just words.'

'It's not the words I want my daughter using.'

'It's good Yiddish.'

'Oh, shmock, shmock,' Heidi said. 'I just don't want people swearing around Natasha in whatever language.'

The table fell silent for a few seconds, as everybody tried to work out exactly what she meant. Eventually Mal said, 'You can't really say shmock shmock. Well you can, but it doesn't work.'

Benny laughed, as the penny dropped. 'No sweetheart you can't. Mal's right. Not if you're trying to dismiss a word. You can say putz shmutz.'

'Sure,' Mal said. 'Or nebbish shmebbish.'

'Or klutz shmutz.'

'Sinai Shminai, even.'

'Of course, Sinai Shminai,' Benny said. 'Absolutely fine.'

'But not shmock shmock. You can't put a "shm . . ." sound before a word if that's how it starts already.'

'On the other hand,' Benny said, 'if you just want to call me a prick, feel free.'

'Benny!' Heidi shouted. But already the party was rolling with laughter. Even Natasha was laughing and she didn't have the first idea what the word meant. 'Oh, you Jews are so bloody exclusive.'

'Heidi!' Benny said. 'Language.'

As the laughter subsided Solly said, 'The invasion doesn't make me feel uncomfortable.'

'You think it's good that Israel invades?' Syd said. 'That we roll our tanks into somebody else's country?'

'Good isn't part of the question. It's just what we have to do.'

'It's aggression. We don't do aggression.'

Solly sniffed and speared the last of his chips with his fork. 'Sometimes to defend yourself you have to fight. It isn't nice but that is life.'

'The moral high ground is the one thing Israel has.' Syd pointed upwards with a single finger. 'You start invading and you lose the moral high ground.'

'What good is the moral high ground if you are dead and buried on it?'

'It wouldn't come to that.'

'Sure it would. The PLO wants to drive Israel into the sea. That's what they always say. They have their terrorists sitting in Lebanon planning only how to destroy Israel. That's all they do. So in this case offence is a form of defence. This is about survival.' Solly took a wooden toothpick from the pot in the middle of the table and began digging at a rogue strand of salt beef that had caught itself between his incisors. 'Do you know,' he went on, 'once there were nearly

100,000 Jews in Latvia. Eighty thousand of them died in the Holocaust. There are just a few thousand left there now. If the Jews of Latvia had gone on the offensive . . .'

'They would all still be dead.'

'They might have had a chance.'

'Not at all.'

'They could have done.'

'Never, I tell you.' Syd Greenspan rested his hands on his slight paunch and fixed Solly with a stare. Solly ignored him and looked away towards the bar below them. He signalled to a waiter to come and clear away plates.

'Anyway,' Solly said. 'We will always have the moral high ground. Hitler, he gave us the moral high ground. By killing our families, your family, he gave us rights in the world.' He felt sure of himself now. This part of his argument, he believed totally. Since his return from Latvia his bedside table had begun to fill with books by Primo Levi and Elie Wiesel and Martin Gilbert, night-time reading that made him wish only for the cool daylight of morning. It was, he had decided, the Nazi genocide of the Jews that had reduced those he had met in Riga to their meagre circumstances. That was why they lived as they did. Their community had been snuffed out by history; they were the forgotten survivors of the Final Solution.

Solly had always known about the Holocaust, of course, in the way family members always know about a relative's chronic misfortune. As a child he had met old ladies who spoke in thick foreign accents and who smelt of rose-water and talcum powder. They always wanted to hug him just a little too tightly. He had been told by his mother to be good because they were survivors and, although he didn't really know what that meant, he had tried not to wince when they squeezed him. When he was 16 he had been sent to shul one Sunday night to watch a film about the liberation of somewhere called Belsen, and had studied the pictures of thin twisted corpses, piled up like rubble, with an adolescent's detached fascination. He had not slept badly that night.

But now he really wanted to know. He needed to know.

Syd shook his head. 'Hah! Do you know the tragedy of the Shoah?'

'No. Tell me.'

'Do you want to know the tragedy?'

'I'm asking you to tell me.'

'The real tragedy is this.' Silence had fallen once more across the table. 'That the Holocaust is meaningless. There is no great truth that we can learn from all this. That the six million are dead does not make us any wiser. It just makes us sadder. It is not one of Aesop's fables.'

'You want to know why it tells us nothing?' Solly said, shaking his head. 'I'll tell you why. It tells us nothing because nobody has paid for what happened. If the guilty had paid then there would be a moral.'

'Tell me the moral? What moral would there be?'

'It would be that you commit evil, then you suffer.'

'And that would make things better?'

'Better, sure. Not right, but better.'

'It is a long way from better to right.'

'Certainly but you have to start the journey or you'll never get anywhere. Instead, you know what happens? Germany is richer than us. They have their big cars and their big money. They go on as if nothing ever happened. And in the Soviet Union there are Jews who can't live the life they want to live. In Latvia, I met dozens of Jews. All they want is to leave but they can't. So this is progress. The Germans go back to being rich and the Jews go back to being persecuted.'

'And how do you think you can change this?'

It was a good question. It was such a good question that Solly almost wanted to answer it. He even had a suggestion, a way to balance things up a little. He didn't know when exactly it had come to him. With

Solly not all ideas struck like lightning; some just came slowly into his mind like high clouds filling up a bright summer sky. It had been that way with this one. Certainly it had begun in the clinic and over cheese-cake with Arnie Sussman. But then it had been merely a distraction. Something to keep the mind working. Now it was much more. Now it was an answer to Syd's question. A serious answer.

Divinia said, 'Salt beef, chips and the Holocaust. This is what I call a birthday dinner.'

'Ach, we serve chips with everything here,' Solly said. 'Apart from with dessert.' It was clearly time to end the conversation. He and Syd could have con-tinued all night but everybody else had had enough. Another nod to a waiter and the lights went out as a birthday cake, flickering with candles, began making its way towards them. Everybody sang out in a dull tuneless roar that made the glassware vibrate and the other diners turn to look. Everybody, that is, except Solly, dark-eyed and intense, who was now too busy thinking amid the guttering candlelight to sing.

Thirty-three

There was no doubt in Barney Dorf's mind. Meeting Solomon Princeton had been the best thing that had ever happened to him. Nothing came close. The day he checked into the clinic had been good, of course, but that was all about bringing something bad to a close. The end of terrible things was not worth celebrating. He remembered a night in his teens when he had been allowed to fumble furtively with a young woman's anatomy in a way he had previously thought would be barred to him for ever. That had been great. Terrific. It had done wonders for his self-confidence. He remembered thinking at the time that it was the best thing that had ever happened to him, and it probably was. But that was a long way in the past now. From another life. From another type of Barney Dorf.

No, meeting Solly Princeton had been in a different league altogether. It was about new beginnings.

He recalled the occasion well, in his cluttered office in Tel Aviv, cooled by a dirty plastic fan that served only to churn up the dust and push the hot air about. Up to that point Dorf had been importing tourist souvenirs, small batches of cigarette lighters decorated with the words 'Jerusalem the Golden' and badly painted panoramas of the city.

'The Americans, they love these,' he said, perching on the edge of a desk swamped by papers, the tassels of his Tallit Katan poking out from under his shirt. He was a short, round man with pink cheeks and a thinning crop of brown hair topped by a blue woollen cupple clipped into place, who still dressed for a British autumn, despite having moved to Israel a year before. A film of sweat clung to his forehead; occasionally he dabbed it away with a new paper handkerchief taken from a box on his desk.

Solly put out his hand and said, 'Can I?'

'Of course. Do.' Dorf placed the lighter in Solly's palm. 'Here,' he said tucking a handful into the breast pocket of his guest's jacket. 'Have a couple more for the kids.' Solly raised an eyebrow. 'Yeah well, lighters probably aren't the best things for kids. The wife, then. Perfect for lighting the Shabbos candles, these are. Work every time.'

Solly studied the design. 'The Dome of the Rock is on the wrong side.'

Dorf laughed and made his way back behind his desk. 'Yeah, I know. Got them done in Taiwan. They reversed the transparency before printing it. Never had any complaints though. They all think it's the Dome that's on the wrong side. Not the lighter.' Solly made to hand it back. 'Nah, keep it. Please. Be my guest.'

Solly thanked him and tucked it into his pocket with the others. Outside a continuous uneven rhythm of car horns and screeching tyres filled the super-heated air.

'Now then,' Dorf said. 'You don't look to me like the kind of man who needs two gross of screwed-up lighters.'

'No,' Solly said. 'I'm looking for someone to help me with a little import-export business.'

'What Barney Dorf hasn't dealt in,' the little man said, his arms spread wide, 'the world don't need.'

'This, I think, is something you have never dealt in.'

'So? Tell me.'

And now Barney Dorf was flying business class across the Atlantic, two boxes of Dorf Corp. product in the hold. Barney Dorf riding in the front of aeroplanes. Who would have thought it? Not Barney, to whom luxury was a second bag of peanuts with his complimentary soda water. A double seat, that was luxury, with the arm rest up. But here, in this business class recliner, he could lie out. Stretch back. Like being in bed. But in the air. Barney Dorf in bed in the air. Perfect for a quick shluf. Lucky Barney.

And for good reasons too. What they were doing wasn't exactly a mitzvah. He knew that. He wasn't deluded. But it was special. Clever. It was the right thing to be doing at the right time. It was time someone did something and on his grandparents' grave he was going to be the one to do it. He and Mr Princeton, they understood each other on this. 'What's to apologize for?' he said to Solly, when they shook on the deal. 'Us Jews, we don't need to apologize. Everyone else, they can apologize.'

He turned to look out the meagre oval of window. They were eight hours out of Caracas now, somewhere over the Sahara, and a thin smudge of purple light was just beginning to spread across the eastern horizon. He peered at his new digital watch, a present from Solly. Not too far now to Cyprus. Not too long until dawn either. Dorf reached down to the case at his feet, pulled out his Tallit and tefillin and, moving carefully so as not to wake the man asleep in the seat to his left, made for the area between business class and economy. Stewardesses, resting their feet in the dead time before the breakfast service, sat on jump seats in the galley, eyes staring blankly ahead. Turning to face the exit he pulled on his prayer shawl. He rolled up his sleeve and began to bind the strap of the tefillin to his arm. Once, he had felt self-conscious about such a public display of faith, but not any more. In the feeling of taut leather against his skin lay the very essence of his identity; such ritual and observance gave to him a comfort he had never found in the therapy groups he had attended. Quietly, the book held before him, he began his morning prayers to the gentle throb of the aircraft's engines.

In the customs shed at Nicosia, where the cool dawn air smelt of rich tobacco and aviation fuel, importers stood uneasily by their cargoes as the officers made their rounds, checking paperwork. Dorf pulled his thick woollen jacket about him against the early morning chill and leaned back on one of his two cardboard crates. He had always been apprehensive about this part of the trip. It was the event he could not control. The delay, however slight, did not make him feel any more comfortable. After ten minutes, when he was just beginning to panic, a tall man in uniform with heavy forearms and the obligatory black moustache approached him.

'I'm looking for Julius,' Dorf said, carefully.

'I am Julius,' the man said, without looking up from the clipboard in his hands. His voice was heavy and raw with the sound of a lifetime's dedication to tobacco and he spoke a rich accented English.

'Good. I'm Barney Dorf. I was beginning to wonder . . .'

'I know who you are. Do you have the papers?'

Dorf handed him the four stapled sheets. Julius glanced at them, drew a line through a listing on his clipboard, then shoved them into his trouser pocket. He pulled out a new set that had been attached to his clipboard and handed it over.

'Is this the cargo?'

Dorf said that it was. The customs man said 'OK. This won't take a moment.' He ripped off the two destination stickers that had the boxes routed from Venezuela to Cyprus and replaced them. The new ones carried Hebrew script plus a further set of initials. Now the boxes appeared to have started their journey at Ben Gurion airport in Israel, stopped here in Nicosia and would end it, via an Air Norway flight bound for Oslo, in Munich.

Dorf said, 'That's it?'

Julius said, 'Yes. It is done.' He reached into his pocket and pulled out a packet of cigarettes.

'You want one?' Dorf took a cigarette but refused a light.

'I'll smoke it later,' he said. He nodded towards the pale sky beyond the customs shed doors. 'It's too early

270

for me.' Barney Dorf didn't smoke at all, but he knew that, here in the Levant, great offence could be taken by the smallest of hospitalities refused. In any case, the exchange marked the end of the deal.

Julius smiled. 'OK then.' He put the packet away. 'Now we nod at each other, like strangers doing business. Then I walk away. We do not shake hands.'

'Of course.'

'We will meet again.'

'I'm sure.' But the Cypriot was already making his way towards the next cargo.

In contrast to his uncertainty about Cyprus, Dorf had been looking forward to the meeting with customs in Munich. This was one he could control. He stood by the crates and bowed his head slightly so that his cupple would be clearly visible, although he needn't have bothered. The German customs officer assigned to his case was six foot three; a blond hulk, long corn-yellow moustache just so. Did all customs officers have moustaches? Barney wondered. This one wore a deep green cotton shirt ironed to a defined crease on the arms and shoes polished to a fetish-shine.

'Mr Dorf?'

'Yes?'

'Mr B. Dorf?'

'Are there any other Dorfs here? I always like to meet relatives. There are so few of us left.'

'It is in the regulations that I must check your name fully.'

'Of course. Regulations are important. I am Mr B. Dorf.'

'May I have your papers please?'

That has a nice historical ring to it, Dorf thought. The German officer asking the Jew for his papers. Only now he says 'please'.

The officer examined the documentation. 'What is Judaica exactly?'

'Items for the Jewish community in Munich,' Dorf said. 'Menorahs, Kiddush cups, Pesach plates, Hebrew books, that sort of thing. The full contents is listed on the sheet beneath.'

'Coming from . . . ?'

'Tel Aviv. My company in Tel Aviv.'

Dorf watched the German's eyelids flutter for a second, as he considered his options.

Judaica from Israel to Germany.

You'd just love to open this box, wouldn't you, Dorf thought. You'd just love to open it up and have a good rummage about.

Judaica.

From Israel.

To Germany. A diplomatic incident in a box.

You'd love to open it up but you can't. You know you can't. You could no sooner open this box than pull out your pecker and piss here on the floor of the customs hall. Dorf laid one hand on top of it and said, 'Would you like to take a look inside?'

The customs officer handed back the papers. 'No, sir,' he said briskly. 'That will not be necessary. Sign here and here.' Dorf did as he was told. 'Welcome to Germany.'

'Thank you.'

Delayed by the wait for his own bags and the queues at customs, the boxes managed to reach the Sinai München on Promenade Platz, ten minutes before Dorf. Solly was waiting for him in his suite on the top floor, the cargo unopened in the middle of the living room.

'How did it go?' Solly said.

'Perfect. You should have been there. I'm telling you. This German customs officer, he was desperate to have a look. Desperate. But he couldn't. Next time you should come with me on the trip.'

'I don't think that's a good idea.'

'No. No you're right. Not a good idea. Still, it was great I'm telling you. Perfect. You're a genius.'

Solly clapped the other man on the shoulder. 'Shall we take a look inside?' They each grabbed a bread knife from the kitchen and slit the tape. Inside the Kiddush Cups, menorahs and Pesach plates lay individually wrapped in plastic.

'These are nice,' Solly said, as he began unwrapping. 'Serious pieces of work. There will be people who will be grateful for these.'

'I know. I was thinking of getting a set for myself.'

'They did us proud.'

'Yeah, proud.'

'Good Argentinian silverwork.'

'Definitely.'

Solly found the two boxes of books below and, leaning deep into the crate, dragged one out. 'Hand me that knife,' he said. He slit open the carton. Inside he found the broad spines to five red leather-bound Hebrew dictionaries, embossed in gold leaf. 'Oh, very nice,' he said, slipping one free. 'Let's just hope we can use these again.'

'Shouldn't be a problem. I was reckoning on two sets of books. As one set comes this way, the others go back.'

'Good idea. And boy, does it weigh.'

'With the paper and binding it should be about two, two and a half kilos.'

'Everything here?'

'If you've got ten books in yours and there are ten in mine, then yes.'

Very gently Solly laid the volume on a coffee table. He ran the pad of his middle finger across the closed edges of the pages until he found the ridge he was looking for. Slowly he opened up the book.

'Look at that,' he said. 'Snug as a bug in a rug.' The two single-kilo bags of cocaine sat side by side in the rectangular hole cut from within the book's pages. Solly looked back at the crates. 'Forty kilos of South America's finest. And you know what's funny. I don't want any of it.'

'Know what you mean,' Dorf said. 'I was anxious, you know, at first. Memories and all that. Me around all this coke, what with my past and all. But I don't feel like that now.'

'No.'

'With God's help . . .'

'Of course.' They both fell silent.

'Help me pack them away,' Solly said eventually, indicating the two open suitcases on the floor by the wall. 'They'll be here in an hour. Then get yourself over to the Bayerische Hof Hotel across the street. There's a room booked for you.'

'Not here?'

'Thought it better we weren't in the same building too much. We can have supper together tonight.'

'Fine,' Dorf said. Quietly, diligently, they set to work.

Thirty-four

Solly had known Barney Dorf was right for the job the moment he laid eyes on him. He was bland. Neutral. A study in oatmeal. For the job Barney would have to do, neutral was good. No, neutral was perfect. Customs men never noticed neutral. They only stopped people who *looked* like drug dealers. That's how they worked. Customs men were not smart.

Solly had recently returned to attending the Drugs Anonymous group, for the sake of what, mentally, he had taken to calling the Project; it had occurred to him, as he sat there once a week trying to work out which of the other members might be of use, that most former drug users had a problem with neutrality. It wasn't in their nature. They could kick the drugs but they just couldn't shift the poor fashion sense that went with them. Even Solly continued to wear his chunky gold jewellery. The bracelets and necklaces hung about him like some glittering tidemark left by the narcotic waters in which he had swum for so long. He knew this, but he couldn't give them up. They were a part of him.

This was not a problem for Barney Dorf. Chunky gold jewellery was not in his repertoire. He was not the kind of man to accessorize.

'Do you know any Drugs Anonymous members living in Israel?' Solly asked Dr Needlebaum, one afternoon, after the weekly session. 'I'm going on a trip there. A religious man? Children of survivors, maybe.'

'Now you're being picky. You want a particular hair colour too?'

'No, any colour. Bald is fine too. It's just children

of survivors, maybe they're a bit more, you know, spiritual. Like me.'

'Maybe,' Dr Needlebaum said. 'Barney Dorf is your man. Lives in Tel Aviv now. Give him my regards.'

To Dorf, Solly said, 'either you like the sound of the Project or you don't. I'm taking risks here. I'm talking to you, telling you everything.'

'I'm good at keeping secrets,' Dorf said, looking out the window of his office at the glued-up traffic below. In his hand he held one of the 'Jerusalem' lighters which repeatedly he sparked up until he burned his thumb on the hot flint. He dropped it so that it clattered to the floor. 'Using drugs is all about secrets, isn't it,' he said, sucking the burn.

'Drugs are about many things. Secrets is one of them. Now we can make them do good too.'

'It appeals,' Dorf said. And then: 'Tell me the system.'

'I stand you security on a loan from bankers here in Israel.'

'You know bankers here?'

'Sure, I know many bankers.'

'Will they know what happens to the money?'

'Why should they know what happens to the money? Why should they?'

'Fair enough. They don't need to know.'

Dorf would wire a down payment to the supplier and follow along to collect the product. It would be routed from South America, via Nicosia into Munich – but re-labelled in Cyprus to look like it was coming from Israel. 'The German authorities will never investigate a consignment of Judaica coming from Israel to Germany.'

Dorf agreed, with a slow nod of the head.

'I'm setting up a couple of charities in Germany. You will invoice one of them for the consignment.'

'This will be a very big invoice,' Dorf said.

'Seven figures big.'

'OK, that's what I was thinking. Seven figures. Go on.'

'The money from the sale of the consignment to the dealers goes into the charity in Germany and then out to you in Israel.'

'The tax authorities on both sides,' Dorf said, 'they won't investigate money coming from a German-Jewish charity to Israel.'

'Exactly. Same principle as getting the coke in there in the first place. You take some off to pay back the loan and for company profits to pay your wages. Pay a bit to Israeli taxes to keep the authorities sweet – and then send the rest back to a second charity in Germany as a donation to the cause.'

'Again,' Dorf said, 'the German authorities won't investigate money from Israel to a Jewish charity in Germany.' A grin was spreading across Dorf's face. 'This is clever. This is a clever plan. So? What happens next?' He moved from the window and sat down, leaning across his desk towards Solly, the thumb burn now forgotten.

'From there the money gets channelled to my charity, the Princeton Trust, in London.'

'Why another charity? Why not just leave it in Germany?'

'I want to get it as far away from the source as possible. The more layers, the more transactions, the harder it is to trace.'

'You've thought about this.'

'I've thought about nothing else for months. But I'm only good on the broad details. Terrible with numbers. I need someone with an accountant's mind on my side.'

'That sounds like me.'

'It is you.'

'We need to agree details . . .'

'Sure.'

'I need one guarantee.'

'Name it.'

'Just the one guarantee. A proviso.'

'I said yes. So name it.'

Dorf hesitated. 'We never sell drugs anywhere else

277

but Germany. Nowhere else. Germany is the only place.'

Solly lifted his hands in surrender. 'This, it's easy to promise. This is what the plan is about. The whole point of it. We make the perpetrators of the Holocaust pay to help the victims of the Holocaust. We keep it simple.'

'Very simple. How many consignments?'

'I was thinking maybe three in the first year, six the year after that. It should net us serious money. First up it's to go help the refusniks, after that, you have any charities you want funded, you just say.'

'Maybe you're running too fast. Do you even have a supplier yet?'

'All of that is coming. It's in hand.'

'How are you going to find them?'

'Same way I found you. Drugs Anonymous is a great way to network with cocaine barons, you know.'

It was true. Drug rehabilitation was a two-way street. For every DA member who had managed to kick the habit there was always another who was failing. And a drug user with a big habit was a perfect link to a drug dealer who was a link to a drug smuggler who was a link to a supplier. In any case, Solly still had contacts from his own past. He phoned up Saul Israelson and the Horowitz brothers and friends of theirs too, took them out to dinner and pumped them for information. Of course, they tried to push drugs on him. This was what happened when you dined with coke heads. They tried to get you to take coke.

'Just a line,' Saul Israelson said. 'For old times' sake.'

'I'm taking a rest at the moment.'

'I heard you were doing more than that. I heard you had taken such a rest you'll never get up again. Turned your back on the catalyst for clear thought.'

'We're here, aren't we? Having dinner?'

'In the old days we never did dinner.'

'No,' Solly said. 'We only did coke. We never ate enough.'

Eventually these dinners would produce results. Drug users could be discreet in front of non-users but when they were with their own they wanted only to talk, share knowledge and insight and intelligence. And Solly was still one of their own, despite his time in the clinic and his religious devotions. Solly Princeton had pedigree which, like his gold jewellery, he would never be able to shake. He was passed from hand to hand, given phone numbers of people who answered to just one name and who never took calls, only returned them. Two months after his first meeting with Barney Dorf he was in Brazil, overseeing the launch of the Sinai Rio, their first hotel in South America, when he received the call. 'Alfred' would be delighted to entertain him for lunch that day, if he was agreeable. A restaurant off the Avenida Rio Branco, in the city's commercial district, was named.

'How will I find Alfred?'

'Do not worry. The arrangements have been made.'

Solly did not have to utter a word to the *maître d'*. He was simply ushered to a corner table at the back. 'Alfred' was a thin man of middle years, carefully dressed in a suit of beige linen. He had perfect white teeth – capped, Solly decided; he had spent enough time in Hampstead Garden Suburb to recognize expensive dental work – and expertly manicured nails that flashed and sparkled beneath the faint lighting. They shook hands and for a few moments made banal small talk about the twin obsessions in Rio: the traffic and the smog caused by the traffic. Then, in a Brazilian accent carrying more than just a hint of a North American burr, Alfred said, 'Shall we do this the Rio way or the New York way?'

'What's the difference?'

'In the New York way we sit and we make small talk for an hour or so while we eat. You tell me about your kids, I tell you about mine – and then over coffee we get to the point.'

'And in Rio?'

'We talk now, then we eat. That way, we disagree, we don't have to hang around with each other talking bullshit.'

'The Rio way, then. I've always hated bullshit.'

'Me too. Anyway I don't have no kids, so I'd have been fucked on the New York small talk.' Solly laughed and slipped his hand inside his jacket to feel for his wallet with its pictures of Joseph and Rachel, just to check it was there. The true family man, Solly thought. He remembers his kids even as he does the big coke deal.

'You want to do business?' Alfred said.

'Indeed.'

'Which territory?'

'Germany.'

'And Western Europe?'

'No, just Germany. I have no interests elsewhere.'

'We have no clients in Germany as yet. Borders are tough to break through.' Two businessmen, discussing trade. It could have been chickens or matzo meal or ready-made kneidlach mix. It wasn't.

'What volume?'

'Between 20 and 40 kilos. Three times a year.'

'A serious venture, then?'

'I would like to think so.'

'You are, I think, new to this kind of business.'

'I was once a consumer.'

'But not any more.'

'No.'

'Perfect. It is wise not to consume our product. None of those in my organization do so.'

'Very wise.'

'If they do I cut off their nose.' He dragged an index finger beneath his nostrils and grinned. Solly sniffed, as of reflex. Was he serious?

'So then, figures.' Alfred took a paper napkin from the middle of the table and wrote down a number.

'Per kilo?' Solly said. Did this man really cut off people's noses? Is that what cocaine barons do?

'Of course. We do not trade in smaller amounts.'

Solly studied the number and then wrote another beneath it, 10 per cent lower. Alfred added a third, right between the two.

Solly said: 'I can live with that. And as a mark of good will I will go up half a point.' Alfred raised his plucked eyebrows.

Solly saw his expression. 'I am not your usual client Mr . . .'

'Just call me Alfred.'

'Alfred, then. I am not your usual client. I am undertaking this business for a specific reason.'

Alfred laughed. 'We all have a specific reason.'

'Mine is more specific than most. As you say, this is not my usual trade. I wish to treat this as a standard business deal, and in my business a gesture of good will is part of the deal, hence half a point. I want you to treat me well. As a second mark of good will I will wire 70 per cent of the funds to you in advance. You fail to deliver and you will have lost a good client. You will have killed the golden goose.'

Alfred said, 'I think we understand each other.' He put out his hand and they shook. 'I will send bank details for the deposit to your hotel as well as instructions for your courier. Departure from South America is included in the price. You will have to arrange for its arrival. As I have said, German borders are tough.'

'That is in hand,' Solly said. He liked the phrase. It sounded like the kind of thing you should say to international drugs barons who cut off people's noses, or threaten to. Everything was 'in hand'. Everything was happening. It just hadn't happened yet.

'Good, then.' Alfred signalled to a waiter who bought them menus. 'We should eat.'

Solly studied the choice but it was listed in Portuguese. 'I will need your help here,' he said eventually. 'You'll have to direct me to the vegetarian options.'

Alfred looked up from his menu. 'Vegetarian? What is this? Vegetarian?'

'Er, dishes without meat. Just vegetables.' Alfred frowned and looked cross. For the first time since he had sat down Solly felt tense and uncomfortable. Had the cocaine baron's ire been raised over the simple issue of lunch? What a stupid way to go, Solly thought, his chest suddenly racing with ludicrous anxiety. Killed for wanting to eat lentil bake. Nose sliced clean off as a warning to others.

Alfred looked back to his menu. 'There is chicken,' he said, his irritation now past.

'Well, actually that's meat too . . .'

'Seriously, you mean just vegetables?'

'I'm afraid so . . .'

'There's a stew of pork. We can ask them to take out the pork.'

'Maybe just some pasta.'

'With a meat sauce? Yes? Just a simple meat sauce?'

'No,' Solly said, his anxiety subsiding too. His nose was safe. 'Pasta without the meat sauce.'

The choice of dish at the Rio lunch was the biggest problem Solly faced while making the arrangements, and even that he survived. Through another contact in Drugs Anonymous he was introduced to a Cypriot customs officer who had turned accepting bribes into an art form. On numerous occasions in the past he had proved willing to turn a blind eye to the small matter of 10 grams of cocaine in return for a certain financial arrangement.

'This will be slightly more than 10 grams,' Solly said, when they met in Nicosia, a few weeks after his trip to Brazil.

'Then it will cost slightly more than $100,' Julius said.

'We understand each other.'

'We do. You know when the first cargo will come through?'

'It's in hand.'

Finally, Solly was introduced to German cocaine dealers who wore Armani suits and ironed their Deutschmarks before placing them in three large Samsonite suitcases. In time Solly would strike a deal with them: for a discount of 30 per cent on the price he was asking, he would receive a percentage of the money from the street, finally giving him control of the retail business he so coveted. But for now it was just the simplest of transactions.

'Do you know when the next consignment will be?' the German asked as he took possession of the first bags of cocaine, brought in under Barney Dorf's care.

'Everything is in hand,' Solly said.

The next morning Solly loaded up a hire car with the three suitcases containing £1.2 million in Deutschmarks, checked and counted by Barney and then counted and checked again. He climbed in behind the wheel and headed south-west along the autobahn; past the town of Landsberg, where Hitler was all too briefly imprisoned, and Memmingen and Lindau, from where Jews had been deported to their deaths. He skirted the shores of the Bodensee, crossed the border into Switzerland and, under a sudden burst of bright autumn sunshine, turned towards Zurich, where a model Swiss banker was waiting to turn the cash into a fat bank balance. No questions asked. No questions answered.

The Jew leaves Germany with a boot full of German money, Solly thought, as the flat river valleys gave way to the expensively upholstered city suburbs. The Jew escapes to Switzerland, with a car boot full of reparations. German money for Jewish victims. Does that not sound good?

Thirty-five

Mal grabbed the copy of the *Jewish Chronicle* from his partner's hands. It was open at a picture of Solly and Judy in evening wear, alongside a number of short, balding Jewish men, their thick glasses glinting beneath the camera's flash. They were gathered before the *JC*'s photographer to mark a fund-raising supper in aid of Soviet Jewry. Mal studied other pictures on the page from similar grand community events. The same short, bald Jewish men always seemed to be at these fund-raising suppers. Maybe you hire them from the caterers, Mal thought. Maybe they come as part of the bargain. Avocado vinaigrette, poached salmon, sauce hollandaise. Oh, and don't forget. We must have half a dozen short bald Jewish men in dinner jackets for the *JC* photographer.

'Does being a big-time philanthropist make you feel good?' he said. A board meeting had just finished and they were lazing in Mal's office at the Square.

Solly shook his head. 'No, Mal, being big in the charity world makes me feel only guilt.'

'Guilt?'

'Chickens die because of me. Thousands of chickens are put to death because of the Princeton Foundation. Every year, dead chickens. It's terrible.'

'I'm lost here. All I see are pictures of short Jewish men in nice shmatte. Explain to me this dead chicken thing.'

Solly sighed deeply. 'You do good works because you want to do good works. Because you have money. Right? Because you think you can do good with the money.'

'Sure.'

'Then eventually someone sees that you're doing good works and says "Let's have a fund-raising dinner in their honour to make more money for good works." And always at these dinner-dances they serve chicken. Always. This terrible, grey chicken. If I hadn't started the Princeton Foundation there would be far less dead chicken.'

'Why should you care? You've made soup out of generations of chickens.'

'Yeah, but my soup is good. Those birds did not die in vain. At these dinner-dances, they cook them so badly, they taste like shit.' He paused for a couple of seconds. 'No, that's an insult to the culinary qualities of shit. These chickens, the way they cook them, this makes shit look like caviare.'

'That is not a nice image, Solly.' Mal turned over the page to the *JC*'s wedding announcements to see if he recognized any names. 'Anyway, chickens deserve to die. They are notoriously stupid. Name one chicken that ever won a Nobel prize.'

'For literature or economics?'

Mal laughed. They sat in companionable silence for a while. 'You and Judy doing anything Sunday night?' Mal said eventually. 'Divinia and me, we're having people over and—'

'We'd love to but it's the Jewish Care fund-raiser Sunday. What can I tell you? I've already pledged for a table.' The excuse was real but Solly was glad to make use of it. These days, too many of Mal and Divinia's guests seemed to be City men who talked in arid numbers, or smug policy advisers from the more obsessive fringes of the Conservative party. Solly was sure his partner didn't enjoy them any more than he did, but still they took place.

'No problem,' Mal said, a little sadly, as if he had expected Solly to say no.

He turned back to the *JC* photograph. 'Solly Princeton, leading figure in the community,' he said.

'I'm almost proud to know you.'

'I'm almost proud to know me too,' Solly said.

It had never been part of the plan, this celebrity. Solly had only wanted to do good. He had wanted to fund secret trips to the Soviet Union by eager Zionist youth leaders, their luggage packed with jeans for the refusniks to sell. He had wanted to fund transit camps and resettlement projects, pressure groups and campaigns. That's all. But to give the Princeton Foundation the legitimacy it needed he had been forced to stage a big public launch and solicit donations, announcing that he would be starting it off with a six-figure lump of his own wealth. The donation, he said, would be repeated each year. That way, no-one would bat an eyelid when cash started gushing out of it, as eventually it would, to fund all the things he wished to fund. The Charities Commission was notoriously bad at scrutinizing the finances of big charities. Millions of pounds of dirty money were using the system as a laundry. Even so a certain amount of effort was necessary to disguise the size of the operation.

'For the project, all I wanted was anonymity,' he said to Barney Dorf, after the second consignment had arrived in Munich.

'For this part of the project anonymity is a good idea,' Barney said, waving at the suitcases of cocaine. 'But otherwise . . .' he gave a long shrug. 'Well, anonymity is for the small people, for people like me. It's not designed for people like you.'

'I'm only five foot six.'

'Don't try being literal with me. It doesn't suit you.'

So Solly wore his dinner suit and went to fundraising dinners and took the applause. He made the speeches and gave thanks and accepted cheques for the cause, which money served as a cover for the much larger amounts coming in from the drug deals. In the City, whenever anybody mentioned Sinai Corp, it was Mal Jones they thought of, the buccaneering businessman whose hotel, restaurant and leisure empire was spreading inexorably around the globe. But in London's suburbs Sinai was Solly Princeton, the great philanthropist, friend of the famous, ambassador for the Jewish community. Silver-framed photographs began to appear about the Princeton living room: Solly with his arm across the shoulder of this film star, of that lounge singer, in a playful sparring pose with the once great boxer now thickening at the waist, greying at the temples. Solly cringed when he saw them. When he was bored he would wander around the room turning them out of view, only to be followed by Judy, who would turn them all back again.

'The Duchess of Middlesex,' Judy said to the ladies who gathered for her coffee mornings, pointing out a new photograph. It showed her alongside an emaciated blonde in a shimmering ball gown, who had been tucked so many times her eyebrows were straining to fly off the top of her head. She looked like a plucked chicken badly wrapped in Baco-foil. Minus the giblets, of course; there surely could be no vital organs inside that withered frame.

'The Duchess of Middlesex?' said one. 'I didn't know you could be a duchess of a suburb.'

'Why not a duchess of a suburb?' said another. 'What's wrong with a suburb that it doesn't deserve a duchess?'

'She's not Jewish,' said a third. 'That hair is natural. Look. No dark roots.'

'Of course she's not Jewish,' said Judy. 'Abigail is a duchess.'

That their hostess should be on first-name terms with a duchess! Such class. Such style. Even if it was a duchess of whom none of them had heard. A duchess was a duchess.

A suburban duchess was the ideal guest of honour at the charity dinner-dances attended by Solly and Judy Princeton. 'Everything about these events is suburban,' Solly said to Judy one Sunday evening, as they sat in their finery staring out over another full ballroom.

'Sure, we come to these places on Park Lane or in Kensington or somewhere else smart in town, but we all might as well have stayed in Stanmore or Hampstead Garden Suburb. That's where everybody else drives in from. Then they all get here and all they talk about is what's going on in Stanmore or the Suburb.'

'So people like a party? What's wrong with that?'

'They forget the cause. That's what's so wrong with it. For them the donation to the charity is the entrance fee.'

'Well, we're here too,' Judy said. 'Sometimes I forget which charity it is we're supporting.'

'I'm here because of the Foundation. That's the only reason. The Foundation. And look over there.' He pointed away to a huddle of short, balding men handing each other business cards. 'See. They're touting for business, these men. That's what they do here. They come here and they tout for business.' A photographer from the *Jewish Chronicle* appeared at their side and they swiftly separated out into a line, all broad grins and shimmering spectacles, to have their picture taken for the next week's edition.

'What's so bad that they raise money for charity and do a little business too? They're happy. The charity is happy. Everybody is happy.'

'How much is this bash costing?' Solly said, checking out the room, counting tables. 'Three hundred people, £50 a head and then some.' He frowned and closed his eyes, giving thanks that Barney was in charge of the sums on the Project. 'A hundred times £50 is £500, no that's £5,000. Times three is . . .' He opened his eyes: '£15,000 right now, right here in this room. Which could have gone to the charity.'

'And tonight they'll raise three times that,' Judy said, kissing her husband on the forehead. Solly scowled. 'Solomon Princeton, you are 36 and already I swear you are talking like an old man. Now come and dance with me.'

Solly knew he shouldn't really gripe; he was only fêted at these dinner-dances because the Princeton Foundation was such a success. Millions poured in from Germany and millions poured out again. At first they concentrated on the refusniks with a little going to an Israeli drug rehabilitation charity, nominated by Dorf. But later, as the situation in the Soviet Union eased, the Foundation had to find new ways to spend the vast and ever-increasing amounts of cash swilling about, untaxed, in its bank accounts. Soon they moved into backing Holocaust educational trusts, helping to set up museums across Europe and funding university libraries. Public buildings carrying the Princeton name were erected, even though Solly resisted the idea.

'I don't want to be remembered as a bit of architecture,' he said. 'Solomon Princeton, they will say, the man with nice brickwork. I remember him. The man with good porticoes. This, I don't need.'

But Judy had insisted: 'Rubbish. What better way to advertise the work of the Foundation?' she said. 'What better way to attract donations?' He could hardly announce that they did not need – nor had ever needed – money from the great unwashed.

And so there were Princeton art galleries and Princeton old age homes and Princeton hospital wards. A London college accepted large grants towards the establisliment of the Solomon Princeton Centre for Holocaust Studies, and in Jerusalem a psychotherapy unit for survivors was named after him. Later, after the governments of the Eastern Bloc countries finally recognized the game was up, the Foundation moved into buying up Jewish lands in Poland, Hungary and Russia, that had been stolen first by the Nazis and then by the Communists. Of course, they could wait to see if the bureaucrats would give the land back for free, which most wouldn't. 'But who wants to wait?' Solly said. 'Fifty years is waiting enough. So now we buy.' Likewise, throughout the dog days of the 1980s and the early years of the 1990s, Princeton Foundation representatives could be seen touring the world's auction rooms, bidding for art treasures plundered from Jewish victims. Those that could not be returned to the original owners or their heirs found their way to a Princeton gallery. It was a neat arrangement.

A damn sight neater than the drug-dealing operation that funded it. Solly could control the way the cocaine came into Germany. He could control who bought it when it arrived. He could control how the money left the country. But once his customers padded across the marble lobby, through the finely appointed doors of the Sinai München and out onto Promenade Platz, his control ended. He knew there were risks. It was his job to calculate risk. He thought about the policemen out there and the judges, the mobsters with their grudges and the greasy-heeled street dealers with their knives. All of these things he considered, in detail and often. And then carefully he filed them away at the back of his mind.

But when it came to the more subtle ways in which 40 kilos of cocaine could cause him grief, his imagination failed him completely.

Thirty-six

He noticed it only slowly, in the less than subtle offers made after meetings or at smart parties thrown by design-conscious restaurateurs and magazine journalists. But by the spring of 1984 Mal was in no doubt. Munich had a serious cocaine problem.

'Here, in Germany, we take our relaxation seriously,' said one wine supplier, after Mal had offered him a contract on the Sinai München's restaurants. 'I would be honoured, therefore, if you would allow me to share with you . . .' So correct. So exact. So unwelcome.

He met the chief of police to discuss arrangements for the hotel's nightclub.

'Obviously we will enforce a strict no drugs policy,' Mal said.

'We welcome your commitment,' the policeman said. 'But today in Munich we must all be, ehm *pragmatisch*. I do not know this in English.'

'Pragmatic, perhaps?'

'Pragmatic? I think so then, yes. These days we have so many drugs here that we cannot always expect that you are finding them all. We are being pragmatic. We are searching only for the dealers.'

Mal described the conversation to Solly. 'Can you believe this? So much coke here that they weren't even expecting us to police it. He said it's not a rich man's drug any more. You can buy it on the streets.'

They were in the suite on the top floor of the Sinai München, awaiting the return of Gerry Bergner from a meeting with city officials, where he was discussing planning permission for a second Sinai hotel in Munich. Solly was staring out the window.

'Did you hear what I said, Solly? Coke is falling in price there's so much of it. What's more, they think it's all coming from the same place. Same grade, the officer told me.'

In a flat voice Solly said, 'Really.' And carried on staring out the window.

'It's a disgrace.'

'Yeah, I'm sure.' And then, 'Come and have a look at this.'

Down below, on the elongated oval of Promenade Platz, a middle-aged man was walking past in lederhosen, suspended over his wide belly on ornate leather braces.

'Can you believe that,' Solly said, pointing. 'They actually wear the things. He's the fifth one I've seen this morning.'

'I know,' Mal said, standing at his side. 'Amazing.'

'Back home, I see someone m a kilt, a Scottish bloke in a kilt, and the worst I think is you pompous schmock.'

'Sure . . .'

'But I see a Bavarian in lederhosen like that and what goes through my mind? You Jew-murdering bastard, that's what goes through my mind.'

For a few moments Mal stayed where he was, staring at the street below. Then he turned and wandered back to the sofa. 'Frankly I never thought you'd agree to us doing trade here.'

'What? Munich?' Reluctantly Solly left the window and sat down before a coffee table bearing a massive bowl of fruit. The sight of so much food reassured him, even though it was resolutely healthy. He pulled off some grapes.

'Munich. Germany. Whatever.'

'There can't be no-go areas for Jews,' Solly said, popping two grapes into his mouth. 'Not now.'

'Simple as that?'

'Sure. We start announcing there's places we can't go and Hitler wins. He keeps the Jews out of Germany by

292

default. I'm not having that. We're in France, Italy and Spain. We have to be in Germany.'

'But you don't like it here, do you?'

'There's other places I'd like to be, that's true. But as long as we're showing a profit I can live with it.'

'And if we start making a loss?'

'We won't,' Solly said, with a wink. 'We're too good at what we do.'

There was a knock at the door and Gerry came m, pushing his glasses back up his nose. He looked harassed and his shirt was wrestling itself from underneath his waistband.

'How did our star German speaker get on with City Hall?'

Gerry sat down on the sofa and pulled out some papers. 'They complimented me on my vocabulary,' he said, with a weak smile.

'I can hear a "but" coming,' Mal said.

'We have a problem,' Gerry said.

Solly said, 'How big a problem?'

'Not a fatal problem, but an expensive problem, maybe.' He looked from one partner to the other. They told him to go on. It's the area,' he said. 'They say the area around the central station is run down, a red light district . . .'

'We know that much,' Solly said. 'We've been there.'

'Let him finish.'

'They say it's run down and that the hotel will stick out like a sore thumb. Cause resentments.'

'You told them it was a different type of place?'

'Yeah, I told them but I think they were only halfway convinced.'

The Sinai München Bahnhof would certainly be a different kind of European hotel from their previous ventures. 'A budget hotel,' Solly had said, when he first proposed the idea. 'Away from the centre, so cheaper, not in competition with Promenade Platz, but complementary to it. We give the punters the big lobby, the fancy restaurant maybe but the bedrooms, the thing they pay for, those are smaller, simpler.' They had found a grand but neglected building right opposite the central station on Bayerstrasse, which was empty except for a strip joint in the basement.

Gerry continued. 'They said Sinai is a luxury brand . . .'

'At least they know who we are.'

'Hush, Solly . . .'

'. . . and that's what everybody will see when we open up. A luxury hotel in a poor district of town.'

Mal shook his head. 'So?'

'So they are minded not to grant planning permission.'

Solly got up and walked back to the window. 'German arseholes.'

'You suggested it was an expensive hitch,' Mal said to Gerry. 'So that means maybe there's a solution?'

'Maybe. They've got a drug problem down that part of town. A lot of street dealing.'

'I know. The police, they were telling me.'

'There's a drugs outreach centre on Senfelderstrasse . . .' He pronounced the word with a natural fluency learned from his refugee parents. 'It's two streets back from the building on Bayerstrasse. Apparently the place is under pressure at the moment, surviving hand to mouth with all the cases coming their way. And I said to them that maybe if we made a donation to the centre, showed commitment to the local area . . .

Solly spun round from the window. 'You what?'

'That we make a donation. Put some money their way. Show willing.'

Mal said, 'How much?'

Gerry pursed his lips. 'I think maybe 150, 200,000 Deutschmarks should do it.'

Solly gasped. 'One hundred and fifty fucking thousand fucking Deutschmarks?'

'Two hundred thousand would be better.'

'To a bunch of German junkies?'

'Most of them are on coke, apparently,' Gerry said. 'They don't inject.'

'I don't care whether they stuff it up their fucking arses. They're German druggies. And you're saying we should bail them out?'

'It would help.'

'No way. No how. Never.' The irony was so strong he could taste it.

Mal said, 'We can't just ignore the idea.'

'Can't we? Why can't we?'

'Solly, if they say no to planning permission we're fucked from the off; and we need this hotel. It's already listed in the prospectus.'

Seven years after Sinai had moved from Mrs Hyman's to Golden Square, the company was about to be floated on the Stock Exchange so that the institutions could recoup their investment. Solly and Mal had decided to sell a few points of their holding for cash but would retain over 40 per cent between them, enough to keep control. The rest was to be sold in the City. Plans for the Sinai München Bahnhof had been included in the prospectus as proof that the company was diversifying out of the luxury market and had plans for future expansion.

'We dump this hotel now and buyers will decide we're already reneging on our promises.'

'So put off the flotation.'

'What are you talking about? Put off the flotation, rather than spend, what, sixty grand?'

'Tax deductible,' Gerry said. 'Donations to charities are tax deductible.'

'It's not the money,' Solly said. 'It's the principle. I told you I don't mind doing business in Germany as a long as we're making profits. But I won't make a loss and I'm certainly not giving money to charity.'

'Solly, you of all people. This outreach centre is for people with drug problems. You know what that's like . . .'

Solly jabbed at his chest with his thumb. 'Me, I

sorted my own drug problems. Me and him.' He
pointed upwards, to the heavens.

'After you spent time in the clinic.'

'Which I paid for. I didn't go to some bloody charity.'

'You paid for it because you could afford to pay for
it.'

Solly waved him away. 'Ach. This isn't about me
and what I paid for. It's about Jew and German.'

'Solly, please . . .

His voice was controlled now. 'This is the thing with
you, isn't it' Mal. You care more about the business
than who you are.'

'You're being pathetic.'

'I'll tell you what's pathetic. A Jew wanting to make
donations to help Germans. That's pathetic.'

'Bollocks. I'm just not obsessed, like you.'

'Who's obsessed?'

'With you it's always "I am the great Jew I am."'

'So now it's wrong that I care about my identity?'
And then to Gerry: 'Help me out here. You must have
a view. After what happened to your parents, having to
run from here. Made refugees. The indignities . . .'

The financial director played with his glasses, as he
always did when he felt uncomfortable. 'This is not my
decision, Solly. This one, I think, is for you. But if you
want my opinion . . .'

'I want your opinion.'

'Then treat it like any other business write-off. If
what's important is that we are always doing business
in Germany then this is a way of making sure that
we're always doing business here. Forget the charity
element.'

'Yeah,' Mal said. 'You said yourself that there should
be no no-go areas for Jews. We step back from this deal
because of a simple sixty-grand donation then—'

'Aw, don't try twisting my words.' He walked to the
door of the suite and reached for the handle. 'This is
about being proud to be a Jew. You decide. Are you
proud to be a Jew or aren't you proud?'

And then he was gone. Outside on the street Solly hesitated for a moment before deciding which way to go. Storming out of a meeting was all well and good but it didn't make much of an impression if all you then did was turn around and go back inside. He ignored the doorman's offer of a taxi and made his way out of the moneyed hush of Promenade Platz. He strolled across the pedestrian squares at the centre of the city and onto Maxilianstrasse, the grandest of Munich boulevards with its bruising architecture. At one end, down towards the river, there was a small Jewish museum which, despite his many trips to the city, he had never found time to visit. It was ten minutes' walk away through a narrow deserted arch opposite the Kammerspiele. A sign directed him up a dull, creaking staircase, wreathed in shadows. At the top he found a single door. The post was decorated with an ornate mezuzah, the sight of which made him feel a little less lonely. He kissed his hand and laid his fingers upon it, before trying the handle.

Of course it's closed, Solly thought to himself, as he pushed at the unyielding door; this is how it would have been whatever day I had come here. It would always be closed. Why should it be easy for a Jew to visit a Jewish museum in Munich? Nothing should be easy for a Jew in Munich. In vain he knocked, already certain there was no-one inside. Eventually he retraced his steps and found himself back on the street outside. He found a café on the next corner, sat down and ordered a drink.

Mal was right, if only on the practicals. Solly knew that now. If Sinai was to carry on expanding, if the flotation was to be a success, it needed the new hotel. And only if the company was a success could the Princeton Foundation also be a success. One gave a certain legitimacy to the other. Still, the £60,000 stuck in his throat. To be forced to help solve a problem you had worked so hard to create. How ludicrous! The waiter brought his coffee and he sat stirring in a large spoonful of sugar as he thought. Over on the wall there was a payphone. Maybe there was a solution. Maybe if he couldn't reach a compromise with his partner, well then, he could reach a compromise with himself.

First he would have to call Mal. He would have to apologize. Always easier to clear the air by phone, at least initially, and then go and see him. Much better that way. The second call would be to an answer machine on another continent six time zones away. Solly did some quick calculations in his head. Another couple of kilos should do it. That was all. Four extra kilos should more than compensate for the donation. Solly stirred a second spoonful of sugar into his coffee and hummed a tune to himself.

Thirty-seven

There were, in the boom days of 1987, many things upon which a rich man could spend his money. He could buy a car with too much engine and not enough leg room. He could trade up from the suburbs to a house of stucco and wistaria or acquire a second home down on the coast, which he would never have time enough to visit. He could learn to fly helicopters or even invest in a racehorse. None of these things appealed to Solly Princeton. He felt comfortable on the soft, creaking leather seats of his old company Jaguar and the house in Hampstead Garden Suburb smelt too fondly now of his family for him ever to leave it. A beach-side holiday home was a non-starter because he could not abide the sea, and helicopters needed landing pads. There were no landing pads in the Suburb. As to the racehorse, he did not think his rabbi would take kindly to him owning a non-kosher animal, even if only for sporting purposes.

'And race goats don't really have the glamour,' he said to Judy. 'Nobody wears top hat and tails to watch goats.'

It was Solly's good fortune, therefore, to be the father of a 13-year-old boy; a thickset lad, prone to a little fat, with heavy black hair and full lips. A 13-year-old Jewish boy was always a good excuse for spending money.

'Have you decided where you're going to hold Joe's Bar Mitzvah bash?' Mal said, six months out from the event.

'It's got to be somewhere that can do big.'

'Funny, I thought you'd prefer a light finger buffet for a dozen.'

'For my boy Joseph?'

'I was being sarcastic, Solly.'

'Oh.'

'Well?'

'I was thinking of keeping the business close to home.'

'The Sinai Piccadilly?'

'Sure. Then I can get it at cost.'

'Invite the company lawyers and you can make it tax deductible too.'

'Don't be cheap.'

Mal looked at him over the top of his reading glasses.

'You were joking again.' Mal nodded. 'Right,' Solly said. And then: 'Actually, now you mention it, if we do invite them maybe we *can* offset it. I'll have to ask Gerry.'

Any savings were ploughed right back into the event. To be under budget was to be cheap. And doing your first-born's Bar Mitzvah on the cheap was not good, particularly when you were Solly Princeton of the Sinai Corporation. The fact was neither he nor Mal could get away with small and intimate any more, and they both knew it. They were running a big, listed company that made big, listed profits. They ran famous hotels and restaurants. They employed thousands of people in dozens of countries. Things were expected of them and none of those things were either small or in the slightest bit intimate.

Of course it helped that neither was part of Solly's nature. So: on the Friday night there was a Shabbat dinner for just their forty closest friends and family; the next morning, when it came to the point in the Bar Mitzvah service where, traditionally, the women threw sweets from the gallery to the men below, they were not lemon sherbets or pear drops that came flying across the synagogue. They were individually wrapped (kosher) Belgian chocolates, handed out by Judy beforehand. Afterwards, there was a lunch party in a marquee in the back garden and the next morning, a smoked salmon breakfast. Finally, on the Sunday evening, it was over to the Sinai Piccadilly and that dinner-dance for 300, complete with champagne fountain. An orchestra played, singers sang and close-up magicians worked the tables to keep the guests amused. Every man received a silver-plated toiletry kit and every woman, a bottle of Chanel No.19. Rabbi Grearson thought to disapprove of the excess until Solly gave a donation to the shul's building fund, large enough to replace the entire central heating system.

'How else do you say you have arrived,' Solly asked Mal, at the pre-dinner reception, 'than by throwing a big party?'

'There's arriving and there's arriving,' Mal said. 'I tell you, if throwing parties were an Olympic sport you'd be in the British squad.'

'I just like to see people enjoying themselves.'

'Yeah,' Mal said. 'I suppose the only other way of announcing you'd arrived was putting up a flashing sign in Piccadilly Circus.'

'A flashing sign doesn't serve canapés.'

Mal spotted a short, vaguely familiar man with loose curled hair, who was scanning the room as if searching for an escape route. 'Who's that?' he said. Joseph was standing in front of him and grinning inanely, hands buried deep in the trouser pockets of his black velvet suit, while trying desperately to look like he wasn't really wearing a black velvet suit.

'Clive Allen,' Solly said. 'Star striker for Spurs.'

'I didn't know you knew footballers.'

'I don't, but a mate of mine, he knows his manager and he sorted it for me.'

'You hired Clive Allen for Joe's Bar Mitzvah?'

'It's not every day you are Bar Mitzvah, is it? What Joe wants Joe gets.'

Joe also received a lot of what he didn't want. By their place setting, alongside their gift, every guest found a gilt-framed photograph of the Bar Mitzvah boy, chin rested on hand, lips parted in a smile to reveal his expensive dental work. The scaffolding had only recently been removed.

'I look a complete dweeb,' Joe said, when he first saw the photograph, a few days before.

'You look lovely,' Judy said, admiring the picture again. 'You look like a perfect little man.'

'I look like a spod.'

'What's a spod when it's at home?'

'One of those,' Joe said pointing to the picture.

'You'll sign one for every guest.'

'I bloody won't.'

'Joseph Princeton, don't you dare swear at your mother,' Judy barked. 'You'll sign these photographs and you'll be grateful for it.' Joe knew the drill. You do not disobey a Jewish mother, in the weeks before a Bar Mitzvah. He signed.

Among the other things Joe Princeton received but didn't want were: eight wallets, four briefcases, five toiletry sets, all cheaper than the ones they were giving away, three personal organizers, two desk blotters and fourteen ink pens.

'A boy can never have too many ink pens,' Judy said as he unwrapped another, over breakfast on the Saturday morning.

'No, Mum, the manager of a pen shop can never have too many ink pens. A Bar Mitzvah boy can easily have too many ink pens. This is too many ink pens.'

'Think of the starving children in Africa and just be grateful,' Judy shouted. Once again Joe decided this was not a good time to argue. Joe was smart.

For much of the party Mal sat alone at his table, sucking on a large cigar and watching, while Divinia disappeared off to work the room. However large and brash the evening was supposed to be he still found it possessed a kind of desperate intimacy that unnerved him. He knew every single one of the people in the ballroom, even if he did not know them personally. He knew their type. He knew their prejudices and their passions. He understood the way that they talked, the rhythms and inflections of their speech, and the furious volume of their voices. Solly lived in this world. He went to parties like this all the time and, while he sometimes disapproved of the way people behaved, he was proud to be a part of it. Solly was content to be identified as one of them. No, not just content. Eager. He was a London Jew and he wanted people to know it. Mal, on the other hand, had always wanted to escape. And yet he could not. He too was a London Jew. Always would be.

His mood was not helped by business problems that continued to roll and tumble around his head, to the rhythm of the orchestra. He had avoided discussing them with Solly, so as not to unsettle him in the run up to the Bar Mitzvah, but that didn't stop them occupying his mind. He shoved the thoughts back once more into the depths, and lifted his hand to take another drag.

Small fingers wrenched the cigar from his grasp. 'They're disgusting,' Natasha said, stubbing it out in the ashtray with such force that the thick trunk of tobacco splintered and broke.

Mal stared at the fragments. 'That was a very expensive cigar,' he said.

'I don't care,' Natasha said. She was wearing a simple black dress and had her bare arms crossed across her chest. 'They're horrible and you shouldn't smoke them.'

'For a 10-year-old you're very . . .'

'Headstrong,' she said, with a satisfied smile. 'That's what Mum says anyway. I'm headstrong.'

'And she's right.'

She put out her hand. 'Now you have to come and dance with me,' she said.

Mal shook his head. 'Not really in the mood, sweetheart.'

Natasha frowned and pouted at the same time. 'Aw, come on, Uncle Mal.'

'Enough with the Uncle Mals.'

'Why won't you dance with me?'

'I told you I'm—'

'If you don't dance with me I'll call you Uncle Mal a hundred times. I swear. Uncle Mal Uncle Mal Uncle Mal Un—'

'All right, all right, you win. Death by Uncle Mal is too much for any man.' She dragged him by the hand to the middle of the dance floor, and wrapped her arms about his waist. He laid his arms on her thin, bony shoulders. She looks more like her mother every day, he thought, as he looked down at her fine button nose and the sand dune curve of her cheeks.

'Why don't you come and see us any more?' Natasha said, above the soft tones of the music.

'I do.'

'No you don't. You haven't been for ages.'

'I've been busy.'

'You're always busy.'

'Grown-ups often are.'

'The term isn't grown-ups. It's adults.'

'Well pardon me. I didn't realize you were so grown-up these days that you would know the term was adult.'

Natasha rolled her eyes to the ceiling. 'Don't try being funny, Uncle Mal.'

'You promised no more of the Uncle Mals.'

She gasped and bit her bottom lip. 'Sorry. I forgot.'

'That's all right.' They shifted slowly and clumsily about the dance floor, trying to avoid the tangle of each other's feet. 'Mum misses you,' Natasha said.

'What?'

'My mum is always talking about you.' A pause for breath. 'Only to me though, not to Dad.'

'What does she say?'

'That you don't come round much any more.'

'You're beginning to sound like a stuck record.'

'Then come round more and I'll be unstuck.'

Mal stroked her soft blond hair. 'You're very funny, Natasha Jones.'

'And headstrong.'

'Of course. And headstrong.'

It bothered Mal that Heidi had noticed his absence. He could explain it, of course. He could explain it all very simply. I haven't been around your home much, dear Natasha, because sometimes I remember just what I feel for your mother. And when that happens, when the memory of an emotion slips back into my mind, well, it's better I stay away. That's all it is. Sometimes my sagging, middle-aged body is overcome by wretched, sagging middle-aged lust. And it's better I stay put. Nothing major. Just grown-up – sorry – adult sadness. You'll make men sad one day too, just the way your mother has. Trust me. When you're grown up, men will wallow in sadness over you. Nothing for you to worry about now, of course.

The song came to an end and she released her grasp. She stepped back a couple of feet and curtsied. 'Thank you, Mr Jones,' she said.

Mal bowed, deep and long and said, 'Thank you, Miss Jones.'

She turned and walked back to where her friends were sitting. 'Just come round soon,' she shouted over her shoulder. 'Or I'll call you Uncle Mal a million times.' At a table on the far side of the room, in the butter glow of a candle, Mal could just make out Heidi, leaning forward, one hand rested fondly on Benny's forearm.

'What do you look so pissed off about?' It was Solly, hands in pockets, red cummerbund belly thrust forward.

'Nothing, mate.' They began to walk back to Mal's table. He felt in his pockets for the thin metal tube carrying a new cigar.

'Bollocks.'

'What?'

'You've been frowning all night. It's my boy's Bar Mitzvah and you've had a frown so deep you could park a bike in it.'

They sat down. 'Sorry, Solly.' He prepared his cigar. 'Just had something on my mind.'

'Anything I should know about?'

Mal tried to manufacture a contented grin. 'Nah, nothing important.'

'Is that not important with a big "I" or a small "i"?'

'Seriously, Solly, it's nothing. It can wait.'

Solly nodded slowly. 'So it *is* something I should know about.'

Mal realized his mistake. 'No I just meant . . .' He broke off to light the heavy trunk of tobacco, pulling hard on the flame from their table's candle.

'You meant there's some shit going down at the Square and you didn't want to tell me about it until after the bash.'

Mal stared at him and released a long plume of blue-grey smoke from the side of his mouth. 'I'm sorry,' Solly said. 'You've got a speaking face. Tells me everything. Right now it says there's a problem.'

Mal leaned over to tap his ash away, avoiding Solly's gaze. 'I only found out a few days ago.'

'Get on with it.'

'And it may be nothing.'

'Mal . . . !'

'Somebody's taking a position in our stock.' There. He'd said it.

'How big?'

'Not reached 3 per cent yet. They don't need to declare themselves until it reaches 3 per cent, which is why I didn't tell you . . .'

'How much so far?'

'By the end of Friday it was 2.85 per cent.'

'What was it at the beginning of the day?'

'One point five.'

'In other words they pretty much doubled their holding in a day?'

'Yeah.'

'Not fucking about then.'

'No.'

'So the minor news you weren't going to trouble me with was that somebody somewhere seems to be limbering up for maybe a takeover bid?'

'That's all,' Mal said bitterly, taking another drag and releasing the smoke through his nostrils. 'That's all it is.'

Thirty-eight

Mal held his glasses in front of his eyes without putting them on, to read the newspaper. He dropped them onto the boardroom table. 'It's one thing to think you've got problems,' he said. 'It's another thing to have somebody else tell you you've got problems.'

Gerry sniffed. 'This is a set-up.'

'What do you mean set-up?'

'I mean the *Financial Times* had help getting this story. A set-up.' The finance director dragged the paper towards him and rested a hand on the three-paragraph report. 'The big buying takes place Friday, right?'

'Sure.'

'So if the *FT* had spotted the movement for themselves they'd have run it in Saturday's paper. Instead . . .'

'It runs in the Monday edition,' Solly said.

'Exactly. So somebody tipped them off over the weekend to have a look at our shares.'

'Either way,' Mal said, 'it's still a story. Our stock doesn't change hands that often.'

'Maybe not at the moment,' Gerry said, 'but the more this sort of buying goes on the more the price goes up, the more people will be tempted to sell. The price is already up 6 per cent.' There was silence. Outside in the square a motorbike growled past. 'Look,' Gerry said. 'We just keep our cool. Maybe it's someone likes the company, and is scooping up a small holding. If they stop shy of 3 per cent we'll know not to worry.'

There was a knock at the door. One of Gerry's assistants stuck his head in. 'Mr Bergner, I thought you'd like to know. We've just had a call. They've bought another tenth of a point.' The messenger withdrew.

The three men around the table stared at each other. 'So now can we lose our cool?' Solly said.

Gerry said, 'They could decide to sit tight for the rest of the day or maybe in ten minutes we'll know who it is. It's hard to tell.'

'How serious is this?' Solly said.

'As I say, it's hard to tell.'

'Gerry, do us a favour and try.'

The finance director stood up and began pacing around the room. 'OK. Here's how it is. With my two points, Benny's two points and the 42 per cent you two have between you we're below having control.'

'A fact of life,' Solly said.

'Sure. We always knew that theoretically it would make us vunerable. Point is we choose which seven other people are going to be on the board and we have the upper hand. As long as they don't gang up on us, we're fine and the way the board's shaped now nobody's going to pull any tricks. We've been careful on that.'

'Certainly wasn't down to luck,' Mal said.

Gerry ploughed on. 'There's maybe another 3 or 4 per cent out there

that's frothy, up for sale. As I say, the price will keep going up, which might bring a few more points on to the market, but either way I don't reckon that whoever this is could manage more than, 8, 9 per cent from loose holdings . . .'

'So we're fussing about nothing,' Solly said.

'After that,' Gerry continued, 'it's down to the big institutions, the single investors. If any of them, any one of them, chooses to sell their holding then our mystery buyer could be up in the mid-high teens . . .

'And we'd have to have them on the board,' Mal said. 'And an unknown quantity on the board in the current climate is not a nice prospect.'

'We're just guessing here,' Solly said. 'We're making it up as we go along. It could be nothing.'

'Sure,' Gerry said. 'It could be nothing. It could be wurscht and eggs for all we know.'

'An ordinary dinner?' Solly said. He liked food metaphors. He understood them.

'Yeah, nothing fancy. Just everyday stuff. But me, I don't like the way it's panning out. Sudden surges in buying, tips to newspapers. Someone, somewhere wants us to pay attention.'

Mal laughed, bitterly. 'They've scored there.'

At any other time they could have ignored the news. They could have gone out to lunch and toasted their new investor, whoever it might be: 2.95 per cent of Sinai stock? What a good buy, sir. Impeccable taste. Now settle back and watch the price rise. Let us do the hard work. But the spring of 1987 was not any other time. It was not about settling back and watching. It was about doing. It was a season of mergers and acquisitions when the laws of nature were reversed. No longer did small fish get eaten by bigger fish. Now the small fish did the eating. Advertising agencies made bids for high street banks; leisure companies made bids for car companies; domestic appliance manufacturers bought arms manufacturers. In the days between the Big Bang and the market crash, those boom months with their own belting rhythm section, money was cheap to rent and easy to get. Anything was possible. All you needed was a little collateral and you were away. Even Mal and Solly were in on the game, standing their shareholdings against massive loans to finance expansion in the Far East. Of course it was secure. Nothing could go wrong. Not in the spring of 1987.

'OK,' Mal said. 'Here's what we do. We get off our arses and we hit the phones. Call our friends at the institutions, the directors, anybody with big stock and make serious nice with them'

'Won't that make them suspicious?' Solly said.

'We keep quiet, then they get suspicious.' He slapped the paper. 'All of them will have seen this.

They'll expect something from us. So, we start with the long-term holders, the ones who have the most to gain from profit-taking now. We tell them everything's on the up.'

Solly said. 'But it is on the up.'

'Right. Exactly. So we're not lying to them We're just telling them, you know, stick with us. Things are good and they're going to get better. Sell now, you miss out on the big money party later on.'

'Some of them may have sold already,' Gerry said.

'So maybe they know who our eager buyer is. Maybe they know something we don't. We try and find out from them We need information.'

Gerry said, 'I think we'll find out soon enough.'

They spent the afternoon dialling numbers.

'Bookings are up, Harvey,' Mal said to one shareholder. 'Everywhere bookings are up. Of course, for you, we can always find room. You want to make a booking, in Paris maybe or New York, you call me.' He hesitated. 'Just don't sell your shares.'

To another he said, Feh! What does the *Financial Times* know from takeover bids?' He listened for a moment. 'OK, the *FT* knows a lot about takeovers. This I grant you. But believe me no-one is going to be taking over Sinai. And it would help in making this prediction come true if you didn't sell your shares.'

To a third he said, 'There is as much chance of Sinai making a loss as there is of Shirley Bassey becoming the next Chief Rabbi. I promise you.'

They agreed to meet back in Mal's office at the end of the day. Solly was there before Gerry.

'How did it go?'

Mal leaned back in his chair and stretched. 'Fine, essentially. Most said they were in for the long run. Some said they weren't planning to sell immediately.'

'Which you took to mean that they might sell if the price was right.'

'Sure. Who wouldn't? They're not charities. I'd do the same.'

'Any on the edge?'

'A couple. I convinced them not to do anything for a few days. But even they said they weren't totally decided. And you?'

'We may have a problem'

'Who with?'

'The lord.'

'Leventhal? What's that shyster up to?' Lord Emmanuel Leventhal, banker and industrialist, friend of politicians, tolerated by minor celebrities, hated by his three former wives, had been one of the first shareholders at flotation, buying 8 per cent for the investment fund he managed as a retirement hobby. 'Money's like manure,' he would say, in his rich mittel European accent. 'You spread it around a bit to make ze young ones grow.' Leventhal said a lot of things like that.

'I got to him just in time,' Solly said. 'He was just about to call his broker.'

'Just because of the *FT* piece?'

'He says he's selling everything, reverting the whole fund to cash, because he thinks there's a stock market collapse coming.'

'Are you serious?'

'Actually, what he said was "Vot comes up must come down".'

'Yeah, I can imagine.'

'He was adamant. Market's overvalued, he says, and now's as good a time to shed Sinai as any.'

'He'd make serious profit.'

'Of course he would. He says it's a "vin-vin deal".'

'Enough, already.'

'Still, I got him to agree to hold off for twenty-four hours.'

'Good man.'

Gerry pushed his way into the office, eyes fixed on a sheaf of fax paper in his hand. 'We've got movement,' he said, without looking up. 'They just went to 3.2 per cent.'

'So?' Mal said, leaning forward on his desk. 'Who are we dealing with?'

'American company,' Gerry said 'Californian.'

Solly frowned. 'Californian?'

'Yeah, San Francisco.'

'What would a Californian company want with us?'

'They're called Petco.'

'What's their business?' Mal said.

Gerry looked up. 'Exactly what it sounds like. Pet care.'

Solly said, 'I'm sorry? This is getting weirder. A Californian pet care company is stalking us.'

'Yeah. Founded mid-Seventies with a pet food delivery business called – oh, you're going to love this. A pet food delivery business called Petty Dejeuner. Do a gourmet delivery business called Pet a la Cart. That's cart without the "e".'

Solly said. 'So fucking Californian.'

'Isn't it.' Gerry continued scanning the pages. 'Core business now is a chain of massive pet care superstores across the States: 136 of them to date.'

'Go back a moment,' Mal said. 'How did you say the business started off?'

'Pet food delivery,' Gerry said. 'Any delivery service works in the States. They go for that sort of stuff'

Mal was leaning back in his chair, a hand clasped over his mouth. 'I don't believe this.'

'What?' they said.

'It's Schaeffer, isn't it? The sinusitis king. You remember, Solly. That morning in the Monarch. Between blowing his nose and dribbling on the table he told us we should start a pet food delivery business. It's Jeremy fucking Schaeffer.'

Gerry flicked furiously through the sheets. 'Mr J. Schaeffer,' he said, baldly, a finger held on the spot. 'Company president, majority shareholder and according to this, he's over here, doing the buying. Taken a suite at the Dorchester.'

The three of them fell silent. Mal and Solly knew

that Schaeffer had disappeared off to the US to work for relatives shortly after his night of patent-leather and stiletto passion with Eddie flowers. They had even raised a glass to him and wished him Godspeed. In the years immediately afterwards, when they were alone, they often talked over what they had done. Each time they wrestled with a moment's shallow guilt, wincing at the thought of their cruelty, before collapsing into laughter. But that was long ago and they had barely thought of him – of his dank top lip, or his pale grey flesh, or his effortless arrogance – let alone referred to how they had removed him from the company, in more than a dozen years. It was the past. Something that had happened in Sinai's adolescence. Nothing important. Now adolescent indiscretions were battering at their door.

Mal said, 'Gerry, would you mind leaving me and Solly to it for a moment?' The finance director placed the fax sheets on Mal's desk and withdrew.

'Do you think he'd hate us enough?' Solly said.

'I'd hate us,' Mal said. 'I'm not sure I'd hate us enough to want to spend all this money. But I'd hate us.'

'Thing is, we don't know what he wants.'

'Oh, come on, Solly. We know what he wants. The man wants revenge. Of course he does. He wants to make us suffer.'

They fell silent again. 'Can you believe that fucking pet food delivery idea of his worked,' Solly said.

Mal was staring out the window. 'It wouldn't have worked here.'

'Maybe not, but he made it work there.'

'Hurrah for Jeremy Schaeffer, pet food maven.'

'We were the shmaltz mavens once.'

'But we're not any more.'

'I don't know about that. We still sell chicken soup. We just sell other things too. You never really escape your roots, do you.'

'You certainly never escape Jeremy Schaeffer.'

Solly said, 'So what do we do now? Sit here for the rest of the week with our thumbs up our arses while he buys our stock?'

Mal reached into his jacket pocket and pulled out a large bunch of keys. He used one to unlock the bottom drawer of his desk and dragged out a heap of tattered paperwork and envelopes, which landed on his desk in a spray of dust. He shuffled through the pile until he found what he was looking for. Solly recognized the manila folder as his partner shoved it across his desk.

'I think we make an appointment to welcome our Jeremy home.'

Thirty-nine

The door to Schaeffer's hotel suite was opened by a pretty, young man with glossy black hair, in sparkling white T-shirt and new jeans.

'Mr Jones and Mr Princeton, please do come in,' he said, his perfect white teeth sparkling through the hotel corridor's gloom. 'Jeremy's on the phone right now but he'll be with you, presently.' Mal tightened his grip on the folder in his hand.

They were led into the living room. Standing with his back to them by the window was a man wearing a immaculately tailored canary yellow blazer, jeans and loafers. The phone's receiver was tucked under his chin and he was holding the rest of the handset, as he listened. 'Albert,' he said, in an accent closer to the west coast than Edgware. 'Listen to me. It's late so go to bed. Yeah. No. I know. Go to bed.' He turned, grinned and raised one hand in hearty salute. 'Yeah, love you too.'

It was all Mal and Solly could do to stop their jaws hitting the floor. Jeremy Schaeffer had short cropped blond hair and where once he possessed only that sweaty top lip he now had a finely cropped moustache. He was tanned a golden honey-brown and it was clear, from the stretch of his T-shirt that could now be seen under his expensive jacket, that his body was toned. In his right earlobe was a large diamond stud and on the fourth finger of his left hand, a simple wedding band. He gestured at them to sit down on one of the two sofas that faced each other across the coffee table. He smiled again as he listened and turned back to the window.

'OK, hon. Sleep well.' He blew a kiss down the

phone. 'I'll call you tonight.' He hung up and turned to his guests.

'Well my,' he said, all smiles. 'Mal Jones and Solly Princeton, has it not been a long time. You guys are looking . . .' He thought for a second. 'Older,' he said, his head to one side. 'But you look good on it.' Before they could respond he turned to the young man who had opened the door. 'Josh, could you be a sweet-heart and rustle us up some coffee.' He made his way to the second sofa, sat down, slapped his thighs with the palms of both hands and said, 'So! Here we all are.'

The folder was resting on Mal's lap. He pulled it towards him. 'You look . . .' It was his turn to hesitate. 'Different.'

'I should hope so.'

'You've got an American accent.'

'Yah think so? Really? Back home everybody says I sound like a Brit. Oh, well. Neither one thing or the other, I suppose.' He lifted his hands and flapped them first to left and then right as he spoke, like an air steward pointing out escape routes. His eyes fell to the folder.

'Aw! Sweet!' He leaned across the coffee table and plucked it from Mal's lap. Mal did not resist. 'You brought some mementoes for old times' sake.' He opened the folder and began flicking through the photographs of his antique night with Eddie. 'Albert will be so pleased to have these. We lost my set when we moved home. Oooh, look at what a flabby little boy I was.'

'Who's Albert?' Solly said.

Schaeffer sniggered. 'Albert's my goldfish,' he said sarcastically, 'because don't goldfish just adore photography.' He glanced up and with a thin smile said, 'Albert's my partner.' He waved the fingers of his hand with the wedding band as if drying his nails. 'My significant other.'

Mal said 'Then you're . . . ?'

Schaeffer half raised his fist in a victory salute while he carried on studying the pictures. 'Oh yeah! Out and proud! Out and proud! That's me.' He closed the folder but kept it on his lap. 'Tell me, guys, just so we know where we are, did you bring these along with the intention of blackmailing me again?' Mal and Solly shrank back into the sofa. 'Only because if that was the plan, I think you'll have to recognize that it's not really a goer any more. My momma's dead and buried and I think – I'm only guessing here – but I think my Albert knows that I'm gay.' Josh returned with a tray of coffee and placed it on the table, his lips twitching as he tried to stifle a snigger. Schaeffer poured. The only sound was of liquid running against bone china.

Mal said, 'Looks like we did you a favour.'

'Oh? How's that?'

'Well, if it hadn't been for that night with . . .' He waved towards the photographs. 'If it hadn't been for that night you wouldn't have come to terms with . . .'

'Hah! You think it was this two-dime whore who helped me come out? You really think that? That's so funny. It was another five years before that happened and I can tell you it had nothing to do with this guy.' He tapped the folder with one finger. 'Believe me I do not wake up every morning and give thanks for Mal Jones and Solly Princeton, the great gay rights activists.'

Solly said, 'Cut the shit, Schaeffer. Why are you here? Why are you buying our stock?'

'Fine. Niceties over with. We'll talk the talk. I'm buying back what's mine.'

'None of it's yours.'

'You stole 15 per cent of Sinai from me.'

'We paid you for it.'

'You blackmailed me.'

'We did what we had to do. You were fucking up the business.'

'You know what I'm worth? I doubt you do because I don't even know what I'm worth, I'm worth so much.

318

If I didn't know business why would I be the success I am today?'

'It's a long way from selling cat food,' Mal said, 'to running a hotel and restaurant business.'

Schaeffer crossed his legs neatly, knee over knee. 'Guys, guys. I can see that you're cross and a little worked up but there's no point losing it. Here's how it is. I'm here and I'm buying stock and then I'm going to be on your board.'

Mal said, 'There's no more shares to buy.'

'Have you asked Lord Leventhal about that?'

Solly said, 'We are powerful people. We can fight you and we will.'

'Of course you will, hon. That's half the fun, don't you find?'

Mal said, 'OK, how about this.' He was trying to keep his temper. 'You leave your holding where it is but we treat you, say, as a consultant.'

Solly gasped. 'Mal!'

'Hush, Solly. We treat you as a consultant on our west coast operation. There will be a retainer, of course. You know the market there and we can—'

'No, I think Solly's right!' And then: 'You're a tease. You know as well as I do that the only way to have control in a company is to own stock. And it's the stock I want. It's the stock I deserve.'

'We can't let that happen.'

Schaeffer stood up. 'We'll see, won't we.' It was clear the meeting was over. He peered down at them. 'You fellas should really get some more sun, you know. You're both looking a bit sick and grey.'

Back at the Square Solly put in a call to Leventhal.

'He says he'll hold off for a couple more hours,' Solly reported to Mal and Gerry. 'Then he says he's calling his broker, and obviously he's selling to whichever of us gets there first. He's already had Schaeffer on the phone trying to sweet-talk him.'

'Gerry,' Mal said. 'How much is Leventhal's holding worth?'

The finance director shoved his glasses up his nose and punched the buttons on his calculator. 'His fund's got, what 8 per cent. I make that . . .' He hesitated: '£24.5 million, give or take penny rises over the next hour or so.'

'Have we got that kind of cash?'

'To lock up in our own shares doing nothing? No way.'

'What about the Far East fund?'

'That's robbing Peter to pay Paul. We raised that money using your present holdings as collateral. Immediately we announced the expansion plans our price went up as people bought in. We now start using that money to buy back our own shares, people will get suspicious. More than we want to buy might come onto the market and then the price goes . . .'

Mal shrugged. 'Shouldn't be a problem. Who else is out there ready to sell? Schaeffer's already got all the slack. People may be suspicious or pissed off but they won't sell.'

'Fine,' Gerry said. 'It's your call but listen, there's no way we can fund the entire buy-back that way. We have to leave the expansion programme in place. I can find you maybe £19 or £20 million that way. Anything in your personal reserves?'

'It's the old problem,' Solly said. 'Worth millions but it's tied up offshore and in untouchable funds. Liquid is a problem.'

Mal said, 'How about £1 million each? That you should be able to do.'

Solly nodded slowly. 'Listen to us. It's like we're trying to split the bill for dinner.'

'Big dinner,' Mal said.

'I always like to go à la carte.'

'Don't. You're making me think of Schaeffer. Anyway? A million?'

Solly said, Yeah, yeah, I can commit to that, I suppose.'

'Which still leaves us £2.5 short,' Gerry said.

The three of them stared at the floor.

'Can't we just let Schaeffer have our leavings?' Solly said.

Mal said, 'No way. I don't want the cunt getting more than he already has.'

'Fine. You used the C word. That makes your feelings clear.' Solly stood up. 'I've had an idea. I'm going to make a call.'

He returned ten minutes later grinning. 'We've got ourselves a deal.'

'Simple as that?' Mal said.

'Sure. A friend of mine, he'll take the last £2.5 million and even assign them to us.'

'Who is this guy? Is he kosher?'

'Hah! Couldn't be more kosher if he had cloven hooves and chewed the cud. His name's Barney. Barney Dorf Runs an import-export business out of Tel Aviv. Part of the Drugs Anonymous mafia. And, you know how it is in that world, we see eye to eye on lots of things.'

'You mean he's a head-banging frumer like you?'

Solly grinned. 'Exactly.'

'Gerry,' Mal said. 'Go make a call.'

Solly watched him leave. There would be no donation to the Princeton Foundation from the latest consignment. That much was clear. But then sometimes you had to make sacrifices, to keep the project on track. Sometimes you had to make strategic decisions. If keeping Schaeffer out of Sinai meant Dorf Corp buying in, then so be it. You had to keep flexible to survive.

Forty

Jeremy Schaeffer did Mal and Solly one big favour. He forced them to listen to Lord Leventhal.

'If there's vun thing my life has taught me,' the peer told them, a single gnarled index finger raised, 'it's that an orgy cannot go on for ever.' The Sinai partners sat, hands clasped over mouths so that their smirks did not escape, trying to imagine the decrepit man before them, greased with the sweat of group sex.

'You've been to a lot of orgies?' Solly said.

The old man shrugged. 'It's a smilley,' he said.

'A smilley?'

'Of course, a smilley.' He tapped his temple, where the skin lay thin as tissue paper. 'A picture of ze mind.'

'Aaah, you mean a simile.'

'That's vot I said. A smilley.'

'Actually,' Mal said, 'I think it's a metaphor.'

'Metaphor, shmetaphor. Listen to vot I'm saying. In ze City, it's an orgy right now. Everybody has ze lust to buy shares, so up go the prices. And soon everybody gets tired, everybody droops. At ze end of orgies this always happens. Believe me, I am old and I know a lot about drooping. My advice is, leave ze orgy before you droop.'

And so they did. A few weeks after buying out Lord Leventhal's shares, they contacted their bankers and announced they would not need the loans they had arranged for their Far East expansion plans, save for the cash already used in the buy-back. It was a wise move. When the stock market crashed in the autumn of 1987 and the Sinai price fell along with everybody else's, it became clear that the value of their holdings would not have matched the cost of the loans on which they were secured. At the time it seemed less a lucky escape than a prudent business measure. Sinai was a solid company with solid assets and it would take more than the vagaries of the market to knock it off course. But later, when the deep recession of the early 1990s began to bite, Mal and Solly gave thanks that they were neither hidebound by debt nor attempting to expand the business. Together the crash and the recession really could have done for the company, as they did for so many others. Instead, Sinai consolidated, shedding hotels that were not working – including, to Solly's intense pleasure, the Sinai München Bahnhof – and concentrating on the luxury product. People with money always had money, even when nobody else had money.

When trade finally did pick up, Sinai was lean enough to go shopping, buying up those firms that had made it all the way through the recession but no longer had the cash to see them out the other side. At First they concentrated on small chains of quality hotels on both sides of the Atlantic, what Solly called 'the Cafetière Outfits'.

'These small hotels, always they serve coffee in cafetières' he said. 'if you ever see a cafetière in the dining room you can be sure there are less than thirty bedrooms upstairs.'

Then it was the bigger hotel chains (the filter coffee boys), followed by nightclubs, restaurants and cafés (espresso machines). City journalists began to take notice of the Sinai partners, these London lads with their grand ambitions to take on Hilton and Sheraton and Mariott. Even journalists from the *Financial Times*. Mal Jones had made it into the pages of the 'journal', just as Samuel Jones had failed to. Reporters wrote of their 'canny' investments, and their 'sharp' deals. No longer was it just their financial results that were reported. Now feature writers were sent out to do profiles. They delighted in the discovery that Mal's real name was Moses, as if they had unearthed the Watergate tapes, or rumbled the Profumo affair. To the hacks he was Moses 'Mal' Jones just as his partner was Solomon 'Solly' Princeton, their most familiar names cordoned off by inverted commas, as if they were the scene of some awful crime.

'They make it sound like I'm hiding something,' Mal said, after reading one feature.

'Let's be honest, mate. You are.'

'Bollocks.'

'OK, so from now on I call you Moses.'

'You do that and I will turn your testes into knishes.'

'Oh lucky soul who gets that dish.'

Headline writers could not resist the lure of the name. One feature was called HEADING TO THE PROMISED LAND; another, with tired reference to the rock canon, MOJO RISING. They loved the Sinai story, these City journalists. After Mal explained to one interviewer that they had met down the side of a synagogue, it became *de rigueur* that the detail appeared in every report whether it was relevant or not:

'Sinai Corp partners Mal "Moses" Jones and Solomon "Solly" Princeton, who founded their company at their synagogue as schoolboys, yesterday announced the acquisition of . . .'

'It makes it sound like we did it between prayers,' Mal said.

'Well,' Solly said. 'In a way we did.'

Sometimes the journalists – usually the Jewish ones – would get it right and report that they had met at Rosh Hashanah, but others were less fastidious with the truth. It was at a wedding, they would say, or a Bar Mitzvah or even at a funeral. By mythologizing their meagre beginnings, these journalists marked out Mal and Solly as scrappy businessmen who had fought their way to the top, the deal makers with their eyes on the prize.

'I see them describe us as scrappy fighters,' Mal said, 'and always it sounds to me like they think we're crooks. We never screwed anyone to get where we are.'

'We screwed Jeremy Schaeffer.'

'Not true. Eddie Flowers screwed Jeremy Schaeffer.'

'We picked up the tab.'

'Then we're generous.'

Solly read these articles and could not help but grin. What they could say if only they knew. What acres of newsprint that would fill! Solly Princeton, drug smuggler. International mastermind. Criminal genius. Oh, and he runs great hotels too. Except it never felt like that. Like those glamorous charity fund-raisers, the drug-running operation was also a suburban affair in spite of itself; cosy in its simplicity, undemanding in its assumptions. The project was now so simple and so regular – so intensely banal – that it felt like little more than a courier business, albeit one with a curious fetishism for confidentiality. Solly and Barney, thickening at the waist, thinning on top, had developed a routine. Four, maybe five consignments a year. No less than 40 kilos, no more than 60. Cash banked in Zurich. Money laundered through the charity network into London. Good being done from bad. Retribution at last.

Often, when Solly was in Israel, he and Barney attended services together, sharing the dead weight of their faith, and never once questioning what they were doing.

'God will judge us,' Solly said to Barney one morning, after they had laid tefillin together. 'It is Him we must answer to.'

'I'm comfortable with that,' Barney said. 'if He calls on us to apologize then we apologize.'

But apology was far from their minds. As the Eastern Bloc emerged from beneath the dark shroud of Communism, interest in the Holocaust increased rather than diminished. From the early Nineties onwards television news seemed constantly to be full of stories about displaced and dispossessed Jews coming forward to reclaim their birthright, before old age in turn claimed then. When there were survivors still about to give testimony, Solly and Barney saw no reason to give house room to doubt.

Julius too stayed in place, the black bristle of his Cypriot moustache now thick with white, the creases of his jowls deeper, the dark tanned skin of his forearms all the more leathery. He rejected promotion, saying that the routine of the customs officer suited him. As did the marble-clad villa by the sea at Paphos and the high-powered speedboat moored nearby. If ever he was questioned by his colleagues he referred to careful investments, family money and luck. This was enough.

if there was one theme to these years for both partners it was repetition. Their deals, and the rewards that these brought them, failed now to surprise. The intrigue lay only in discerning the slight differences between the business plan they were drawing up now and the business plan they drew up last year. Bigger growth here, smaller growth there. Larger market share and higher market profile. More cocaine sales. Bigger grants to charity. Finer charity fund-raisers.

More.

Of the same.

There were diversions: a second home in the pine and scrub cluttered hills of Majorca for Mal, complete with helicopter pad; a growing circle of friends in Jerusalem for Solly; a small private jet on lease at Heathrow for both of them. But these were merely toys for giants, shrinking in the massive palms of their hands.

'I am 45 years old,' Mal announced to Divinia one evening in the spring of 1995 as they lay in bed watching television. 'And I have realized all my ambitions. I am a millionaire. I run a world-famous company. I have a wife. I have two sons. I don't know what to do with myself. I think maybe I am about to have a mid-life crisis.'

'Then you better find something else to do,' she said, and switched channels. 'And would you mind putting your wife and children before being a millionaire, if you ever come up with that list in public.'

Two months later the partners met for lunch at the Sinai Diner on Baker Street. It was a ferociously hot day, a reminder of the opening night almost twenty years before. But now the restaurant had air conditioning which filled the room with a gentle background hum.

'You hear about Natasha?' Mal said, as he dug his knife into the bowl of chopped liver between them.

'No? What?'

'Oxford University.'

'Accepted?'

'Yeah. To read English.'

'Bright girl.'

'Like her mother.'

'Heidi went to Oxford? Don't be silly. She didn't go to Oxford.'

'No, but she's bright. I meant she's bright.'

'Oh sure.'

'She'll be a journalist, a writer one day.'

'Who? Heidi?'

'No, Natasha.'

'Of course.'

'Bright girl.'

Solly chased a little liver round his plate. 'And your boys?'

'Simon and Jonathan?'

'You got any other boys?'

'Don't be smart.'

'So?'

'They're fine. Simon will be a barrister, I'm sure of it. Got a mouth on him.'

'Joseph too.'

'Has he got rid of that beard yet?'

Solly laughed. 'No, but he's started plaiting it. Tying ribbons on the end. Think he's trying to goad me. Judy hates it.'

'Does it work, his goading?'

'Nah, I just tell him he looks like a Hasid and he sulks.'

'He go to shul? With a beard like that he should go to shul.'

'Joe? Nah. Hasn't been in years. Breaks his dad's heart.'

'You can't force that stuff down his neck.'

'Who's forcing? Just once in a while it would be nice if . . .'

'Listen to you. You sound like your mother.'

'May she rest in peace.'

'Of course.'

'You know I don't think Joe could say the Kaddish for me if I dropped dead tomorrow.'

'Are you planning to drop dead tomorrow?'

'No but, you know, I might. And is it too much too ask that a son be able to say prayers over his old man's body? I say prayers for my old man.'

'Solly, I couldn't say the Kaddish, not without a phonetic version.

'You should be ashamed of yourself'

'Why should I be ashamed of myself? I don't believe in God. Why should I want to say the prayer for the dead?'

'Technically it's not the prayer for the dead. It is a prayer in praise of God. But we do say it when someone dies.'

'Don't go all yeshiva on me.'

'What's so wrong that I should try and educate you in Judaism? You're a Jew whether you believe in God or not. He believes in you. This stuff matters.'

'To you.'

'One day it will matter to you too.'

'Bollocks.'

'I despair.'

'Of my heathen soul? Your despair is wasted. Better to despair of a waverer. Despair over Divinia. With her it will be appreciated.'

A waiter came to clear their plates ready for the next

course. Mal turned to watch him go and then stayed twisted in his chair looking around the room.

Solly said, 'What?'

'This place,' Mal said, turning back. 'It needs redecorating. Wood panelling needs revarnishing. It's all looking, you know, shabby. This is our flagship diner. And look at it.'

Solly said 'Oh', and ran his tongue around his teeth. 'What?'

'I was just thinking.'

'What?'

'I was just thinking what a pity.'

'What, this place? It's only decorating . . .'

'Nah, didn't mean that. I was just thinking how nice it was. We weren't talking about the business. We were talking other stuff Important stuff, about our kids, Judy and Divinia, and then . . .'

'I start talking business again?'

Solly shrugged. 'It was nice not to talk about Sinai for once.'

Mal sat back as the waiter laid down two salt beef plates. When they were alone Mal said, 'Would you like it if we didn't have to talk about Sinai ever again?' He shoved a lump of salt beef into his mouth, breaking up the fibres with his tongue.

Solly laughed. 'What? Make it taboo? That's no way to run a business.'

'No, I mean . . .' He sprinkled salt on his chips. 'I mean no longer being involved with Sinai.'

Solly put down his knife and fork. The other talk had been the preliminaries. Kids' talk before real talk. 'What's on your mind, Mal?'

'I've had a visit from the lord.'

'What? Leventhal? He's beginning to repeat on us like a kipper. When's he going to retire?'

'It was a favour for a friend.'

'What friend?'

'Geoffrey Katz.'

Solly knew the man. He owned a chain of bowling

329

alleys, some cinemas, a few restaurants and a hotel business in the US. His company, Faithful PLC and Sinai Corp had competed over purchases in the UK. They were competitions Sinai had always won.

'Katz is looking to expand.'

'Katz is always looking to expand. He does more looking than expanding, mind . . .'

'The lord came to see me on his behalf. Katz wanted to know if we wanted to co-operate on a couple of projects.'

'What sort of projects?'

'Doesn't really matter now because discussions have moved on from there.'

'Thank you for bringing me in on this.'

'Look, we all got talking and, well, there seemed no point mentioning anything until we had it sorted.'

Solly raised his hands in surrender. 'Go on. Go on. What's the plan?'

'A kind of merger. We buy Faithful shares for Sinai shares. It will look like we're buying them because we're the bigger company, but really it will just be the two companies coming together.'

'We'll control huge chunks of the leisure market.'

'Sure, our combined share price should be a lot more than just the two prices added together. By merging with Faithful we'll be removing one of our big competitors.'

'And this is the way by which we don't have to discuss Sinai ever again?'

'I was getting to that.'

'Go on.'

Mal settled back and looked about the room as though he did not recognize his surroundings. 'Sinai's, what? Twenty-six or twenty-seven years old. It's big. Bigger than either of us ever planned.'

'I didn't plan anything. You had the plan.'

'You know what I mean.'

'Yeah. But you had the plan. Not me.'

'Sure. But . . .' Mal sighed. 'I'm bored. I find it hard

to get out of bed in the morning. To go into the Square. There's the odd deal that excites me but mostly . . .'

'It's not there any more.'

'What can I tell you? And I think you feel the same way. You'd like to spend more time on your Foundation work.'

'I was thinking of buying a place in Jerusalem.'

'Well that's what I'm saying. Your thoughts are elsewhere. You're thinking about things that are more important to you.'

They sat in silence as their food cooled. Finally Solly said, 'Are you suggesting we bail out?'

'The terms of the merger will require golden handcuffs. We'll probably be bound in for a year. But then, with Katz in place, he says we can sell up and get the hell out. We leave him as chairman, keep whatever shares we don't need to cash in and go on to other things.'

'Have you got other things?'

Mal laughed. 'I don't know. I was thinking about getting into IT. A new start-up. I was thinking of working in the US and—'

'But have you really got other things?'

Mal hesitated and stared at his hands. 'No,' he said quietly, as if he had been rumbled. 'That's one of the reasons I want to get out. I need other things in my life. I'm not going to find anything while I'm chained to a desk at the Square.'

Solly said, 'What's the catch?'

'No catch. It all depends on Faithful shareholders voting it through. The only proviso is that the Sinai share price mustn't go down or they'll be getting less for us acquiring their shares. To be honest it would be better if our share price went up, but the interim results should be good so—'

'You want to do this?'

'No, the question is, do you want to do this?'

Solly felt a weight lifting off his shoulders. 'It's time,' he said. 'Arrange a sit-down with Katz.'

And that should have been it. The beginning of the last act for the Sinai Corporation, the world-beating multinational founded so many years before in a dog-turd clearing down the side of a prefab synagogue in Edgware. And it would have been. Or to be fair it still was, but not in the way either of them intended. All disasters have small beginnings and this one was no exception. If it hadn't been for a bowl of raw minced lamb, that stood resting for just a little longer than was healthy on a kitchen table in Nicosia, Mal Jones and Solly Princeton would indeed have been guaranteed their fresh start. They would have had it all. A cash fortune, easy celebrity and their freedom.

Instead, because of that bowl of sweaty meat, Mal Jones was destined to watch the sick, grey waters of the sea ebb and flow onto the shingle beach at Herne Bay, a place whose name he was yet to learn. What's more, he was destined to watch it ebb and flow time after time after time.

And he hated the sea.

Forty-one

Julius Economaides trusted in routine, much as priests trust in the scriptures. Routine gives you something upon which to drape your life, he would always say, as he stroked his bristle moustache. Routine is like a hanger for a fine coat or a shoe tree for hand-stitched boots. It helps your life to keep its shape. Only when your life has an obvious shape do people not examine your affairs too closely. For what is there to see in an ordered life but more of the same? What is not the same, those delicate wrinkles in the spread of routine, can then go unnoticed. Order is the best of disguises.

And so every Thursday evening, before the start of his shift in the customs shed at Nicosia, Julius would eat his supper at a cheap taverna on the edge of the airport called the Red Lanterns, although it was a long time since he, or anyone else, had referred to it as that. To the many ground staff and cabin crew who used it as an unofficial canteen it was known as the Landing Lights on account of the red neon sign outside, which pilots swore could be mistaken for the start of the runway. When an aeroplane passed overhead on its final approach, causing the aluminium cruet sets to rattle in their holders, diners would often look heavenwards and cross themselves, as they offered up a silent prayer that tonight the pilot would not be mistaken. To the uninitiated the Landing Lights could appear in high season to be the dining room of some curious seminary, where every ninety seconds the devout on one table or other would look up and make the sign of the cross at the rattle and whine of decelerating jet engines.

But this was the third Thursday in October 1995 and the high season was long past. Only four flights flew over Julius's head as he sat at his usual corner table eating his usual Thursday evening dish of meatballs and rice with tomato sauce. In any case the rhythmic pulsing of the jets could not distract him from the young waitress who had recently started working there and the deep, dark promise of her plunging cleavage as she leaned down to serve him. He did not register that the spheres of meat broke up in his mouth more easily than they should have done. Nor that at their centre they were still stone cold, although the temperature of the separately cooked sauce was largely responsible for masking the meatballs' meagre acquaintance with the oven. He did recognize that it was not the greatest dish he had ever eaten, but you did not go to the Landing Lights for great food. You went because it was cheap and convenient and employed pretty waitresses with large breasts. Halfway through dinner he decided he had eaten his fill. But then Julius realized that, without a plate before him, he would have no excuse to stay and ogle. So he picked up his fork and, like a builder shovelling sand at the end of his shift, began eating once more.

It would be wrong to suggest that Julius Economaides's body did not know what had hit it. The victim of a mugging may not know who it was who did for them, but they will still know it was an enemy. Equally the customs officer's guts may not have been able to put a name to the toxic bacterium breeding in the meatballs but they were determined to have nothing more to do with them. An hour after coming on duty, therefore, Julius Economaides found himself on his knees vomiting copiously onto the cool concrete floor. His colleagues stood around sucking on their cigarettes and watched. Each of them shared the same uncomplicated thoughts: that they would now be short-staffed for the rest of the night and that they would have to share it with the stench of vomit and ineffective disinfectant.

Barney Dorf knew nothing of the Red Lanterns or the Landing Lights. He knew nothing about waitresses with big breasts or about toxic meatballs with rice and tomato sauce, undercooked or otherwise. All he knew was that at ten o'clock the previous morning he had telephoned Julius Economaides from Caracas and conducted the usual cryptic conversation they had enjoyed four or five times a year for over a decade.

'I hear a cold front is heading your way,' Barney would say, after they had asked after each other's health.

'There is no cold front tonight,' Julius would answer. 'The weather is clear.'

'Then my journey should be smooth.'

'You should have a comfortable descent.'

Accordingly the cargo had been loaded and he had settled down in first class for the transatlantic flight, content that the crooked customs man would be waiting for him in Nicosia, to see that everything was organized for the next leg of its trip to Munich. Dinner on the plane. A nice shluf in his recliner seat. A few Belgian chocolates. What more could Barney Dorf want?

In the customs shed he noticed his contact's absence but for the first five minutes thought nothing of it, instead sniffing the acrid smell of bile on the air whenever a gentle wind blew into the hangar from the runway beyond. Soon he began scanning the room, with a careful jut of the neck, casually looking for the man who served as the vital link in the chain. He will be here, Barney thought. He told me he was on shift tonight. This morning he told me. So why should he not be here? Why should he lie to me?

But he was not there. Around the shed there were other familiar faces among the officers. How could there fail to be after a dozen years? These were men he had seen once every two months. He knew them to smile and nod at and now they smiled and nodded at him. But none was the familiar face he wanted to see. That he needed to see. Barney took short shallow breaths and tried to contain his panic. In the early days he had worked hard to prepare himself for the possibility of discovery, imagining his protestations in court; his grand statements about retribution and making good come from bad. The Jews making the Germans pay. An honourable crime. But as the years passed and the smuggling operation developed a comfortable rhythm those thoughts had slipped to the back of his mind. To believe in failure was to bring on failure, he decided. Why have bad thoughts when bad things weren't happening? That was merely to invite the inevitable. And discovery need not be inevitable. Nothing was inevitable. Everything was possible.

But now those thoughts came flooding back to him and he was unprepared for their intensity. By the time he was approached by a slight, dapper customs officer with a shining bald globe of head like a polished melon, Barney was panting like a dog.

'Your papers, sir.'

'I'm waiting for Officer Economaides,' Barney said, squeezing out the words. He backed off towards his carton.

The customs man did not look up. He scribbled on his clipboard. 'Mr Economaides is . . .' He sniffed the air as if to remind himself 'Unwell.'

'Unwell?'

'Something he ate,' the man said, resting the palm of his hand flat against his stomach.

'But he wasn't unwell . . .'

'When wasn't he unwell?' Now the officer was interested. Why should this Mr Dorf know anything of Julius? Why should he care who cleared his cargo? He let the hand holding the clipboard hang slack at his side and studied the little man with the woollen skull-cap on his head.

'Sorry?'

'You say he wasn't unwell. When was this he wasn't unwell?'

Dorf sank his hands deep in his pockets and tried desperately to look like he was casually scanning the room, as he fought to regain his composure. 'Oh, the last time I was here.'

'Why should he not be unwell now, then?'

'Big fella,' Dorf said. 'Sturdy chap. Always looks fit.' Good answer, he thought to himself Very good. Sturdy chap. Julius exactly. We'll get through this. We're already through this.

'How often your friend Mr Economaides, he opens your boxes?'

'Eh?'

The customs officer cleared his throat impatiently. 'These boxes? Your boxes? How often? He open? Them?' He slapped the top of one, so that a dull thud echoed deep inside.

'I'm not sure what you're talking about there. Opening the boxes.'

'Is simple. I want to know how often he look inside.' The customs officer eyed the cargo greedily.

Barney shivered and unconsciously began backing away past the nearest of the two cartons and towards the large double doors of the customs shed.

'He . . . well he sometimes . . .' He was stammering.

'I think we should look in this cargo,' the officer said briskly, turning away from Barney and waving to colleagues on the other side of the shed to join him. It seemed as if customs officers were swarming around the boxes now, withdrawing heavy-handled blades from sheaths at their hips to cut them open. The bald-headed officer began to advance down the room, matching Barney's retreat step for step.

'Sir, you come back.'

'But he said . . .'

'You come back here while we open boxes. It won't take long.'

'He said to me . . . he told me . . . he said to me.'

'You must not leave customs until we have cleared your cargo.'

From the corner of his eye Barney could see other men in carefully pressed shirts and slacks walking towards him, their dark black eyebrows shuffling up and down in surprise. Then he felt the gentle burst of early morning air upon his cheek and smelt sweet aviation fuel and realized, with a curious sense of freedom, that he had backed through the vast hangar doors, out of the customs shed, and onto the concrete apron that led to the runway. The boxes, his boxes, seemed to be shrinking in size as he continued to back away, his feet scuffing against the hard ground as they tried to gain purchase. Back away far enough and the boxes would become tiny. Then he wouldn't be able to see them. Then they would have nothing to do with him. They wouldn't be his boxes any more.

He heard his heartbeat rattle through his body as the blood pumped in his ears. Barney began to concentrate on the sound, focus on it, until the heavy thud-thud-thud jumped in speed and then jumped in speed again to become a single burst of roaring noise. It seemed the men were shouting at him now, the sinews in their tanned Cypriot necks drawing taut against the effort. But Barney couldn't hear what they were shouting. He didn't want to hear. He just wanted to get away. There was the gentle wind and the roar of his heartbeat banging in his ears, growing louder, always growing louder and that was all he wanted. Noise. The escape of noise.

Everybody in the customs shed, passengers and officials alike, was staring at him now. Shouting. Waving their arms about. Why were they waving their arms? Why should they do that? But they weren't advancing on him any more and that was a relief. They'd given up, as if they didn't wish to get too close to him.

Barney Dorf didn't even see the two-seater Cessna which was drawing up to the customs shed, before the propeller began chopping away at his shoulder, in a

338

shower of blood and tissue and bone. The spinning blades dragged his body further and further into their blur of metal, hacking away at the stocky drug smuggler's neck, swiftly severing an artery, and only releasing his corpse to fall to the ground when they had neatly lopped off his topmost nine inches. His head flew into the air and traced a gentle parabola towards the customs shed doors, bouncing three times across the ground before coming to rest, eyes wide open as if still registering surprise, just a few inches in front of where the crowd stood. For the second time that night a customs officer fell to his knees and found himself vomiting onto the concrete floor, while his colleagues watched.

The bald officer – who had managed to hold down his supper – rested the palm of his hand flat against his stomach again and said, 'Now I think for definite we should be opening these boxes.' He called for a knife and began to cut away at the plastic tape that kept the lid closed.

Forty-two

Just as Barney Dorf was undone by food so Solly was
saved by it, at least for a few days. He had long insisted
that the coffee shop at the Sinai München on
Promenade Platz stock baked cinnamon cheesecake,
imported from New York. It sold poorly – if at all – but,
as Solly reasoned, he was the company chairman and
if the company chairman wanted to make a loss on
cheesecake he was entitled to make a loss on cheesecake. This Friday morning he was seated at the coffee
shop bar, fork in hand, chipping away at a large slice,
while he waited for the separate arrivals: first of the
consignment, then of Barney, and finally of his customers. But cinnamon cheesecake was a serious
business and it did not surprise him that time escaped
his grasp as he worked his way from the apex of his
slice towards the sweet pastry crust. He only realized
how much of his attention it was holding when the two
German drug dealers appeared at his side in their
expensive suits and short haircuts.

'Mister Princeton?' said one. They always made his
title sound like a first name.

Solly looked up irritably from his plate. 'What are
you doing down here?' he said. He looked at his watch.
'Go up to the room. Mr Dorf will let you in.'

'There is nobody in the room,' the German said, restlessly running his fingers through the stubble of his
hair as if to check its sparse covering was still there.

Solly forked away another lump of cheesecake. 'The
cargo?'

'The porter says he has placed it in your room, but
he will not let us in there.' The man looked about the

340

coffee shop as if he expected to be arrested by a waiter at any moment.

Solly sighed. 'Barney must be caught in traffic.' He checked his watch again. He dragged the electronic pass card to his room out of his pocket and handed it to them 'Let yourself in. Go play with the mini-bar.'

'You are not coming?'

'I'll be up shortly,' Solly said, returning to the plate before him. 'I've business to attend to.'

Five minutes later Solly was disturbed again by a young man he recognized as one of the hotel's duty managers. Dieter. Or Frederick. Or Tristan. Something formal and slightly fey.

'Herr Princeton . . .'

'What?' he barked, eyeing the remainder of his cheesecake.

'I am sorry to be disturbing you but there are police-men here in the hotel.'

'So?'

'They wish to be allowed to search the hotel.'

Solly took another mouthful. 'Do you always check with the chairman before taking a decision? what would you do if I was not here?'

The German gave a slight but defined bow and said, 'In any circumstances I would of course take this de-cision myself, this being the essence of my training . . .'

So bloody formal, Solly thought. So bloody typical. This being the essence . . . So bloody German. 'Get on with it.'

'But, Herr Princeton, it is your suite they wish to search, so I thought perhaps . . .'

At first Solly tried not to register any surprise at all and then thought better of it. To be too blasé about a police search of his rooms would be to arouse sus-picion. Instead he contrived a delicate raise of the eyebrows and said, 'We cannot stand in the way of the law, can we. I will just finish this—' he chipped away at the *pâtisserie* once more with his fork '—and then I will be up to find out what they want.'

But Solly knew what they wanted, even as the hotel manager backed away wringing his hands. He was now certain Barney was not caught in traffic. He was caught elsewhere in some other kind of situation from which he could not extricate himself why else would the police be here? In his rooms there were two boxes containing 52 kilos of high-grade cocaine and two of Germany's most notorious drug dealers. Soon the room would contain a large number of policeman. This was not a good mix for a party. Not a good mix at all.

He took one more mouthful of cheesecake, savoured the sour-sweet tang of its centre and the fragrant burst of cinnamon, before reluctantly laying down his fork and pushing the plate away from him. He patted his inside jacket pockets, left and right, to reassure himself that he was carrying both his passport and his mobile phone, and then slowly clambered off his bar stool. He left the hotel by the coffee shop entrance and hailed a taxi to the airport.

In the car Solly made three phone calls. The first was to Mal's villa in Majorca. He wanted to check his partner was still staying there alone, working on the last details of the Faithful merger. To his relief his call was answered by the cook, who confirmed that Mal was indeed there. 'Tell Mr Jones I will be arriving late this afternoon,' he said, and hung up before she could transfer the call to her employer. Next he telephoned the pilot of Sinai's jet at Munich airport. The aeroplane was due to fly the short hop to Zurich later that afternoon from where it would collect Solly after he had deposited the cash. Now the pilot was told to file a flight plan for the Balearics and to prepare for departure.

Finally Solly called home. Joseph answered.

'Joe? what the hell are you doing there? why aren't you at university?'

'Nice one, Dad. Make me feel welcome, why don't you.'

'I said what are you doing there?'

'I'm home for the weekend.'

'How long for?'

'It will be the usual weekend. Two days. Saturday and Sunday.'

'Don't be smart.'

'Why not? You paid good money for me to be smart. I might as well use it.'

Solly allowed himself half a smile.

'Is Mum there?' he said.

'Not a sign. Just got here. Deserted. It's like being an orphan.'

'You make my heart bleed, Joe. If only I'd known how deprived you were.'

'When you coming back? It would be good to chill with you for a couple of days.'

Solly felt a wave of regret break over him. How long would it be before Joe knew what was going on? Before Rachel knew? Before Judy knew? Christ, how long would it be before Solly knew for sure? 'That's the thing. I've got to go and see Mal.'

'Where is he?'

'Majorca.'

'More to the point, where are you?'

'Munich. On the way to the airport.'

'Cool.'

'It isn't cool, Joe. It's bloody German. Look, tell Mum when you see her that I've got to go see Mal. Tell her that . . .' He looked at his watch again and realized suddenly that time was short. 'Tell her I'll call her tomorrow when Shabbos goes out.'

'Fine. Whatever.'

'And Joe. Tell your mum . . .

'Yeah?'

'Tell her I love her.'

'Dad?'

'And I love you too. And Rachel. Take care. And shave off the bloody beard. I can hear it rustling against the mouthpiece.'

Joe rang off in gales of laughter that echoed along the

diluted electronics of the phone line. So simple a call. So domestic. So unburdened by threat. To Solly it felt as if he were working to some unconscious plan; a set of chess moves sketched out in advance for the occasion when things went wrong. But he knew there was no plan save that he should get himself far away from trouble to give himself time to think. In his own mind he was now on the run. He was doing it expensively, by private jet and private helicopter and GSM mobile phone. But he was still on the run. Fleeing. This is what Jews do, he thought. They flee. I am a Jew so now I flee.

First from the airport and then from the satellite phone in the jet he tried to make one more call, to Barney's office in Tel Aviv, but for much of the day there was no answer. Only when he was on the ground in Palma, waiting for the helicopter to take him across the island did he finally get a reply.

'Is Barney there?'

A sob rattled the line. 'No,' his secretary said, in a whisper. 'He's not here.'

'It's Solly Princeton calling.'

'Oh Mr Princeton . . .' Another sob.

'Where is Mr Dorf?' And then, encouragingly,' Talk to me. Where is Barney?'

'He's dead,' she whispered, as though she had killed him herself

'When? How?'

'Last night.'

'Talk to me, please. Tell me what you know.'

'Last night in Nicosia. At the airport.'

'How?'

'They didn't say.' She sobbed again. 'Just that he is dead. An accident. Some kind of horrible accident. The police, they called me at home an hour ago. Asked me for numbers of relatives. I only came into the office to . . .' Her voice collapsed into gasps and snuffles and hisses of disbelief Solly tried to make soothing noises, then rang off

344

In the helicopter, to the juddering of the blades above his head, he sketched out a scenario. Barney dead in Nicosia. Boxes opened, contents discovered. Boxes allowed to go on their way, followed all the time. Arrive in hotel and are delivered to chairman's suite. Police raid suite, find drugs, find drug dealers. Gain confession.

And then the bartering – shorter sentences in return for names – begins in earnest.

No more cinnamon cheesecake. For a moment that was all he could think about. No more full plates of cheesecake. No more shards of sweet pastry. To focus his mind he began quietly to recite the Kaddish for his friend, now dead in some accident unspecified. Killed on a foreign airfield. He took comfort in the soft repetitions and familiarity of the Hebrew words, and let his thoughts clear away, like an early morning mist burned away by sunlight.

The helicopter skittered across hills of scrub and honey sandstone, through a clear late afternoon autumn sky of diluted ink. Long shadows stretched now across the curves and rocky outcrops below, and an exhausted sun hung bloated and red over the hills to their left. Friday afternoon and sundown was not far away. In the villages below, lights were coming on; the last patches of sunlit earth were being smothered by the gloom and the trees were turning from a luminescent green to the colour of a stormy sea. Solly leaned forward from the back seat to the pilot and shouted at him to increase his speed but the pilot merely pursed his lips and shook his head.

And then they were there, the helicopter cresting a ridge and following the contours of a gentle hill towards the large white villa with its terraces and balconies and red tiled rooves. The swimming pool shone blue and clear for a moment from the underwater lights until the surface was broken by the down draught from the helicopter as it began to land on the pad sixty yards away. Solly could see Mal standing to one side in shorts and a shirt, billowing in the wind to reveal stretches of pale brown belly. He was crouching down and shielding his eyes against lumps of grit and sand picked up from the fields of rocky scree below his expensively cultivated gardens. Finally the blades began to power down and Solly clambered out.

'Solly, mate, for Christ's sake what's going on?' Mal was shouting over the still heavy engine noise. 'I've had phone calls here from the manager of the München all afternoon looking for you.' He wrapped his arm around Solly's back and in a crouch forced him to run up across the lawns to the house.

'What did you say?' Solly asked when they had made it to the terrace.

'That you were on your way here.'

Solly nodded. 'OK,' he said. He looked up at the sky, at the colour swiftly leaking away. 'I'm in a bit of trouble,' he said, quietly. 'I need your help.'

'Name it,' Mal said, remembering the kind of trouble Solly had once been in. 'Anything you want I'll try and do.'

'At the moment there's just one thing I need,' Solly said.

'What's that? Seriously. Name it.'

'Two candles. Box of matches. Candlesticks. It's Shabbos.'

Forty-three

It was early Sunday morning and Mal was in the swimming pool, sitting astride a lilo. His legs dangled either side and the weight of his body, positioned with expert care, caused the inflatable to buckle in the middle so that one end rose up the water to give him a back rest. The lilo glided towards the side of the pool. When it reached its destination, Mal kicked out with his feet, causing it to plough off through the water towards the other. He trailed one hand across the surface and watched the baby wake form behind it.

He had been sitting here alone like this, rolling back and forth across the pool, for almost an hour. He knew it was the behaviour of a moron and for a moment imagined the poolside to be crowded with thousands of his shareholders all staring in silence at the slack, waterlogged chief executive. Look at that. The man who controls an international hotel empire. What a klutz. But the bald repetition, to and fro, back and forth, helped him to think. And God knows he had a lot to think about. Occasionally his mind would wander to the flabby stretch of his belly, the folds made all the more obvious by his posture. He reached down with one hand and grabbed an unforgiving mound of flesh. Can I pinch more than an inch, he muttered to himself recalling an advertising slogan for some ancient diet plan. I should bloody say so. He grasped a second lump of fat on the other side and squeezed them both, so that it looked like he and his stomach were shaking hands. An inch here and an inch there. And an inch here. And here. Keep going like this and I'll have a foot. A foot of belly. A foot for a belly. A belly for a foot. The one thing wealth can buy you that you don't want: a really bad body. The lilo collided with the side of the pool again and the straining rubber squeaked against the tiled surround. He looked up and away over the empty scrub hills and remembered what he wished he could forget.

Solly had said nothing all Friday evening, retiring to the room Mal gave him to light his candles and say his prayers. The next day he maintained his silence, hiding away in his room. Shortly before lunch Mal knocked on the door and, getting no response, barged in. He found his partner sitting on the edge of his unmade bed in boxer shorts, vest and cupple, head bowed over a prayer book in his lap. The room smelt heavily of sleep.

'Solly mate, it's lunch.'

'Baruch ata . . . later, Mal . . . adonai elohainu melech . . .'

'Come down and have some lunch. We'll talk.'

Solly closed his eyes and raised his head. 'I'm praying,' he said, with an irritated sigh.

'You look to me like you're having a furtive wank. That book's not big enough to cover anything.'

'Have some respect,' Solly barked.

'And you could do with a shave. One faint breeze and you'll be able to hear your stubble rustling.'

'I'll come when I'm ready.'

'Shall I wait lunch?'

'Is the only thing you can think about food?'

'Now I've heard everything. Solly Princeton accusing someone else of gluttony.'

'I'm praying,' Solly said, and bowed his head again over the pages of Hebrew.

For a moment Mal stood watching his partner and then slowly, a knot drawing itself tight deep in the depths of his belly, he left the room and closed the door.

Solly refused to take phone calls too, and of those there were many. First was Judy wanting to know where her husband was. Policemen had been to the house looking for him. Mal was sitting by the pool under a wash of bright, warm autumn sunlight, the cordless phone pressed to his ear. And still he shivered.

'What did they say?'

'Just that they wanted to talk to him, Mal, what's he been doing? Tell me. I have to know. I deserve to know. After all I've been through with that man, I deserve to . . .'

'I don't know, sweetheart. Honestly. He won't talk to me.'

'Mal, I'm scared.'

'I'm sure it's nothing. Probably a parking ticket', and he tried on a reassuring laugh, but he knew it was only the sound of discomfort. 'Look, I'll get one of the lawyer boys round the house. Don't say anything to the police until you hear from me or Solly.'

Next came Divinia, worried about Judy who was worried about Solly. And there had been policemen at their front door too. what did they want, these stern men in their sensible slip-on shoes? What were Mal and Solly involved in? What was it? What had they done? She had a right to know. And what will the neighbours think, police cars drawing up into the drive like that? The shame!

'I've done nothing,' Mal said. 'Solly's upstairs. Won't say a word. The moment he tells me I'll tell you. Believe me. In the mean time I'll get one of the lawyer boys round to keep you company. Don't say anything to the police.'

Next Gerry.

'Gerry, mate, I have no idea, seriously . . . Solly's upstairs, praying his fat head off, like his life depends upon it. what did the police say to you? . . . Only that? . . . No indication of what they wanted? . . . What did you say? . . . Fine. You gave them my number here? Just fine. Great . . . No, no. I know you had to. I can see that. Look, I'm going to get one of the lawyers to come round your place, keep you company. Don't say anything more to the police until you hear from me.'

Then Joseph, worried about Judy. Then Judy again, wanting to know if Solly had said anything yet. Next Heidi, because she had heard from Divinia, and a little later Benny, because the police had finally been round to see him too. More lawyers.

At 4 p.m. a phone call from an Inspector Brown in London. Or Black. Or Blue. Mal saw it only as a wave of dull colour breaking over him.

'We are eager to speak to Mr Princeton, as are the authorities in Germany. Can you tell us when he'll be returning?'

'Mr Princeton's asleep right now, after his long journey yesterday. Can you tell me what this is about?'

'We have been asked to investigate the whereabouts of Mr Princeton on behalf of the German authorities.'

'Can I ask why?'

'In connection with an incident on Thursday at one of your hotels, Mr Jones. Perhaps you could ask Mr Princeton to call me the moment he awakes.' Mal took down the telephone number as the line fizzed and crackled and went dead.

Mal finally snapped when he took a call from a City journalist for one of the Sunday newspapers who asked for confirmation that a breaking scandal in Munich would cause the delay or cancellation of the Faithful merger. Mal shouted, 'No, it bloody well won't!' into the mouthpiece and then, as a more satisfying alternative to ringing off, chucked the cordless handset high into the air so that it crashed down onto the terrace and shattered, sending components ricocheting into the pool. Back in London an intrigued journalist stared at his own handset, and decided it was well worth making a few more calls on the Sinai story.

Early on Saturday evening Solly emerged from the

house dressed and shaved. He ignored his partner, who was still sitting out studying merger papers, and went to stand at the very edge of the pool, as if to dive in. He looked upwards to the darkening sky and when he had counted stars said, 'Mal mate, I've got a bit of stuff to tell you about. None of it's easy stuff but then lots of things aren't, are they? That's just the way life is.' He pulled up a seat opposite Mal's and leaned forward, forearms resting on his knees. 'First thing is I'm sorry for the shit you're about to have to go through on my behalf really I am. But I just want to tell you, you've got nothing to worry about. Nothing at all. I'm gonna take full responsibility for everything. In fact I want to take responsibility. It's time people knew what I've done and why. I don't apologize for it. I'm just going to explain.'

Mal said, 'Enough preamble. Talk to me.'

Solly sat back and considered his fingernails as if a prompt script lay there, and said simply, 'For the past twelve years I have been smuggling cocaine into Germany.'

'Solly, for Christ's sake . . .' Solly raised one hand to silence him.

'You'll have to let me finish everything, then ask me questions.' He hesitated for a second, let his hands fall into his lap and stared away over his partner's head. 'I only ever sold into Germany and the money raised, which was substantial, went to charity. I never benefited at all.

'For almost an hour Solly talked and whenever Mal tried to interrupt he would silence him with a dark stare and the words 'Let me say my piece. I've got to say my piece.' He talked about retribution and making good come from bad. He talked about Latvia and the refusniks and the Foundation and Drugs Anonymous. He talked about the cause and the project. Finally he said, 'It just all came together at once. You know how ideas sometimes do. Everything fits into place and you can see it's right. You can't get away from the idea. You can't escape it so you just have to give yourself up to it.'

Mal nodded because Solly was staring at him and he couldn't handle the expectation in his gaze. But then he shook his head as if trying to rouse himself from sleep.

'This is incredible,' he murmured.

'I don't have to convince you, do I?' Solly said, with a shrug. 'You've had enough phone calls from people looking for me to know it's true.'

'Why are they looking for you now?'

'Don't know for sure. The cargo was coming through Nicosia, something happened and the man who was accompanying it was killed.'

'What was this bloke's name, this colleague of yours?' Mal was thirsting for information now. He wanted detail. Anything with which to bring what he was hearing into focus.

'Dorf,' Solly said. 'Barney Dorf.'

'I recognize that name. Why do I recognize that name?'

Solly looked away. 'Don't know.'

'Dorf Dorf.' Mal jumped up as if his seat were electrified. 'Of course. I know why I know his name. Dorf bought the Leventhal shares we couldn't afford back in '87.'

'What of it?'

'What money did he use? Tell me the money was clean. Tell me it wasn't drug—'

Solly waved him away. 'Completely clean.'

'Do you mean clean-clean or do you mean laundered-clean?'

'What difference does it make?'

'It makes a huge fucking difference.' Throughout Solly's explanation Mal had found himself shrinking back in his seat. It had seemed almost impossible to admonish his partner for what he had done. What words could he find to match the offence? What could he say to challenge such certainty? But now, here in

352

the detail of the Leventhal deal, Solly's infected drug money seeping into the clean wells of the Sinai finds, he had a point of contact.

'You contaminated the company.'

'I saved the company.'

'You poisoned the firm.'

'I made sure Schaeffer didn't get his hands on us.'

They were both standing now, staring each other in the eye. 'Anyway,' Solly said, 'Sinai isn't just yours. It's mine too. I had the right to do what needed to be done.'

'Yeah, but you didn't have the smarts to do the right thing.'

'You know what, mate, you want to know what was great about running coke into Germany? what was really great? I'll tell you. It was my business. You ran the firm. Me, I ran something far more complicated and I didn't need your sodding help. I did it. I raised millions of pounds and I made Jewish lives better with it. It was mine. All mine. Not yours.'

'Is that what all this is about? Solly Princeton becomes drug dealer to purge inferiority complex about his partner?'

'I took control of my life.'

'And fucked up other people's lives.'

'What lives?'

'German lives.'

'Feh! Fuck them. Why should I worry from German lives?'

They fell silent once more. For the second time that night, Mal was incapable of finding the right words. He turned and stood with his back to Solly and stared up at the endless vault of the sky just as his partner had done an hour before. Usually he revelled in the glitter-tossed star fields above him but now they seemed tarnished and devalued. Beneath these stars he had learned terrible things. They had eavesdropped on his loss of innocence and in turn they too had been defiled.

Defiled.

Devalued.

Loss of value.

Loss.

His mind turned over the words.

'What are your plans now?' Mal said to the darkness.

'Tomorrow, day after, I'll fly home. Turn myself in and then I'll have to go to Germany. Stand trial, the whole bit.'

'You think you've thought all this through don't you?'

'I've had time, mate. I've done a lot of thinking.'

'The deadline on the Faithful deal is Wednesday.'

'I know. Can't be helped. You'll just have to take all the glory by yourself. Sure you'll prefer it that way, taking the glory. Always have.'

'You still don't get it, do you?' He turned to Solly, who tipped his head to one side.

'This is a share swap. Sinai stock for Faithful stock. It's only gonna go through if our price stays up.'

'So?'

'Christ, Solly. At least try and think. Give it a go. Just for once. You go home. You're arrested. Shit all over the papers about the Sinai chairman who uses one of the company hotels as the centre of his bells and whistles drug-running operation. You want to know what will happen? Everybody's going to be flogging our shares like just talking about them, they'll contract gonorrhoea . . .'

'You don't know that for sure.'

'Of course I know that for sure. That's what's going to happen. This time next week our shares will be worth tuppence and so will we. And Judy. And Joe. And Benny. And Heidi. And . . .'

Solly began to mumble. 'I didn't mean to . . .'

'Oh yeah. Of course you didn't mean to. What weird fuck-up means to? Who ever means to?' And then, 'You arsehole.' It seemed the most appropriate thing he had said all evening.

And now it was Sunday morning and Mal was in the

pool, gliding back and forth, and what bothered him most was the injustice of it all. Sinai was a good company. No, it was a great company, with solid assets and big profits and a future. It wasn't overvalued and it wasn't undervalued. The share price was spot on, a fair representation of the firm's profit potential and the worth of what it owned. They had built this great institution. And no longer was it about chicken carcasses and soup-making machines and salt beef bars. No longer was it about giving Mrs Roth and Mrs Silverstein what they wanted. They weren't an Edgware firm any more. They were a world firm and Mal wanted them to stay that way.

If only the company co-chairman wasn't about to be arrested for smuggling cocaine. City opinion wouldn't like that. They wouldn't like it at all.

But the share price had to stay up.

What he had to do was influence City opinion.

So the share price would stay up.

Or even just make it look like he was influencing City opinion.

So that the share price *did* stay up, regardless of what people thought.

It didn't matter how it was done, just so long as it was done.

The solution appeared in his head immediately. what was it Solly had said? Sometimes you can't escape an idea so you just have to give yourself up to it. Mal could see no alternative. Slowly he paddled back to the side of the pool nearest the house. He pulled himself out and walked dripping to his chair and reached for the cordless phone he always left within arm's reach to make a call to London. Only then did he remember that it was lying behind him in a broken heap where it had landed the day before.

Forty-four

The stockbroker arrived later that day. He had the charmless walk of a man about to make a lot of money and a black leather briefcase big enough to carry it all.

'Solly,' Mal said, laying a hand on his partner's shoulder. 'You remember Piers Grafton.' They were standing on the lawns as the helicopter powered down its engines, so they had to shout.

'How could I forget?' Solly barked. It had been more than fifteen years since he had clashed with the thin-faced, golden-haired City boy who had run their estates office, but the memory did not fade. The hair was receding now so that its only clear feature was a savage widow's peak like an arrowhead, and his cheeks were thin and gaunt. But, to Solly, he still had the lazy posture of an SS officer convinced he had won promotion.

Grafton grinned, and said, 'I'm here to save your Israelite *arse,* dear boy.' He stamped his feet like a dray horse, and hooted and honked with laughter.

Mal stared at his own feet, finding comfort in their stillness. 'Yes, well,' he said. 'We have a lot of work to get through.'

Solly said, 'We must be in trouble. If we're relying on scumbags like this to get us out of a hole.'

Grafton buried one hand in his trouser pocket and jangled his change. 'Shall I just pop back on the old helicopter then, matey? Because I *really* don't mind if I do. *Your* call.'

'Piers, go on up to the house. The cook will show you where to drop your things.' Mal gripped Solly's shoulder tightly, to stop him following.

When he had gone Mal stuck his face close to Solly's. A soft wind blew off the hills and the air smelt of warm dust and pine. 'Understand this. You have no say here. No say whatsoever. All you are going to do is what me and Piers Grafton tell you to do.'

'You seriously don't mind using a shyster like him?'

'The Israelite crack is just him trailing his coat tails 'cause he knows how much it winds you up. Anyway, I've been working with a shyster like you for twenty-five years, haven't I? Difference is, you got us into trouble. He's going to get us out.'

'You have no self-respect.'

'Fuck it Solly, I do not need this. I really do not need this.' He lifted his chin and sniffed the air and wrinkled his nose. 'You want to know the truth? The real truth? Well I'll tell you.' He stared his partner in the eye. 'Sinai is all I have. OK? There it is. I've said it. Sinai is what I am and what I've always been and it's going to be hard enough to find a life outside it, without the whole outfit going west. I need the Faithful deal to work. I need to get out with my dignity, with people still thinking of me as the deal maker so I can have a future. It goes wrong and those bastards in the City who have been staring down their nose at this upstart Jew boy the past twenty years will be in heaven.'

Solly took one step back. 'You really don't have any self-respect, do you?'

Mal pretended he had not heard him. 'They will love it. Seriously. And I'm not up for that, whatever it takes. At the moment we are that fucking close—' he held his thumb and forefinger millimetres apart – 'to it going that way because of you. OK? You understand now? Because of you.' Solly stepped back another foot. 'Right,' Mal said, with a jerk of his head. 'Not another word.' He turned away and walked back up to the house.

They sat outside on the terrace in the sweet shade of a fig tree. The only noise came from flies buzzing the last of that season's fruit, and the pool's filtration system, which fizzed and bubbled. Grafton dug sheaves of paper out of his bottomless briefcase, as if clearing space for his commission, and laid them on the coffee table that stood between them.

'Right, gentlemen,' he said rubbing his hands together, the big player at the biggest poker game in town. 'For what we are going to do you have to think of your shares as your children. In a few days, of course, the whole world is going to think that your children are the worst-behaved brats on the street and all because of some nasty rumours about one of their parents.' He turned to Solly and threw him a wink; Solly looked away.

'Of course, we know that your children are awfully bright and well-behaved and that they shouldn't be written off just because of what their folks have been getting up to.' Solly huffed. Grafton acknowledged his discomfort with a thin smile. 'Our job is to make everybody realize that too. In other words, gentlemen, we have to control the market in opinion and I am here to tell you that that opinion comes at a premium.'

If the Sinai partners could buy their own shares everything would be rosy, Grafton said. Just pukka. Because then they really could control the market in opinion. As everybody else sold, forcing the price down, Sinai would step in and buy back the shares, forcing the price up once more. 'But that is a no-no, I'm afraid, gentlemen. It's somewhat illegal for a company to deal in its own shares so close to a merger, so instead we have to get other people to buy your shares for you. And then these other people can tell the rest of the world just what super kids your children are.'

Grafton selected a set of papers from the pile in front of him and held them on his lap. 'Of course getting other people to support your share price is also rather less than legal but what the eye doesn't see, eh?' He passed the papers over to Mal. Each one was a profile

358

of a leading businessman, plus a photocopy of a photograph. Mal read them and then passed them on to Solly who glanced at them before passing them back to Grafton.

'These are your saviours, gentlemen,' Grafton said. 'Thought it important you know who is prepared to assist you. Each of them has helped us in the past. Been very amenable.' Mal was impressed and surprised. These were big names; chairmen and chief executives of public companies, with high profiles and lots of shareholders and reputations. They were scions of banking families and captains of industry, the embodiment of propriety. And they were on the take. Grafton pulled a cheap plastic cigarette lighter from his pocket and as each sheet was passed back to him he set fire to it, allowing the burning paper to flutter to the terrace where it turned into ash. 'No extra paperwork we don't need, eh.'

Each, he said, was prepared to purchase a block of Sinai shares as they came onto the market. However, they would need guarantees. 'You'll have to sign your own holdings over to a trust I will control.'

'Why?' Solly said. 'Why our shares? They're worth millions, these shares.'

'Exactly, chap. Anything goes wrong, and the price falls after they've purchased. You'll have to give them more shares to compensate them back to the value of their outlay.'

Solly took a sharp intake of breath, as if he had been stung.

'Not that it will come to that. Just a precaution. My clients like precautions.'

'What's the target price?' Mal said. 'At what price do these white knights start getting their hands on our stock?'

'Ah,' Grafton said, with a brief nod of his head. 'I'm glad you asked me that.'

Mal and Grafton began furiously discussing thresholds and guarantees, yields and deadlines and margins and commissions. Buying short, selling long. Escrow accounts and transfers. Solly tried to keep up but the more they talked the less he understood. The only thing he'd ever understood was profit and loss, whether a business was making money or not. And even then his knowledge had come more from intuition than balance sheets. With a balance sheet he was always confused by the time he reached the third row of figures. Instead, he would know instinctively by the number of punters through the door whether it was working or not. That, he always felt, was why he was so good at what he did. He looked at people, not figures. Only people. It was why he'd needed Barney – may he rest – on the drug-running operation. It may have been his business but he still couldn't work the numbers. Someone else had to do that. Always someone else for the numbers.

Grafton and Mal talked on and on. For a while Solly considered saying nothing. Why should he speak? They didn't want him to speak. Look at them, foreheads inches apart, talking in machine code, muttering the numbers at each other like computers on heat. But this was too important for him to keep silent about. He was involved too. Wasn't he? Up to his chin in it. Going under fast.

He closed his eyes and said, in a loud clear voice, 'I'm afraid I do not understand what you are talking about.'

Mal and Grafton fell silent. Solly opened his eyes. They were both looking at him as if he were the tiresome younger brother playing gooseberry on a hot date.

Then Mal spoke. 'You,' he said slowly, 'do not have to understand anything.' He pointed at him with one outstretched index finger. 'All you have to understand is that you got us into this and we're getting you out. There's things I don't understand about you and believe me there's things I don't want to understand. So let's just think of it as a fair trade. My lack of understanding for yours. All you have to do is what we're telling you to do. OK?'

Solly looked away to the pool, like a petulant schoolboy.

'I said, OK?'

Solly said, 'Yeah, OK.' Why fight?

Grafton spoke again. 'A couple of last things, gentlemen. We keep the circle on this small?'

'Of course,' Mal said. 'Us three, we're the only ones who need to know from this side.'

'What about Gerry?' Solly said.

'Him particularly,' Mal said. 'He's to know nothing. Keep him clean. Gerry must always be whiter than white.'

'Fine,' Grafton said. 'Good that we're agreed.' Although Solly had agreed to nothing. 'Then the second point, chaps, and this is just a precaution – because we like precautions, don't we – can I suggest you put all your assets into your wives' names now, so that if anything goes a little awry . . .'

'Did you bring the relevant papers?' Mal said.

'Of course.' Another pile of snow-white documents spilled onto the table. More space cleared in the briefcase for more commission.

One by one, page by page, Mal Jones and Solly Princeton set about signing away their lives. Out went the offshore funds and the exotic properties, the high-yield investments and the long-term holdings and the careful earners for their future and their children's future. That invisible empire of possessions and riches, built up over twenty-five years, slipped in the scratch of pen across paper, from one set of names to another.

Until, by the end of that warm Majorcan evening, Divinia Jones and Judith Princeton were officially two of the wealthiest women in Britain.

Forty-five

They arrived back at Heathrow airport early on the Wednesday morning, to a cold overcast autumn day that made Solly think about the *pâtisserie* on Edgware High Street; of customers with hot fresh bread pressed against their cheeks for comfort against bitter winds, and the smell of clarified butter and ground almonds out back. Judy was standing at the arrivals gate, flanked by an honour guard of Sinai salary men, her soft, sagging face fixed beneath a hard screen of make-up. Mal stole a glance at her lips and remembered the cracked ceiling at Mrs Hyman's. Inappropriate memories always came to him when he was under pressure.

'Solly, this is Mr Gold,' she said, pecking her husband on the cheek, and pushing forward a man with skin to match the colour of the terminal's grey marble floor. 'Mr Gold is a successful lawyer and you will do what Mr Gold says. For once in your life you will do this, if not for me then for Rachel and Joseph. And you will shave, for heaven's sake. You will give me a rash with that stubble. What will the police say, when they see you with that stubble . . .'

'Judy, leave it. I will not be kissing the police-men . . .'

'Do as I say,' she barked. 'God forbid you should think of your family for once . . .'

'Judy . . .'

'After all, Mr Gold has certificates. *He* has been to university. *He* is an educated man. Where have *you* been? Majorca, that's where you have been, sunning yourself while your family has been under siege from policemen and journalists and . . .'

The Sinai party was moving off now towards the airport terminal doors, the two Sinai drivers using Mal's bags to shove their way through the crowds. There was a shout of 'Over there!' and, before they could escape, bulbs flashed magnesium bright from within the crowds of passengers. The photographers and reporters were upon them, firing questions, demanding answers.

'Mr Princeton, do you have any comment to make about this morning's story?'

'Judy,' he hissed 'What story? What's he talking about?'

'I told you,' she said. 'Journalists all weekend. But will you listen to me? Do you ever? No, you just—'

'Mr Princeton, will you be going to Germany?'

'Not now, Judy, please . . .'

'Mr Jones, is the Faithful deal still going ahead?'

'Never will you listen to me. And now look where you've ended up . . .'

One of Sinai's PR staff, a little man in a big man's suit, struggled along behind trying to keep up, his tasselled loafers slipping and sliding against the shiny floor. 'Look, guys,' he yelped. 'I mean really, guys . . . give them a chance, because look . . .'

Mal raised his head and without breaking pace said, 'My office will be issuing a statement within the hour. We have nothing more to say. Thank you.'

'Yeah,' said the PR man, who knew nothing about the statement. 'Within the hour. A statement. We'll be issuing . . . One of—'

But they were out of the terminal now and clambering into their cars: big, black Mercedes with tinted windows, high-powered engines and thick tyres; scandal-motors designed for escaping from airports. Solly, Judy and the lawyer went in the first, Mal and the PR man in the second.

As they pulled away the PR man handed Mal a copy of that morning's *Financial Times*. He was apologetic, as if he were presenting the corpse of a dead puppy. The headline said FAITHFUL DEAL IN DOUBT AS SINAI

INQUIRY WIDENS. Mal didn't read the story beneath. He pulled a piece of paper from his briefcase. On it was one paragraph, handwritten.

Mr Solomon Princeton, co-chairman and chief executive of Sinai Corp, this morning presented himself at Paddington Green Police Station, accompanied by his solicitor, to help police with their inquiries. He has agreed to answer all questions and will shortly be travelling to Germany to assist the authorities there. He has been charged with no offence and is giving his time voluntarily. The merger between Sinai Corp and Faithful PLC will go ahead as planned, subject to agreement.

'Put that out the moment we get back to the office,' Mal said and settled back in his seat.

I didn't wish him luck, Mal thought. I said nothing to Solly. I just let him get in the car and drive away. I didn't wish the little shmock luck. To his surprise he felt guilt battering hard at the walls of his stomach.

Gerry and Benny were waiting in the lobby at the Square when Mal's car drew up, hands in pockets, pacing out the floor.

'We're down five pence since opening, already,' said Gerry, the moment Mal made it through the door.

'What's going on?' said Benny.

'Our shares are in freefall.'

'Talk to me, mate.'

'We won't make the target price.'

'Say something, Mal. Tell me something I need to hear.'

Mal looked at the receptionist, a young blond woman who wore her hair up in a style he'd always liked. She managed a weak smile. So even you are panicking, Mal thought. Even the small people are panicking. All of you, worrying for your jobs. The building seemed to hum and grind with panic, like a runaway train desperately trying to pull itself to a halt before hitting the buffers.

'We'll be fine,' Mal said and climbed into the lift with his brother and the finance director.

Up in Mal's office Gerry ran to one of the share-trading screens that had been fitted on his desk at the tail end of the Eighties, and hunkered down in front of it.

'Down two more pence,' Gerry said, shoving his glasses back up his nose. 'Down again. Confidence has been marginalized. Profit-taking is maximized.'

'You're rambling,' Mal said. 'Stop it. You're not making the situation any better.'

'We're taking a battering. Losing value.'

'I said stop it.'

'We're being barbecued.'

'I said . . .'

Gerry stood up straight, tensed his jaw and pushed his glasses back up his nose once more. He'd had enough. 'The fucking fuckers are fucking fucking us, you mad fucking fuck,' he bawled. 'And you're doing fucking nothing.'

There was silence in the room. Benny stared anxiously at Mal. Mal stared at Gerry and Gerry stared back, eyes blinking behind his lenses. Then Mal began to laugh, slowly at first, his chest barely moving. It picked up speed and intensity and volume, made his shoulders dance and his soft belly quiver. Benny caught the laugh and finally so did Gerry, who made a worrying noise like a cat hawking up a furball, until all three of them were standing in the room, their heads thrown back, howling at the ceiling.

When the laughter subsided Mal said, 'Fellas, this will be a difficult day but trust me, it will go through.'

Benny said 'I have to say, mate, if we were a horse I wouldn't be putting money on us right now.'

'Exactly,' Mal said. 'That's what I'm saying. You always lose so of course you wouldn't put money on us.'

'I don't bet any more. It's, you know, an image. And anyway I don't always lose.'

'Mostly you lose. The big ones you lose. This is a big one so you would lose.'

Gerry interrupted: 'What has Solly been doing?'

'He'll have to tell you about that himself.'

'There are rumours.'

'There are always rumours.'

'These are not nice rumours.'

Mal went to his desk. He took off his jacket, sat down and stared at the screen for himself. Dropped another penny. 'Since when have rumours about Jewish businessmen ever been nice?' he said. And then, without looking up, 'Gerry, go phone your friends at Faithful. Make nice with them for an hour or two. Tell them everything's fine. Just a glitch.'

'But is it a glitch?'

'We own a lot of very big hotels. People pay us a lot of money to stay at our very big hotels. The business is solid. So believe me, it's only a glitch. And Benny, go keep an eye on our PR guys. Those klutzes can't even spell statement let alone issue one. I'll have something more for you in an hour.' Benny and Gerry seemed reassured now they had something to do. Mal had been right before. Why should he get it all wrong now? Granted, it didn't look good. Still, Mal understood the business. He worked the numbers. He was Sinai. That was what he did. If they couldn't trust him on this, they couldn't trust him at all.

They left him alone.

But still the share price kept dropping. It had started the day three pence above the target price for the Faithful merger. Now it was ten pence below. Then another tuppence down. Now Mal wondered whether he even trusted himself.

Five pence.

One penny.

Three pence more. Value is falling off these shares like leaves off autumn trees, Mal thought. These shares are wilting before my eyes, dying. His share-dealing screen was solid with red now, the company's blood rolling in an electronic surge across the pixels. And where was Grafton? What was that damn anti-Semite goy shit stockbroker doing to stem the flow of this blood? Why was his finger not on this perforated money artery, pressing hard, keeping the fluids in, saving the patient? Mal reached for the phone and dialled the man's number.

'Grafton, I'm dying here,' he shouted. 'I'm being slaughtered.'

Grafton gasped. 'Get off the line, you arse. You don't call me here, not today.'

'I tell you, I am dying. My guts are ruptured.' Mal slapped the screen with the back of his hand. Sweat was breaking out in beads across his top lip. 'Here, on my screen, ruptured. I'm dying.'

'Don't call me again,' Grafton barked and hung up.

Mal took deep breaths, steadied himself and then phoned upstairs to his brother.

'Benny, I want you to issue another statement.' He squeezed the receiver in his hand as his brother replied, so that his knuckles went white. 'I know it's bad. That it looks bad. I can see it here too. It's on my screen too. So listen to me. I want to issue a statement. Put out this statement. Say this. Say that the chairman and directors of Sinai have faith in the company and have no doubt that our price will pick up in time to satisfy the conditions of the Faithful merger. OK. You've got that? Fine. Put it out.' He threw the phone back onto its rest.

At two o'clock that afternoon Gerry went to see Mal. He was studying his shoes and holding a long white envelope which he gently passed to Mal without looking him in the eye.

'What's this?'

Gerry fiddled with his glasses again and looked up for a second. 'My resignation.'

'You what?'

'I need to get out, sort a way to sell my holding.'

'Am I hearing this?'

'I can't take the risk, Mal, I'm sorry.'

'I can't believe I'm hearing this.'

'Most of my money is in those shares. I can't afford to lose it all.'

'You can't sell your shares. Not now. It's illegal. Not so close to the deadline.' Mal crossed his fingers.

Gerry scoffed. 'There are ways. You know that. There are always ways.'

'No wonder the price is falling, now even the directors are selling their shares. This, I suppose, is loyalty. In the 1990s this is what passes for loyalty.'

'You have to understand, Mal. I have to do this. Look at the price. Look. Our shares are in the toilet.'

'Of course our shares are in the toilet. You're selling them. So they fall. You do this, the finance director tries to sell, and the price will go through the floor. Why should anybody else keep our shares if even the finance director doesn't want them?'

'I'm sorry Mal. Really I am. I have to try and do something.' And then he was gone.

Half an hour later Benny came to see him.

'Now even my brother,' Mal said, when Benny had announced he was going to try and offload too. 'My own flesh and blood?'

'What can I do, mate? I don't have lots of offshore accounts like you.'

I don't either, Mal muttered to himself Not any more. 'Look,' he said, trying to keep calm. 'Don't sell. Don't do it. You do that and we're really finished. I'll re-imburse you, whatever you lose, I promise. Which you won't because—' he waved at the screen – 'this is just a glitch.'

'Mal. Listen to me. We are 112 off the target price. The markets close in two and a half hours. We are screwed. Do I have to spell it out for you? The horse has gone lame. It's pulled up. It's thrown its rider. The horse is lying in the middle of the course and right now they're coming out with their pistols and they're going to put the bloody animal out of its misery. And I can't afford to be in at the kill.'

Mal hit the screen with his fist. 'The price will pick up!' he screamed.

'It won't.'

He hit it again. 'It will.' His eye caught the roaring tides of red on the screen and he felt his throat tighten. Was he about to cry? Here, in front of his younger brother. Break down and weep? Was that what was going to happen? 'It will,' he said again, as if words alone could make the wished-for happen. 'Believe me. It will. It will.'

It was only then that he saw it. A flicker down at the bottom of the screen. It would have been nothing on any other day. What was one penny to Sinai? Nothing. A fraction of a shaving of a piece of an empire. But today was not any other day. Mal leaned towards the screen. He wasn't imagining it. The price really had stopped falling and had risen a penny. Then, as he was watching, it rose another penny. One more delicious, rounded penny.

In a thin choked voice he said, 'It is.'

'What?'

'It is. It's happening.'

'Mal, give up.'

'I'm telling you. Come look.' Now it was up another two pence. Bit by bit the price was climbing again. 'Here, on the screen. It's happening.'

Benny came and stood by his elder brother's shoulder. 'You messing with this screen, mate?'

Mal shook his head. 'Don't need to. Because its happening. Here. I told you. It's going up.' Without looking down he opened a desk drawer and pulled out a piece of paper. 'Give it an hour,' Mal said, 'then release this to the press.'

Benny read it: '"The chairmen and directors of Sinai Corp are delighted and humbled by the faith shown in their company by investors and look forward to finalizing details of the merger with Faithful PLC as planned."' He said: 'You were so confident this was going to work out that you wrote your victory speech in advance?'

Mal giggled. 'I know my business, mate.' On the screen the price was climbing steadily upwards.

'You do, don't you.'

'Just go release the statement,' Mal said. 'And see if you can find Gerry and stop him selling his shares. Tell him I refuse to accept his resignation.'

At ten to five, forty minutes before the deadline, the Sinai Corp share price went back over the target price for the merger. Sinai and Faithful would now become one. Mal pulled a big fat cigar from a box in his desk and lit it, following the rituals he had been shown so many years before by Syd Greenspan. Here's to Piers Grafton, he thought to himself as he took a puff, a grey-blue cloud of smoke breaking over the blinking eye of the share-dealing screen. He took another long draw, tumbled the smoke around inside his mouth for a moment and then sat back and exhaled. And here's to my freedom.

Forty-six

Late morning the next day Solly appeared in Mal's office. He was wearing a clean suit and shirt and he had shaved but he still looked tired. There were dark grey circles beneath his eyes and his head hung low on his neck, as if he didn't have the strength to hold it up.

Mal said, 'You look like shit.'

Solly rnanaged a weak smile. 'Thanks. I worked very hard at it. I think it's what they call police station glow.' He pulled at the bag under his right eye with one index finger. 'Very exclusive this. Only really important criminals get to look this bad.'

'Don't flatter yourself, Solly. There's scarier people out there than you.'

'I know,' he said. 'Shared a cell with one of them last night.'

'It was bad?'

'It didn't fall into the category marked good.'

'When they release you?'

'This morning, at eight. The lucky recipient of police bail.'

'That's lucky.'

'Cheers, friend.'

'No I just meant . . . well I thought . . . someone done for drugs.'

'I'm not charged with anything here. Only in Germany. I gave myself up voluntarily, so I'm not seen as a risk. Promised to co-operate an' all that. Had to leave my passport of course, but apart from that . . .'

'Well I'm pleased.'

'Yeah. Me too. Been home, seen Judy. The kids were

there too so that was . . .' His voice trailed off and he turned to study the view from Mal's office windows, although he knew exactly what was there to look at.

'The deal went through,' Mal said.

'I heard. Congratulations.'

'Congratulations to you too. It's your firm as well.'

'And everything was . . . ?'

'Everything was fine. Cut it a bit close but all that matters is that it went through. Gerry tried to bail out but we got him back on board just in time.'

'Right.'

'Yeah.'

Solly sank his hands into his expensive trouser pockets and his shoulders sagged. 'You busy?' he said.

'Well there's papers from yesterday to go through . . .'

'Only I was thinking it would be good if we had lunch.'

'What? Today?'

'Yeah. You and me. You know. Lunch. There's a place I want to try, a fish restaurant and I just thought.'

Mal hesitated. There were papers and there were meetings and there were people who needed talking to. All of which was just an excuse for not talking to Solly. There would always be papers and there would always be meetings and there would always be people. He said, 'I'll get one of the lads to drive us.'

'Nah, let me drive. Car's outside. I want to drive.'

'I didn't know you still knew how to.'

'I got my chauffeur to give me lessons.'

They crossed the traffic clutter of central London, Solly cursing as he crunched the unfamiliar gears of the Jaguar, and weaved through the narrow streets south of the river to the wider, more forgiving spaces of the motorway. Heavy autumn clouds scudded across a watery sky.

'I didn't realize we were going abroad,' Mal said.

'Kent,' Solly said.

'As I say, abroad. Are there any Jews in Kent? We'll be the only two, won't we?'

'You never heard of the Margate Ghetto or the great Rebbe Shlemiel of Broadstairs?'

'I knew the Jews had wandered but I didn't realize they got that lost.'

Solly grunted out a short laugh and fell silent again. The soft hills just beyond London gave way to the flat flood plains of the Thames estuary; tired, mottled fields edged by ragged hedgerows stretched away to the horizon where the distant reflection from the sea made the sky seem thin and anaemic. An hour and a half after they had started their journey, just when Mal had begun to wonder if they were simply going to drive off the edge of the country, Solly left the motorway and turned into a town announced by a sign that read WHITSTABLE, HERITAGE COASTAL TOWN.

'Not my heritage,' Mal said.

'Everybody says Whitstable is very nice.'

'It's a fishing town. When have you ever been interested in fishing?'

'I'm interested in fish. To get the best fish you go to source.'

Narrow lanes of red-brick shops and houses, shyly aware of their own prettiness, led down to the seafront. Solly pulled into a car park just behind the high concrete sea wall. They locked up and went to stand on the platform behind the barrier to study the unfamiliar view. A wide beach of raw shingle, carved up by breakwaters of dark sodden wood, stretched off in both directions. Sailing boats were drawn up high on the beach, canvas wrapped tightly about their masts. They huddled there against the wooden oyster houses and red-brick villas, these skiffs and yawls, as if trying to escape the shore breeze, which carried on it only the sound of surf and the smell of salt.

'Odd thing, the sea,' Solly said.

'Can't see the point of it myself,' Mal said. 'Don't know what to do with it.'

'Can't build on it.'

'Nah. You can't buy it either.'

'And you can't walk on it, even though your bloody mother always thought you could.'

'And like your mother thought you'd sink.'

Mal laughed. 'No, but my dad always thought I would,' he muttered. He pulled his jacket tightly around him against the wind. The banter didn't stop him feeling edgy and uncomfortable, here on the fringes of such a gross, uncompromising expanse of water. He watched the weight of the sea crush the shingle, and shivered.

Solly said 'Come on. That should be the restaurant over there. Let's go eat.'

It was a bright, airy room of brick and bare floorboards, filled by sunlight and the sound of the waves. Solly glanced up at the blackboard that held the menu and when the waitress came to take the order he said, 'I'll have the lobster.'

Mal said, 'Solly? What in God's name are you doing?'

'That's the whole lobster, not the half. And a bottle of champagne, the house.'

'Er, I'll just have the brill,' Mal said. Then, when the waitress had sorted out side orders and left them alone he said, 'What you doing? Lobster's tref.'

Solly reached for the brown bread, tore a piece off and stuffed it in his mouth. 'You care?'

'Well no, but I thought you did.'

'I'm reminding myself of what it's like.' The champagne arrived and Solly poured them each a glass. 'I want to remember what it's like to have choice and I want to feel a bit of guilt. That way, when I'm inside I won't be tempted to stray.'

'I would have thought you already had enough to feel guilty about.'

'Told you . . .' he sipped his champagne and licked his lips, 'I feel sorry about the fallout, but not about what I did. It had to be done.'

Mal shook his head and knocked back the rest of his glass. He didn't want to argue. Not now. The past week had taken it out of him. They fell silent and sat gazing out over the room's casual chatter.

Eventually Solly said, 'We had a good run.'

'What? Sinai?'

'Yeah, it was fun.'

'Good memories.'

'Of course.'

'All our own work.'

'The money was grand but it was the early days I remember most.'

'At Mrs Hyman's?'

'And before. You remember trying to touch Max Schaeffer for the cash in shul?'

'How could I forget?'

'You seriously gave it to that tosser of a son of his. Kicking him in the shin like that.'

'One of those blows. Know what I mean. You aim your toe and bam, it finds its target.'

Solly giggled. 'Do you think Max knew?'

'Probably. Hated his son almost as much as we did.'

'We were outrageous.'

'We had ambitions.'

'We were going for it.'

'Yeah, remember when we planned the first shop over Mrs Hyman's body?'

'That was you, not me.'

'I was enthusiastic.'

'You were a bit bloody hasty.'

'Mrs Hyman didn't mind.'

'She was dead. She didn't have any say in the matter.'

Their food arrived and they filled their glasses and emptied them and filled them again and set to work. They talked on: of the Princeton *pâtisserie* and Mrs Hyman's and building up the company and eating ice-cream in Chalk Farm; of buying Plantagenet and selling Sinai Kitchenware. Of the ill-defined geometry that is success. Solly pulled apart his lobster as if its deconstruction were a noble task.

'I forgot how good this tastes,' he said, dragging lumps of meat from the claw.

'I never could work out how you could deprive yourself.'

'Willpower, mate.'

'You always had such big appetites.'

'Which is why I need willpower.'

'There was food. And there was cocaine of course. And then there were women.'

'Women?'

'You always had more women than me.'

'Judy's my girl.'

'Of course she is, but I mean before that. Everybody knew you were a player. Everybody knew that you played the scene.'

Solly frowned a little as he picked at his plate. 'No, Judy's the only one.'

'Of course, but before . . .'

'Nah, you don't get it, do you. Judy's the only woman I've ever, you know . . .'

'You what?'

'Yeah. I lost my cherry to her. Grand, isn't it. This lobster really is something.'

Mal laid down his fork. 'Hang on. Then what was all that stuff you used to tell me?'

'What stuff?'

'Up in the store room at the *pâtisserie*. I spent hours listening to you talking about what it was like to have sex. You made me feel like a seven-year-old, all your spiel about shiksas saying thank you for sex.'

'Oh that.'

'Yeah, that.'

'What was I supposed to do? You looked up to me. What was I supposed to say? "Actually I'm a virgin and I've never done it"? What would you have said then?'

'But Judy gave you that . . . On Rosh Hashanah she . . . You told us, all of us. Out back, you said.'

'Made it up.' He concentrated on his lunch, refusing to look Mal in the eye. 'I mean obviously she did eventually give me a blow job. Quite a number actually, very good at it she was, so she deserved her title.'

'But that first one, that was a line?'

'I just liked the gag about her blowing my horn while the rabbi blew his. That was all.'

'I am shocked.'

'Mal Jones, you must be the only man I know who could announce that he's shocked because I *didn't* get a blow job in the rabbi's room. Anyway, you're not exactly high in the gigolo league, are you.'

'What do you mean?'

'Well Divinia, she's your one and only too.'

Mal sniffed and hoped he wasn't reddening. 'Yeah. Yes. Yes she is, my only one only. Maybe that's the secret of success in business. Marry as a virgin.'

Solly laid down his tools. The lobster was now just a mess of shell and flake. He dabbed at his lips with his napkin and drained his glass. He was a little drunk now and his shoulders were slumping. 'Mal, you'll look out for Judy and the kids when I'm, you know . . .'

'It may not come to that.'

'Believe me it will come to that. They'll want to put me inside. For what I've done, they'll want to put me away. I knew it was possible. Still, I just, I mean, I want you to promise you'll look out for them. Joe trusts you and so does Rachel and of course Judy's always been very fond of you . . .'

Solly's eyes were reddening now and Mal wondered if he might be about to weep. He could see why he might want to. He could imagine there were things he wanted to weep about, just as he had wanted to cry in front of the dealing screen the day before. But the room was too sunny and light for that; it was not a room for weeping in. Mal reached out and squeezed his partner's hand. 'You have nothing to worry about on that score. Promise you. I'll look out for them.'

Solly said, 'Let's pay and get out of here. Let's go for a drive.' He dragged his wallet out of his inside jacket pocket and threw it onto the table where it landed with a thump, as if marking a full stop to the conversation.

Forty-seven

Solly took them out eastwards from town, along a coast road that soon left behind the knowing sweetness of Whitstable. The buildings here were of old brick and raw, blistered paint; a grey and dowdy sulk against the energetic slab of sea they overlooked. For a while they were driving along an exposed ridge, the shore thirty feet below. A harsh sea wind blew inland that made the Jaguar rattle and shake on its axles and forced Solly to tighten his grip on the unfamiliar steering wheel. Even so the car weaved along the road, which Mal put down to the alcohol now seeping into his partner's bloodstream.

'Are you OK?' Mal said, but Solly ignored him. He bent his arms and stooped down over the leather-clad wheel as if he were being crushed into place. Below them white-crested waves broke across a darkening sea, and churned against the shingle. The light was failing now, and any blue sky was being snuffed out by late afternoon cloud.

The road dipped downhill and then turned inland onto a flood plain dotted with pebble-dashed semis and crazy-paved drives that for a moment reminded Mal of the Edgware of his youth, each house a model of careful self-improvement. A fragment of suburbia isolated here on the salt-drenched earth, where people came to nurse their sadness. Then they were turning back again to kiss the shore and the car was slipping into the opposite lane as they took the bend too fast.

'Solly! You're on the wrong side of the road!'

Solly yawned and burped and pulled back into line with a heavy downward jerk to the wheel, that made the car's rear slide in one direction and then the other. 'Sorry,' he said, when the motor had steadied. 'Bit sleepy. Got to pay attention.'

The sea was to their left again now, and ahead of them the dull buildings of Herne Bay stretched away on the curve of the shore; a cluster of sharp-edged blocks and rectangles pressed up against the rounded coast. A few miles distant the dark, skeletal finger of a pier reached out from the centre of town, as if trying to make its escape. Solly pressed his foot down on the accelerator and Mal gave thanks that there was little traffic on the road. Then, suddenly, they were braking again and the Jaguar was coming to a halt at the kerb. Mal closed his eyes and took a deep breath, grateful the journey was over, at least for now.

'This will do,' Solly said, turning off the engine and pulling out the keys. He stumbled out of the car, slammed the door and made his way round the front to clamber over the high grass verge that led down to the beach. Mal jumped out after him. The smell of salt water and ozone and the sharp, biting wind caught him by surprise. Christ, but he hated being here, by the sea. It didn't suit him, this proximity to the elements. They weren't his style.

'Solly,' he shouted, cupping his hand over his mouth, but either his partner could not hear him now because of the wind carrying the call away, or he had decided not to hear. He was scrambling down the shingle, his expensive leather-soled, hand-stitched shoes sliding into the clefts and dips made by the shifting pebbles. Mal had no choice but to follow, cursing the wind and the beach and, most of all, the man who had brought him here. Only when he was within five feet could he make himself heard. Solly was standing at the water's edge, watching the surf lap the toes of his shoes, hands stuffed in trouser pockets, collar turned up against the wind.

'What are we doing here?' Mal shouted and then again, 'Why are we here?'

Solly turned to him and raised his thick dark eyebrows in welcome as if he had been joined in some solitary pursuit by an unexpected friend. Then he looked out to sea. Mal went to stand next to him.

'There's a place near here,' Solly said. 'A stretch of sand. Only comes out at low tide. It's like a walkway. It's called the Street.'

'What of it, mate?'

'. . . and at low tide you can walk on this sand road right out into the sea. But if you stay out there too long the water just comes back in and you can't get back and you drown.'

'You came here for sand? Jews spent forty years trying to get out of the desert and now you come here for sand?' But Solly wasn't up for gags.

'It's an image,' he said.

'What of?'

'Me. My life. My, you know, career. An image. A smiley.' He grinned to himself. 'A big bloody smiley.' He let out a deep sigh. 'Thing is, you can see the sea on either side and you know you could drown in it, but when you fall in, it still catches you by surprise. Stupid, isn't it.'

'You're not drowning.'

'I've already drowned.'

'Bollocks.'

'Whatever. If it makes you feel better.'

'You'll get back from this.' But Solly didn't respond. He looked at his toes and kicked pebbles into the foam. The wind blew wiry tangles of black and grey hair over his eyes.

'I don't think I'll make it in prison,' he said.

'Of course you will.'

'The food was . . .' He shuddered. 'It was these baked beans in something that tasted like strawberry jam and this potato which was grey and lumpy and dry like sawdust and . . .' He swallowed, as if forcing down a lump of police station potato. 'That was only the police cells. Imagine what real prison food . . .'

Mal put his arm around Solly's shoulder and gave him a squeeze. 'It will be over quickly.'

'A day was enough.'

'Why did they hold you for so long?' Mal said. Solly looked up at his partner and frowned, as if trying to remember. He shook off Mal's arm and put a few feet of cold beach air between them.

'That's the thing, isn't it?'

'What is?'

'Yesterday in the police station.'

'What? What about yesterday in the police station?'

Solly turned back to the sea. 'First it was just a couple of blokes checking out that they weren't going to have to get me extradited to Germany. That was a formality, swift. Dealt with in half an hour.'

'And then?'

'Then there was our own drug squad, the boys from the Met. Wanted to be certain I hadn't brought anything in here.'

'And you reassured them?'

'Suppose I did.'

'How long did that take?'

'Three, maybe four hours.'

'And afterwards?' There was something in the way Solly was standing now, all hunched up, protecting his guts, that Mal didn't like. As if he were trying to bury the words deep inside him.

'Afterwards was when the other men came.'

'What other men?'

'The ones from the Serious Fraud Squad. In the expensive bad suits.'

Mal took a step backwards. 'What are you saying, Solly? Talk to me.'

'I *am* talking to you. I'm telling you. Men from the SFO. In expensive bad suits.'

'What did they say?'

'That they'd been watching our shares all day.'

'And what did you say?'

'Christ, this is an interrogation. I don't need an

interrogation. One of those I have already done. Three of those, even.'

Mal gritted his teeth and said, Then just bloody tell me what they said.'

Solly ran his tongue around the inside of his mouth so that his cheeks bulged. 'They said that they'd been watching our shares all day and the movement was unusual. They wanted to know if I could help them with an explanation . . .'

'What did you . . .?

'Let me finish. So I said I hadn't been in the office all day, that I'd been here in this stinking police station eating terrible food and answering questions. But the thing is Mal, they just kept on . . .' He turned to face his partner. 'They kept on and on and on. Asking me things about share deals and price maintenance and conspiracies and I was tired, so damn tired. You don't know what it's like to be interrogated like that.'

Mal could barely breathe. 'Please, tell me something I want to hear. Anything.'

'So eventually, this has been going on two, three hours and I've already done maybe four hours with the other men and they're going on and on. So I think to myself damn it, with what I've done I'm in for so long a bit of fraud is neither here nor there. What can they do, I think? For share dealing? Kill me? Of course they can't kill me. Maybe I tell them, I think, so they go away and they leave me alone and they won't investigate any further and—'

'You told them? For fuck's sake Solly, you told them? All you had to do was not say anything. Keep a secret. That was all. You've kept enough secrets in your time.'

'But with those secrets nobody asked me, so they were easy to keep. When someone asks me, then it becomes harder to keep a secret. I thought I was doing you a favour. Believe me. I thought I was. I was going to take the blame for all of it.'

Mal stood, his feet apart, hands covering his face.

'Oh Christ. How could this be a favour? Oh Jesus fucking Christ.'

'And it would have been fine,' Solly said. 'I'm sure of it. Take a plea, few extra years from the judge, simple. But the thing about it is, the really bad thing is, that then they start asking me details. They want to know how the plan worked. They were asking me all these questions, about thresholds and commissions and surpluses. So many questions. And I'm telling you I'm up to here with questions.' He slapped the underneath of his chin with the back of his hand. 'All day it's questions.'

Mal let his arms hang lank at his sides. The wind was whistling in his ears and the waves were breaking inches from his feet but his gaze was fixed only on his partner.

'And maybe I'd have been able to convince them,' Solly said. 'Just maybe, but the problem was I couldn't answer their questions. Because I didn't understand how it worked. None of it. I told you, when we were up the house with that shyster Grafton, I told you, didn't I. I said Mal, I don't understand. And you said what's to understand? You don't need to understand. And I said I should understand but you said I was to do as you said and—'

'Did you mention me? Tell me you didn't mention me.'

Solly had been firing out words, blustering out explanations and descriptions. But now he let out a deep hiss of breath and hung his head low and spoke in a slow murmur. 'No. I wasn't the one who mentioned you. They were the ones who did that. They told me I couldn't have done it and it must have been you; that you were the one who understood this stuff and must have been responsible because I couldn't have been.' Solly turned and gripped Mal's upper arm with one tight hand. 'And I told them, honestly I did. Time and again. I said no. They kept asking and time and again I said no. He wasn't the one. Mal Jones is

384

clean in this, I said. Those were the words I used. Mal Jones is clean. I told them that.'

'But they didn't believe you?'

'They just kept going. And I was tired, and I was cold and I was hungry from that bad food, so I think to myself just to get out of there, why not take the rap? Take the rap by telling them something they want to hear and they will let you go. And then I heard myself saying it . . .' Solly took a deep breath and closed his eyes. 'Before I could stop myself I heard myself say that you only did it because of me. And if it hadn't been for me you would never have done it at all.'

Solly heard his partner roar and when he looked up, recognized in his face a blood fury that he recalled seeing only once, when Schaeffer had stalked their offices over twenty years before.

'You arsehole.' Mal thrust Solly away with both hands to his lapels so that he stumbled backwards, until he was ankle deep in sea water. 'I've taken so much shit from you over the years.' He pushed him again and now they were both splashing about in the dark shallows.

'Your moods. The drugs. Christ, the drugs.' Another shove.

'Your lax bloody business sense.' A slap to the cheek.

'Your big fucking mouth.' And another, harder this time.

'But this . . .'

For a few seconds Solly took the blows, stumbling backwards into deeper and deeper water, as if he accepted that this was what he deserved. These punches and these slaps and shoves, here in the afternoon-black sea.

But now he snapped. 'Fuck it, Mal. I'll take everything that's coming to me. But remember this. If it wasn't for me, you'd have been nothing. Nothing at all. You never had a single good idea in your stinking sodding life. You want to know the best idea you had? I'll tell you the best idea you ever had. It was talking to me. That was your best idea.'

With a howl of rage Mal launched himself at his partner and they tumbled over into the water. They tasted salt and suffered the pressure of cold liquid rushing deep inside their heads; they felt rocks on the sea bed digging into their backs as they turned over and over, trying to hit each other. But neither of them managed to land a punch. They had no experience of fighting like this, not even a childhood memory to pull on; Jewish kids didn't do this kind of thing, not all flailing arms and rushing fists. Not in Edgware. Slowly, they gave up, the weight of the water and their sodden clothes making it feel as if they were threshing about in glue.

And then it was over. Solly was stumbling to his feet and onto the shore, his rich black wool suit leaking the gallon of sea water it had soaked up back onto the shingle. Mal was still in the surf, but on his knees now, trying to drag air into the depths of his ragged, untended lungs.

Solly pressed the back of his hand against his nose, checked it for blood – there was none – and said, 'All you had to do was explain it to me. That was it. Nothing else.' He took another breath. 'But even that you couldn't manage. You had to keep it to yourself. Sinai always had to be yours.' He shook his head one last time and spat out the words, 'You really are a shmuck.' Then he turned and walked away up the beach to the car, his wet trousers squeaking as he moved. Mal watched him go, a stocky silhouette against the fading autumn light, almost as broad as he was tall. He clambered up over the verge and into the car, started the engine and drove away along the coast road, disappearing from Mal's view. Until all that was left was the call of the engine and the crunching of gears and the smell of the sea.

Forty-eight

Dawn had broken over Herne Bay an hour ago, and the water was quiet and still in a way it can only ever manage in the earliest hours of the day. Mal stood by the bedsit window, looking out over a spread of grey sky and grey sea. Natasha was sitting, legs crossed, on the sagging double bed, wrapped up in his blankets against the top-floor chill. Mal had talked through the night and now it was the morning of Yom Kippur.

She said, 'And that was the last time you saw Solly?'

'Last words we ever spoke to each other. And he calls me a shmuck.'

Mal was arrested at home late that evening when he arrived back in London by train, his clothes crusted in salt from their fight in the surf Benny Jones and Gerry Bergner were already in custody by then, trying to work out exactly what had happened to them and just how much Mal was to blame.

'Syd Greenspan had a massive stroke and dropped dead within an hour of hearing the news that I had been arrested,' Mal said. 'And Divinia, of course, blamed me. A few words to our boys and it's a hat trick, the whole family blames me. Perfect Jewish blame. I got it wholesale. Cheaper that way.'

'They'll all come round,' Natasha said.

'You think so?'

'Given time.'

Solly's car was found abandoned on cliffs to the east of Herne Bay, but there was no sign of the driver. There were obvious conclusions to be drawn, but without one, squat, hairy body, there was nothing with which to back them up. As far as the police in two countries were concerned Solly Princeton had disappeared and was still wanted for international drug dealing and fraud. The City, however, didn't need a body or even a trial to help it reach its conclusions. Within days the Sinai share price had collapsed and the Faithful merger was off. Mal and Solly's shares ended up in the hands of their sleeping partners (until they, too, were arrested, along with Piers Grafton) and trading in the company was suspended by the Stock Exchange. Benny and Gerry saw the value of their holdings wither, only adding to their animosity towards Mal. They were eventually released without charge on the strength of his statement to the Serious Fraud Squad. Nevertheless, they refused to forgive him.

The Sinai empire, and the thousands of jobs that depended upon it worldwide, was only saved by the intervention of an American businessman who bought up the shares at rock bottom prices. His name was Jeremy Schaeffer.

'That hurt the most,' Mal said. 'Divinia announces she wants a divorce and it made a kind of sense. It was never a great marriage and we weren't making each other happy any more. It was inevitable. If blaming me for Syd's death made it easier then fine. I understood. We all need our reasons. But Schaeffer? Owning Sinai? Twice I had fought that man off. Twice. And then, when I can do nothing about it, he just walks in and . . .'

'He got lucky,' Natasha said. 'He didn't do anything clever.'

'That's true. I just did something really stupid.'

'You didn't mean to break the law. You were just trying to make the company hold its real value.'

'I should have had you as my barrister,' Mal said. And then, 'You know something sweetheart, Solly was wrong. He said the only idea I ever had was talking to him . . .'

'Of course he was wrong.'

'Yeah, because I had one other idea. The share-dealing operation. All my own work that was. Grafton did the detail but I came up with the basics. Solly was nowhere near it. I carved him out of it. Kept it to myself The only idea of mine that Solly didn't inspire.'

Mal left the window and slumped down on the bed next to Natasha. He was tired and cold now and because he was denying himself food, he was craving breakfast even though it was still a while before he would usually eat. 'I spent my entire career trying to make Sinai a big, mainstream British company. To get it out and away from Edgware.'

'You mean you were trying to make it less Jewish.'

'I was trying to make it international.'

'You were trying to make a company called Sinai, which built its fortune on a chicken soup machine, less Jewish?'

'I shouldn't have bothered.'

'That's what I'm saying.'

'At the end, you know what I was? I was Moses Jones, the Jewish criminal.'

'I saw those articles.'

'There was nothing I could say. No way I could argue with them.'

'You're a Jew and you were found guilty. But when they read out the charge sheet your Jewishness wasn't listed as an offence. You didn't do what you did because you're Jewish.'

'To read those articles you'd think . . .'

'Since when have you paid attention to anti-Semites?'

'Me, I don't even go to shul. Don't believe in God. And yet I was Moses Jones, Jewish criminal.'

'You want to wallow in other people stupidity, go ahead. There's no profit in it. In any case,' she said, looking about the magnolia walls of the room, 'you've paid for what you did. Prison wasn't exactly a picnic, was it. And then this place. There's a legal term for making Jews live in bedsits in Herne Bay. It's called a cruel and unusual punishment. You wanted to come here and atone for your sins, to where you and Solly last argued, then it seems to me that you've done it.'

Mal looked at her for a moment, investigating the soft, familiar contours of her young face, before pushing himself up and off the bed. He went to stand by the window. Through the walls, they could just make out the muffled chiming of bells from the nunnery below and next door. The first cars were edging their way along the seafront and a gull hung uneasily in the morning air. Mal pressed the fingertips of one hand against the cold, dirty glass and said, 'I wish it were that simple.'

'It is that simple.'

He shook his head and closed his eyes. 'It isn't. You know if I believed in a God it would be easy now. I could atone for my sins to Him. But I don't so I can't. That was Solly's bag, not mine. If I want to atone—' he opened his eyes and turned to Natasha '—it's you I have to look to.'

'I've already said you have nothing to—'

'But I do, you see. I do. The way I told you it finished on the beach? The way I told the police? Solly and me fighting? Him walking away and driving off?'

'Yeah?'

'It didn't happen like that. I wish it did, but it didn't.' He turned back to the window and the wretched, taunting plain of the sea. 'It really wasn't that simple. But then I suppose with Solly nothing ever was.'

Forty-nine

Mal closed his eyes for a few seconds as if trying to drag the memory back from its hiding place. 'I heard Solly say the stuff about telling them I had done it, but only because of him. I heard him say it and something snapped inside. Like that.' He clicked his fingers. 'Just went. I pushed him away, two hands to his lapels. Shoved him. And he stumbled backwards up the beach because he was drunk. I've already told you that, haven't I? That he was drunk?' His eyes were still closed. Natasha said he had, but nothing more.

'I was shouting at him. I've taken so much shit from you over the years, I was saying. Going on at him about his moods and the drugs. I was pushing him. And then I gave him a slap.' Natasha recoiled against the wall at the sound of the word, as if she too had taken the impact. 'And then another. And another. He'd talked. That was the thing. He'd confessed when he didn't need to.'

Now Mal opened his eyes. 'For a few seconds Solly took it all. He was still stumbling backwards of course, trying to keep his footing on the beach. But he was taking everything I threw at him. It was almost as if he thought that this was what he deserved. All these punches and these slaps. But then he came back at me. He was shouting too. Laying into me. If it wasn't for me you'd have been nothing at all, was what he said. He told me I'd never had a single good idea in my life. He said the best idea I'd ever had was talking to him.'

There was silence in the room. The chiming of bells had been replaced by the wash and rush of the sea against the shingle as the morning breeze set in.

Natasha said, 'What happened then?'

Mal stared at her. 'I gave him one last shove. This time he lost his footing and fell backwards. I remember his arms tracing these futile circles in the air, in an attempt to regain his balance, but he didn't. He landed heavily, really heavily, his head flicking back on his neck and hitting the shingle. There was this dull thud, like a rock landing on damp earth. You know what I mean?' Natasha said that she did. 'And then there was a rush of noise as the air was pushed out of his lungs.'

Mal leapt astride him, he said, one knee on either side of his partner's chest, and grabbed him by his lapels, lifting him bodily off the shingle.

'I called him a selfish little shmuck. I remember that. And then I was bawling at him: Do you have any idea what you've done to me? All of that.

'Solly's mouth was hanging open and his eyes were wide open too but as I pulled him upwards, they rolled backwards in his head until only the whites were showing. I shook him again.

'It was only then that I saw the blood.' It was spreading out from the back of Solly's head and across the stones, Mal said, varnishing them with a violent, crimson glaze. It washed into the holes between the rocks and pebbles and trickled towards the sea, soaking into the creased skin of his stubbled neck and down the back of his jacket collar. Slowly Mal let go of the handfuls of lapels.

'I was calling his name. Quietly, you know. Like it's the middle of the night and you're trying to work out if someone is asleep or awake. I patted him on the cheek.' Mal reached out one hand, palm open, to recreate the action. 'I was gentle at first but then I was doing it harder to get some response from him, so that it made this really loud slapping noise. I remember thinking someone might hear us, because the noise was so loud.'

But there was no response from Solly, apart from movement in his left hand; a set of involuntary

twitches and shakes, as if he were surreptitiously conducting an orchestra. A blue tinge was spreading
across his top lip now and the flow of blood from the
wound was increasing. Carefully Mal lifted himself off
Solly's chest and knelt down by his side. He slipped
one hand under his head.

'Don't worry, mate, I said, we'll just have a look at
what's going on here.' He hesitated. 'And that's when I
saw it.'

'Saw what?'

'It was horrible.'

'Tell me, Mal. You've come this far. You've got to tell
me.'

'Really, it was grim.'

'Mal!'

He took a sharp breath, trying to suffocate the physical memory of rising bile. 'It was this wound,' he said.
'This huge bloody wound. I could have buried my fist
in it, the thing was so deep.' He folded up the fingers
of his hand to demonstrate the size. Natasha curled up
her nose and grimaced.

'Exactly,' he said. 'Disgusting. Really grim.'

'I think I'd have been sick.'

Mal shrugged. 'I was. Right there, next to his . . . next
to him.'

After he had vomited Mal wiped strands of saliva
from his mouth with the back of his hand. He turned
back to Solly and, remembering scenes from movies,
pressed an index and middle finger against his neck,
searching for a pulse. But there was nothing. He placed
his ear next to Solly's mouth to listen for breathing but
all he heard was the wind and the sea and his own,
snare-drum heartbeat.

He was panicking now, he said, his mouth dry and
his flesh clammy with sweat, despite the chill coming
off the water. 'Hang on in there, Solly,' he gasped into
his partner's ear, hunkering down beside him, paranoid that someone might hear or see them, these two
middle-aged Jews in expensive suits, lying by the sea

on a darkening autumn afternoon. But the beach was deserted, and on this shingle slope they were out of sight of the road. 'Hang on in there. Don't go. Just hang on.' For a few minutes he stroked Solly's forehead, brushing back his hair, imagining he was doing some good. But already his skin was cooling and felt thick and unnatural beneath his fingers.

'I tell you, Natasha it had only been ten minutes but I didn't need a death certificate to tell me what the situation was. At times like that you don't need paperwork to tell you the truth.'

For an hour Mal remained beside Solly's body, hugging his knees up against his chest and sobbing. Before him the sea. Behind him the beach. All that space and nowhere to go. Above him the sky turned from an autumn grey to a deep blue before the colour drained away altogether. Only then did he act. It was not a plan. Just a means of survival.

'I stood up, gripped Solly by his ankles and began to drag him down towards the water. I remember thinking to myself that I was already a criminal because of all the things I'd done so it didn't matter what I did now. My mind was all over the place. You know. Racing. I remember thinking how the police would hold this dead body against me if they caught me doing what I was doing. And then I was laughing because of how it sounded, having a dead body held against you. Like I was a pervert who had a thing for corpses.'

Natasha managed a thin smile.

'Then I looked down at Solly's dead eyes and felt another wave of nausea and I thought I was going to be sick again. Anyway I realized I was in shock. That was why my mind was working that way. I just tried to keep my mind on the job.'

The thick-hipped body proved cumbersome to move, even though the pebbles beneath it acted as mini-rollers. As Solly slipped down the beach his arms stretched up above his head and snagged on occasional rocks as if he were trying to hold onto the ground, and his cranium bounced up and down over ridges of pebbles, with a troubling thud. Then Mal found his hands slipping against the smooth fibres of his partner's expensive silk socks. He stopped and rolled them down to expose enough hairy skin to enable him to gain purchase, then returned to dragging. Only when he was up to his knees in the water and Solly's body was half into the sea did Mal remember the car keys. He would need those.

'I dropped his legs, forgetting just how heavy they were and what sort of a splash they would make. So now I was soaked right up to my ribs in ice-cold water.' For a few seconds he stood stock still, shivering in the darkness in case anyone had heard him. But it sounded like cars up on the road were continuing on their way into Herne Bay. 'I remember wondering why anybody would want to drive into Herne Bay. That was how confused I was. I had Solly's ankles in my hands, I was soaking wet and all I could think about was what a shithole Herne Bay was.' He looked out the window at the desolate seafront. 'I was right about that, of course, wasn't I. So maybe I wasn't so crazy.'

Mal turned back to Natasha. He had stumbled back onto the edge of the beach, he said, and, kneeling down on the stones, dug around in the jacket pockets until his hand found the hard outline of the car keys. He pocketed them and then waded back in to continue dragging Solly into the water. The moment Solly's head floated free of the beach caught him by surprise and with one last tug he found himself falling backwards and under the surface. He thrashed his way back to the cool evening air and regained his breath, one hand rested on Solly's floating stomach for balance.

'I only managed another three minutes in the water, it was that cold. I was floating Solly's body further and further out to sea, but I became convinced the cold was about to get the better of me and that I needed to get back to shore or I would be dead too.' He waded out and for a few minutes stood there dripping in the darkness trying to work out where Solly had fallen so that he could lob the blood-smothered pebbles into the surf

'That would be a simple mistake, I thought. Might as well leave a big neon sign on the beach. X marks the spot. I even dropped down on my hands and knees and felt around, looking for rocks covered with Solly's blood.' Only then did he hear the fizz and splash of water on water coming from behind him. Turning his face upwards to the night sky he realized that it was raining, and heavily.

'I said thank you to the night sky. Thank you so much. I decided the damn rain could do the job. The elements could take control. I reckoned that I shouldn't be there any more. That I needed to get away.' He stood up and patted his trouser pockets to check that Solly's keys were still there.

Finally he stumbled back up the beach to where the car had been parked ninety minutes before.

'But I tell you, Natasha,' Mal said. 'That ninety minutes felt like a whole lifetime.'

Fifty

Mal pressed his hand against the window glass again as if trying to push his way out and said, 'I killed my best friend, out there on the beach. That's what I have to atone for. That's why I'm here in this godforsaken place staring at this godforsaken, bloody water.'

Natasha pulled the blankets tighter about her shoulders and said nothing. He looked small and scared, standing there in the dull morning light. As if the world outside posed an unspeakable threat. She didn't want to add to his discomfort, enrage him with some ill-chosen word.

'He deserved punishment,' Mal said, 'but he didn't deserve that. He didn't deserve to die. He was a good man. Trustworthy. A real mensch.'

'He was a drug dealer,' Natasha said, in a whisper.

'Yeah, but for a reason. He believed in something. Me? I never believed in anything. The business, maybe. Success. All of that. But it isn't a cause. I didn't have a cause. He did. You might not have approved of his methods, but at least he had a cause.' Mal hesitated. 'And I killed him.'

'It was an accident,' Natasha said, finding her voice now.

'Which was my fault.'

'No it wasn't. It was his. He was drunk.'

'I was the one who pushed him. I was the one who made him fall. If it hadn't been for me he wouldn't have fallen over.'

'If he hadn't drunk most of a bottle of champagne maybe he wouldn't have fallen over.'

'But he had and he did and now he's dead.'

'It's not murder, Mal. Manslaughter, at a push. Maybe even accidental death. You could have seen to it that he got a better burial, I suppose . . .'

Mal allowed himself a weak smile. 'Never swim in the sea around here,' he said. 'Current will have you out in no time. All the while I was in Class I kept expecting Solly's body to be washed up and then the questioning to begin . . .'

'And what if his body had been washed up?'

'What do you mean?'

'Exactly what I'm saying. What difference would it have made? The car was found up on the cliffs. Everybody assumed he had committed suicide anyway.'

'Yeah, but I was the one who put the car up on the cliffs. I must have spent an hour sitting up there using the Jag's heater to dry off I thought about jumping, you know.'

'I can imagine.'

'It might have been simpler.'

'The coward's way.'

'Maybe that's what I am. A coward. Solly wasn't a coward. Wasn't his style.'

'Chunky gold jewellery was his style.'

Now Mal laughed. 'Awful, wasn't it?'

'The pits.'

'Told him it made him look like a Stanmore bathroom but he wouldn't have it.'

'His own style.'

'You know the one thing I'd love, sweetheart? You want to know what it is? I'd love to hear his voice again. Just the once. Hear him talk the talk. That's what I'd love.'

Natasha stared furiously at the tired old weave of the blanket wrapped around her chest. 'Maybe you can,' she said.

'Sorry?'

'I said maybe you can.' She looked up, nibbled her bottom lip for a moment and said, 'Pass me my bag.'

Mal grabbed the handles of her shoulder bag and heaved it off the table, dropping it into the well made by her crossed legs. She opened it up and dug around inside. 'I received this about four days after Solly disappeared,' she said.

'What? Received what?'

'Hang on.' She thrust her hand deeper inside. 'This,' she said. It was a single letter-sized envelope of thick, ridged beige paper. The expensive kind used for Bar Mitzvah invitations and accountants' bills. Mal's name was typed on the front but there was no address. She passed it over.

'Solly's note just said that I should give it to you either when you were acquitted or when you got out.'

'Nothing else?'

'Sent me his love.'

'Sweet man.' Mal opened a drawer in his bedside table and found his reading glasses. He placed them far down his nose, ripped open the envelope and studied the letter inside.

'What is it?' Natasha said.

Mal looked at her over the top of his frames, then back to the note. 'Don't know. It's not from Solly. It's from a bunch of London solicitors. Attend their offices at my earliest convenience, it says.'

'Don't you love lawyer-speak.'

'Deal with matters of a personal nature.'

'Maybe Solly has left something there for you.'

'Probably a new recipe for chicken soup,' he said, with an uneasy grin. He wasn't sure he liked the idea of a letter from a dead man, particularly one he'd killed. You could never answer back to dead men. He took off his glasses and rubbed the unfamiliar feeling from the bridge of his nose. 'Is this why you came here? To deliver this letter?'

Natasha wrinkled her nose and for a moment Mal thought how much she looked like her mother. 'That,' she said. 'And because I wanted to check my father was OK.'

Mal leaned towards her. 'Sorry?'

'Don't try it on, Mal. I think the moment for that sort of stuff has passed. Don't you?'

He studied her face, the curve of her cheek and the gentle line of her delicate lips and considered trying to deny it. But what was the point, given all the other things he had admitted to overnight? And none of those had anything to do with Natasha. This one did. He remembered the door to Heidi and Benny's flat in Maida Vale closing behind them on the night the first Sinai Diner opened in 1976 and Heidi saying 'Benny will be hours' as she reached up to caress his cheek. He remembered an embrace in the hallway and then that first kiss.

'Did you marry the wrong Jones brother?' he had said.

'I married the one who asked me.'

'Was that my mistake?'

'Maybe mine too.'

'I wouldn't have walked out on you tonight like he did.'

'You didn't, did you. You're here with me.'

'Finally.'

They kissed again and Heidi wrapped her hands round his hips and pulled him hard towards her. And later, after they had made love in his brother's bed, she said thank you.

Then, two months later, a conversation between them in a quiet moment at a noisy family party.

'It's yours.'

'How do you know?'

'Because Benny can't.'

'Maybe the doctors got it wrong.'

'OK Mal, I'll be frank with you. Because Benny didn't. Not at the right time.'

'So it's definitely mine?'

'It's either yours or immaculate conception and there hasn't been much of that in Maida Vale lately.'

'You sure he won't suspect?'

'My Benny? Suspect? Believe me, he has no idea. He thinks a menstrual cycle is a kind of exercise machine.'

'What do you want me to do? Tell me. Name it.'

She held his head in her hands and kissed him softly on the lips. 'Nothing, darling. I'm delighted. Really. Just keep it to yourself I thought you'd like to know is all.'

Could he really now deprive Natasha of acknowledgement?

'How long have you known?' he said.

Natasha relaxed and laid her head back against the wall. 'It would be great now if I told you I'd known for years. You'd hate that, wouldn't you.' And on cue Mal shivered. 'The idea of me knowing a secret all that time. Seeing you at parties and stuff and knowing the truth. But you can relax. Mum told me last night. Said if I was going to come and see you now there was something I should know.'

'Are you . . .' he paused. '. . . all right with it?'

'All right? I'm delighted. Two dads.'

Mal gasped. 'Please Natasha. Benny doesn't know. He mustn't find out . . .'

'And he won't. Ever. There's no need. He's still my father. He's still the one who brought me up. It's just nice to know that my favourite uncle is also my father.'

'I'm your only uncle.'

'You're not my uncle at all.'

Mal sat down on the bed again and took her hands in his. 'If there's ever anything you need . . .'

She leaned over and kissed him on the cheek. 'Thank you. It's very sweet. But to be honest at the moment I think you're the one who needs help.'

'Maybe you're right.'

'So . . .?'

'So what?'

She flicked the solicitor's letter that he was still holding. 'What are you going to do?'

He opened up the crumpled piece of paper and looked at it again. 'Attend at my earliest convenience,

I suppose, which is probably some time today. Go and pay a visit to—' Rather than put on his glasses again he held the paper away from him to compensate for his short sight – 'Mr Green. Time I left this place. Before I start turning magnolia.'

'And then?'

Mal shrugged. 'I have friends. My Uncle Morri has said I can stay with him or there's cousin Shirley, wrote to me while I was inside. Said I could have their spare room as a stopgap. Not sure I fancy it, though. There's always a hotel, of course. Divinia may have all my assets thanks to Grafton, but she's put a bit aside for me. Says I'm still the father of her kids, which is something, I suppose.'

Natasha threw off the blankets and stood up, straightening out the wrinkles in her T-shirt. 'Don't be ridiculous. You'll come and stay with us.'

'But Benny . . .'

'Our house is a matriarchy. Mum and me, we'll sort it. We're in the majority. Anyway, he wants to see you. He's just too proud to admit it. Give us a call from town when you're done—' she raised her sable eyebrows conspiratorially '—with Mr Green.'

She gathered her things together and they made their way back down the dank, creaking stairs. By the door they embraced but this time they didn't need silence.

Mal said, 'Thank you for coming . . . when nobody else would.'

'Wouldn't have missed it for the world.'

'You're a saint.'

'I'm your daughter,' she said with a grin. And then, 'The Solly thing. It won't go anywhere else. Doesn't have to. You don't have to say anything either. It's up to you, of course, but if I were you, I wouldn't.'

He considered her for a moment and then said simply, 'Thank you.' And although he must have said it thousands of times before to thousands of people he didn't think he'd ever really meant it until that moment.

Fifty-one

Mal found London unnerving after Herne Bay: the noise and clutter of Victoria Station; the dark whistling tunnels of the underground that smelt only of soot and old grease; the constant mutter and growl of the city traffic. It came at him from every side and made him feel empty and stateless. Once too cosmopolitan for a dead seaside town. Now so hypnotized by the endless wash and roll of the sea that he was unsuited to the city. Neither here nor there. Not one thing or the other. He was relieved to find the offices of Blum, Green and Blum, Solicitors, with its subtle lights and thick carpets and silence, in a tall town house on the Marylebone Road. It was late afternoon now and hunger from the fast was beginning to make him dizzy. The city noise only made his head spin all the more.

The reception area was empty, save for a rotund middle-aged woman behind a desk, a newspaper open before her. She saw Mal and swiftly folded away the paper.

'Can I help you?'

Mal looked around the empty room and felt foolish. 'I should have phoned ahead,' he said, proffering the letter. But phoning ahead would have felt like announcing himself to London and that was something he did not feel he had a right to do. He wanted to be able to slip in unseen and unquestioned. Without what Syd Greenspan would have called 'palaver'. The receptionist held the note away from her, to compensate for her own poor eyesight, and Mal relaxed.

'Was it Mr Green you were hoping to see?' she said

'Mr Green or anybody else who can . . .'

'Because I'm afraid Mr Green isn't here today. Very few in today actually. Skeleton staff.'

'Oh. I see.'

'It's the' – she leaned forward across the desk and whispered – 'Jewish Day of Atonement.'

Mal mentally slapped his forehead at his own stupidity. 'Yes, it is, isn't it.'

'So both Mr Blum and Mr Blum aren't here. Nor Mr Green, of course. Very quiet. Rather nice, actually, if you know what I mean.' She threw him a little wink.

'I think I do.'

She studied the letter again. 'Still, there's a reference number here so we shouldn't have much trouble. Young Mr Forsyth is in, minding the store.'

'Young Mr Forsyth wouldn't have cause to observe the Jewish Day of Atonement, would he?'

'No, not young Mr Forsyth,' she said with a comforting smile. She bustled off through a doorway into the guts of the building to find the one man in the firm of Blum, Green and Blum who could be guaranteed to have eaten lunch that day. Forsyth appeared minutes later, clutching a file. He looked like the kind of man to wear shin pads under his trousers in case his boss called an emergency game of rugby. He was broad-chested and had pink cheeks and a prominent Adam's apple.

'Mr Jones,' he said in a soft Morningside accent. 'Do come through.'

He led Mal to an expensively furnished but empty office, bare of pictures or even a calendar, and sat him down on one side of a desk while he occupied the other. He placed two envelopes on the table, similar to the one Natasha had given him the night before.

'I'm sure Mr Green will be very sorry to have missed you.'

'I do understand. I should have called ahead.'

'Not at all, Mr Jones. Not at all.'

Suddenly Mal realized that, for the first time in two years, someone was deferring to him Once he had been used to this treatment, expected it even. It came with the job of being rich and powerful, was part of the money package. But that was before Solly parked the car on the outskirts of Herne Bay and stumbled his way down to the sea.

'Everybody's been most accommodating,' he said.

'To be frank Mr Jones—' he leaned forward across the desk '—we're rather grateful for something to do on days like these.'

'I can imagine.'

The two of them stared silently at the two envelopes until Mal said, 'Would you mind if I opened them alone?' and Mr Forsyth scrambled to his feet and rubbed his hands together and said, 'Of course not. Forgive my presumption. I'll just be out in reception if you need me.'

The two envelopes were marked with his name and there was the single letter 'A' written in the top right-hand corner of the one nearest him. The second carried the letter 'B'. He picked up A and studied the front for a few seconds, putting off the moment. Then, with one sharp intake of breath he ripped it open. Inside was a sheet of paper, dated the day they had gone to lunch in Whitstable a little under two years before, and filled with Solly's handwriting. Mal patted his jacket pocket and found his glasses.

Mal mate,

If you're reading this then it seems I had the guts to do it. Not the smartest thing in the world, topping yourself but sometimes, you know how it is, needs must. Couldn't see another way. Prison wouldn't have suited me. I couldn't have made a go of it. And anyway what use would a jailbird be to my Judy and my Joe and my Rachel? None, that's what. So I made my bed and now I've got to lie in it and that's all right, really it is, because me and him upstairs, we've got an understanding. I'll take what comes to me.

Thing is, I wanted to apologize to you. Mal, you didn't deserve the shit you had to go through for me, really you didn't. I'm sorry and all that. It wasn't part of the plan. Because the truth is, whatever I've said in the past you always looked out for me. You looked out for me even when I wasn't looking out for myself You were always a mucker to me, a total mensch, and I'll always love you for that.

Judy and the kids are sorted as far as money goes, thanks to your chum Grafton. Made it a lot easier, he did, getting us to sign everything across. So I suppose more thanks are in order. Just keep an eye on them all the same, will you? Do that for me. I wouldn't trust anybody else.

There's one last favour I have to ask and it's a bit of a touchy one . . .

Mal read the last paragraph, looked across at the second envelope and began to laugh. Solly would make a good Jew of him yet. Even if only from beyond the grave, he would see to it that his partner did the right thing.

Mr Forsyth stuck his head round the door. 'Is everything all right, Mr Jones?'

Mal's laughter was subsiding. He took off his glasses and folded them away. 'Everything's fine,' he said. He folded up the letter and put it in his inside pocket alongside the second envelope, still unopened. 'Everything seems to be working out just fine.'

Back outside on the Marylebone Road he considered his options. He needed somewhere suitable. The right place for the job, where a bad Jew could go to become a good Jew. Somewhere that Solly would have approved of or, better still, somewhere that he would have chosen himself Mal looked up at the sky. It was six o'clock now and although it wasn't completely dark, he reckoned he'd done enough. Sure, Yom Kippur wasn't over yet but the fact was he'd fasted and now he was starving. He'd seen out the Day of Atonement. He'd unburdened himself. And maybe he hadn't done it by the book, and maybe he hadn't followed the halakha to the letter. But then how many Jews did that these days? Very few. Everybody chose their own way. Or improvised. Mal was no different.

Then it came to him. He knew where he had to go. He turned right and stepped out the short distance to Baker Street.

The restaurant was still there but now, under Schaeffer's ownership, it was called the Manhattan Diner. Mal peered through the window, cupping his hands around his eyes to get a clearer view. To his relief he didn't recognize any of the staff Then again he barely recognized the restaurant. He went in and stood for a while by the door, studying the room, empty still of customers. It had been completely redecorated. The wood panelling had been removed in favour of raw red brick which Mal knew to be just as fake as the wood. The panelling had only covered up a shell of breeze blocks which must still have been there underneath. The *faux* Norman Rockwells had gone and in their place were cheesy Hollywood portraits of Bogart and Monroe and Groucho Marx. The bar remained but instead of the wood and brass construction, it was built out of the same red brick as the walls, only topped in zinc. Up behind the bar where once had hung a certificate from the Beth Din certifying it as a kosher establishment, was the achingly familiar picture of James Dean, shoulders hunched, as he walked down Broadway.

A waitress approached him.

'Can I help you, sir?'

'I'd like a table for one.'

She frowned. 'For one?'

'Just for one.'

She turned to her colleague preparing the bar for the evening's service but he merely shrugged and went back to polishing glasses.

'How about this table?' she said, pointing to one in the window.

Mal looked past her and said 'No I'll take that one, the first one on the second terrace.'

She squinted in the direction he was pointing as if she didn't recognize her surroundings.

'The restaurant's empty,' Mal said. 'It shouldn't be a problem'

'No of course not,' she said, clearly uncomfortable with a customer being so particular. She led the way to the table and said, 'I'll bring you a menu.'

Most of the dishes Solly and Reuben had put there over two decades before had gone. There was no chopped liver or chopped herring or salt beef or latkes. Just burgers and ribs and the brutal kitchen chemistry that was Tex-Mex. Only one familiar starter remained.

'I'll have the chicken soup,' Mal said, handing back the menu. 'I'll choose a main course later.'

When she was gone he took the letter and the envelope from his pocket and read the last paragraph again.

There's one last favour I have to ask and it's a bit of a touchy one. You see, suicide may have been the solution for me but the rabbis don't go for it much. Not really recommended in the Talmud, is suicide. Even if they found my body, and knowing the currents out there they won't have done, I wouldn't have been buried in a Jewish cemetery. And, of course, without a body there's nothing to mourn over. (Well, if there wasn't a body you can let people see this letter and they'll know what happened to me, won't they.) But that still doesn't sort my problem. Thing is, no-one will have said Kaddish for me. I know we never saw eye to eye on this stuff but maybe you could make an exception? Just this once? And don't worry about not knowing it or not being able to read Hebrew. You'll find a phonetic version in the second

408

envelope, along with a little something extra for you. All you have to do is choose the right place and say Kaddish. That's all it is. I know you won't let me down. You never have before.

All my love.

Your friend Solly.

Mal picked up the second envelope. Inside, as promised, was the phonetic version of the Kaddish, too many consonants crammed together around too few vowels. Clipped to it was a second short note from Solly.

Mal mate,

I'm only guessing here but I reckon all of this has probably left you a bit strapped for cash. It was always a risk. I hope this makes up for it. For the past few years I've been putting something aside for you in your name for a rainy day. Don't worry. It's all clean. Came from my Sinai earnings. Not the other. Tax is paid too. So it's all yours. Should be about £2.5 million by now. Enough to get you back on your feet. Bank details are below. Take care.

Mal read the note one more time, before folding it up and burying it in his inside pocket. He felt sick and grateful at once. Absolution and escape, in a simple beige envelope. Not what he had expected. Not what he had expected at all. And there was nothing he could do in return except this one last act.

The waitress brought his soup and placed it down in front of him with a stagey kind of care, as if sudden movements would scare him away. He looked up and smiled and said thank you and she gave a tight nod before retreating behind the bar where she felt safer. Mal studied the bowl of hot chicken soup, sniffed the gentle curls of steam lifting off its surface, and remembered the very first time he had watched Solly at work so many years before in Golda Princeton's kitchen.

'My son,' Golda had said, 'is the Einstein of the kitchen. There should be a Nobel prize for cooking. I tell you. Who cares about economics? Adding up never saved your life. But cooking, we all need to eat.'

And she was right, Mal thought. She was absolutely right. We all need to eat. I need to eat. He flattened out the piece of paper bearing the words of the Kaddish, lifted his spoon and began to work his way through the soup. Between sips, as the bowl of his spoon dipped down beneath the surface, he said the words on the piece of paper out loud in a soft but certain voice. There were no witnesses save the waitress and the barman and it was better that way. From a distance Mal looked like nothing more than a shabby middle-aged man sitting alone talking to himself A lonely man in a lonely room with nothing for company but his imagination. You had to get closer, much closer, to realize what was going on. You had to be at the next table or standing beside him or better still, sitting right across from him to understand; to know that these mutterings in a curious foreign tongue were not the deluded words of the desperate or insane, but simply the sound of a wiser man saying a last goodbye to a friend.

Recipe for chicken soup

This is my Great-Aunt Muriel's recipe and it is entirely possible that it found its way to Solly Princeton via his mother Golda. After all, Aunt Muriel and Golda Princeton never lived that far from each other in north-west London and things have a way of getting about inside the Jewish community.

Serves six

Ingredients
1 large boiling chicken or 1 chicken carcass and
    2 packets of giblets weighing a pound
1 large onion, quartered
2 carrots cut into chunks
1 leek
2 celery stalks and leaves, cut into large slices
2 sprigs of parsley (optional)
salt and pepper

Put the chicken, quartered, into a large pan with three and a half pints of cold water. Bring to the boil and remove the surface scum. Add all the other ingredients and simmer on a very low heat for at least two and a half hours, adding extra water as necessary. If you are using a whole chicken you can remove it after an hour or so to take off the meat, but do return the bones to the pan.

At the end of cooking you can use a Pollo-Matic, if you have one, both to strain the liquor of vegetables and stray bones, and to remove the fat or shmaltz. Be careful to turn the tap off before the shmaltz follows the soup down. Otherwise you'll have to strain it with a standard sieve and then leave it to stand for a couple of hours or overnight in the fridge, until the shmaltz hardens on the surface and can be lifted off with a knife. Add salt and pepper according to taste.

Other people will have other recipes for chicken soup, but you think I care? In my family what Great-Aunt Muriel says, goes. Trust me. This one is the best.

Enjoy.